SOME FINE DAY

SOME FINE DAY

Kat Ross

SKYSCAPE

SKYSCAPE

Text copyright © 2015 Kat Ross
All rights reserved.

Published by Skyscape, New York

www.apub.com

Amazon, the Amazon logo, and Skyscape are trademarks of Amazon.com, Inc., or its affiliates.

ISBN-13: 9781477849378
ISBN-10: 1477849378

Cover design by Hideki Sahara
Library of Congress Control Number: 2014916803

To Dad, who I have never seen, even once, without a book.

More than once, a society has been seen to give way before the wind which is let loose upon mankind; history is full of the shipwrecks of nations and empires; manners, customs, laws, religions— and some fine day, that unknown force, the hurricane, passes by and bears them all away.

Victor Hugo, Les Misérables

CHAPTER ONE

At first, the logistical problems seemed insurmountable, and of a magnitude never before faced in human history. But the alternative was equally unthinkable.
From Armin Delacour's Descent of Man:
The Transition Years 2050–2068 *(banned)*

Rain streaks the window of the train as the white-gloved waiter sets a cup of coffee on the table. Like the plates and silver and linens and everything else in the dining car, it is finely made, porcelain thin as a rose petal with a gold band around the rim. As he clears the remains of the meal, I add a generous dollop of cream. The coffee is hot and strong, even better than I expected.

Outside, sheep dot the countryside, humps of grey in the steady downpour. We cross a trestle over a deep gorge, and then sunlight breaks through the clouds, casting pools of light and shadow on the emerald slopes far beneath. It's an impossibly beautiful scene, and my throat catches a bit, as it always does.

My uniform is hot and a little tight. I haven't slept in more than twenty-four hours. But I start to relax, sipping the hot coffee and letting my eyes soften into the mist rising from the valleys.

Suddenly, without warning, everything is gone, the sheep, the rain, the green. In its place is a featureless red desert.

"Jake," I say.

I hate it when he does that.

"You act like it's real." He moves his hand back a couple inches from the console on his armrest.

He's sulking because I'm looking out the window instead of paying attention to him. And he's right. It's not real. None of it is real. What's real is that we are on a magnetic bullet train speeding through the darkness at four hundred miles per hour, and that train is about six thousand feet beneath the Earth's surface.

But I was still enjoying the view.

"Come on, Jansin. Seven hours to Raven Rock. Holidays, remember?" He grins, and I have to grin back.

Jake wears the same uniform as me, navy blue with two black bands around the left arm, and has almost the same haircut, except shorter. He has bright blue eyes and brown skin and dimples. The overall impression is very wholesome.

"Let's go watch the live feed," he says, and I'm too tired to argue, so we pay the bill and walk two cars down. It's almost empty at this hour, and we get a corner booth all to ourselves.

"Alecto," he says, grabbing a remote. "She's hot this week. Energy burst from the Equatorial Current."

Alecto is one of the younger hypercanes, only about fifteen years old. A baby next to Megaera, which has been tearing up the surface for half a century.

The words HYPERCANE NETWORK! shimmer on the screen, then dissolve into six boxes. The upper left is a satellite view of the cane, its Cyclops eye now peering down on what the caption identifies as the Sino-Russian Prefecture. A crawl at the bottom gives real-time updates on latitude and longitude, sustained wind speed, central air pressure, and predicted path for the next seven to ten days. Jake has always been fascinated by the storms. He can watch them for hours.

I can't really blame him for his fixation. The HYPERCANE NETWORK! is the only thing we get besides the news that has any variety. The movies and TV shows are from the old days. By now, we've seen them all a million times. Westerns are my favorite, because of the wide-open scenery and the horses and the crazy, doomed love stories, like in *The Unforgiven*.

Jake gives a low whistle and settles back, putting an arm around my shoulders. I snuggle in, opening the top two buttons of my uniform where they pinch my neck. I turn my face for a kiss, and get one, but it's half-hearted. His eyes never leave the screen.

"They all look the same to me," I say.

The other boxes are ground views from unmanned weather platforms. Alecto's wind speeds average about four hundred and fifty mph, with gusts up to six hundred. I see surging seas, airborne debris that flies past too fast to identify. When Jake turns up the volume, the sound is deep and eerie. Like something alive.

Then an ad cuts in, synth guitars wailing our national anthem, and a montage of images depicting athletic-looking young men and women speaking rapidly to computers, belly-crawling through caves, sparring Jiu-Jitsu style with lots of flashy aerial throws, and finally, marching in perfect formation down a wide avenue as crowds cheer from the sidewalks.

"Thinking about your future?" a smug male voice asks. "Think you've got what it takes to serve in the most elite fighting force ever to . . . *blah blah blah* . . ."

"I need to sleep," I say, and he smiles and kisses the palm of my hand. Jake can go without rest for days and seem perfectly fresh.

"Go. I'll wake you half an hour out."

The compartment is large by bullet train standards. Even in second class, you get one thousand-thread count sheets and a mint on the pillow. I'm so exhausted, I'd curl up on the floor without complaint. But after folding up my uniform and brushing my teeth, I take a minute to find the sheep again and fall asleep with the image of sunlight pouring through the clouds onto the valley floor.

Jake gets me exactly thirty minutes before arrival. More strong coffee in the dining car, and then we're pulling into the station. The platform is crowded, but I see my father right away. He's a big man and looks even bigger in full dress regalia, with a chest full of medals and shiny black shoes. Jake gives him a salute. "At ease, cadet," he says, and hugs me tight until my toes barely touch the floor.

He summoned Jake and me for midterm break a week early, and I wait for him to explain, but he just takes my bag and hustles us out to the car. His long-time driver Archie nods at me and I nod back. Traffic is heavy around the station, the streets full of shoppers and people getting out of work. There's light everywhere, white, red, yellow, blue, twinkling in the semi-darkness, and it seems so cheery and full of life after the drab grey of the Academy, like waking up after months of hibernation. We creep through the city center, then accelerate as the commercial district gives way to factories and hydroponic farms, the glow from their high-powered grow-bulbs illuminating flurries of snow.

Which, of course, is also artificial.

Apparently, people start to go crazy without any weather at all. In the first years after the Transition, about a quarter of the population fell into a clinical depression. A lot of them killed themselves. So the scientists invented machines that made rain and snow and day and night. And they created the network that lets us watch the storms. All five of them.

After about an hour, we turn up the winding drive to my house. My mother stands silhouetted in the front door. She's small, like me, with the same tilted eyes and dark hair. She pecks me on the cheek and holds her arms out for Jake, who gives her an awkward hug. He's always a little nervous around my parents. And it's the first time he's been invited to stay for a whole week.

4

I shower and change out of my uniform into a nice floral-print dress, and then we all sit down for dinner in the solarium. My mother is an agronomist, and she's made this room the most beautiful in the whole house, with pineapple lilies and rare orchids and a hundred other flowers I don't know the names of.

"Tell me about school," she says, and Jake gives a gung-ho recital of our latest training.

This term we've been studying small unit tactics, advanced light weapons and close quarter combat. Jake is a better shot, but I'm faster with my hands and feet. I've dropped him on the mats nearly every time, which he pretends not to mind but does, just a little bit.

We have squash soup, followed by poached leeks and synth steaks in a mushroom cream sauce. It's heavier, richer food than I'm used to, and makes me drowsy. I'm glad to be home, and I think about the next seven days of freedom: walking in the gardens with Jake, curling up in the worn pea-green armchair with the good lamp and mismatched ottoman for my feet and re-reading some of my favorite books, maybe taking day trips into the city. Pretending that I'm a normal teenager. Soon, we'll graduate and get our assignments and everything will change. I'm not sure I want that to happen. Not yet.

Jake listens politely as my mother talks a little about her work. She helps run the massive cryobanks where they keep thousands of plant and animal species frozen for rejuvenation someday, everything from grizzly bears to brain coral. It's still only a tiny fraction of the life that once existed on the surface, but better than nothing. Her specialty is food grains, and she spends most of her time experimenting with different varieties to see which ones do best in underground growing conditions.

Then my father shares a long look with Jake and clears his throat.

"I have a very exciting announcement." His eyes are sparkling, and so are Jake's. "We're going up."

"Up?" I'm confused. "Upstairs?"

My father laughs. "A little farther than that."

I don't know what to say.

"The surface, honey. We're going to the surface."

Jake's watching me. Clearly, he knew about this and didn't tell me. For a second, I'm irritated. But then the news sinks in and excitement bubbles up from my toes like a kettle starting to boil.

"Are you serious?"

"Entirely. I pulled some strings and we got seats on a mole going to Archipelago Six day after tomorrow. Storm window looks good, nothing for a thousand miles." He chuckles. "Nothing except sun and sea."

He hands me a brochure. I touch play and see a girl in a bikini frolicking on a beach with stunted palm trees in the background. "Topside Travel offers all-inclusive packages to Archipelagoes Five through Twelve." Her voice is rich and husky. "Our secure pods whisk you to the surface in perfect comfort, where you can dine under the stars and enjoy spa treatments, yoga classes, snorkeling or simply soaking up the sun. The five-star accommodations include valet service and an exotic menu designed by renowned chef Henri Petit . . ."

A series of pictures unreels: laughing couples strolling hand-in-hand through the surf, a silver-haired man in a tuxedo sipping a glass of wine underneath a gauzy white tent, little kids tossing a beach ball on a rocky shore.

The girl holds up a pink cocktail glass as the words "All bookings subject to last-minute cancellation due to unforeseen weather events" slide by on the bottom of the screen.

Sun. I've never seen the sun, not in person.

Jake looks about ready to explode, and I decide to forgive him the deception.

We're going to the surface.

❧

The next day is a flurry of activity.

We have to get shots for malaria and typhoid, and of course I don't own a bathing suit or much else suitable for a tropical vacation. It's always exactly seventy-three degrees in Raven Rock, which is supposed to be the ideal temperature. I go shopping with my mother in the city, and choose a yellow bikini with two tiny plastic fish dangling from the top.

When I show it to Jake, he waggles his eyebrows suggestively and I pretend to put him in a sleeper hold. We start wrestling on the living room floor, where my father finds us and Jake jumps up, abashed.

"Just getting in some sparring," I say.

My father snorts.

"Keep it clean," he says.

But everyone is in a good mood, my parents more affectionate with each other than I've seen in a long time. Jake's restless, spending hours in the media room, flipping from one live feed to the next.

I finally go to bed, but I can't sleep, trying to imagine the smell of the ocean, the feel of real sunlight on my skin. We spend an hour or so a week under ultraviolet so we don't get rickets and other bone diseases, but I doubt it's the same, or even similar.

My room hasn't changed much since I first went off to the Academy. The daisy-print wallpaper is fading and the air has a musty, unused smell that makes me a little sad. I take down a stuffed tiger that I loved nearly to pieces as a child and hold it for a while. Then I get up and repack my suitcase, just for something to do.

I pray the weather stays clear.

Very few people ever get to see the surface. You need more money than God, or serious connections to the military, or both. I wonder what kind of strings my father had to pull. He's a two-star general, middle-ranking, but attaché to the head of inter-prefecture relations. That means he has to travel a lot, so he wasn't around much when I was growing up. He's very devoted to his job, and

I know how important it is to him that I do well at the Academy. He probably arranged for this trip as a reward for my imminent graduation. I've always been scared of disappointing my father, even though he doesn't intentionally put pressure on me. It's just that carrying on the family tradition is a huge deal for him.

I'm too wound up to eat breakfast in the morning, but Jake wolfs down a stack of pancakes and an obscene amount of synth bacon.

"I've heard the moles can be a bumpy ride," I tease.

"Cast iron stomach," he grins, patting his torso. Jake's built like a bulldozer, broad and hard and crushingly heavy.

We drive half an hour to the Raven Rock launch station and get on line. There are ten departure gates, each leading to a group of moles behind closed doors. A perky blonde in pumps and a short grey dress checks our papers, then ushers us to a second, shorter line. A holodisplay ticks down the minutes to launch. Thirty-two. Everything is sleek and white and shiny. I smile at a little red-haired boy just ahead of us in line. He doesn't smile back.

There's an edge of anxiety in the air. Talking and laughing just a little too loud. Most of us have never been inside a mole before, although we know how they work: back end a simple pod with seats, front end a boring machine that drills through rock and dirt and whatever else gets in its way. They move faster than you'd expect, but it's still a long way to the surface.

Jake squeezes my hand. "Lucky seven," he says, looking at our gate number.

Finally, when the display reads fifteen minutes, the doors open and the line starts moving. A final desultory scan of papers, and we enter the hangar. There are three moles. They look like tin cans with teeth.

The first is carrying security, contractors by the looks of them. Jake sneers a little. They're heavily armed and joshing around with each other, totally at ease. Not their first trip.

The last mole will take the science officers and support staff. That's the deal between the government and the adventure companies. One detachment per trip to repair the weather stations and gather data. Botanists, meteorologists, a shrink or two. I watch as a woman in a lab coat supervises the loading of equipment crates. She looks frazzled.

So we're second in line.

"How long will it take, Daddy?" I haven't called my father "daddy" since I was eight.

"A few hours, sweetheart. Don't worry, there's movies, snacks, games. Network feed, of course. Everything is soundproofed."

He's dressed casually, in slacks and a blue button-down, but his back is still straight as a board and he oozes authority. The attendants fawn all over him, and my mother rolls her eyes.

"Who's the goon squad?" Jake asks as we settle into our seats.

"Mandatory," my father says.

"That's a lot of firepower they're packing."

"Toads have been known to take a big hit and keep coming."

"Toads? I thought they stayed at the pole."

"They do. Usually."

And then one of the attendants is reviewing safety procedures and telling us to turn off all electronic devices and I feel a hum under my seat as the huge motors start warming up.

Captain Dan comes on the intercom, gives us a pep talk and says he hopes we don't get too bored, eliciting groans from a couple of the passengers.

The mole ahead of us, the one with the contractors, rumbles off into the darkness of the hangar. Twenty minutes later, it's our turn.

Six hours to Archipelago Six.

CHAPTER TWO

*If one imagines the Earth as an apple, the engineering
feat proposed by the Intergovernmental Consortium
merely entailed pricking the skin.*

We haven't always lived like this. Most historians call it the Transition. It happened a while ago, when my parents were just little kids. And it happened fast.

The seas warmed past fifty degrees, and hypercanes or superstorms or whatever you want to call them began to form, and instead of eventually losing strength and going away they got bigger and stuck around. Some of them are the size of continents now.

So a decision was made to go underground. But there wasn't room for everyone. Not even for most.

That's why some call it the Culling.

"Beverage?" the attendant asks, and I thank her and take a soda. We're an hour or so in, and the trip is actually turning out to be kind of boring, just like Captain Dan said.

The red-headed kid is across the aisle on my left, hammering away at a game. His parents are nursing cocktails. The mood has gone from apprehensive to lethargic and half-drunk, by the glassy looks of some of the passengers. The mole is very smooth, soundproofed as promised, no hint of the rock being explosively vaporized a few feet away. Just a slight upward tilt to my seat.

I doze off, thinking about the sheep and the valley and the sun breaking through the rainclouds. It's become my favorite daydream.

Then I feel Jake's hand on my arm. "We've stopped," he says.

And I realize that there's no hum under my seat anymore. It must have just happened, because no one else seems to have noticed.

"Is that normal?"

"I have no idea."

I expect Captain Dan to get on the intercom, but he doesn't. Half the passengers are asleep, the others reading quietly or watching the cane network. Tracking the storms is something of a national obsession.

Then a guy toward the back yells, "It's not moving. Why is it not moving?"

His voice slurs a little, and there's an edge of panic there.

Uh-oh, I think.

"Now sir," an attendant says, gliding down the aisle with a fixed smile on her face.

But the cat's out of the bag now. A low murmuring begins, as people start to grasp what's happening. The attendant holds up her hands. She's young and pretty and immaculately groomed.

"There's nothing to worry about. The mole ahead of us snapped a rotor on some bedrock. It's being repaired. We expect to be moving shortly."

"What does that mean? How shortly?" the man calls out. He's half risen from his seat. The middle-aged woman next to him, wife or girlfriend, puts a restraining hand on his arm and he shakes it off.

The attendant knows better than to tell him to calm down, which usually has the opposite effect on people. "Why don't I just check with the captain and get an update?" She disappears into the forward cabin.

No one speaks for a minute. I know it's my imagination, but the temperature in the mole seems to go up a few degrees.

"How much air do they carry on these things?" someone asks.

I sip my soda and share a look with Jake.

"Moles have redundancies built into their redundancies," he says quietly. "Foolproof."

I don't really want to be the one to say it, but we're all thinking it anyway, so I go ahead.

"Black Dome."

Jake snorts and looks away, like he's disappointed in me. But before he does, I see a flash of fear.

Black Dome.

It happened six years ago. I was only ten, but I remember every detail. My parents tried to shield me, unsuccessfully, since it was all anyone talked about for weeks.

Five moles, twenty-five passengers and crew each. Departed from Black Dome launch station on August the nineteenth. Fair skies above, a perfect window for an excursion to Gallia Archipelago.

Ninety-three adults, thirty-two children.

The tremors started about halfway up, the mole equivalent of turbulence on an airplane. Ice rattling in glasses, maybe a bag or two toppling from the overhead bins. No one's too alarmed at first. But then they get stronger.

Subterranean quake, six point six in magnitude. The epicenter was two hundred miles away, so the moles weren't just crushed like the glorified tin cans they are. What happened was worse.

They got trapped.

For thirty-seven days.

The military tried to send in diggers, a smaller, more maneuverable version of moles, to reach the stranded passengers, but the rock was too unstable to get close. Their com uplink still worked, although after a couple of weeks, people stopped talking.

Rescuers got in eventually. They're probably still in therapy.

I sip my soda and stare at Jake until he looks at me.

"That was totally different," he says.

I don't bother to answer.

There were seventeen survivors. It doesn't take too much imagination to figure out how they managed that.

A few more minutes go by, and someone emits a low sob. My father gets out of his seat.

"I'm going up front," he says.

But before he can turn around, the drunk guy pushes past him and starts heading for the forward cabin. He has thinning brown hair, and the back of his neck is red and splotchy. My father grabs his arm.

"Get your goddamn hands off me," the guy hisses, swinging one fist around in a wide arc that catches my father in the side of the face. It shatters his glasses, and a thin line of blood runs into the crease of his nose.

My body is moving before my brain even tells it to. High sweeping kick to the chin, followed by a gut punch on the way down. The guy drops like a sack of potatoes.

I feel hands on me, Jake's, and the guy's wife or girlfriend screaming. And then the hum of the engines starts up again.

The attendant comes rushing through the door, takes in the scene, and stops in her tracks.

"Everyone back in their seats," she says.

I comply, ducking my head to avoid the stares of the other passengers. Jake and my father carry the unconscious guy to the rear of the mole and lay him out on the carpet. No one says anything.

The rest of the trip is pretty uneventful.

CHAPTER THREE

The earliest years of the colonies, later known as prefectures, were marked by deprivation and psychological trauma to a degree not anticipated by the architects. But the human species adapts; we are curiously, even ruthlessly proficient at it.

Everyone has to put in special contact lenses before we exit the mole. Apparently, it takes a couple of days for our eyes to adjust to the glare. Of course there's plenty of light underground. Everything runs on geothermal now, which is a practically inexhaustible energy source. But it's not the sun.

We line up in the aisle. The guy I kicked is awake, bruised but not broken. If I'd wanted to hurt him permanently, I would have. We studiously avoid looking at each other. Once he sobered up, he approached my dad and apologized. They shook hands. No hard feelings. My dad has a little cut on his eyebrow, but my mother remembered to bring his spare reading glasses so he's not too upset.

"Thanks for choosing Topside Travel," the attendant says, smiling, and I can tell she's glad to be rid of us.

She opens the hatch and light spills into the cabin, not the light I'm used to, this stuff is different, brighter and stronger and *hotter*, and it is followed by a warm breeze that smells like nothing I've ever smelled before. Equal bits salt and earth and decay; I don't mean rotten or spoiled, just living matter breaking down into its component parts. We shuffle forward, suddenly uncertain, Jake grinning like a madman ahead of me. There's a short flight of steps leading down, and then we're standing on hot, coarse sand, with the sea about thirty yards away.

I've seen pictures. They are nothing, absolutely nothing, like the real thing.

A man and woman approach the mole. They're wearing stacks of flower garlands around their necks, which they proceed to drape all over us.

"I'm Sissy and this is Mac, we're your check-in coordinators," the woman says. "The welcome tent is right over there." She points at a white pavilion about twenty yards away.

I shed my sweater and wander down the shoreline, unsteady on my feet. All my senses are jammed up by a torrent of weird new data, as though I've crash-landed on an alien planet, and I'm not the only one. The red-headed kid is standing stock still with his mouth agape, just staring at the sky. I follow his gaze up, up, up . . . and for a dizzying second I feel like I'm on the edge of a cliff, like everything is turned upside down and if I take a step I'll plummet into the bottomless blue, with nothing to break my fall.

They say that about one in thirty tourists is stricken with agoraphobia so bad they can't leave the mole. Of course they give you a psych evaluation before booking, but the reality of the surface is just too much for some people, even the well-adjusted ones.

It's almost too much for me. So I sit down, hard, on the rocks and wait for the world to stop spinning.

Archipelago Six. The brochures I read on the mole said it comprises about three thousand low-lying islands scattered like a string of pearls along the Atlantic seaboard, just above Greenbrier Prefecture. That's the one adjacent to ours. Raven Rock doesn't have very good diplomatic relations with its neighbors, which is why they need people like me and Jake.

The storms intensify in fifteen-year cycles and Archipelago Six hasn't taken a direct hit for a while, so there are palm trees and even a few white birds. Seagulls, I guess. They're gathered near the welcome tent, watching it with sharp, hungry eyes. There must be food in there.

"You OK, honey?" my dad says, hoisting me to my feet. "Pretty nice, huh?"

Yes. It's pretty nice.

The water flashes like a field of blue-green crystals. And the air. It moves. The living breath of the planet, I think, feeling romantic and foolish and suddenly sad. We've lost so much. More than I ever imagined.

"Don't stare," Jake says. "Even with the contacts in, you can go blind."

I realize I've been looking straight at the sun and tear my eyes away. Black afterimages dance against the horizon. It's smaller than I expected. But harsher too.

My mother spots the third mole erupting through the sand a little way away, beyond a cordon, and says she thinks she knows the science officer, the woman who was supervising the loading. They met at a conference two years ago.

"Carlsson," she says. "René. Or maybe Rebekah. She had some interesting ideas about nitrogen uptake. I'll have to say hello once they've settled in."

"Shop talk," my father grumbles. "We're supposed to be on vacation."

"I know you'll end up triple-checking the security protocols and bossing those poor fellows around, so I guess we're even," Mom says.

We look over at the contractors. They got here first, and they've already dug trenches at either end of the pebbly beach and set up a discreet perimeter of motion detectors in the underbrush. They're wearing civilian clothes, slacks and T-shirts, so us tourists don't feel like we've been stuck in an internment camp. But they're too big and bored and competent to be anything but soldiers.

"Is all that really necessary?" Jake asks. "I mean, what are the toads going to do, swim a thousand miles from Novarctica?"

My father says, "They can swim farther than you think."

Toads. Newly emerged life form, amphibian but with primate characteristics. As in bipedal, as in crudely intelligent. Also, if you hadn't guessed, not friendly. No one knows where they came from. One day, they just appeared. In biology, it's called punctuated equilibrium, a fancy way of describing the rapid evolution of a species when it's put under severe environmental stress. Some cold-blooded species are apparently very good at this. Better than we are.

"They've never been known to attack a large party," Jake persists.

Strictly speaking, this is true. But every now and then, a surface expedition doesn't come back. The camps are found abandoned, ransacked, the people just gone. No hard evidence that the toads did it. No evidence that they didn't, either.

But Jake is right about one thing. They've never been spotted this far south.

"It's a legal liability issue. The travel agencies have to offer security or we'd shut them down," my father says, and I take Jake by the arm and drag him over to the welcome tent. Enough toad talk. I want to put on my little yellow bikini and see what that water actually feels like.

Inside, there's a table piled high with fruit and cheese and cold cuts and pastries. I bite into a slice of ham and almost choke. It's real. Not synth ham, which, like all "meat" products, is actually a kind of fungus that supposedly has the texture of flesh. This is real ham. From an actual pig. It's like the difference between ice cream and cottage cheese.

I think I've eaten meat from an animal about four times in my life. It's that hard to get.

I decide I'm really going to enjoy this vacation.

Jake and I get fruity concoctions from the bar and take our plates to the shore while my parents sort out the check-in process. The meteorologists are setting up their equipment at the far end of the beach. They assemble a satellite dish, solar panels, and Doppler LIDAR, which stands for Light Detection and Ranging, a laser system that measures temperature and wind speed along the beam.

"I think you're getting a tan already," Jake teases.

"Not likely with the two hundred SPF I slathered all over myself. But I appreciate the lie."

He smiles. Jake has the best smile, honest and open. Like a puppy.

"There goes the guy whose ass you kicked."

I look over my shoulder. He's walking with his lady friend toward the sleeping tents, which look plush. They're laughing together, and he leans over and pecks her cheek.

"I did not kick his ass."

"Oh right, sorry. You kicked his face in."

"Jake."

"OK, OK. I would've done it if you hadn't gotten there first, sweetie."

I swat him on the leg. "Let's go swimming."

I change in my assigned tent. It's not plush. It's palatial. I can hear the ocean through the gauzy walls, which are thin enough to let in plenty of light but not completely immodest. Thick oriental rugs cover the ground, and my bed is four-poster, mahogany, another unimaginable luxury.

The advance crew arrived days ago, and they seem to have anticipated anything I could possibly want. There's a mini-fridge stocked with food and drinks, fresh flowers everywhere, and an exquisitely carved oval standing mirror in which I am now checking out my bikini. I've gotten more muscular in the shoulders and thighs these last months, though Jake probably still has a hundred pounds on me. At the Academy, they call me the Speck because I'm shorter than everyone else. Not in an affectionate way either. But looking at my reflection, with no one towering over me for comparison, I feel good. I just wish I had longer hair.

We've trained in pools since we were five, but I'm still nervous when I walk down to the shore. The waves aren't all that big. It's the size of the ocean that intimidates me. Not to mention what's out there, somewhere beyond the horizon. It's sunny and calm, but I can't forget the hypercanes churning their way across the surface, obliterating everything in their paths as efficiently and remorselessly as the moles blast through bedrock. I can't forget that I am up here with them, instead of safe down below.

Jake's already in the water. He's swum out past the breakers and waves when he spots me, an anonymous head identifiable only by his massive shoulders. I stick a toe in. It's very warm. I suddenly wonder what else lives in there.

"C'mon, Nordqvist," Jake yells. "Don't be a cherry."

I've gone through so much worse than this in training, I remind myself. Rappelling down the sheer sides of lightless subterranean caverns with god knows what at the bottom. Fighting guys twice my size with no weapons except my hands and feet and superior intellect. Survival stuff I don't even want to think about now because I'm on vacation. This should be a piece of cake.

My knees are knocking as I take a deep breath and march into the beautiful blue-green water like I've been summoned to the commandant's study. A big wave rolls in, and I time it wrong and get shoved off my feet. The world goes topsy-turvy. I lose all sense of up and down and start to panic. But then my training kicks in. I stop struggling and make myself go limp, and my own buoyancy pulls me to the surface.

I float on my back, just letting the surges push me around. I think my contacts get washed out, because everything is suddenly brighter, almost blinding. So I close my eyes and savor the salt on my tongue and just float for a while. I haven't been this relaxed in months. Maybe years.

Then something grabs my foot and I think it's a barracuda, but of course it's only Jake.

He chases me down and we try to throw each other in the surf and after a while, I stop worrying about giant squids and just want to see him get a royal snoutful of ocean. My skin stings. I have sand in my bathing suit. And it's the best time I've had in a really long while.

CHAPTER FOUR

Food, air and water; these essential commodities were as valuable, and scarce, as if we had relocated to another planet entirely.

Dinner is an elaborate affair. After showering and modeling nearly every item in my suitcase in front of the mirror, I settle on a simple white linen dress with delicate flowers embroidered on the neckline and sleeves. My mother loans me her diamond studs, and I go minimal with the makeup, just a little lip gloss and mascara. Strappy white sandals, for which I painted my toenails a bright coral. I think I look pretty nice.

There are tiki torches burning all along the shore, and about a dozen tables with white tablecloths and elegant flowery centerpieces. Most of the adults have gathered at the open bar in the welcome center. My mother is chatting animatedly with René, or maybe Rebekah, and my father, as predicted, has gravitated towards the chief of security, a stocky man in his late forties with dreadlocks and an amiable expression. They appear to be hitting it off.

I notice a couple of guys with earplugs and bulges under their sports coats hovering in the background. The rest are probably in the trenches, looking at girly mags and eating synth spam.

The sun is low, and the color of the sea has changed to a darker blue streaked with copper and gold. My first sunset.

I suddenly don't want to go back down, not ever, and the feeling is so strong that my heart starts to beat really fast and my chest hurts. I know we can't stay. It's impossible. The storms terrify me. But still, I want to, I want to so bad. We're not supposed to live down there, I think. We're supposed to live up here.

"Hi gorgeous," Jake says, handing me a glass of juice with a little umbrella sticking out of the top. He makes a show of looking me up and down. "Very alluring, though I've always been partial to a woman in uniform."

I think about confiding in him. Reject that idea immediately. He's not built to think outside the box.

"Especially when she drop-kicks you like a can of beans," I say instead.

He laughs. "Yeah, especially then."

We hold hands and watch the sun sink below the horizon.

"Jan, do you ever think about when training is over?"

"All the time."

"I don't want to lose you."

I keep quiet. I'm not sure where he's going with this. Everyone knows we have no control over our cell assignments, and they're kept secret until after graduation. Once we're in the field, contact with family and friends is minimal.

"What if we could work together?" Jake says. He's wearing a white button-up shirt with a navy blazer slung over one shoulder. His skin glows caramel in the twilight.

"You know that's not going to happen."

"But what if we could?"

"I don't know. Why are you asking me this?"

He shrugs. "Just wondering."

"That would be great," I say.

The truth is, he's my protector, and we both know it. Before Jake came along and took an inexplicable interest in me, the bullying by other cadets was merciless. Now it's tolerable. I'm grateful and all, but I wonder if maybe he's as infatuated with my father as he is with me. He seems to take my devotion perfectly for granted too, like I've won the lottery or something. And now that my eight years of hazing are almost over, I just want to move on. Leave the Academy—and maybe Jake, too—behind and start fresh. Part of me feels disloyal. But another, bigger part is ready for something different. Not just ready, if I'm being honest. *Craves* something different.

"You don't sound like you mean it," he persists.

"OK, fine." I turn to him, suddenly annoyed. I didn't want to do this now, but I've thought about it a lot lately and he needs to hear it. "The reality is, we're going to get our teams, and go do our jobs, and someday you'll marry a very nice lady and have lots of kids and you'll be bringing them on nice vacations like this one."

He lets go of my hand.

"That's bull."

"I'm not the one you want to end up with, Jake. Trust me."

"Why not?" His eyes narrow, and I know I'm wounding him, but I can't stop. "Just tell me why not."

"Because you're a dog and I'm a cat," I say.

"What's that supposed to mean?"

We're the elite of the elite, Jake and I. He'll make a fine field agent someday. He has a perfectly rigid value system and plays by the rules, always. I can't imagine him refusing a direct order to do anything. Anything at all. That's one way we're different.

"It means that as much as I appreciate what you've done for me, we're about to graduate and go our separate ways. I didn't make the plan. That's just how it is."

"Wait a second." He shakes his head. "Appreciate what you've done for me? And what is *that* supposed to mean? I thought you cared about me. I thought . . ." He trails off. "I don't know what I thought. But it sure wasn't that you think I'm doing you some kind of favor."

"I didn't say that. It came out wrong. Look, can we not fight about this?"

I like Jake. I do. He's smart and handsome and loyal. But there's something missing. He never seems to suffer from a single shred of self-doubt, for one thing. He's like one of those lizards I read about in biology that change color to blend with whatever they're standing next to. Jake lives in a world of absolutes, black and white, us and them. I envy him that sometimes. It must make life a lot simpler.

"I go out with you because I like you, Jan. I thought you felt the same way."

"I do," I snap, suddenly tired of the whole conversation. The truth is, my feelings for him are so conflicted and mixed-up that I can hardly make sense of them myself. "I just have a lot more on my mind than our relationship at the moment."

He looks at me long and hard and walks away.

In retrospect, I probably could have handled that better.

Jake is polite but cool to me at dinner. We're sharing a table with Dr Rebekah and her assistant Miles, a strapping lad of about twenty-five who keeps sneaking glances at me underneath his long dark eyelashes, which doesn't escape the notice of Jake. Rebekah has a dual degree in biology and weather sciences, mainly so she could get on the surface trips, and she's captivating the table with factoids about the hypercanes.

After a while, even Jake stops pouting and gets into the conversation. It's his favorite subject, after all.

"So how close have you ever gotten to one? I mean, personally?" he asks, sawing into a steak like it's his last meal on earth. I watch him chew his meat and wish I wasn't sitting right across the table from him. It's amazing how physical attraction can do a one-eighty under the right circumstances. Did I seriously used to let this guy put his tongue in my mouth?

I'm greasy and stuffed, and it's only the second course. The new sandals are chafing my feet, so I kick them off under the table and plunge my toes into the cool sand. After living in combat boots for the last eight years, it's pure heaven.

"Once we took a mole up into Megaera's eye," Rebekah says. "It's about two hundred miles across, but still a tricky operation since she's travelling fast."

Jake almost pees himself. "You were in the eye?"

Rebekah smiles. "I saw the wall. It's so high, it actually punches through the stratosphere."

"That's badass." He looks at my father. "I mean, very cool."

"It was," Rebekah agrees.

"What about Tisiphone? I never really understood why she doesn't move like the others."

"That's a good question. Tisiphone is the smallest, of course, and the only one located in the northwestern hemisphere. No prefectures below, no islands above, just open ocean. She's pinned down by opposing jet streams that let her rotate but hold her more or less in place."

Waiters arrive, replacing the steak with a creamy bisque and sautéed asparagus with lemon. Wine glasses are refilled. I stick with ice water. The rich food and gentle surf sounds are making me sleepy. It feels like a hundred years since I carried my bags to the car this morning.

"Have you ever considered a career in private security? Plenty of surface time," Rebekah says.

"We've invested too much training and money in this kid to let him go," my father interjects. "Besides, Jake's a company man, right?"

I don't like the look that passes between them. It's conspiratorial.

"So Miles, what's your specialty?" I ask, and he blushes furiously.

"Biosciences," he says. "Animal genetics. Cross-breeding."

"I hear that's a hot field right now."

Jake scowls and takes a big sip of red wine. He's still a year below the drinking age, but no one seems to care tonight. I just hope he doesn't get drunk and do something stupid.

"Yeah, it is," Miles says. "I work mostly with sheep and pigs. Modifying the genome for optimal survival in subterranean conditions. We've made some progress with fruit bat DNA, but it's still in the early stages."

It turned out farm animals don't do very well underground. In fact, the majority of them die before reaching adulthood. No one's exactly sure why.

"Sounds fascinating," I murmur.

He blushes again.

"We brought Miles along in case we run across any interesting life forms," Rebekah says. "Not many big mammals left, but there are some avian and insect species that appear to have adapted."

And the toads, I think. They've adapted.

"I bet there's more we don't know about. Ecosystems are more resilient than you'd think," Miles says. "Of course, the food chain was radically disrupted. But look at the gulls. They're still here."

I remember their sharp eyes, watching us. Tough little buggers.

Later that night, Jake stumbles tipsily up to my tent. He looks lost and sad, so far from his normal cocky self that I feel guilty and let him in against my better judgment.

"Why are you acting this way?" he says, collapsing onto my bed and staring up at the canopy.

"What way?"

"You know."

"You'll have to be more specific," I say, already regretting my decision.

"Like you don't care."

"You're drunk, Jake," I say. "And if my dad catches you in here, he'll kill us both."

I'm really starting to wish he hadn't been invited on this trip. At school, there's no time for reflection. We're too busy training in black ops and hostage extractions and how to kill a man with our bare hands in a hundred different ways. Jake and I have our routine—eating together in the mess hall, spending the one hour of evening downtime watching the storms in the rec room (his idea of a perfect date), sneaking kisses between class—and I don't really question it. But spending entire days with him up here . . . I'm having major second thoughts about our relationship.

"Your dad loves me," he slurs.

"And vice versa, I'm sure," I say tartly. "But you still need to go back to your own tent." I peek out the flap. "Oh my God, someone's coming. Move! Hurry!"

I grab him by the arm and drag him to the door.

"Can I at least get a—" he says, lips puckering, as I give him a mighty shove between the shoulder blades.

I listen to his muttering fade into the distance, until I'm sure he's not coming back.

The rest of this vacation is going to be seriously awkward, I think as I crawl under the covers.

After breakfast, I go swimming again, and this time I figure out the rhythm of the waves and don't get bashed around so much. My eyes are adjusting well without the contacts. The weather is perfect, bright sun and puffy white clouds. I find a patch of smooth sand and lie there for a while, just watching them drift overhead. The sky is so *huge*.

"I'm glad you're getting a chance to see the real world," my mom says, dragging a plastic chair up beside me and settling in. She's wearing a plain white one-piece bathing suit and big straw hat and looks about a decade younger than her thirty-eight years. It's easy to see why my dad's still madly in love with her.

"God, the last time I was on the surface I was only four," she says. "The thing I remember the best is my dog, Jimmy. He was a Shepherd-Rottweiler mix. My father would take us to the park on Sunday afternoons. Once we got caught in a big lightning storm— they seemed to come more and more frequently, sometimes out of a clear blue sky. Poor Jimmy was so scared, whining and hiding between my father's legs. But not me. I thought it was the most exciting thing. Like a fireworks display." She closes her eyes and sighs. "We packed up and moved below a week later."

"What happened to Jimmy?" I ask.

"My parents said he couldn't come. No room. I cried for a month." She smiles wistfully. "I still think about that dog sometimes. I wonder what happened to him. If he found a way to survive."

Most often when I hear about the Transition, it's just this big abstract thing that happened. It hardly even seems real that people once lived up here. My father's never spoken of it to me, not about himself personally, and this is the first time I can recall my mother telling a story about it. I always figured they were too little to remember much. But now I think about Mom's dog, imagine him wandering the streets, alone and scared, and it suddenly makes it real in a way that years of dry history lessons never did.

"Hey, let's go into the jungle tomorrow and gather some samples to take back," she says, noticing my troubled expression. "I'm dying to see what kinds of plants have migrated to this latitude."

"Plants migrate?" I reapply sunscreen and flip over onto my stomach.

"Of course. Most thrive within a narrow temperature range. When it gets too hot, they seek out cooler climates, just like animals. But as their territories shift, they encounter new species, so it can get complicated. We scientists call it ecosystem reshuffling." She sees my eyes glazing over and laughs. "Call it a mother-daughter hike, OK? We need to catch up."

"Sure, mom, Sounds fun."

I glance past the beach volleyball net to where Jake is napping in the shade of a palm tree. He looked a little green at breakfast and I'm relieved he's keeping his distance.

Five days left. I try not to think about it, because the thought of getting back into the mole, this time with my seat at a slight *downward* tilt, makes me deeply depressed.

I lift one strap of my bikini and see a faint line. By God, I'm starting to get a tan.

Jake is already brown, but he was born that way. I wonder how many generations it will take before the melanin is leached out of all of us for lack of any evolutionary purpose, and we all look the same, a bunch of pasty cave-dwellers. That thought, too, is depressing.

"What's with the long face?" my father booms, leaning down to kiss my mother on the forehead. He's a big, energetic man with thick, still black hair, crinkly blue eyes and a square jaw. At home, I'm used to seeing him either in uniform or dark, conservative clothing. Today, he's wearing mirrored sunglasses and a garish floral-patterned shirt. It's a completely surreal image.

"You look lovely, my darling," he says. "As beautiful as you are brilliant."

"Oh my, Anker." Mom grins. "How many mimosas *have* you had today? It's not yet eleven."

"I am intoxicated only by your beauty," he says solemnly, then offers me a hand. "Come on, pumpkin, let's walk."

So I peel myself off the lounge chair and we set off down the beach, gulls wheeling and squawking over our heads. The dark green mounds of other islands dot the horizon. A soft breeze ruffles my hair, carrying a mosaic of scents too complex to unravel. All I know is it smells great.

"Do you like it here?" he asks.

"Yes," I answer simply.

"This may be the last real time we spend together as a family for a while. I wanted it to be special."

I put my arm around his waist and give a squeeze. We pass the science camp, and Miles waves at us. We wave back. He's doing something to the LIDAR, while Rebekah looks over his shoulder. No holiday for them.

We walk for a while more, slowly so we don't get to the trench too soon. I get the feeling my father has an agenda. And sure enough, he stops as soon as we're on a deserted stretch and takes off his sunglasses. Here it comes.

"Honey, you know I can't talk much about my work, but six days ago, our intelligence uncovered a troop buildup in the caverns near Greenbrier's northern border. Probably related to the trade embargo. Nothing to worry about yet, but . . . Well, we have to anticipate that the situation could deteriorate in coming months."

Military-speak for impending war, I think.

"Nu London is a staunch ally. But how the other prefectures will react is unclear. We're working all the back channels now. There's always a chance for a diplomatic solution."

The heart of our dispute with Greenbrier is fresh water. It's the most precious resource underground. We get air through vent tubes that go to the surface, and abundant energy from the Earth's core. The mines produce a wealth of various metals and ores. Water's a different story. There's a finite amount. And we need a lot of it, for climate control and agriculture and industry and sanitation.

About a year ago, Greenbrier depleted its own water supply and starting tapping into our aquifer. It wasn't the first dispute we've had with them. Tensions have flared over mineral rights and who controls the bullet train system and a million other things. That's why we have the Academy, and they have something called Subterranean Operations Command. The irony is that we both started out as part of a centrally administered network of prefectures. That was the original plan. Kind of like the pre-Transition states. Well, it fell apart pretty quick.

Our water conflict with Greenbrier has been getting uglier in recent weeks, though we're still short of all-out hostilities. War on the surface was bad enough. War underground . . . The idea makes my blood run cold.

"We're putting together a special team," my father says. "Intel, sabotage. Missions of that nature. I want you on it. I want Jake on it. We need the best."

Jake knew about this, I think. Just like he knew we were going to the surface. What else isn't he telling me?

"I thought you'd be happy," my father says. "You and Jake seem good together."

I almost laugh, though not out of amusement. Could his timing be any worse?

"Good together how?" I ask warily. "As a team or as a couple?"

"Well, both, I guess. So what do you say?"

"I don't know. I need to think about it." And if I take long enough, maybe I won't have to make a decision at all.

My father squints at me, the way he does when he's displeased and trying not to show it. "I don't know what you have to think about, honey. This would really get your career started on the right footing. Some key people are going to be watching this team very closely. Plus to keep Jake in the picture . . . I thought you'd be over the moon."

"Yeah, well, as to that," I say, deciding I should just tell the truth. "I'm not so sure about Jake. I don't think we have that much in common anymore. Like we've drifted apart."

My father stares at me, stunned, as if *he's* the one being broken up with.

"Wow," he says. "I didn't see that at all. I thought you two were doing so well. He's a fine young man. He loves you. He told me so. We talked about it last month, he called me, and we decided that if you guys could just spend some quality time . . ." And then he sees my face and realizes that he made a serious strategic error by admitting that the two of them had been plotting out my future behind my back and tries to change tacks but I'm already gone, walking back down the beach toward my tent, which I wish had a door so I could slam it hard.

I pass Jake, who might be an ass but isn't dumb and steers well clear of me.

War. We're going to war. Maybe. Probably.

What a bloody mess.

I decide to get a massage while I still can.

CHAPTER FIVE

Within a few short years, the billions left to their fate became as a dream, erased from the collective memory. Pre-Transition population estimates in most textbooks were radically revised downward.

The raid comes in the middle of the night.

This time, I was the sulky one at dinner, picking at my food and answering in monosyllables until everyone stopped trying to talk to me. I hate it when I get like this, but I'm so mad at Jake and especially my father that I can't help it. My dad has the decency to look mildly embarrassed. We never fight, I hardly even see him, so it's feels weird to be giving him the silent treatment. I'm usually agreeable and cheery, a total daddy's girl. But I'm sick and tired of everyone else making decisions for me. I'm sixteen, not six, and it's time he noticed that.

I deliberately looked my worst, selecting a ratty tank top and hideous paisley skirt from years before that I'd packed in case of an emergency like, I don't know, cleaning fish or something. No makeup. Just a permanent frown.

Anyway, the raid. Speaking of bloody messes.

Four am on the dot. The hour when a person's defenses are at their lowest ebb. The military knows this, and so did the raiders.

They come from the jungle side, and they come fast and sneaky. They've done this before. By the time the sensors go off, it's too late. I wake to small arms fire popping in the darkness, followed by the deep boom of the artillery guns in the trenches and the rapid staccato of automatic weapons set to the fully open position.

I roll out of bed, pulse racing, just as a spray of bullets rips through my tent, shattering the standing mirror and sending glass shards flying in a deadly rain that rakes across my shoulders. Wood splinters explode in the air. My bed has been decapitated, and the falling canopy nearly crushes me as I crawl across the floor and try to find an exit.

There's definitely something stuck in my back. Right between the shoulder blades. It hurts bad, but I can still move my arms so I guess my spine isn't damaged. I want to stop, to get it out, but I can't. First I need to find out what's *happening* out there.

Could it be toads? What else? There's nothing else.

The firing stops for a minute, and I creep under the edge of the tent, lifting it high so it doesn't catch on the thing in my back. My pajamas are spotted with blood, black in the moonlight. Figures move in the distance, but I can't tell if they're human or what. It's so hard to see. And then I realize that I have blood in my eyes too, and I swipe it away with a hand that is trembling uncontrollably.

OK.

Basic training. Find cover. Assess the enemy position. Launch a counterattack.

I have no weapon. But the contractors do. And the trench sounds like a really good place to be right now. So I start crawling on my stomach down the beach, stopping periodically to shake the blood from my eyes. Scalp lacerations are always gushers.

Someone screams off to my right, and there's a fresh burst of gunfire. More shouting. The man who punched my dad, the man who was just yesterday pecking his girlfriend on the cheek, suddenly runs out of the darkness, his shirt and hair on fire. He runs straight past me into the surf and flounders there. A big wave comes and the next second he's gone.

I crawl another twenty yards, into the shadow of the medical pavilion, and that's when I get my first good look at what's attacked us.

Not toads. People.

They're ragged and none too clean, but they're human. Men and women both. Some have guns, others are carrying crude wooden clubs. The sand is littered with bodies, ours and theirs, but it's a matter of numbers at this point. And there are more of them than there are of us. A lot more.

I see with something close to all-out panic that they've already overrun the trenches.

A group of three raiders suddenly materializes out of the shadows not five yards away. I freeze, pressing my body against the side of the tent. They're silent as rats and pass close enough that I could have reached out and touched the bare ankle of the one closest. A moment later they're gone, and I'm struggling to make sense of it, but I can't, because the whole situation is impossible. Who *are* these people? And, even more mystifying, *how did they get up here?* After endless fumbling in the darkness, I locate the tent flap and crawl inside, but there's not much that is useful as a weapon, just basic first aid supplies to treat bug bites and sunburns and things like that.

I don't think I can go any further without dealing with the thing stuck in my back so I reach around, biting down against the pain, and my fingertips brush something smooth and sharp. A glass shard, probably from the mirror. I work it loose, and steady myself on a gurney until the bout of nausea passes. I need a pressure bandage to stop the bleeding but I can't do it myself, not between the shoulder blades. Instead, I grab a jacket hanging from a hook and button it up as tightly as I can. If nothing else, I feel a little better knowing I won't be going out there in just my PJs.

When I creep through the flap, two things happen simultaneously. I spot Jake. And I hear the low rumble of a mole's engines fire up somewhere nearby.

They've formed a circle around him, three of them, including one who makes Jake look like a skinny ten year-old kid. Oh God, the guy is big. Jake's holding them off with a tent pole, but barely. I give him another minute or so before he's down.

"Evac! Evac!" someone shouts behind me. It's the security chief, and he's still trying to work his radio, but nobody appears to be alive to listen.

"Jansin!" He grabs my arm, points off to the right. "Go, get your ass into that mole. Your mother's there, your father too. He's says he won't leave without you, but Lord almighty . . ." He eyes my bloodstained hands and face. "There's a medikit on board, just get out of here. I think there's more coming through the jungle."

The urge to run, to turn my back on the carnage and not look back until I'm through the hatch, is overpowering.

"One minute," I say. "Jake's pinned down. Do you have a backup sidearm—"

But the security chief's radio is crackling, he's got contact, and he turns away, ignoring me, as a frantic voice starts begging for reinforcements that don't exist.

I stand there for a moment, frozen by indecision. If I go to help Jake, I could end up getting killed too. It's a strong possibility. I realize that I not only don't love him, I barely even like him anymore. Meanwhile, I can see the mole now, twenty yards away. Any anger I felt at my father has burned off in the cauldron of extreme fear. I know if I can just get to him, everything will be OK. I'll be safe.

I hear a cackle of hysterical laughter down the beach followed by screaming and I'm not sure if it's them or us.

In the end, there's no real choice. Not for someone who's spent the last decade training for situations like this. Rule one is you don't turn tail and run away. Under any circumstances.

It takes ten seconds to cross the rocks. I'm terrified, but I try to push the fear away, lock it up in a place where it won't cloud my judgment. I've been scared plenty of times in training, but not like this. This is real world.

On the way, I pull a club from the hand of one of the dead raiders, a blonde boy barely older than me whose body is still smoking from laser fire, and use it to crack the big one in the back of the head as hard as I can. He staggers, falls to his knees, tries to get up. The guy is an ox. Before he gets far, I deliver a flurry of kicks to his face that leave me feeling faint. He hits the ground like a load of iron slag. But I crack him on the head again anyway, just to be sure.

Jake turns to the woman to his right, while I face the third, a smaller guy who takes one look at me, one look at the colossus sprawled face-down on the sand, and hightails it into the jungle. If we weren't in such deep trouble, it would be almost comical.

The woman is made of sterner stuff. She's tall and lean, with shrewd black eyes and an intricate braid that nearly brushes her butt. A long white scar bisects her tan face from eyebrow to jaw.

"Better get back to your mole," she says, in a crisp accent that rings of Nu London.

The cluster of figures milling around the trenches is starting to head in our direction.

"Let's go, Jake," I hiss.

But his temper is boiling now. Boys are such fools sometimes. He swings at her, and she neatly sidesteps the hook punch and punches him in the side. No, stabs him in the side. I see a blade slick with blood slide out from between his ribs, and Jake's eyes go round with shock. I kick it out of her hand and then something that feels like an armored truck hits me from behind and my feet leave the ground as I'm seized in a bone-crushing bear hug.

I can't believe it, but the big one is on his feet again.

"Get down!" someone screams, and I try to duck as a gun goes off, four shots in quick succession.

It's the security chief. He manages to hit the woman in the shoulder, and I think the ox too, but now there's dozens of figures running toward us down the beach, closing in from about thirty yards, and I can't shake loose, I can hardly breathe. I try kicking Goliath in the crotch, but it's like kicking a boulder.

The mole is moving, I can see it, the hatch still open, arms waving from inside, beckoning. *Hurry up!*

Security chief points the gun directly at the giant's forehead and pulls the trigger. The hammer clicks down on an empty chamber. It's the worst sound in the world.

And then the giant lumbers off, still holding me in a death grip, and over his shoulder I see the mole slow and pick up Jake and his savior. The gap between us widens. For a split second, I see my father's face. I hear him call my name.

The hatch closes.

CHAPTER SIX

The spirit of cooperation that permitted the Consortium to complete its work amid global chaos soon disintegrated under the weight of political pressures and looming famine. Communication between the far-flung colonies was severed.

I watch with a kind of sick numbness as the mole points its nose down and starts burrowing into the sand. The first wave of raiders hits before it's completely submerged and starts pounding on the steel-plated sides with their clubs. It's useless, but a mob instinct has taken over and they have to vent their rage on something.

I don't want to think about what's going to happen to me next, so I try to analyze the situation the way I've been taught, work the angles, see things from their point of view.

First off, it's a disaster that some of us escaped.

Their lead time to take the loot and run has now shrunk dramatically. Six hours back to Raven Rock, say two more to scramble a fleet of moles or diggers packed to the gills with soldiers, another six hours for the return trip. It's one thing to hit a bunch of tourists in the middle of the night, quite another to face hundreds of heavily armed, highly disciplined troops who specialize in counterinsurgency and scorched earth tactics.

I wonder if I can stay alive for fourteen hours.

The ox finally puts me down but keeps one hand the size of an oven mitt clamped firmly around my arm. I don't bother trying to shake it off. My knees are wobbly, and I'd probably keel over if he wasn't holding me upright.

The woman with the braid approaches us, barking out orders. Her face is tight from the bullet wound in her shoulder, which must hurt like hell, but she's calm and in charge, which is reassuring. At least there's a chain of command here.

In the light of the burning tents, I see figures hauling off the wounded and scavenging through the debris. The heaviest activity appears to be around the scientific equipment, but the food services pavilion is a close second. And the open bar. The air reeks of charred flesh and urine and the acrid stench of burning plastic. I try to keep my face impassive, but my eyes are watering and I feel like I might be sick.

The woman eyes me up and down. I'm barefoot and about a hundred pounds soaking wet. Still, she looks at me like I'm some kind of venomous insect. Not a major threat, but perhaps best crushed anyway. Then her gaze lingers on my coat, narrowing slightly. She cocks her head, as if considering something.

"Take her to the *Solar Wind* and put her below," the woman says finally. She starts to walk away and the beach tilts at a dizzying angle. "Unless she bleeds out first."

And that's the last thing I hear before the darkness takes me.

In my dream, I'm back in uniform, not the navy blue of the Academy but the solid black jumpsuit they wear in special ops. We're a team of four, and we're all wearing balaclavas, but I know the big guy in front of me is Jake.

It feels like late afternoon by the quality of the light, although its source is indeterminate, as it always is underground. We're in

Greenbrier, one of the poorer districts. The streets are deserted. Jake holds up a hand, gestures to the windows of the housing complexes on either side. *We're being watched.*

I unholster my sidearm but keep my finger loose on the trigger and the muzzle down. There's so many windows, thousands of them. I don't see anyone, but the hair on the back of my neck is tingling. Yes, we're being watched.

Jake gives a signal and we crouch down, backs to the graffiti-covered wall. The agent next to me has bright blue eyes and a medium build, could be a man or a woman. I check the hands. They're smallish and fine-boned. So, probably a woman. The other has brown eyes and gloves. Perfectly androgynous.

A bus rolls past the end of the street, empty except for the driver hunched over the steering console. It's electric, like all vehicles, and very quiet.

What's our mission? I can't seem to remember.

It's something important though.

I'm filled with a sense of urgency and I'm terrified we'll fail. But fail at what?

Then I feel something warm running down my face and pull off my balaclava. My hand comes away red. Blood. I have blood in my eyes. I think if I can just wipe it away, I'll be able to remember. So I use the mask like a cloth, but it keeps coming, soaking my jumpsuit and boots.

"There's the target," Jake says.

I see a little red-headed boy of about eleven step out from a doorway across the street. I recognize him. He was on the . . .

"Your hit, Nordqvist," Jake says. "Take him out."

I look down at my gun. It's a 9mm semi-automatic with an extended magazine that holds thirty rounds. Some of us carry fancier laser stuff, but good old-fashioned bullets never went out of style. I know this kid. How do I know him?

"Target's on the move," Jake says, as the boy starts walking towards us. He's looking straight at me, his face expressionless, naked except for a dirty white T-shirt.

"Mission window's closing," Jake says. "They're coming for him, goddammit. That's a direct order, Nordqvist!"

I flick the safety off, get the target in my sights. He's close enough now that I can see the spray of freckles across his nose. He's a skinny little thing. Barefoot.

I lower my gun.

The mole. He was on the mole.

"I'm sorry," I say. "No kids. I don't do kids."

Jake turns to me, his eyes full of love and pity. And then he shoots me in the face.

I wake up breathing hard, a pain in the center of my back that feels like someone drilled a hole there. I'm face down on the floor, but the floor is *moving*, a slow lateral roll with the occasional forward pitch thrown in for good measure.

For a few seconds, I have no idea where I am. More than a few seconds, actually. I'm resting on rough wooden boards, and the walls are creaking. I hear a rhythmic rushing sound all around me. The faint cries of seagulls.

Seagulls.

It starts coming back, fragmented images of dead bodies, burning tents, the sharp wail of the motion sensors. My father's face as the hatch slams shut. I push up to my hands and knees and the room cants hard to the left, sending me sliding across the floor into a line of barrels. The impact is agony.

It's too dark to see well, though dim light is seeping in from a little round window. Something smells awful. The ceiling is disconcertingly low, just high enough to sit. When I look out the window, I realize I'm on a ship. That should have been obvious, I suppose, but I've never been on one before and the all-over pain makes it hard to think. A few dozen other boats, small and weather-beaten, keep pace to the side. We must be pretty far out to sea because the water has changed to a gunmetal grey color. No engine sounds, so I guess it's a sailing ship, a fairly big one.

I know almost nothing about boats. Our naval capabilities withered to zero when we retreated below the surface. Same for aviation, although we have flight simulators at the Academy. The military is supposed to be experimenting with planes that can fly through the storms, but it's all very top secret, just rumors around the Academy.

The ship shoulders through a mountainous swell and skims down the other side, and my stomach follows suit. Partly from seasickness, but also despair.

So much for fourteen hours to rescue.

Archipelago Six stretches for more than five hundred miles and contains almost twice that many islands. The perfect hideout for pirates, or whatever these people are. As long as they keep moving. Because by the time the satellites spot them and the moles arrive, they'll be long gone. The thing I don't understand is how they avoid the hypercanes. I've seen the storms on TV and they're simply monstrous. The surface of the Earth is about as hospitable as Mars for any prolonged period of time.

I guess they've found a way or I wouldn't be here right now. But drifting on this vast expanse of water, I still feel uncomfortably exposed. The more I think about what's out there, the more I feel a weight pressing down on my chest. It gets worse and worse. I start dripping with sweat. So I look around the hold, try to focus on the details, to actually *see* what my eyes are looking at instead of the scary movie playing in my head.

Other than the barrels and a few crates, the space is empty. There's no door, just a square hatch in the ceiling that must be bolted tight from the other side because it doesn't budge when I give it an experimental push. I lie on my belly, mouth full of dust, and must fall asleep for a while since it's dark when I open my eyes again. The motion of the ship has altered, more forward pitching, less side-to-side. Maybe we changed course.

I'm hot and my skin feels tight, like my head and hands are a few sizes too big. It occurs to me that the awful smell might be my wounds.

I drift in and out, and think I hear voices above me, a loud argument. One wants to help, and the other, a woman, keeps saying there's not enough to go around. She repeats a word that sounds like *pika*. I try to call out but my throat is too dry to make a sound. The blackness is so total it's like being buried alive. Only the creaking of the walls reassures me that I'm in a ship's hold instead of a grave. Then there's a flickering light, something stings my arm, and I slip into nightmares of tiny spiders, fangs glistening with poison, creeping out of the cracks in an endless, horrible flood.

A long time later, hours or maybe days, I'm not sure, dawn comes and I cry a little just to see the walls again. It's been ages since I did such a thing. I'd almost convinced myself I'd forgotten how, which is ridiculous. Anyone can be broken. *Anyone.* I'm not there yet, though the darkness got to me worse than it should have, considering I've spent long periods hooded and bound in stress positions during RTI, resistance to interrogation training. I think about this for a while and realize the crucial difference is that no matter how bad it got, I knew there was a limit. I knew what was coming. With these people, I don't know the limit. I don't know anything about them. Maybe there *is* no limit.

Raindrops lash the porthole, a word some pedantic part of my brain recalls from a book, maybe one of the Wilbur Smith epics. *Porthole.* I place my hand against it, fingers splayed wide. It's small enough that they touch the rusty metal rim, but it would be so much worse without it, I think. So much worse.

There are stitches over my left eyebrow, which I discover by accident when I cough and it feels like someone hit me in the head with a rock. There's also a bottle of water in the corner that I'm certain wasn't there before. I drink the whole thing and don't care that it has an unpleasant, salty aftertaste. The fever seems to have broken, and my back is better too, still sore but not in the inflamed, deadly manner of infections.

I think about Jake. If he was lucky, someone on board the mole had surgical skills. Abdominal wounds can get very bad, very fast. But this makes me remember the dream, and I don't want to remember it right now, so I lie in front of the porthole and watch the heaving horizon. For a long time it stays the same, featureless and boring, although fixing my eyes on a single point seems to help with the sickness. Then islands start appearing, some no more than a single bunch of trees, others much larger and dark green. From a distance, they look like mossy boulders.

After a while, the pain in my back turns to a maddening itch. I peel off the filthy, blood-stained coat I took from the medical pavilion and gingerly reach around behind me. There's more stitches back there. Someone sewed me up. There's also a clean spot on my right arm that bears a faint puncture mark, like from a needle. Antibiotics, hopefully. I must have slept through the whole procedure.

I have to wonder at the kind of people that would doctor me and then throw me back down here without even a blanket to lie on. I wonder why they're bothering, why they didn't just kill me or leave me on the beach. Unless they're criminally stupid, they must understand that a hostage situation would be suicide.

In school, we were told that within a year of the Transition, of the Culling, there was no one left on the surface. Those who didn't succumb to disease or starvation or war were swept away by the canes. This is gospel. Chapter and verse. I've never questioned it.

Maybe a remnant of a remnant survived.

I work it through as I stare out at the dark water, endless in every direction. There's no more coral reefs, or apex predators like sharks. They vanished decades ago. The marine food chain was radically disrupted. Jellyfish seem to like the warm, acid oceans just fine, but they're in the minority. I guess other species could have adapted though. That's a food source. And while there's obviously no kind of large-scale agriculture, a small group could forage enough fruits and vegetables to survive. They grow stuff, too, I can see container gardens on the decks of the other boats.

And what they can't grow or forage, they take from us.

But again, that's not the biggest problem, not by a long shot. The biggest problem is how to avoid the canes. It's what drove us underground in the first place. Nothing can withstand the storms. Adapting is not an option. There is only one option, I've always been told. Go down and go deep.

I think back to the beach. Their behavior after the attack. *The heaviest activity appears to be around the scientific equipment . . .*

If they had the LIDAR and other instruments, they could see the storms coming. Track them, and move accordingly.

They could run.

I can't believe military intelligence doesn't already know about this. Which in turn explains the presence of the contractors. They weren't worried about toads. They were worried about humans.

Could my father have known?

Could he *not* have known?

At least I'm sure he and my mother made it to the mole, Jake too. Not knowing if they were dead or alive would just consume me.

I doze for a bit, and when I wake up, I have to pee. They didn't leave me anything, just the water bottle, but the top is way too narrow and I'm too exhausted to even try. So I crawl to the hatch and pound on it, the stitches tugging painfully every time I lift my arm.

"Hey!" I yell, and it feels good to hear a voice, even if it's my own and it sounds both puny and too loud in the enclosed space.

Finally I hear boots above. There's the sound of a key turning in a lock and the hatch swings upward.

"What?" an exasperated voice says.

"I have to go," I say, squinting in the sudden light of a lantern.

"Go?"

"Yes," I say. "To the bathroom. You must be familiar with the concept."

"Bloody hell."

"Please."

"Ah Jeez . . . Captain said . . . oh, all right then." A hand reaches down and roughly hoists me up. "The head's that way, last door to starboard."

The head? I think. Whose head?

"Bathroom," he says, noting my bewilderment. "On the right."

He is a guy in his mid-twenties, lanky but strong, about six-foot, with a short carroty beard and matching hair just a touch longer than would be permitted at the Academy. His hazel eyes are not openly hostile, but neither are they at all friendly.

He marches me down a dim passageway, then stops and leans against the wall. I open the door to the "head" and discover a coffin-sized room almost entirely occupied by a dingy steel toilet with no seat. Add the pitching of the ship and it's like trying to thread a needle inside a urinal during an earthquake. Barefoot. I try not to touch anything or look too closely at the floor. God knows what kind of microscopic civilizations are thriving in here.

When the unpleasantness is completed, I'm tossed back in the hold. As the guard's footsteps recede overhead, I press my face against the porthole and this time I see stars and a sliver of moon. They keep me anchored in the darkness until the rocking of the ship eases me into unconsciousness once again.

CHAPTER SEVEN

A decade in, it became clear that the superstorms were only growing stronger. There would be no return to the surface.

The next six days are a miserable blur. I bang on the hatch when I need to use the head, and it's either the redhead or another one, even taller with ebony skin and cornrows. Neither will speak to me or answer any questions. They give me one meal in the evenings, usually a cup of lumpy potatoes mixed with black seaweed. It's stiflingly hot down here during the day, but cold at night. At least the fever hasn't returned. I don't know if I could survive it in my current state.

The first day after discovering the stitches I spent hours trying to get the barrels open, hoping they might contain food or something that could be used as a weapon. It's pointless, they're made of stout wood and the tops are nailed shut. My nails are cracked and bleeding by the time I give up. After that, I fall into a kind of lethargy. I dream about my mother, and Jake. About food, and clean sheets, and mugs of hot tea. Term must be starting by now. It would have been my last.

I scan the empty blue sky through my porthole, imagining there's a satellite up there taking a picture of the ship and beaming it on to the ones searching for me. I know it's unlikely; the whole thermosphere got screwed up by carbon dioxide, and many of the satellites that still work have erratic orbits. Thousands are just space junk now, since we can't send maintenance crews and have no launch capabilities. But enough still send signals that reach the meteorological substations.

If there was a clear window above the ship at some point, and *if* a functioning satellite was passing over, and *if* military intelligence crunches the data in time . . .

Well, it's something. Otherwise, there's no hope at all.

On the seventh day, the hatch opens in the morning, which has never happened before, not without my banging on it. I expect to see one of the regular guards. But it's someone new. A boy, a little older than me, somewhere between eighteen and twenty, I'd guess. Tall, with tan skin and a long, dark blonde braid. Jeans cut off at the knee and a clean white T-shirt. He has the high cheekbones and close-set blue eyes of a Northerner who'd probably be pale as milk if he didn't spend half his life under the blazing sun. He takes in the dirt and the smell and his face hardens, but he doesn't say anything, just offers me a hand. It's much gentler than the usual. He seems to know where I hurt and makes an effort not to put too much strain on my arms.

"This way, please," he says, leading me down the passageway to a door just past the bathroom.

I've never gotten a *please* either.

The room beyond is small and plainly furnished: bed, table and chair, shelving with wooden rails to keep the contents from spilling when the ship rolls. There's a sandwich on the table, and a bottle of water. My stomach rumbles.

"Go ahead," he says, in a faintly clipped accent I've never heard before. "I brought it for you."

I pick up the sandwich. It's white bread with some kind of synth meat that doesn't smell very fresh. Probably the contractors' spam rations. We always ate well at the Academy. The accommodations were Spartan, sex-segregated dorms with standard issue metal cots and a three-drawer dresser to hold our meager personal items. But the food was good and plentiful. It had to be, since we were burning about three thousand calories a day in training.

The sandwich tastes as nasty as it looks but I gobble it down in four bites. My hands are so dirty they leave black smudge marks on the bread. I feel like a feral cat that's been coaxed into the light with a scrap of food, fur on end and bracing for a kick at any moment. But the boy has the decency to pretend not to notice, looking me in the eye with neither animosity nor disgust. I sense an anger simmering there, though I'm not sure who it's directed at.

"If you don't mind, I'd like to have a look at your back," he says. "You're lucky; whatever injured you missed the right lung by less than an inch."

"Are you a doctor?" I ask warily.

"I'm a physic," he says. "I help sick people, if that's what you mean."

I sit awkwardly on the bed, trying to keep my nightgown from riding up, as he inspects the wound. He doesn't touch me. I appreciate that.

"What was it?" he asks.

"Glass shard," I say, pulling my coat back on.

"Yes, I thought something like that. The edges are sharp and neat, no tearing. Deep puncture though, infection is what we need to be on the lookout for now."

He reminds me of the Academy medic, a brisk but humane woman who was ruthlessly proficient at putting our battered bodies back together again.

"Can you tell me how long we've been at sea?" I ask.

"Nine and a half days."

I picture the beach at Archipelago Six, no doubt still crawling with military. I'm sure my father is among them. He'd be pulling out all the stops, especially when they fail to recover my body. I have no idea how far a ship can sail in that amount of time, but it must be hundreds of miles at least.

"What are you going to do with me?" I ask, wishing he'd offer me some more food.

"That depends on Captain Banerjee," he replies evenly.

"Are you the one who sewed me up?"

He looks at me and I notice that his left iris is slightly bluer than his right, which is more of a slate grey color. "Yes, I am. You were in bad shape. Some of us thought . . ."

"It wasn't worth it?"

He shrugs, embarrassed.

"What's your name?" I ask, thinking I should try to make friends with the ones who don't seem to want me dead.

He hesitates, but only for a moment. "It's Will."

"OK then, thanks Will," I say. "I guess you saved my life."

He shrugs again, as if that's not a burden he really wants to carry. "It's my job. I'm sorry I didn't come to check on you sooner. You shouldn't have been left like that. I've been stretched thin these last few days." He points to the corner. "There's a bucket there, and a towel, if you want to clean up a little."

I nod. Anything to prolong my time out of the hold. The thought of going back fills me with dread. We could be at sea for weeks. I'm afraid I'll go crazy if they leave me in there.

He excuses himself, locking the cabin door behind him. The saltwater burns like fire on my half-healed cuts and scrapes but it leaves me feeling human again, even if I have to put my dirty clothes back on at the end. When I'm done, I lick the last crumbs off the plate and sit down on the bed. I don't wait long.

A minute later, the door bangs open. It's the woman with the scar and the braid. Her left arm is in a sling. She doesn't have to tell me that she's the law around here. It's evident in the way she holds herself.

"You're a bloody tough one, aren't you?" she says without preamble.

This doesn't seem to require a response, so I keep my mouth shut.

"OK, listen up. We need another physic. Will's overwhelmed, and we took a lot of casualties last week. I'm not in the habit of picking up strays, but you're a special case. You have skills." She pauses and her gaze narrows a fraction. "Just don't mistake my generosity for weakness of character. If I have reason to think you're making any less than a wholly committed effort to patch up my crew, I'll throw you overboard myself." She says this in a very pleasant, cultured voice that is much more convincing than shouted threats would have been.

"Yes ma'am," I say. "But I'm not sure I understand. Physic?"

Banerjee's eyes are hard and black like onyx, her face more handsome than beautiful. She's probably in her middle forties, although there's an ageless quality that makes it hard to pin her down by a decade either way.

"Don't play with me," she says coldly. "We're way past that now. Your people are gone, and so is your old life. The sooner you accept that, the easier it'll be for all of us. Sick bay is overflowing, and I have no patience for misguided courage."

Her eyes flicker over my coat, like they did on the beach. I look down and notice a small white nametag on the right breast pocket that says *L. Davidson, R.N.* She thinks I'm a nurse. I briefly consider trying to play it off, but I'd probably end up killing my patients. Not that they don't deserve it.

"It's not mine. I borrowed it," I say. "I'm sixteen. And my name's Nordqvist. Honestly."

Banerjee's expression darkens. Suddenly her hand whips out and seizes my chin, turning my face into the light. She scrutinizes me for a minute, then curses softly and lets me go.

"That's too bad," she says. "We're not very big on dead weight around here. Damn Will for convincing me to waste antibiotics on you." She sits down at the table and rubs her forehead. "Any technical knowledge of remote sensing equipment? Solar panel maintenance and repair?"

I shake my head.

"Navigation? Botany?"

"Not really."

The list goes on, and I feel more useless by the minute. By the time I tell her that no, I can't cook, hunt, work metal or weave on a loom, I've come to the humbling realization of how few things I actually know how to do. Down below, we get everything we need from the factories and the hydroponic farms. I guess I should know more about plants since that's my mother's specialty, but I've hardly been home for the last eight years. Clearly, these people lead a much more primitive existence.

"I'm afraid we have a problem, Nordqvist," she says. "I'll be honest. This group is not in a position to take on another mouth to feed, another body to clothe, without a compelling reason."

"Maybe you could just drop me off," I suggest weakly.

The captain stares at me like I'm the dullest cadet in a remedial logic class. "Drop you off? Where exactly? We're in the middle of the ocean."

"But I saw islands . . ."

"They're far behind us now. I can't turn the whole fleet around."

I don't say anything, afraid whatever comes out will only make things worse. There's got to be something I can bargain with. I just have no idea what it is.

"According to our charter, any person who endangers the group is subject to expulsion, effective immediately." She lets the significance of this sink in. "By definition, a pika like yourself, in the absence of any mitigating factors, is a threat to the group. You don't fit in, and they'll be looking for you."

That word again. "Pika?" I say.

"Underground burrowing rodents. Ring any bells?" She sighs. "Look, you're young, I don't hold you personally responsible. But your people left their people to die up here. The ones that are left nourish a grudge, and I can't say I blame them."

"You said their people. Aren't they yours too?"

"I used to be one of you," the captain says. "In another life. But that's none of your concern."

There's a pained silence. "Look, I'm nobody special," I say. "I am . . . I was a military cadet. But my family's poor. My dad's a bus driver, my mom's a teacher. They don't have any political influence. I've probably already been written off as missing, presumed dead. End of story."

I'm not sure if Banjeree's buying it but I hold her gaze without wavering.

"That's nice," she says finally. "Very reassuring. I wish it was enough. Unfortunately, we still have to cut you loose." She looks away, but not before I see a flash of pity in her black eyes. "Maybe someone else will pick you up. Who knows?"

Obviously, the odds of that happening are slim to none. It's a death sentence, and not even a quick one. Suddenly, as hard as I've prayed to escape from these people, I'm terrified they'll abandon me.

"Hold on a minute," I say desperately, but she's already out the door.

When she comes back, she's not alone. The red-headed guy is with her, face carved in stone. He yanks my arms behind me and walks me down the passageway and up a circular metal staircase. Captain Banerjee opens a door and sunlight hits my face. It's blinding after so many days in the darkness, but I can't throw up a hand to shield my eyes so I just stand there blinking like a troglodyte. My heart is hammering in my chest. I close my eyes and breathe the salt air deep into my lungs, and it's indescribably clean and fresh after the stench of the hold.

A bunch of people are on deck doing things with the sails and the complex web of ropes shrouding the double masts. There's no land in sight, not even a distant speck, just white clouds mounded on the horizon. Even the gulls are gone. Captain Banerjee walks up to an older man and says something I can't catch, and he looks over at me, a troubled expression on his weathered face. They converse for a moment, and he finally nods, starts moving through the crew and saying a few words to each one. Heads begin turning my way.

"What's going on?" I ask the red-haired guy, who's let go of my arms but stayed close enough to grab me if I try to bolt. As if there's anywhere to bolt to. He doesn't answer, and won't meet my eyes.

"All in favor?" Banerjee calls out, and hands start going up across the deck. I notice the older guy keeps his down, and a few others, but they're a small minority.

"Bring the prisoner astern, Rupert," Banerjee orders, and he drags me to the back of the ship, where our foaming wake trails out for a quarter mile or so until it dissolves into the blue emptiness of the ocean. Everything is happening so fast. I didn't think it would happen so fast.

"Wait!" I scream, as Will bursts from the wheelhouse and is seized by the nearest crewmen.

"Don't, Captain," he says, not loudly but with a note of authority that makes the others pay attention. "We can still use her in sick bay. You know I need help. Let her change bedpans if it's punishment you're after."

"You already have Lisa," Banerjee responds calmly. "This girl is nothing but a liability. The crew agrees."

I scan the crowd, and what I see there is not encouraging. The ones that don't hate me outright seem resigned to executing an unpleasant but necessary task. Most are way too young to have witnessed the Transition firsthand, but they still look old and tired and like they've never had enough to eat in their lives. Rupert forces an orange life vest over my head and pulls me to the edge, where I seize the rail with both hands. For some reason, the vest scares me worst of all. It means they're really going to do it.

"This is nothing but murder," Will says, and now there's heat in his voice. "You all know it."

Banerjee lifts her chin. She's standing in the middle of the deck, her body shifting smoothly with the rolling of the ship as though it's a part of her, and she radiates such command I can see why the others follow without question. "Your objections are noted for the record. Also for the record, I'll add that I do what I have to do to keep this group alive. That's my first priority."

Will curses and fights to break free but he's being held firmly by three crewmen.

I look over the edge and picture the fall, the waves closing over my head, then watching the ship as it sails off, and night comes, and there's nothing but me and the terrifying vastness of the sea. Of all the ways I have imagined dying, and some were very bad indeed, drowning in the ocean, *on the surface*, was never even a remote possibility. It feels utterly wrong. A major mistake has been made somewhere.

Adrenaline floods my mouth in a hot, coppery burst. When Rupert reaches for me, I'm ready.

With his left hand, he grabs a fistful of life jacket. His right seizes my arm just above the elbow. This is the easiest way for him to dispose of me. A little tug, a little lift, and over I go.

In a split second, I reverse my hand so it's gripping his arm, instead of the other way around. Then I jerk his weight down, forcing his knees to bend and bringing his head into perfect alignment with the elbow that's already on its way. It makes contact with the sweet spot just behind his jaw, and Rupert's out before his body even hits the deck.

The whole thing happens so fast that Banerjee and her crew don't know what to make of it. I lift the life jacket over my head and drop it on Rupert's chest.

"Well, damn," someone says.

The rush ebbs away. I'm inches from falling over and never moving again, but I can't. They need to think I'm stronger than that, even if I'm not really.

I've got an idea. A traitorous idea that goes against every value they beat into me at the Academy. But in the end, when I'm forced to choose, I choose a chance at life over loyalty. I can't help it.

"How many of your people died last week?" I say loudly, steadying myself against the rail as the ship wallows through a deep trough.

There's a moment of heavy silence. Then Will answers. "Seventeen," he says. "And twice as many injured."

I look around, choosing the ones that seem the least belligerent and holding each of their stares for a few seconds. "What I just did to him, I can show you how to do to your enemies," I say. "Turn their own skills and strategy against them."

Banerjee crosses her arms. "Go on," she says.

"I know weapons, I know single combat." There's a few snickers, which I ignore. "I can teach you stuff that'll cut your casualty rate by half, maybe more."

"That's quite a claim," the captain says. "What I just saw was a man caught by surprise, and a lot of dumb luck. Even a rabbit will bite when it's caught in a trap."

There's more laughter at this, and I feel my tenuous reprieve start to evaporate. So I say something reckless. "I'll prove it then. I'll fight whoever you want." As soon as the words are out of my mouth, I know they were a mistake. I should have held out for better terms.

Banerjee's smirk turns to a broad grin. "How about it? Should we let her?"

There's a ragged cheer from the men and some of the women. They probably don't get much live entertainment. Will and the older guy just look worried.

"Let's do it then," the captain declares. "Time's a-wasting."

I let go of the rail and my right knee starts to buckle. I grip it again fast and hope no one noticed.

"I want my stitches out first," I say.

Banerjee frowns. "No."

"Afraid to give me a fair chance?" I say. "You've starved me and left me in the dark for more than a week. Prior to that, I was stabbed in the back and had my head cracked open. All I'm asking is to let the doc get my stitches out so I can move right."

Everyone looks at the captain. One or two are nodding. I realize that they live by a code, these people. They aren't completely without honor. And neither is Banerjee, as much as she wishes to be rid of me.

"You've nothing to lose," I say quietly. "I, on the other hand, have everything to lose. I'm only asking for a fair chance."

She scowls deeply, then gives a short nod. "Fine. But do it soon. I want to get this farce over with. Oi! Bob!"

A huge figure lumbers into view from behind one of the masts. My heart sinks. It's the giant from the beach.

"Fancy a sparring match?" Banerjee asks.

He looks at me and rubs his head thoughtfully. "With her?"

I'm hoping he'll find it beneath his dignity to fight a wee girl, but Bob doesn't seem to care much either way. He's like a wrecking ball, happy to demolish whatever's placed in his path.

"Yeah, OK," he rumbles.

"Excellent." Banerjee turns to me, black eyes glittering. "I'm sure you're anxious to dazzle us all with your strength and agility, but for now there's work to be done." She strides to the wheelhouse. "Set a port tack! We make land tomorrow."

And with that, it's over. The crowd starts to disperse, everyone returning to their duties. Everyone except for Will, whose unreadable gaze follows me as I'm taken back below.

CHAPTER EIGHT

The problem then became one of simple mathematics.
How many lives can a closed system support?

The next morning, I can tell something has changed. There's a lot of activity on deck, feet pounding up and down. I look out the porthole and see flocks of birds, some small and brown, others hot pink with comically long legs. We're running about a mile offshore of the biggest island I've seen yet. It pokes out of the sea like the top of a jungle-covered mountain.

Maybe that's what it was, once.

A deep lagoon appears ahead and the ship turns toward it, muscling up a huge white-capped swell and rocketing down the back side. Then we're in calmer waters, so clear I can see the sandy bottom far beneath. Faint shouts from above, they must be dropping the sails, and we coast for so long that I think we might run aground. The light dims and the water splashing against the sides of the ship takes on a strange echoing sound. Rough rock walls glide past. We're inside a cavern. Which makes perfect sense if you think about it.

Because the last major problem is how to elude the satellites.

They leave me waiting for a good hour, which feels like an eternity when your imagination keeps conjuring up scenarios of what's about to happen, each worse than the last. What was I thinking? I'm in no condition to fight anybody, let alone Bob. I should be in a hospital bed.

Finally, Will comes. I'm glad it's him and not one of the others. He takes me to the same cabin as before and gives me a bowl of tasteless grey porridge, but also something unexpected: a hard-boiled egg.

"Go on, you need your strength," he says.

His kindness is almost tougher to take than if he were openly antagonistic. I pick up the egg and peel off the speckled brown shell. My stomach is tied into knots, but I eat it because he's right.

"This was yours, wasn't it?" I guess.

"I'm not hungry," he says with a smile that's supposed to be reassuring but just looks funereal.

"Thank you," I say. "And don't worry about me, I can take care of myself."

He doesn't say anything, but his expression conveys serious doubts about the truth of this claim. Doubts I share, but don't care to admit.

Will watches me bite into the egg and I am acutely conscious of my dirty legs and greasy fingers. I try not to eat so fast this time, but there's not much food anyway and it's gone in a minute or two.

"I hear you knocked him out before," he says, as we walk single-file down the passageway and ascend the stairs to the deck. "During the fight."

"The truth? I hit him from behind with a club," I say. "Twice. And that only worked for about a minute."

He stops and turns to me. "What's your name? Your first name, I mean."

This catches me off guard. "Jansin," I say.

"You don't have to do this, Jansin," he says, and my name sounds strange in that clipped, flat accent, like it belongs to someone else, although it also sounds like maybe that's how you're *supposed* to pronounce it. I'm half northern stock myself, after all.

I try for a withering look. "Unfortunately, I do."

Will's eyes go flat. "You don't get it. Listen to what I'm telling you, for God's sake. I've seen him tear people apart. I don't know where you come from, what you think you know, but trust me on this one. You're not even remotely a match for Bob. And don't think he'll hold back, because he won't."

This irritates me. When you're short, and a girl, nobody takes you seriously. Until you convince them otherwise. "You're right. You don't know me. You don't the first thing about me," I say haughtily. "And they were about to toss me into the sea, in case you've forgotten. The captain made it clear that us pikas are pretty well despised around here. Unless we have something to offer, something you need."

"And what do you have?" he asks in a sarcastic tone that irritates me further. "Besides excessive optimism."

"You'll see," I say, stepping out to the deck.

It's cool up here and not too bright, which gives my eyes a chance to adjust to the outside world again. The cavern is immense, extending back about a hundred yards, where the water disappears into a wide fissure. We climb down a ladder to a waiting rowboat and Will takes the oars, facing me. His eyes are a stormy blue-grey and his nose is slightly crooked, like it's been broken a few times.

"Do you have family on board?" I ask.

"They're dead," he says, eyes fixed on a distant point over my left shoulder.

"Oh," I say. "I'm sorry."

"It was a long time ago," he replies, in a tone that discourages any more questions on the topic.

I chew on my bottom lip. Long silences are not my strong suit. They make me prone to babble, especially when I'm already nervous. I try to size him up without being too obvious about it. His dirty-blonde hair is twisted into a topknot, and he's wearing the same jean shorts, this time with a frayed T-shirt that might have been black once but is now just a colorless grey.

As a matter of habit, my first instinct on meeting a new person is to try to figure out if I could beat them in a fight. At the Academy, this is not idle speculation. Will's a lot taller. Not bulky like Jake, but with hard, lean muscle on his chest and arms. I'd say he has about sixty pounds on me. I bet I'm faster though. So probably an even match, if he's had any training.

"Where'd you learn medicine?" I ask after a while.

"Books. I know a lot about plants, so I make natural remedies when we run out of drugs."

"Does that happen a lot?"

"All the time."

"You mean, like paper books?"

He looks at me oddly. "Yes, paper books."

This amazes me. "Hardly anyone uses those anymore. They cost a fortune. Where do you get them?"

"Here and there."

Thick forest slides by on our right. Many of the trees are missing their canopies. It looks like a giant hand came down and snapped off the trunks halfway up. My fear of the storms, which until now has taken a back seat to my fear of Bob, comes surging back.

"Are there animals on these islands?" I say, trying to distract the panicking, lizard part of my brain that just wants to dig a deep hole and hide there.

"You ask a lot of questions."

"Just curious. If there are people, maybe there are animals too."

Will turns the rowboat toward the sandy shoreline of the lagoon. "Some small game, but anything too big to hide got wiped out. The ones that could, moved on a long time ago, mainly toward the poles. Birds do the best. Most species are programmed to migrate anyway, and they sense when the storms are coming, days or even weeks ahead."

More boats are pulled up on the shore ahead of us, mostly rubber Zodiacs with electric outboards, and I see several dozen people unloading crates and carrying them into the jungle. There are kids too, which surprises me a little. The older guy, the one who voted against drowning me, is supervising the assembly of the LIDAR and other equipment, which they're partially camouflaging under a pile of palm fronds. Everyone on the beach knows their assigned task, and the whole operation is smooth and efficient.

Will pulls hard on the oars and we coast the last few yards into the shallows. Everyone stops working and stares as we cross the sand. It's weird to walk on something that doesn't move, like reverse seasickness. I keep my head high and meet their eyes until they look away, uncomfortable. Most do. Not all. The ones that don't are the younger ones who think they're tough.

I wonder how many would even survive my last eight years of training.

We follow a footpath through the forest until we reach a small clearing. The main camp must be someplace else, or else they just spread out in small groups. There's a few people setting up a mess tent and digging pit latrines off to the side, but they don't pay us much attention. On the way, I think hard about running. What stops me is the fact that we're on an island. They'd hunt me down eventually. And I know nothing about surviving on the surface, where to find food or water.

Will leads me to one of a group of plastic tarp structures. There's a rusty cot with a blanket, and a table with a cracked water jug. There's also a woman inside. She's very tall and thin, and her skin is a blue-black color that almost glows. She's wearing shorts and a tank top. Her head is shaved to the scalp. Nose straight and wide, with high cheekbones.

She's holding a tray of surgical instruments, which she sets down on the table.

"This is my assistant, Lisa Gueye," Will says. "Do you mind if she observes the procedure?"

"Fine by me," I say.

Lisa smiles in a neutral way. Her teeth are crooked but clean.

"Good," Will says. "OK, I need you to get those clothes off."

I stare at him until he turns around, then lower the top half of my pajamas and lie face down on the cot.

"This may hurt a little," he murmurs. I hear the clank of stainless steel on metal. "Gauze, please."

Something wet and cold presses down between my shoulder blades.

"Healing nicely. No redness or swelling. There'll be a scar, but it's not in a very visible location."

"Does it matter which one you start with?" Lisa asks.

"Not really. We'll go top down."

There's a tug on my back, but it's not particularly painful. More of a tickling sensation. The whole thing lasts about fifteen minutes.

"All set," Will says finally. "You'll feel a bumpy ridge there, but it should flatten out in two to three months."

Unspoken is whether I'll be around in two to three months. Or two to three hours.

"Thanks," I say. "It feels better."

"Just try not to rip it open," Will says, not looking at me as he bags the dirty gauze. "We're already running low on everything again."

"I'll do my best," I say, more lightly than I feel.

Lisa leaves and Will moves to follow her, then stops and turns back. "I still think you're a fool. But since I can't talk you out of it, I'd advise you to kick him in the . . . you know. It's your best chance. I'm really not in the mood to patch you up again. We're out of painkillers entirely."

"Thanks for the pep talk," I say. "But I don't plan on needing your help. Bob might though."

I mumble the word "quack" under my breath and disguise it as a cough.

Will seems on the verge of saying something else, and then two guys are outside the tent. I get up before they can tell me to and we walk back down the path to the beach. The children are gone but all the adults are there, at least a hundred people. I spot Bob right away. He's squatting on the sand at the edge of the crowd, which has formed a rough semicircle. He's staring into space and when we get closer, I realize he's humming to himself. God knows what he's thinking. Probably what he's going to eat for lunch after he breaks every bone in my body.

The murmur of the crowd grows silent as we approach. I take slow, deep breaths. I've fought plenty of guys before, I remind myself. And won, too.

Not this big, though. Not even close.

The thing is, Bob's an unknown. If he's been trained in any kind of formal fighting system, I'm in trouble. If he's a lot faster than he looks, I'm in trouble. One plus is that Bob will almost certainly underestimate me. How could he not? I'm wearing my pajamas, and two of me probably still wouldn't equal one of him.

"Right!" Banerjee says loudly, stepping to the center of the circle. "Let's recap. The prisoner issued a challenge. Bob accepted. If she wins . . ." Banerjee looks at me in a way that implies the probability of such an outcome is vanishingly small. "If she wins, she earns the right to food and shelter for the duration of our stay here. She will also teach anyone combat who wants to learn."

I notice she doesn't say, "stay with us, period," but I'll take what I can get.

"And if she loses?" calls out the older guy from the boat.

"Well, Charlie," Banerjee says calmly, "there's an atoll six degrees northwest of here that's suitable. If you'll recall, we left a rapist there two years ago." She turns to me. "Don't worry, a storm came through not long after. He won't be there anymore. You'll have the place all to yourself."

Curiously enough, this doesn't make me feel any better.

The sand is hot under my feet as I walk up to the ring of spectators. They move back as I pass, clearing a path to Bob, who's waiting just above the high tide line. There are no taunts or jeers. The crowd is restrained, solemn even. Blood pounds in my ears, the sound mingling with the crashing of the surf until all I hear is a dull roar.

"There will be no weapons," Banerjee pronounces. "And I'd prefer it if no one is killed. This is not blood sport. It's a demonstration of skill." She steps back. "Proceed."

As I hoped, Bob immediately charges, head lowered like a bull. If he were experienced, he'd wait to see how I move, what I know. And he wouldn't open with something so obvious, and so easy to counter. I wait until the last moment, then pivot to the side and let him blow by. He comes at me twice more, and both times I sidestep the attack. He's getting winded, and frustrated too, so on the next rush, he pulls one giant fist back for a haymaker. With Bob's raw power, if he lands a single punch like that, the damage will be major. I lean back and his fist whistles past my face, but he's off-balance now, his weight too far forward, so I step onto his bent right leg and spring back to give myself room for a round kick to the face. My shin connects squarely with Bob's cheekbone, and he staggers. His bell's been rung, but not for long. I need to break something. Put him in shock. It's the only way to stop him.

Bones can be set. I figure an arm or leg would be perfectly in line with Banerjee's directive.

Bob recovers and kicks sand at my face, but it's dry and powdery and all I have to do is turn my back for an instant to let it pass harmlessly by. Then I drop onto my hands as he rushes again and donkey-kick him in the stomach. There's a whoosh of stale breath, he hunches over, and I spin clockwise and grab his right wrist, intending to pull him down into an armbar, but he suddenly stands up. His face is bright pink, rage and consternation twisting his childlike features. I pull harder but Bob's got to be upward of two fifty, two sixty pounds and I just don't have the power to bring him down. So I switch tactics and let my upward momentum take me to where I can wrap my left leg around his neck and squeeze.

My entire body weight is hanging on Bob's right arm and shoulder, he's starting to arch backwards, but I'm out of leverage. In another few seconds, he'll shake me off like a dog drying itself after a bath. So I push my right knee into his lower back and pull back with my left. That does it, and Bob goes down.

Someone in the crowd lets out a hoot. We're locked together on the ground. I've got him half in the armbar, one foot propped on his ribcage and the other still hooked around his neck. I strain as hard as I can to fully extend the joint lock on his elbow and bring it to the edge of snapping. Pain and compliance. But Bob is crazy strong. He flexes his bicep, which is the size of a grapefruit, and I feel myself rising. So I sit up, hug his wrist tight against my chest, and lie straight back down again. Bob's arm stretches out a bit more but his elbow's still crooked just enough to thwart the armbar. Then he grunts with effort and begins to turn toward me, and I can feel his arm, the fine blonde hairs slick with sweat, start to slide through my hands and down my body.

I can't let him break free. He'd be on top of me in a second. I raise my bent right leg and smash it down into his solar plexus. His mouth opens and shuts, but no sound comes out because his diaphragm is frozen. Before he can recover, I straddle his hips and start whaling on his face with everything I've got, fists and elbows, at the same time using an open palm to whip his head from side to side. I've had this done to me before, much less hard than I'm doing to Bob right now, and it's almost impossible to regroup because besides the pain of getting hit, your point of focus is constantly shifting. It's like being inside a nightmarish gyroscope.

This goes on for ten or twenty seconds—I'm not really sure, time slows to a crawl when you're fighting flesh-on-bone—and then Bob pulls it together somehow. Instead of using his hands to try to block the flurry of blows raining down on his face, he grabs me around the waist and bucks upward with tremendous force. It's like being launched from a cannon. I fly through the air a good fifteen feet to the edge of the waves. The half-healed scar on my back breaks open; warm liquid spills down my ribs. I push up to hands and knees, disoriented and plastered with sand. I tried to tuck and roll into the landing, but it was still jarring. The faces of the crowd are all blurry, like they're drifting under a foot of water.

Almost too late, I remember to look back over my shoulder to see what Bob is doing.

His face is a mask of blood. He's absolutely maddened. And what he's doing is coming down on me like an avalanche. Bob makes a sound like a kettle about to boil, his hands reach for my throat, and I suddenly register the cool sand under my fingers. *Not dry, wet.*

I spring forward. My right hand parries his left fist down and away. I swing myself around behind him and drag my pinky across his eyes, digging in for the choke.

When I was a third-year cadet, a boy got his cornea scratched during a fight. He said later it was the most painful thing he'd ever endured, worse than a direct hit of pepper spray.

Bob hisses in agony, clamping his hands to his face. I get my wrist hooked against his airway, closing the vise with my left forearm.

Everything is slippery with blood. His body is pressed tight against mine, I can smell him, and it's not a bed of roses. I wrap my legs around Bob's waist, arch backward and start counting. Seven seconds later, he's gone. In a full airway choke, the body plays possum. It's a reptile brain defense mechanism. Seven seconds, every time.

Unless you're panicking. Then it's less, because the brain uses up its supply of oxygenated blood even faster. Bob sways, limp in my arms. The final question is which way he'll fall. And it's just my luck that he starts to go down backwards. On me. I twist his head to the side and his body obediently follows, sparing me the experience of being buried under two-fifty-odd pounds of sweaty giant.

When it's done, I slump back. The sun is blazingly bright. I watch a tiny blue crab scuttle along the waterline. It occurs to me that I probably stink too, I just can't smell myself anymore.

I only want to be left alone, but eventually people come and carry us both away.

CHAPTER NINE

The late Fifties witnessed a series of minor rebel-
lions among Raven Rock's disaffected classes, easily
quashed. This consolidated the power of the quasi-
authoritarian state, although civil institutions and
liberties were not dissolved entirely.

Will sews me up again, and is very obviously not happy about it. Then they give me a tarp-tent with a cot. I stay there, rising only to hobble to the latrine. Twice a day, Rupert brings me the usual cup of gruel and seaweed. So much for improved cuisine now that we're on land.

In the afternoons, the rains come. This is not the fake driz-zle I'm used to at home. No, this sounds like someone turned a fire hose on the roof of the tent. Within minutes, the clearing is a muddy quagmire. Every time the wind gusts, sheets of water sweep through the two-inch gap in the door flap. I curl up and try to sleep, but the noise is just deafening. I obsess about whether one of the canes has caught us, even though I know we wouldn't still be here if that was the case.

The bumps and bruises are healing but my agoraphobia or whatever it is just keeps getting worse. I didn't feel like this when I first got to the surface. The difference is that I knew the moles were waiting to take me home at the first hint of danger. Even on the ship, at least we were moving. Here we're just sitting ducks. Nowhere to run. Nowhere to hide.

On day three, Lisa drops by and gives me a shirt and shorts she says belonged to her daughter, Fatima. Also a pair of rubber flip-flops about three sizes too big, but I'm glad to have them. My feet are filthy and bruised from going barefoot to the latrines.

"How old is your daughter?" I ask as Lisa lays the clothing out on a small plastic table.

"Just turned nineteen." Lisa grins. "Won't listen to a damn thing I say anymore. She's a sharp kid though. Charlie's teaching her to stormcast. He says it's more of an art than a science. All I know is when he makes the call, we head for the boats."

"Stormcast?" That makes me sit up.

"Yeah, you know. Calling the evac. Knowing which way to run."

"Has a hypercane gotten close before?" I ask, dreading the answer.

"Aye. We have to be ready. Sometimes there's only a few hours warning. The surge can hit faster'n you'd believe, right out of a blue sky. Once it smashed up some of the boats and swept a bunch of tents away, some with people inside."

Great. Just what I wanted to hear.

"Why don't you come out and have dinner at the fire tonight?" Lisa says.

I make a noncommittal noise. "Maybe. I'm still a little tired."

I look at my grey skin and ask for a bucket of water to wash with. Soap too. Lisa brings both things, and I scrub until I'm raw and tingling all over. I get dressed, savoring the feel of clean clothes. Then I go back to bed. If it was less muddy, I'd sleep under my cot. Instead I just hide under the thin blanket they gave me.

Four more days pass. I keep making excuses to stay in my tent. After a while, I can tell Lisa's not buying it. So when she shows up with Will and the captain in tow, I'm more or less resigned to whatever they plan to do to me.

"You're a surprise, Nordqvist," Banerjee says, looming at the foot of my cot while the others wait by the door. "And I'm not a person who's easily surprised."

"Thank you, ma'am," I say.

"We kept our end of the bargain. Now you need to keep yours. Are you holding back on me?"

"No, ma'am," I say. "I'm just . . . not quite right."

"In what way?" Her black eyes bore into me.

"I don't know," I say, feeling miserable and sorry for myself. "I just don't want to . . ."

"Don't want to what? Get on with it."

"Don't want to go out there," I say in a rush.

Will steps forward. The tent is tiny and with four of us in here, the air feels thick as jelly.

"Surface sickness," he says.

The captain rolls her eyes. "Are you sure she's not faking? She did fine fighting Bob."

"No, I'm not sure," Will says. "But look at her hands. The way she's clutching the cot like a lifeline. That's fairly typical from what I've read. Of course, I've never seen an actual case myself. But it's a recognized disorder."

I force my fingers to uncurl and rest at my sides. They lie there like dead spiders. I hadn't even realized I was doing it.

The captain lets out a long sigh through her nose. "OK, assuming it's real, how do you treat it? I won't have her lying around all day like a bloated tick. She'll make herself useful or I *will* leave her on that atoll."

"Understood," Will says. He turns his cool gaze on me. "What is it precisely that worries you?"

I've been afraid for so long that it comes as a relief to be annoyed for a change. One, that they're talking about me as if I'm not here. Two, that he could be so dense. Not to mention pompous.

"What is it?" I say. "Well, let's see. Let me think. Oh, here's something. We're on an island, surrounded by water, *living in tents*, and there's fivehypercanes ripping up the planet somewhere, maybe headed this way, and we have no way of tracking them until it's too late. I'm mean, your lives are basically one long game of Russian roulette." I laugh. "Or maybe a short game. Very short. Am I the only person around here who sees that?" My voice has risen to an embarrassing, cracked sort of screech and I shut my mouth with an audible click.

Banerjee and Will exchange a look.

"I'll take her to Charlie," he says.

"Good idea." Banerjee leans over me. "I want you teaching in two days. I want you hauling water and checking nets. In short, I want you to be a functional part of this group. There's work to be done. So pull it together, Nordqvist." She tosses the last words over her shoulder on the way to the door. Lisa steps aside to make way.

"Or what?" I yell at her back. "I'll die? That's going to happen anyway."

Banerjee doesn't bother turning around.

I scowl and pull the blanket tighter around my shoulders.

"Get up," Will says, not ungently.

"Where are we going?"

"Not far." He sees the naked fear in my eyes. "Come on. You go to the latrines, don't you? Well, Charlie's tent is no farther than that."

"You promise?" I sound like a little kid and heat rises to my cheeks.

"I promise," he says solemnly, and my anger at him dissipates. "Come on. You marched down to that beach to meet Bob like it was nothing. You can walk across a clearing."

I take a deep breath and let the blanket fall. "I knew where Bob was. I knew what he looked like. I knew when he'd attack. With the canes, you don't know any of those things."

Will offers me his hand. It's calloused and dry, despite the humidity.

"That's where you're wrong," he says.

Charlie turns out to be the old guy from the boat, one of the few who didn't vote to throw me overboard. Up close, he looks like some kind of friendly brown gnome. Bright blue eyes, random tufts of white hair. Skin so leathery he could be seventy or a hundred and seventy, it's impossible to tell. After handing me a cup of water and gesturing for me to sit down, he tells me his job is to watch the sky, watch the ocean, watch the barometer and the LIDAR. I can tell he trusts the first two more than the latter.

"There're lots of natural signs if you know to look out for them," Charlie says, clearly enjoying a chance to talk about his favorite subject. "Cloud formations on the horizon that look like rooster tails, swirling out from the edges of the cane. The height of the waves and the distance between the troughs. If they increase to twelve feet and seven seconds, you probably have a cane less than seventy-two hours away."

These early signs are critical, he tells me, because by the time the wind picks up and the barometer drops like a stone, the monster is already on you.

"I've seen 'em do strange things," Charlie says. "But that's why we keep ready. Captain's drilled on evac a thousand times. We can be in the boats and underway in two hours now. Ain't never caught us yet."

It makes me feel a little better that Charlie's in charge of the stormcasting. He's obviously not a novice. But I still have a million questions.

"What if there's nowhere to run to?" I ask. "Hypercanes are huge. What if two of them come at us from opposite sides?"

Like a trap closing.

Charlie thinks for a moment. "Well, they just don't do that. Now, normal hurricanes, the little ones, they won't form over land. All their energy comes from warm ocean waters, right? And as soon as they do hit land, they start to die. Hypercanes are different. They're so blessed big they can steamroll right over a continent and not even slow down. But none of 'em can cross the equator. It stops 'em sure as a giant invisible wall. Those that live in the northern hemisphere have to stay there, and the same for the ones in the southern hemisphere. It's a consequence of the Coriolis effect."

I have no idea what he's talking about but I nod anyway.

"I ain't seen a hypercane come off the continent in more than a decade. That leaves the ones out to sea. So we keep along the shelf and run north or south as necessary."

"Why don't you just stay at the equator?" I ask.

Charlie laughs. "That's a dead zone," he says, leaning his hands on his knees. He's wearing shorts and an unbuttoned shirt that might have been plaid about a century ago. "Water's too hot for fish and the air's too hot for anything else. You'd be cooked through in a day, and if you lasted any longer than that, you'd starve to death. Anyone with half a brain went north." He glances at Will, who's sitting quietly on the floor between us. "Like his people."

I want to ask Will about where he comes from, but then I remember him telling me that his parents are dead and decide it's probably not a topic he's dying to talk about with a complete stranger.

"So what's the average warning time that a storm is coming?" I say instead.

"Plenty long," Will jumps in, eager to change the subject. "Usually a whole day or more, wouldn't you say, Charlie?" He shoots him a look only a complete idiot could miss.

"Oh," Charlie says. "Absolutely. And what you have to understand is that when we catch the first signs, the cane itself is still at least thirty-six hours away."

"That sounds pretty close to me."

"Well, it is and it isn't," Charlie says. "Like I said, we can be gone in two."

"And you can outrun a hypercane? In sailboats?" I say.

"Yep." Charlie grins. He's got about six teeth. "The wind's usually good at that point."

He and Will laugh like it's the funniest thing ever. I've never seen Will laugh before. I mean, the boy barely smiles. It makes him seem his age instead of like a forty year-old actuary trapped in the body of a teenager. Of course, when I tell him this he stops laughing and looks mystified, which makes me and Charlie laugh even harder.

"What's an actuary?" Will says, as he walks me back to my tent.

"It's someone who analyzes risk and tries to minimize losses." I don't tell him that actuaries contracted by the military were the first to propose we go underground. They said there was a three percent chance humanity would survive if we didn't. "They tend to be very serious people," I say.

We pass the central fire pit where some of the crew eat together. I hear them talking and laughing together in the evenings.

"Charlie knew, didn't he?" Will says.

"There used to be lots of actuaries," I explain. "Especially when things started falling apart. Corporations, governments, everyone wanted to understand what this whole cascade of natural disasters would mean for them. What they would cost, in money and lives. The probabilities of different scenarios occurring. The past was no longer any guide to the future, and people were panicking. Charlie's old enough to remember."

"So you think I'm serious?"

I shrug. "It's your job, right?"

Will stops in front of my tent flap. His face is closed again, like a window has slammed shut. "It's not just my job. This is how we live. I don't know what you expected, but you're right about one thing. People die all the time here. They die of rotten teeth. They die in childbirth. They die from bites and stings and burns and a million other things I can't fix. I can't fix them because I don't have proper medical supplies. Because we have nothing except the trash you guys leave behind. So, yeah. I guess I'm a serious person."

He stomps off and I remind myself that one boiled egg and a shot of penicillin does not make someone a friend. In fact, these people *attacked* my friends. Maybe even Will and Charlie. Who knows what's they've done to survive? I just have to wait. And I won't let myself get too close to any of them. Not when I know what will happen when the extraction teams arrive.

My people are not gentle with those who wrong us. We will kill fifty of you for every one of ours. And the search will not stop until I am found, one way or another.

It's getting dark. I lie down on my side and listen to the rain. The downpour has eased to a gentle patter, dripping from the trees and magnifying the earthy forest smells. I watch a bug make its way across the underside of the tarp. It has a tiny orange body and eight long, jointed legs as fine as eyelashes. There's a lot of weird insects up here I've never seen before. At home, we have streets and buildings and little oases of carefully manicured parks under grow lights and the rest is rock. Just miles and miles of rock. It comes in different colors and textures, but it's still rock and it's still reliably dead. Up here, every square inch seems alive with *something*.

I touch a green shoot poking out of the ground near the leg of my cot and it suddenly strikes me that this place was inhabited once. Not one of the megacities, with the buildings so tall their tops pierced the clouds, because there would still be ruins. Even the canes couldn't sweep all that away, not in a few decades. But people lived here, I'm sure of it. The eastern coast of the United States of America was very densely populated before the ocean reclaimed it. I scan the grass and the trees, looking for something, I don't know what, some sign, but there is nothing. What came before has been erased as perfectly and inexorably as a footprint below the tide line.

Early the next morning, Rupert comes to summon me to Banerjee. He seems to feel bad about what happened on the ship, or maybe he's just scared of me now, but he smiles when he gives me my porridge, displaying a row of mossy stumps. I guess Will wasn't kidding about the dental care around here.

I decide that I feel reasonably OK about going outside. For one thing, I actually slept through the night for the first time since I got here. No nightmares about flaming men drowning in the surf or, far worse, the vague, paralyzing sense of dread I haven't experienced since my early days at the Academy. My mind is clear and thanks to Charlie, I no longer feel helpless. I know what to look for.

The captain's tent is set off in its own clearing near the beach. It's bigger than mine, but not by much.

"How's your recovery coming along, Nordqvist?" Banerjee says. She's wearing a leather vest and her arms are ropy with muscle. I wouldn't want to fight this woman, even if she is twice my age.

"Fine, thank you."

"You spoke with Charlie?"

"He set me straight, ma'am."

"Did he? Well, I'm glad. Because we need to commence the training immediately."

My heart lifts a little. "Are you expecting an attack?" I say, trying not to sound hopeful.

"I'm always expecting an attack. Do you think we're the only group in these parts?" The captain somehow found a swivel chair, the kind they have in offices, and she sits in it like a throne. "Not all are a problem. In fact, most are trade partners. But there's a few that would be perfectly happy to gut every last one of us and take our ships and supplies. It's my job to prevent that from happening."

"How big will my classes be?" I've never taught before and the idea makes me nervous, even though I know the material inside and out.

She smiles. "I can't force anybody to do anything they don't want to. That's not how we operate. I'll put the word out and it's up to you to do the rest. But I expect you to recruit and train a core group that can help protect this camp." She holds up a finger. "In addition, you will get on the work roster. We're restocking the fleet, food and water. The sooner that's finished, the sooner we can be underway. I have no desire to linger here." She stares at me like she sees what a liar I am, even though she couldn't possibly know who my parents really are. "You can go now."

Will and Lisa come later to take my stitches out. He's polite to a fault. I'm rude. Lisa keeps looking askance at us, trying to figure out what's going on. I spend the rest of the day lying on my cot pretending I'm in the flight simulator at the Academy. It's always been my favorite escape. The program lets you pilot anything from Harrier jump-jets to the space shuttle, which always depressed me because it represents everything we lost. I guess the Mars 2020 Rover and Venera-D, the probe that the Russians sent to Venus, and all the others going back to Cassini–Huygens and even earlier are still out there somewhere. There's just no one to answer their signals anymore.

Early the next morning, I head down to the beach to check the sky. It's clear, with a light westerly breeze. I time the swells. They're slow and steady, about three feet and ten seconds apart.

No hypercanes. Not today.

I let the water lap at my toes. The sun feels pleasantly warm, not searing like it gets later in the day. The captain's posted a lookout on one of the rock outcroppings along the shore. They wave. I wave back. If any of the mercenary types she told me about tries to sneak up on the island, at least we'll have some warning.

My stomach's churning a little as I walk back up the path to the clearing. I'm scared, both that no one will show up, or that they will. Beating Bob bought me a chance to prove my value. If I fail, Banerjee's made it clear that there won't be any more chances.

The camp is still waking up and only a few people are visible, hauling water or cooking breakfast over open fires. I scope out an open area away from the other tents that's reasonably level and free of rocks. Then I sit beneath a hardwood tree with big, gnarly roots. The air smells of wood smoke and wet leaves. It's already hot, even though the sun hasn't cleared the treetops.

Boy, do I miss coffee.

After a while, three girls about my age come over.

"Is this where we learn how to fight?" asks the boldest one. She's skinny, like everyone, with mahogany skin and big, round eyes. Her black hair is knotted into a long braid, perhaps in imitation of the captain. The other two are tall and fair and look like sisters.

"This is it," I say, standing up. "I'm Jansin."

"I know," she says. "I'm Nileen, and this is Ezzie and Matty."

We nod at each other. They don't seem very enthusiastic, and I get the feeling Nileen roped them into coming here.

I glance down at my wrist, but of course the band isn't there. At the Academy, every minute of every day is accounted for, down to the second. I still find it disorienting not to know the time.

"Let's just give it a few more . . ." I begin.

Nileen interrupts. "No one else is coming," she says flatly. "They're scared you'll embarrass them, or they claim they won't hit a girl, or they don't like that you're a pika." She says the word without malice, just a fact.

"OK," I say. "Let's give it a few more minutes anyway."

I start the girls on a grueling routine of sit-ups, push-ups and jumping jacks. A few people watch us out of the corners of their eyes, but Nileen's right, none of them come over. Eventually, the camp empties as everyone heads for their assigned jobs.

After about fifteen minutes, I survey my students.

They're lying on their backs, completely winded. Perfect. The point is to exhaust them before we even start. Muscle memory happens ten times quicker when you're tired and operating under duress.

"On your feet," I say firmly.

They groan and stand up, Ezzie bent over and leaning with her hands on her knees. Then Nileen's eyes fix on something behind me. I turn and find myself staring at Bob's chest. So I tilt my head back until I catch his watery blue eyes. The left is still badly bloodshot.

"Hey, Bob," I say.

"Hey," he rumbles.

"Is there a problem?" I say, sliding my right foot back a couple inches and tensing to duck.

He looks confused. "No, man. I just thought . . . can I sign up?"

I blink. "You want to take my class?"

"If you don't mind. I understand if you don't want to." He shuffles his feet and turns pink. "Ah, it's OK. I just thought you could teach me to get a little faster on my feet, you know?"

It hits me then that in the same way I've always hated being small, Bob's size is not something he relishes. *Ox. Giant. Behemoth. Clumsy and slow.* But I've known men nearly as big as him who moved like lightning, and landed feather-light on their toes after kicking higher than ought to be humanly possible. It just takes practice.

"I can teach you that," I say, and he smiles. "In fact, your timing is exquisite. OK, guys, want to see something cool?"

They all nod.

"I'm going to show you how to break a bear hug." I turn to Bob. "Go ahead. Grab me as hard as you can."

He squares his massive shoulders, steps forward and lifts me up off the ground, crushing my face against his chest. I love this move because it doesn't matter how big and strong your opponent is. Unless you've been trained, it always comes as a horrible surprise. It only works if you're facing the person though. Otherwise he never would have overpowered me on the beach and I wouldn't be standing here right now.

My arms are pinned to my sides, but my hands are loose. So I just reach around, grab the flesh on his back just above his hips, and twist as hard as I can. Bob shrieks and drops me like a burning coal.

"What the hell was that?" he bellows.

"It doesn't really have a name," I say. "But it works."

The girls are laughing behind their hands, so I decide I'd better even the scales before Bob feels picked on. I demo some chokeholds on Ezzie, which sobers everyone up in a hurry. Then we review basic fighting stance, left foot forward and knees slightly bent, weight mostly on the balls of the feet. Eyes straight ahead, chin tucked. They're swaying by the time we get to punching and kicking drills, so I bark at them until it's obvious no one has any juice left.

It feels so good to be moving again, to be training. I tried to channel Sergeant Jackson, my first drill instructor, and I don't think

I did too badly. After class, I turn to go back to my tent but Nileen stops me.

"Come eat with us," she says, adding, "Captain's orders," when I hesitate.

"OK." I'm a little tired of sitting alone on my cot anyway.

"You ever cast a net?" Nileen asks as we fill two bowls with vegetable stew and find seats in the shade. About a dozen people have gathered in the clearing for the noon meal. A couple of them stare at us, but Nileen ignores them and they finally turn away.

"No," I say.

"I'll show you then. Work sched says you're on net duty all week. Me too." She shrugs. "There's worse jobs, for sure."

"Like what?" The stew's not half bad. I swallow the last spoonful and look wistfully at the pot, but nobody seems to be going back for seconds.

"Like hauling water. Makes your arms near to fall off after a few hours. The closest spring's a good two miles inland, but it's too rocky to camp there. Got to fill five hundred barrels before we go. Enough to last a few weeks at sea."

"The captain said something about making me do that," I say, thinking about the freshly healed wound on my back.

Nileen laughs. "She was prob'ly just threatening. They put the really big guys on barrel duty. Like Bob."

We both look across the clearing. Bob's sitting alone on a log, eating methodically with his head down. I haven't been here very long, but I know a pariah when I see one. Mainly because I was one myself at the Academy. Rich girl, daddy's a general, barely tall enough to pass the entrance physical. Three strikes. Everyone assumed I'd gotten some kind of free lunch, so I had work twice as hard as the rest of them just to prove I'd earned it. I always hoped it might make them stop hating me but it made them hate me more.

"Let's go." Nileen stands up and brushes off her hands. "It's gonna be hot down there but at least we'll be standing in the water."

"One second." I walk over to Bob. His small eyes squint up at me suspiciously.

"You did alright today," I say. "See you tomorrow, same time?"

Bob nods slowly. "Yeah, see you tomorrow." He looks down and starts spooning stew into his mouth again. I guess the conversation's over.

"Well, ain't you nice," Nileen murmurs as we walk down the path to the beach.

"Don't get used to it," I say.

"Most people's scared of him. He's a loner, you know."

"Maybe not by choice," I say.

"It ain't just that he's big," Nileen says as we reach the shore. The sun has burnished the ocean to a bright, metallic sheen. "It's who he used to be."

We walk down a ways to a row of buckets. Nileen grabs one and carries it to the waterline.

"You can get your own tomorrow. Today, we'll work together. A good cast takes practice," she says. "Now, see these weights? That's called the lead line." She pulls a fine mesh net out of the bucket and carefully shakes it out. It's about eight feet across, with lead sinkers around the perimeter. "You got your loop." She snaps a thick black band around her wrist. "That keeps the net from getting away from you. Don't forget it. This here's your drawstring and Braille lines. They'll pull the net tight when it's full and you're ready to haul it in."

We wade into the shallows and Nileen demonstrates a couple of casts, swinging the net with both hands and letting the weights carry it out. Then she walks backwards with the drawstring over her shoulder until it cinches shut. A few others are also fishing in the surf a ways down the beach. Nileen points to a slender girl, about our age, with honey brown skin and lots of short braids. Even at a distance, with the sun in my eyes, I can tell she's extraordinarily pretty. Something in the way she holds herself, every movement precise and graceful.

"That there's Fatima," Nileen says. "Lisa's kid. Dad died of bone-rot when she was a baby. Well, she's the reason we got Bob."

I watch closely as Nileen hurls the net in a soaring arc, try to memorize what's happening with her arms and legs and hands. "She gave me clothes," I say. "So what's the story?"

"You don't know?" Nileen says, clearly relishing a new person to gossip with. "Here, hold it like this." She reels in the net and hands it to me. "Now throw as hard as you can, it's heavier than it looks . . . Not bad. Try again, with your legs a little farther apart . . . Anyway, Bob's only been with us four years. He used to be one of the Lord's Redeemers. They're bad juju. Recruit kids to raid other groups. They beat 'em and drug 'em up and whatnot till they'll do anything they're told. Till they get so brainwashed they like it."

Nileen casts the net and this time she lets it settle into a wide circle on the water and waits.

"Where do they find the kids?" I ask.

"When they hit a camp, they kill all the grownups and take the ones under twelve," she says matter-of-factly. "Well, they hit us one day. Snuck up in the fog. We was getting our asses kicked pretty bad when Bob sees Fatima and it's like love at first sight or something. Even at fifteen he was huge. Almost as big as he is now. His mates wanted to grab her but he wouldn't let no one near her. Killed a dozen men that day, none of 'em ours." Nileen hauls on the drawstring and I see flashes of silver in the depths. "Finally, his mates broke and ran. Captain said he could stay. Some weren't crazy about that but no one cared to speak against him. He's dead loyal to her now."

"What about Fatima?" I ask. "How'd she feel about that?"

Nileen sucks her teeth as we pluck a dozen fish from the net and drop them in the bucket. The littlest ones she tosses back. Then she shows me how to hang the net for drying.

"She don't fancy him if that's what you mean. But he saved her life. I don't think she'll ever forget that."

"So what? He just moons around after her, knowing she'll never love him back?"

"Yeah, basically." Nileen points to the bucket. "You're the newbie, you get to carry it to camp."

"Well, that's pretty pathetic," I say, hoisting the bucket and wincing at the burn in my shoulder. "About Bob, I mean."

"Yep."

The sun's low on the horizon as we walk into the trees. I'm suddenly exhausted and can't wait to topple onto my cot. It seems like weeks since I've stood on my feet for more than a couple of hours.

"Well, you sure pumped me for information today," Nileen remarks as we enter the camp.

"I so didn't," I mumble, stifling a yawn. "You volunteered everything."

"Whatever. Tomorrow you're telling me what *I* want to know. Like all the fancy food you pikas get and . . . other stuff."

"Like what?"

"Like I don't know. Real houses. Pretty clothes. Hot tubs."

"Hot tubs?" I start to laugh.

"Yeah." She glares at me defensively. "I read about 'em in a book."

"OK, OK." I drop the bucket by the mess tent. "I'll tell you all about my life of luxury tomorrow. Ever heard of a mani-pedi?"

Nileen comes to my tent later and tries to get me to eat with the crew but I pretend to have a headache. I'm starting to like her and I don't want to.

When night falls, my surface sickness comes back with a vengeance. It's funny, but the thing that makes me feel better isn't the womb-like tunnels and caverns of home. Instead, I pull the blanket over my head and imagine in I'm in the cockpit of a British-made Hawker Nimrod fighter. With my eyes shut tight, I see green fields of alfalfa below, winding country roads with white fencing and mottled black dairy cows. Then the sea, blue and endless. And beyond, only the gentle curve of the Earth.

CHAPTER TEN

*Not surprisingly, what began as a military-run proj-
ect gave rise to a rigid social and economic hierar-
chy. The most notable example of this is Raven Rock,
which in many ways came to resemble the ancient
city-state of Sparta.*

I'm waiting under the tree the next day when Bob, Nileen and
Ezzie arrive for class. I guess Matty had second thoughts once
she realized it was full contact. They're all walking stiffly, and I
remember what it was like for me the first year at the Academy,
when I'd go to bed crying every night, so sore I could barely hobble
to the bathroom to pee. I was only eight.

"You ready?" I ask as we warm up.

Nileen gives me a dark look. "Dunno, boss. I got knocked
down about a hundred times yesterday."

"Today it'll only be ninety-nine," I say. "The main thing is you
keep getting up. Now give me a hundred push-ups."

Nileen doesn't answer, largely because she can't breathe.

We cover the same ground as yesterday. It'll be a long time
before they move on to anything more advanced. I make a point
of praising Bob when it's due and making sure everyone gets their
fair share of being the crash dummy. About halfway through class, I

notice the captain and Will across the clearing, watching us. They're talking quietly together and I'd give almost anything to hear what they're saying but I have to pretend to ignore them. Frustration makes me push my students harder than I should, and I hear Ezzie cursing under her breath as she stumbles away.

As it turns out, my fears are grounded. The two of them have been plotting against me. Moments after I dismiss class, they walk over, the captain smirking, Will impassive as usual.

"How's it going, Nordqvist?" Banerjee inquires. Her mouth is smiling while her black eyes dissect me, examine the pieces, and put me back together again.

"Just fine, ma'am," I say.

"So glad to hear it. If I were you, I'd be getting a bit bored, restless even."

"No ma'am. Frankly, I couldn't think of a nicer way to spend my vacation."

She barks out a laugh. "Good." Leans toward me. "Because I've been thinking. It's time you start contributing even more to the community. We don't need dead wood around here."

I brace myself for latrine duty or some other odious task no one else wants.

"I know you were casting with Nileen yesterday but I've decided it's a pity to waste your pika education on manual labor. So here's the deal. Will's volunteered to teach you some rudimentary physic skills. You're lucky we'd just requisitioned supplies when you were hurt. But most medical treatment is undertaken with herbs and plants. Will is an expert in their identification and usage, and you will help him on his scouting trips in the jungle."

I can tell from the way she said "volunteered" that she really meant "been ordered", and wonder if latrine duty wouldn't be less unpleasant.

"We'll shift your classes to afternoons. Is this arrangement acceptable?" Banerjee's tone makes it clear that this is not a question.

"Yes ma'am."

"Good. Have a pleasant day, Nordqvist."

"I'll come an hour after dawn," Will says. "Please be ready."

I check that no one is looking and make a horrible face at his back.

The next morning, Will walks into my tent. He doesn't say good morning or anything at all, just dumps a pair of muddy hiking boots on the ground and walks out.

We're off to a promising start, I think as I lace them up. They're a little loose, but I know from experience that's far better than too tight.

Outside, he hands me a backpack, and starts walking into the woods. He's tall, with long legs, and I have to jog to keep up.

"Where are we going?" I ask.

"Up the mountain."

"Thanks. I never would have figured that out."

We slog through the undergrowth, crossing shallow streams and steadily ascending towards the higher ground in the island's center. He pauses occasionally and plucks a flower or leaf to stow in his pack.

"*Cassia angustifolia*," Will says, showing me a handful of yellow blossoms. "Also called senna."

"What do you use that for?"

"It has laxative properties, among other things."

"Remind me not to get on your bad side," I say perkily.

"Too late for that."

"Oh, my God. Did you just make a joke?"

"No."

Will sets a hard pace, but I keep up without too much trouble. I think this surprises him a little, though it's hard to tell since he's got his actuary face on. At some point, we stop and eat lunch on a shaded hilltop. I open my backpack and find a crab salad thing that's a refreshing break from the usual gruel.

"So what were you doing on the surface?" he asks.

"Holiday," I mumble with my mouth full. "With my family."

"Brothers and sisters?"

"Only child."

"Your parents. Did they . . . ?" He looks away, seeming to regret asking.

"They're OK. They escaped in a mole. I got left behind."

Will drinks some water, then hands me the bottle. He has nice teeth, improbably white and even.

"Did you go the surface a lot?"

"It was my first time. Talk about unlucky." I beam my best fake smile at him.

"But why go at all?" he says. "Don't you have everything you need down there?"

I shrug. "I guess so. But it's not the same. I mean, we don't have all this." I open my arms to indicate the trees, the grass, the sky. "I'd never seen the sun before."

"That's crazy." Will leans back against a boulder. "Where does the air come from?"

"We have ventilation tubes that bring cooler air from the surface into the prefectures and bullet train tunnels. They're booby-trapped, for obvious reasons."

"Are there farms?"

"Of course. We use hydroponic agriculture. It's a way of growing crops without soil."

"How do the plants photosynthesize if there's no sun?"

"You ask a lot of questions," I say.

"I'm a physic. That's what we do."

"OK, OK. Fluorescent grow lights."

He grills me for the rest of the afternoon until I'm forced to remind him that *he's* supposed to be teaching *me*.

"The captain sent you to check me out, didn't she?" I say, putting my hands on my hips. "Admit it."

"What? No." He flushes and I know I'm right.

"You think I want to be here? You think I'm some kind of spy?"

"Don't be ridiculous."

"Look, I didn't even know you people existed until a couple weeks ago. In school, they told us everyone was dead. That we were the only survivors. Now I'm stuck up here." Lightning flickers, thunder booms, and the skies suddenly open up. "And it's pouring!"

"Would you calm down please?"

I don't answer, just turn and stomp down the mountain.

Now we're even.

There are no clocks or calendars, so in my mind, I start dividing the days into morning, noon, and rain. Apparently, the region once known as Virginia has a monsoon season and we're in the middle of it. This makes it harder to tell if a hypercane is coming because the barometers are up and down all the time.

The best thing about the rain is there's plenty of fresh water, but the food is still meager, mostly vegetable soup with whatever else turns up, usually seaweed and small portions of fish. They keep four dairy cows and a few chickens, with a strict rotating schedule for who gets the eggs. I think with longing of the synth meat sandwich Will gave me on the ship.

I think I would literally kill someone for a piece of fruit.

The supplies are weirdly random. Like, I ate breakfast this morning with a gold-plated spoon, but there's no salt or pepper.

Toothpaste, but no toothbrushes. We use twigs instead, which works better than you'd think.

After a few days, my classes start to acquire an audience. Teenaged boys, no surprise there. Girls fighting girls has some kind of universal appeal that transcends race, caste or culture. Girls fighting Bob is probably a draw too. Eventually, one of them gets dared to sign up, a moonfaced kid with an unpronounceable name whose ancestors probably hailed from Eastern Europe somewhere, when there still was an Eastern Europe. He turns out to be a quick study, and doesn't seem to mind getting dumped repeatedly in the mud.

Soon two more boys join in, and then the whole lot. Some more girls too. After a while, men and women in their early twenties show up, wanting to know why their snot-nosed siblings are suddenly getting the better of them.

We fight with our hands and feet, and we fight with sticks. I teach them how to neutralize guns and knives. The method you learn at the Academy has nothing to do with style or grace. It's based on disabling your opponent as brutally and quickly as possible. Nileen is my best student, so I've promoted her to helping teach some of the rookies in small groups. I'm trying to condense their training so they learn enough to defend themselves in a real fight if the mercs hit us. I don't know how much time we have here. Charlie says the storms always come, eventually.

One morning, a month or so after Will first pulled the rowboat onto the beach, I walk out of my tent and find about thirty people waiting in the clearing. And that's the first time I know, really know, that I'll be OK. I have a purpose here. At least for a while.

That night, I eat dinner on a log with Charlie. I've been hanging out with him sometimes after class. He doesn't seem to harbor any animosity towards me, not like some of the others who still see me as a pika. I've given up trying to hate Charlie and Nileen. Ditto my other students. Even Will, who tells me anything I want to know about a seed or root but clams up at the merest hint of a personal question.

I needed to hate them. Because if I didn't, I'd have to be afraid for them.

Sometimes I wonder if Raven Rock has given up the search. But I know my father. He won't let that happen, not ever.

I wonder this: If I begged him for their lives, will it make any difference?

Once or twice I've even wondered if I still want to be found.

For some reason, being with Charlie soothes down all those roiling, conflicted feelings. He likes to talk and is always kind and tolerant of my questions. When I ask about Banerjee, he tells me that she's a defector from the Nu London army. Went to the surface on assignment, decided she just couldn't go back. She survived on her own for nearly a year before hooking up with the group.

I always knew Banerjee was tough as bedrock but that amazes me. Not just that she made it alone, but that she did it as a pika, like me, knowing nothing about the surface. Clearly, the woman is on a whole other level of hardcore. She comes to watch my classes sometimes and seems satisfied with what she sees. I find myself craving her approval, the way I did the toughest instructors at the Academy. She has that effect on people, once you get past the scary bird-of-prey eyes.

I realize I still don't understand the inner workings of the group so I ask Charlie if Banerjee's word is law, like the commandant.

"More like the equivalent of an old-time mayor," he explains as he reads the barometers and makes notes in a battered spiral notebook. "Her say counts for more, but we all vote on the big things."

Charlie looks up at me with watery blue eyes. "It's not good when a few people have too much power. Bad decisions get made. I've been with a few other groups over the years, and this is the best one. Cause of her."

"I remember you from the ship, Charlie," I say. "You voted with Will to spare me. How come?"

Charlie puts the notebook away and stares into the fire. He's one of the oldest people in the whole crew—definitely old enough that he remembers the Culling firsthand and ought to hate me even more than the rest.

"People are people," he says finally. "Thinking otherwise is what got us into this mess in the first place. That and refusing to face reality when it was plain as day that all the cars and the factories and the power plants was wrecking the planet." He laughs. "And throwing a young girl into the sea to die is still wrong, no matter how we got to live now. But Banerjee was just doing what she thought was right for the rest of us. You can't fault her. I'll tell you one thing. Life goes on. Some things bounce back, some things don't. But life goes on. It always does. It's *civilization* got left behind."

I think about the island, the way new growth is moving in to fill the holes left by the superstorms.

"Nature abhors a vacuum," I say. "Someone famous said that."

Charlie smiles a sly old fox smile. "Aristotle, my dear."

I grin back. "Why Charlie, I think you're right."

"I did go to proper school," he says. "Till fifth grade anyway. Then I went to work as a picker in Jersey's biggest e-waste dump, recycling bits of computers and cell phones and such. Maybe I'm lucky I didn't end up there. Full of poison, that stuff was. Anyone picked long enough they got real sick. One guy was covered in these red bumps. It scared me."

We've never talked about the Culling, about *before*. I was too shy to ask. But I feel like everything I thought I knew about the world and my place in it is starting to turn upside down. They've lied to us about so much. I'm afraid of what Charlie might tell me, but I need to know the truth.

"Where are you from?" I ask. "Originally."

He looks up. "Little shantytown near old Atlantic City, nothing special. It's gone now."

I take a deep breath and say in a rush, "My grandparents all died before I was born. The first generation of elderly people didn't do well underground. It was too much of a shock. And the history classes at the Academy were pretty dry, mostly the technical stuff, like the collapse of the oil economy in 2043, the final melting of the Greenland and Antarctic ice sheets, the mass migration from the coasts and the formation of the Intergovernmental Consortium."

He nods slowly. "Yeah, I remember some of that."

"How old were you when it happened?" I ask.

"Sure you want to talk about this?"

"If you don't mind."

So Charlie tells me. How he was thirty when the first superstorm landed, that would be Megaera, and the government gave up any pretense of governing and put everything into building the underground cities. How all the infrastructure—highways, bridges, airports, the whole electrical grid—was already shot from decades of one hundred and twenty degree heatwaves, catastrophic flooding in some places and record-breaking drought in others. The starvation and the riots. The national lottery that used social security numbers to decide who got a place in the evacuation.

How National Guard tanks dispersed the crowds at the entry points leading down, because people panicked at the end and refused to believe they would be left behind. How his sister was shot right next to him, and he almost drowned when the tsunami came but managed to climb onto the roof of a high office building where a chopper picked him up. Private charter pilot, scouting for survivors.

"Sea levels had been rising for a while already," Charlie says. "But the end came so sudden, faster than anyone expected. It's funny, I remember being a little kid and seeing all the beachfront mansions on the Jersey shore and wishing I'd get rich enough to buy one someday. Then we started getting hit regular by canes, and nobody wanted to live there no more. The rich people moved inland and the cheapest shacks you could find were right beach-front. Didn't matter that they got knocked down every season, we'd just build 'em back up again."

He rises to get a bowl of soup and toss another log on the fire. We don't need the warmth but the light is cheery. "The ones who made it afterwards were the ones who found boats and learned to read the weather," Charlie says. "Cause the flooding was bad, but the storms were worse. Much worse. Now the young ones here, they don't remember any of that. Never had a country, don't even know what it means. I think some of 'em don't believe there ever used to be airplanes and televisions and cars. Think I'm making it up."

"They don't talk about it much anymore," I say, feeling physically ill. Charlie's story is a far cry from the sanitized version of history we were fed at school. "My people, I mean. They call it the Transition, and pretend there was no choice."

"Well, maybe there wasn't," Charlie says, "though everyone knew it was rigged. Sure, they took some poorer folks to do the hard work. That's who won the so-called lottery. But most of the spaces were already taken, either through political influence or straight-up bought and paid for. The scientists, I understand. They were needed. Hell, they'd been warning us about what was coming for decades and no one listened. But when push came to shove, weren't no congressmen or billionaires left out in the rain. It was the same all over. We got people in our group from everywhere in the world you can think of, though that's one thing that changed real quick. Don't matter now what color you are, man or woman, long as you pull your weight and fit in."

I try to imagine the billions of people and how the end must have been for them but the magnitude is just too enormous to grasp. "How many survived?" I ask quietly.

Charlie thinks on this for a minute. "Can't say exactly. I only know the eight hundred miles or so we claim as our range. There ain't many, but there's enough. We communicate with a few other groups by short-wave. When we have a meet-up, sometimes we'll pick up new folks, or folks will leave. They're free to do so. If they got a special skill, like Will, they just need to 'prentice someone else before moving on."

"Is the whole world like this? Just islands?"

Charlie laughs. "Oh no. There's plenty of bigger land, some of it right nearby, but trust me, you don't want to get stuck there when a cane hits. Ain't nowhere to hide. Better to keep moving. I'll tell you one place nobody goes though, and that's up north. Toad country. Ships sail too far, they don't come back."

The fire burns low and we're quiet for a while. Charlie moves to stand, then turns to me. "Tell me something," he says. "Did you like living down below?"

Like? There wasn't anything else. I consider it for a moment.

"Not really," I say, and I realize that's it's the truth.

"Hard to imagine," Charlie says. "I've seen some bad stuff, but I'd still rather have the sun. People just aren't built to live like earthworms." He smiles, and his homely, weathered face is almost handsome.

I haven't seen any animals yet, but there sure are lots of bugs. By dusk, the clouds of mosquitoes usually drive everyone into their tents. Sometimes though, if there's a breeze, people will sit out and tell stories. Some are like myths, and involve sea serpents or mer-people or underwater cities made of coral and gold. Others recount narrow escapes from the hypercanes, and the rogue waves, hundreds of feet high, that can appear out of nowhere on a calm day and swallow a fleet whole. My favorites are the ghost stories, set in the watery, skeletal remains of megacities like Jakarta and Shanghai and Houston.

One evening, about ten of us are sitting around the fire when Nileen turns to me.

"Your turn," she says, arching her thick black eyebrows.

I try to say no, but she starts nagging and the rest join in until I throw up my hands.

"OK, let me think."

"Something romantic," declares Fatima, who used to be quiet around me and now, like Nileen, views me as a font of information on the sweet pika life.

"Pish," Nileen says. "I want adventure."

"Blood and guts," urges the kid with the unpronounceable name.

"But funny too," Ezzie chimes in.

I think hard for a minute, and then it comes to me. Ancient, but still a classic.

"A long time ago," I say, "in a galaxy far, far away . . ."

I'm just getting to the part where Luke's fighting the beast in the trash compactor when I see movement at the edge of the fire. It's Will. He's never joined us before, and his presence throws me off a little. I stumble over my words, but quickly regain my composure and tell the rest with relish, including a James Earl Jones impression that's not half bad.

Everyone got a bit of what they wanted, so they're happy. As usual, Will's harder to read. I did see him actually smile a couple of times. And his eyes never left me, though I pretended not to notice. When it's over, he vanishes back into his tent without a word. Nileen watches him go, but the scowl on my face discourages her from commenting.

Then lightning splits the sky and we kick dirt over the fire and scatter for our tents. The air is thick and heavy, the way it gets before a big storm. Charlie told me there used to be something called seasons in these parts, and that every year a bitter cold would come and all the plants and trees would die and then be reborn. Now there's just hot and hotter.

Later that night, when the rains finally come and I'm lying on my cot with nothing to do but stare into space and worry about what's going to happen to me, what's going to happen to all of us, the door flap rustles. Will ducks in, wearing an army-issue poncho with water streaming down the sides. The flickering candlelight reveals an enormous lump in the front, which turns out to be a stack of books. From the way he handles them, taking care not to let a single drop touch the covers, I can see they are precious to him and I feel oddly moved that he risked bringing them over in the downpour.

"I brought your homework," he says, setting them down on the foot of my cot.

"My homework?"

"Yes. You have to study hard if you're going to learn how to be a physic. It takes years, you know. You're lucky to have me as a mentor. I had to train myself."

I don't know if it's the knowledge that we probably won't have weeks together, let alone years, or if it's just his arrogance in assuming I should be grateful when he only tolerates me because Banerjee ordered him to, but something in me snaps.

"How typically humble of you," I say.

"If you don't want them, that's fine," he says evenly, picking up the books and turning to go.

What's wrong with me? I know he's trying to be nice. Why am I compelled to poke him with a sharp stick every time I see him?

"Wait!"

He stops but doesn't put the books back.

"I'm sorry. Yes, please, I'll take them. I just don't know why you think I'm cut out to be a physic." I laugh hollowly. "I'm a killer. That's what I'm good at."

Will looks at me for a long moment. Then he sets the books down.

"You should start with this one, it gives a basic overview of herbal medicine," he says, handing me a heavy hardcover. "For the others, focus mainly on the equatorial zones. The books are old, and these latitudes are much warmer now, so we're seeing a lot of the species that used to be much farther south."

"OK." I glance down at the book. The title, in spidery black letters, is *An Encyclopaedia of Vintage Remedies*. It seems strange reading words on real paper, with pages that I have to turn by hand. But I like the heft of it, and the way it feels in my palm.

"Thanks."

He nods. "Goodnight, Jansin."

I read until my single candle burns too low to see anymore.

CHAPTER ELEVEN

Ironically, the technological advances that made the Transition possible proved to be a high-water mark. Humanity's ambitions narrowed to a single imperative: survival.

Where'd you find all those books anyway?" I ask as we move through a valley with huge moss-covered boulders. The sun comes out and the air has a moist, earthy smell. I feel really happy to be alive for the first time in a long while.

"I trade for them when we meet other groups," Will says, holding a branch so it doesn't smack me in the face. "Most people just want fiction. Two years ago I found one that has amazing hand-drawn illustrations. They're perfectly detailed, which is important because some of the poisonous species look very similar to the ones with curative properties."

He finds something called spiny amaranthus that's used to control high blood pressure, and other plants I can't remember the names of. Will moves through the woods with a natural, animal-like grace that I envy. All the exploring I've done has been in caves, and my feet keep tripping over hidden roots and hollows.

The island still bears the scars from earlier hypercanes: downed trees, patches of earth scoured clean by the wind, heaps of tangled brush. But like Charlie said, life is a remarkably resilient thing. Everywhere, new shoots have thrust out of the dirt, meadows taking over where once there was only forest, and before that, people. I wonder what it will look like in ten or twenty years. Something completely different, maybe.

"So what did you do for fun?" Will asks as we descend into a valley. Late afternoon sun slants through the trees and the woods are alive with the buzzing of insects.

"I flew planes," I say.

"Seriously?" He turns around. "I've never seen one. I thought they were all gone."

"Well, not real planes. I flew in a simulator at school. You can choose from hundreds of different programs. Anything from World War Two to the Fifth Gulf Conflict. I spent so many hours in there, I could probably fly anything. I mean, if we had actual aircraft. Which we don't."

"You have satellites though, don't you?"

"A few. My dad says–" I cut off abruptly. "Well, most of them broke years ago. But we use the ones that are left to track the storms."

"And search for hostages?" Will asks casually.

"What? I don't know. Maybe. I mean, I seriously doubt it." I realize I'm babbling and figure I'd better at least start babbling about something else. "Did I ever tell you about our political system? The satellites are actually the reason it turned out the way it did. See, we started with a federal government, just like the old days. There are five prefectures: Raven Rock in Pennsylvania, Greenbrier in Virginia, Cheyenne in Colorado, Kirtland in New Mexico and China Lake in California. All of them were dug out of existing underground bases. The builders just went deeper, a lot deeper." I pause for breath. "Well, they were supposed to communicate by satellite but the orbits became erratic. It was twenty years before full contact was resumed, that was when they built the bullet trains. By then, Greenbrier had declared independence and Kirtland followed suit shortly after."

Will's staring at me and I could swear, if I didn't know him better, that he's trying not to smile, though for the life of me I can't see why.

"And which one is yours?" he asks.

"Raven Rock," I say. "We were the first capital. The seat of government. I don't think the people running things ever got over the fact that the other prefectures seceded from the union. All except Cheyenne . . . Oh hey, isn't that echinacea?" I pluck a purple flower that looks like a daisy and hand it to him.

"You've been studying," he says, twirling the stem between his long fingers.

I bat my eyelashes and heave an internal sigh of relief that we've moved on to a new topic. I'm getting careless around him, and that could be fatal if he's reporting to Banerjee. "Every night, professor."

"Well, keep it up. I'll make a physic of you yet." He holds my gaze with those stormy grey eyes. "And please, no more nonsense about your worth, Jansin. I see how you treat the outcasts like Bob. You're a good person. Like us, if you'd only see it."

We hike down the mountain in silence. I feel more confused than ever. Will can be maddeningly aloof and arrogant and starchy, but then he goes and says nice things that make me like him even more than I already do.

Which, I realize with a sinking feeling, is a lot.

The days pass, and my hair gets long enough to start falling into my eyes, so I take to tying it back in a yellow kerchief Nileen gave me. I'd actually forgotten that my hair was curly, it's been short for so long. But I like the silky feel of it when I take a bucket shower, and my skin feels smoother too from living in the open air. I study the books Will gave me every night. I can identify about two dozen herbs now, and even more flowers, which are easier for me because they look so distinctive. Learning his craft reminds me strongly of my mother, and how she used to take me into her greenhouse when I was a little girl and let me help water her beloved flowers. I think the two of them would have hit it off big time. They're both quiet and precise and with prodigious memories for detail. Once I saw a spiky orange and blue flower I remember was one of her favorites, and I thought how excited she would be to see it growing in the wild. When I asked him, Will said it was called bird of paradise. I think my mom would be happy to know that there are still a few beautiful things in the world.

The more I read, the more impressed I am at Will's vast store of knowledge. I can point to pretty much any plant during our hikes and he will tell me not just the common name, but the Latin name. Sometimes in the evenings we play a game where I open a book at random and try to stump him with obscure references. He usually wins.

I feel his eyes on me sometimes, when I'm gathering in the forest, or when we're eating lunch. He still wears his indifferent stoneface in public, but when I catch him staring, I see something else before he looks away. What I see is a kind of simmering heat that's about as far from Will the Actuary as it's possible to get. It makes me nervous and intrigues me at the same time. He's so different from Jake, in every conceivable way. Jake was goofy and open and easy to read. Will's another country entirely.

I asked Nileen about him once when I was helping her repair a pile of nets. She's basically the local scandal-monger and will tell you anything you want to know about anybody, including fact, rumor and idle speculation. Anyway, she said they picked Will up about eight years ago. He was alone on a small sloop at the northern range of their territory. From the state he was in, they guessed he'd been drifting for weeks. He didn't speak for a very long time after they found him, and then he claimed he couldn't remember how he got there.

I think I'm not the only one around here with secrets.

"So tell me some more about your city," says Nileen, who trades in information like a fishwife hawking the day's catch.

We're scrubbing pots down at the beach, using handfuls of gritty sand to scrape off the burned bits of food from the bottom. It's late afternoon. A fresh sea breeze discourages the flies. Fatima is washing a pile of plates next to me. She has long, slender brown fingers and hazel eyes that both Nileen and I envy. Unfortunately, she's also super-nice so we can't hate her.

"City-state," I correct primly. "Anyway, it has four zones: Industrial quad, that's where the factories are. Ag quad, where we grow the food. Capitol quad, which is government buildings and university. And Barracks quad, where we live. It's not actually military barracks anymore, we have normal houses. But that was the name they gave it during construction and I guess it just stuck."

"So everybody's rich like you, huh?" Nileen says.

"I'm not even that wealthy," I say, guiltily thinking that just the contents of my old room would be a treasure trove on the surface. "There's people with a lot more. But there's people with a lot less too. Especially the ones that work in Industrial quad, and the miners."

"What happens when you get too old to work no more?" Fatima says, setting aside the last clean plate and grabbing one of my pots, the biggest and nastiest. That's how she is.

"Some people go live with their families. But we keep a tight lid on the population. We have to. Zero growth policy. That means they sometimes end up on their own, if they don't have kids or their kids don't want them. Some go to Chalktown. It's like a squatter camp. It's supposed to be illegal."

"Supposed to be?" Nileen says. She never misses much.

"Well, there's no place else for them. So the authorities have a bit of a problem."

"That's messed up," Fatima says in her slow drawl. "Look at Charlie. He's crazy old. But we'd never ditch him just cause he's useless or some kind of burden."

"But he's not useless," I say. "He's one of the most important people you've got."

"Maybe so," Fatima says. "But it don't make no difference. Look, he's teaching me to stormcast, ain't he? If he was scared about getting replaced, he wouldn't do that, would he? But he knows we take care of each other. He got nothing to worry about." She thrusts her hand into the recesses of the pot and lets out a yelp. "Damn," Fatima says, examining her palm. "Something bit me."

Nileen pokes cautiously at the pot, which has rolled onto its side. A second later, a small brown spider comes scurrying out. Nileen tries to stomp it with her flip-flop but the creature's too fast, vanishing into the rocks.

"What was it?" Fatima asks, clutching her wrist. There's an angry red welt on her left hand, and it's starting to swell.

"Not sure," Nileen says with a frown. "I didn't get a close look. Coulda been a brown recluse. Except I think I saw a yellow band around the body."

"Well, it hurts fierce," Fatima says.

"Let me see." I examine the bite without touching it. I can see two tiny holes where the spider's fangs sank in. The skin at the edges is starting to turn black, and fine red lines are already spreading out from the wound. I don't know much about spider bites, but this seems like a rapid, extreme reaction.

"We'd better go find Will," I say.

Fatima is starting to sweat. "Good idea." She's sitting cross-legged and leans forward, propping her right palm on the ground like she's going to stand up, but nothing happens. Her voice is scared when she says, "I can't feel my legs. They're like, numb."

Nileen and I exchange a look. "Go get Bob," I say. "Bring him back here. And tell Will what happened and that he needs to prep the infirmary."

She nods. "You gonna be OK, Fatima," Nileen says, and then her skinny knees are pumping at a dead run toward the jungle path.

"What's a brown recluse?" I ask, mainly to keep Fatima talking and distracted from the pain.

"Just regular," she says with a shrug. "Black widows is worse. But I never heard of one of them doing nothing like this." She shivers, and then she's falling to the side. I get an arm around her just in time and prop her head on my shoulder. Her braids tickle my cheek. We sit that way for what seems like forever. I watch the waves wash in and out, and feel her twitching against me as the venom attacks her central nervous system.

Then Bob appears. For such a big man, he's moving incredibly fast. Even Nileen can't keep up. He scoops Fatima into his arms without a word and starts running again, carrying her weight like it's nothing.

The camp is quiet. Most of the adults are still out fishing, cleaning and repairing the boats or tending the container gardens. A few young children and their minders stand in wide-eyed silence as Fatima is brought into the medical tent. I follow Bob inside. He lays her down on the table Will uses as a surgery. Almost immediately, she turns her head and vomits on the ground.

"Where's Will?" I demand.

"Here," he says, ducking through the tent flap, and seeing him makes me realize how absolutely terrified I felt a moment ago, and how much better I feel now.

His grey eyes assess the situation in an instant and then he's issuing orders.

"Bob, fetch a bucket of clean water. Nileen, I need Lisa." He looks at me. "You were there?"

I nod. "A spider bit her hand. Nileen said it looked like a recluse, but that it had a weird stripe."

Will has one forefinger pressed against the pulse in Fatima's neck. His other thumb is lifting her eyelids to check the pupils, which are hugely dilated. When I describe the spider, he looks up sharply.

"What color?"

I try to remember. "Yellow, I think."

"Are you sure?"

"Yes, I'm sure. She said a yellow band."

"Damn." Will prods the bite and winces. It's now the size of a grape and the color of an eggplant. "That's the ramped up kind. Genetically altered to be thirty times as venomous."

"Altered by who?"

"Old-time scientists, I heard. Some experiment that got loose. There was a lot of that happening at the end, when things broke down." He looks at Fatima. Her eyes are closed and her breathing is rapid and shallow. "They're rare. I've never seen one. But I've been told about cases by other physics."

"What can we do? Will she live?" I feel stunned. We were just having a normal conversation not twenty minutes ago. For the first time, I understand how casually life can be snuffed out on the surface, without hospitals or machines or technology. For thousands of years, we were Earth's top predator. Now we're the prey again. And sudden, violent death is always a heartbeat away.

Will doesn't answer the second question directly. "We need to excise the skin and draw the venom out, like a snakebite," he says. Fatima gags again and he turns her head so she doesn't choke and his calm façade cracks a little bit. "Where the hell is Lisa?"

I shake my head mutely.

"Then you're filling in," Will says. "I need shepherd's purse, sage and plantain. There's a box in my tent. We'll make a poultice. I'll hit her with the last of the antibiotics. It's the best we can do." He lays a hand on her forehead and I feel a stab of jealousy. What's wrong with me? Fatima's throwing up on his shoes, for God's sake, and possibly dying. I must be losing my mind.

Will starts prepping the needle and I get going before we make eye contact and he sees the shame and confusion there. Bob passes me on the way in with the water. He looks shell-shocked. Nileen is nowhere in sight; I guess she's off looking for Lisa and my heart fills with pity at the thought of her finding out what happened to her only kid.

Will's tent is just across the clearing. I've never been inside. I expect it to be neat and orderly, buttoned-down like him, and I'm surprised to find the sheet rumpled and a balled-up T-shirt hanging off the foot of his cot. There's a body-shaped indentation in the middle and my attention lingers on it until I realize what I'm doing and get focused in a hurry. His possessions are pitifully few—a smooth black river stone, a feather, other boy stuff—so I spot the box right away. It's finely made, bound in brass like a pirate's chest. I open it and grimace. The box is overflowing with small plastic vials containing dried flowers, roots and leaves, and everything's labeled according to some arcane numbering system known only to Will. I wish I could say I've become such an expert that I can instantly recognize what he's asked me for, but that's not the case. So I just grab the whole box and run back to the infirmary.

Bob boils water while Will and I get clean linens and make the poultices. Then Will heats a scalpel in the fire and cuts away the necrotic skin around the wound. I've never seen anything like it. The fang marks are oozing a clear liquid and it's almost as if her flesh is decaying, dissolving, like a corpse. Fatima goes in and out of consciousness. It's a mercy when she's under, and nerve-racking

111

every time she comes to. Her screams echo through the camp. Lisa comes and strokes her good hand and cries. We take turns holding Fatima down. It goes on for hours, and I wonder what kind of people meticulously engineered an insect to do such a thing.

We change the poultice every fifteen minutes. Will says it will draw the poison to the surface. But the necrosis keeps spreading. The antibiotics are gone. Everything's gone except for Will's herbs. Finally, Will says we can't wait anymore. He'll have to take the hand off. If he doesn't, she'll lose the whole arm, or just die. Lisa sobs and fights him. But in the end she knows he's right. So he does it. We have no anesthesia, not even a bottle of whiskey, and I realize I was wrong when I thought she couldn't scream any louder. His face is like a stone when he saws into her, and his hands are steady. I can't even imagine the strength of character it takes to do that.

When he cauterizes the stump, Fatima finally passes out and mercifully stays that way. I have no idea how much time has elapsed. It's been dark for hours. I stayed to help because Lisa was such a mess, and because Fatima was nice to me, and because I was there from the beginning, which is the way it happens sometimes. I haven't had a second to stop, to do anything except boil more water or clean up puke or hold the stick between her teeth, but now I kind of topple into a plastic chair and just put my head in my hands.

"You did well," Will says.

Not *did good*, like Fatima or Nileen would say. *Did well*.

His voice is heavy with exhaustion, but there's a steadiness too. The resigned courage of the battlefield surgeon. You do what has to be done because there's nobody else to do it. You partake in these horrors and then you lock them in a box, like the chest you keep in your tent. And you wear an actuary face for the world because it's the only way to function with a semblance of normality.

"Why don't you talk like the others?" I say, unable to bring myself to discuss what we just did. "You speak so precisely."

"I learned English from books." Will takes the chair next to me. We watch Fatima's chest rise and fall. She looks about ten years older. "Danish is my first language."

"Can you teach me to curse?"

Will smiles, but it's half-hearted.

"She was cleaning my pot, you know," I say. "If she hadn't finished hers first and wanted to help, that would probably be me."

"You didn't tell me that." Will's eyes move over my face, and I remember almost touching his sheets. My cheeks warm and I look away.

"I didn't really think of it until now. I was too scared." I have literally never uttered those four words to another human being before. I put my chin up and wait for him to say something sarcastic but he doesn't and I realize that Will wouldn't. Jake would, but Will wouldn't.

"You said it got away?" he asks.

I nod.

He runs his hands through his dirty-blonde hair. "We need to call a meeting first thing in the morning, tell everyone what happened and warn them to be on the lookout for a spider that appears to be a brown recluse but with a yellow band. I am not doing this again."

"Have you before?" I ask.

"Yes. But only fingers and toes. Never a whole hand before."

Only.

"How old are you, Will?" I say. "If you don't mind my asking."

And he says, "Seventeen."

A week after the spider incident, I wake up extra early after a bad dream whose details I can't recall, only that it was red and loud. As is my habit, I go down and watch the sun come up alone on the beach. Everyone's been subdued since what happened to Fatima.

She's going to make it, thanks to Will. He saved the rest of her arm. She's young and strong. She's got Bob and Lisa with her every minute of the day, and the rest of visiting in shifts too.

It could have been much worse.

Of course, the next time it might be. And there's always a next time up here in the crazy ruins of Western civilization.

But despite that, despite the horror and the sadness, I watch the sun rise and I wonder how I could have gone without this my whole entire life. It's not living down below. Just existing. I realize I haven't thought about rescue at all lately. I realize I don't want it anymore.

The truth is I've been on my own for years now. I went through the agony of losing my parents when I was eight and they packed me off to the Academy. Those wounds scarred over a long time ago. I had no close friends. I was good at what they taught me but I didn't relish it, the way some did. The best thing I can say is I knew my place there, knew what was expected of me and what to expect in the future. In the military, there's a plan for every contingency. Nothing is left to chance. That's the hardest part about life on the surface, I think. The not knowing, from one day to the next, what will happen. I don't just mean the storms, or genetically-engineered spiders, but lots of things can kill you up here. Anything from cancer, what they call bone-rot, to an infected hangnail. The food's terrible, there's no climate control, and the only creatures that seem to be thriving are the mosquitoes.

And yet.

I can deal with it. The fear and the strangeness. *The not knowing.* I don't have my place yet, my niche, but I could someday.

If Raven Rock will let me.

Late afternoon, my favorite time of day. The captain says we'll be leaving soon. So we build a huge bonfire on the beach, with dancing and singing in different languages. Fatima is out of bed, walking around again. She's lost a lot of weight and says I should take some of her clothes until she gains it back. She gives me a dress, blue with thin straps that cross behind my back. It fits perfectly. I feel shy at first, but people keep coming up to me, students and their families, Charlie, Nileen, Lisa, offering a bite of fish or a sip of milk, still warm from the udder. Even Banerjee herself, who looks me up and down and nods approvingly.

"You don't look like a pika anymore, Nordqvist," she says.

I hadn't really thought about it that way, but she's right. My skin is brown and I'm leaner than I used to be, although the hikes with Will and daily fighting practice have kept me strong.

It's not just that. I've changed inside too. I feel lighter, easier. Like I've shed a suit of clothing that didn't quite fit.

"Thank you, ma'am," I say.

Banerjee stares at me for a long moment and seems satisfied with what she sees there.

"Welcome," she says, and embraces me in a formal way that has the weight of ritual. The captain holds me long enough for the others to see and take note, then steps back.

I don't know what to say, and suddenly Will is beside me.

Banerjee smiles. "Go, little sister," she says, loud enough for everyone to hear. "Enjoy the party."

Will leads me through the crowd and it takes forever because people keep stopping me for a quick hug or kiss on the cheek. They call me daughter or sister. I hug them all back, but my head is spinning a little when we finally break free and reach the edge of the sea. The sun is setting and the waves are gilded a fiery orange at their crests.

"Walk with me," Will says. The actuary must be on leave; there's a light in his eyes tonight, like he's thinking of a great joke and I'm the only other person in the world who gets it.

I kick off my flip-flops and we head down the beach until the buzz of voices fades away and the only sound is the liquid rush of the waves lapping at the shore.

"What just happened?" I ask as we stop to rest side by side on the sand.

"You're one of us," he says.

"So my probation is over?" I smile. "Does that mean I get on the list for eggs?"

Will gives me a quizzical look. "I don't know that word."

"Eggs?" I tease.

He grunts. "No, probation."

"It means a test."

He considers this. "Then yes, your probation is over. We'll never leave you, Jansin." Will stares out to sea. "We'd die for each other in this clan. Loyalty means everything," he adds, and it's a like a knife twisting in my heart. I resolve to tell Banerjee the truth tomorrow, whatever it costs. I know about loyalty. My whole life has been about loyalty. The catch is I was never given a choice about who and what I was loyal to. This is different. This is *my* decision. I can't put the group at risk any longer. I can't put Will at risk. They at least deserve to know what's coming for them.

I want to say all this but the words stick in my throat.

We watch the daylight seep from the sky like honey through a sieve, red and purple giving way to the cooler tones of evening. I wish I could take his hand again but there's still a distance inside him, a gulf I'm not sure another person can cross. So I content myself with lying there, feeling his fingers inches from mine.

"What do you know about the canes?" he asks after a while.

I glance over. His skin glows golden brown against his white shirt, a sight I find very distracting. "Um, there's five. They're big and I hope I don't ever see one up close. Let's see . . . Alecto is the youngest, Megaera the oldest. Kelaeno's the speed demon.

Aeolus seems to have the most erratic path, no one knows why. But it means she's a favorite of long-odds gamblers." The horizon stretches clear and flat as a pancake, but it still gives me the creeps talking about the canes. "That leaves Tisiphone. She's the recluse of the hypercane family. Locked in place, out in the boonies, no satellites above, no ground views either. Look, Charlie's really the person you should ask."

Will gets up on one elbow and looks at me seriously with those mismatched eyes. "What if there was a place the canes didn't reach? A land mass."

"Go on," I say.

"I know it sounds crazy, but my mother used to tell me stories when I was little. She was Inuit, though my dad was Danish and yellow-haired like me. Anyway, she got the stories from my grandmother, who lived through the Big Melt. About an island that's hundreds of miles across and sheltered from the storms somehow."

It's the first time he's ever mentioned his family, but I don't think he even realizes that, he's so lost in memory.

"My sister Greta would get angry and say it was all just a grown-up fairy tale, but I believed it. I mean, I *wanted* to believe it, but there was a ring of truth. The details were so vivid. The thing is, Jansin, I've heard the same story from other people we trade with. A few are crazy cultists. Wrath of God, reaping the whirlwind, that kind of stuff. But I've talked to people from all over the world. Most think it's nonsense, but a few say they've heard it too, from relatives or elders." He leans back and stares at the sky. "I'm just saying, there might be something to it."

The first star comes out, bright and solitary.

"What if there is a Promised Land out there," I say. "How do we find it?"

Will sighs. "I don't know."

"Sounds a little like wishful thinking," I say. "I mean, wouldn't you have met someone who's actually been there? Wouldn't *everyone* want to find it? It's a nice idea though."

I roll to the side and Will lightly touches the tattoo on my back, just under the nape of my neck. I'd almost forgotten about it. Goosebumps rise under his fingertips.

Ubi maior, minor cessat.

"I've always wanted to ask you what that means," he says.

"It means the weak capitulate before the strong. That's my school motto."

"Nice. Sounds vaguely fascist."

"What do you know about fascism?" I ask, laughing in surprise.

"I know about all kinds of things."

"Do you now? Such as?"

"Such as constellations." He points up at the sky. "That's the Big Bear. See the paws and the tail? And that one is the Archer . . ."

We lie quietly for a bit.

"There's a picture of a wheat field in that book about North American horticulture," he says. "The first time I saw it, I couldn't believe it. I kept flipping back. That's what a real farm should look like, Jansin. Just big open sky and miles of grain. If we could only plant crops up here, everything would change. But we can't."

Because the canes would sweep them away.

"So you think that if you could just find this place, this safe place, you could jumpstart surface civilization again?" I say.

"Yes," he answers simply.

I think of the sheep and the sun breaking through the clouds. Wasn't that my favorite daydream once? Before I saw the real thing.

"Well, sign me up then," I say.

It's too dark now to see his face, but I know Will is smiling.

∾

Usually we take bucket showers in a makeshift enclosure, but since it's still nice the next day, Will and I pack a picnic lunch and hike up into the hills. He says there's a stream up there that runs into a deep pool perfect for swimming.

I went looking for Banerjee first thing after breakfast, but Fatima told me she'd gone off with Rupert in one of the smaller boats to check out a freshwater spring on the next island. Her absence was both a relief and a disappointment. I'm so tired of lying all the time, of constantly watching what I say. It's like a heavy weight I just want to walk away from and never look back.

I decide I'll spill my guts to the captain tonight even if I have to camp out in front of her tent.

After we climb for an hour, the ground starts to open up and the island spreads wide behind us. I can see the shore, and the line of breakers beyond it. The ocean is a dozen different shades of blue, turquoise in the shallows and fading to deeper cobalt in the depths. A thin veil of dirty white clouds has spread across the sky.

We move high up the mountain, farther than we've gone before. Will spots some guarana, whose large brown seeds are used to treat migraine headaches, urinary tract infections and a bunch of other things. I sit on a fallen tree while he gathers handfuls of the red outer pods and stows them in his pack.

A few minutes later we reach the pool. It's surrounded by mossy rocks, with a pebbly bottom. We dive in with our clothes on and float on our backs for a while. Will's more relaxed than I've ever seen him, like a different person. It turns out he has a gift for accents, and he absolutely ruins me with impressions of Banerjee and some of the tough-talking boys in my class. When I manage to stop laughing, I find the bar of soap I pilfered from the bucket showers and sit on a flat rock near a trickle of water coming down the slope above. I start to comb out my tangles and then I feel his fingers on mine, gently drawing my hands into my lap.

"I'll do it," he says, and I'm very aware of his closeness and his hands in my hair, his breath next to my ear. I sit very still. He smells like cool water and clean, sun-warmed skin.

I feel like such a fraud.

"Can I ask you something?" I say.

"Of course." His voice is low, husky, as his fingers stroke my curls.

"Did Banerjee make you take me on? Do you tell her what we talk about?"

Will freezes and his hands drop to his sides.

"Why do you think that?" he says neutrally.

"I don't know. I just . . . I thought you hated me. It didn't make any sense."

"Jan."

I turn around to face him. He's giving me his intense look, the one I could just drown in.

"First of all, I never hated you. I tried to save you, remember? You just have a talent for rubbing me the wrong way sometimes."

I smile a little. "Sounds strangely familiar."

"And second, it was my idea. You're obviously smart. And fit." He eyes wander over the wet clothes clinging to my body and he clears his throat. "Anyway, Lisa's great but she's a diabetic. She doesn't like people to know, so keep it to yourself. But strenuous exercise is too dangerous for her without insulin."

"And that's all?" I say, feeling unaccountably bold with him today.

"And I like talking to you," he admits. "You're different from anyone I've ever known before."

I swallow. "What if I'm not who you think I am?"

"What do you mean?"

I take a deep breath. There's no going back now. "What if I'm a general's daughter? What if my presence is endangering the entire group? They'll never stop looking for me, Will, never." I bury my face in my hands.

"Hey." He scoots closer and puts an arm around my shoulders.

"Don't you hate me now?" I mumble.

"No, Jansin, I still don't hate you. I kind of figured that anyway, from the way you talked. I'm not a complete fool. Have you told Banerjee?"

"I was going to today." I peek at him through my fingers. "What if they leave me behind? It's the only smart thing to do."

I realize I've just articulated my greatest fear, one I didn't even want to admit to myself. Will takes my hand and pulls me to my feet.

"Then I'll stay too," he says, and I can tell he's perfectly serious.

That does it. The emotional release of confessing everything I've pent up for weeks makes me cry a little, which Will can't handle at all.

"Please don't," he says desperately. "Everything will be fine, you'll see. She'll never get a majority to vote against you now, even if she wanted to, which she won't. And the ones that try . . . Well, we'll get Bob to pay them a visit. He worships you almost as much as Fatima, you know."

"OK," I sniffle, wiping my face with the hem of my tank top.

"Plus I packed a really special lunch!" Will cries, bounding over to our packs. He rummages through his own and pulls out a cloth bag. "There's fried fish and rice," he says, setting out a plastic container, "but in light of your current state, I'd suggest we skip straight to dessert."

Will whips out a small brown square and presents it to me with a theatrical flourish.

"Is that . . . ?" I whisper.

"Chocolate. Sweet-talked it from the cook."

"Oh. My. God." I start laughing through my tears. "I think I love you."

Will's eyes lock on mine for an instant, then he tears his gaze away and grins. "Don't get carried away," he says.

There's nothing better than a good cry, unless it's a good cry followed by a piece of dark chocolate. I close my eyes and let the sweetness mingle with the salty tears in a glorious explosion of endorphins.

We eat the rest of our picnic lunch in peaceable silence, letting the sun dry our clothes. Then the sky darkens and the air takes on a heavy quality. It's probably my imagination, but I can almost feel the pressure dropping. The high, wispy cirrus has given way to thick, low clouds crawling in from the sea.

"I hate to say it, but we should get going," Will says, brushing the last grains of rice fish from his hands. "Charlie told me the rains are coming early this afternoon."

We pack up and head back the way we came as thunder rolls through the valley. It starts to drizzle, so we put our ponchos on. Pretty soon, the drizzle turns to rain, which turns to a soaking deluge. I can hardly see through the horizontal curtains of water.

Lightning forks down and an ear-splitting boom follows almost instantly. Will looks back. "We need shelter," he calls. "Come on, I know a place ahead."

We slog along for another few minutes and then he turns toward an overhang in the side of the cliff, not exactly a cave but deep enough to be dry at the back. Will drops his pack and strips off his poncho, then helps me do the same. The rain encloses us in a cocoon of white noise. A cool breeze hits my skin and I shiver a little.

Will stands in front of me, watching the storm. "I'm really sorry for what happened to your people," he says after a while.

His face is turned so I can't see his expression. We haven't talked about this since the first day we went up the mountain together. About the night at Archipelago Six.

"It's just . . . you have to understand. There're things we need, things we can only get from the camps. Medicine, but also food, clothing, weapons. The cities are all looted or flattened or under water. There's nothing left from the old days. Some of the clans raid each other, but we don't do that. Most of the time, we hit after the tourists are gone and pick through the scraps. It's safer that way, but you never know what you'll find." He pauses. "You probably think we're savages. But I've never killed anyone. And I hope I never have to."

I wrap my arms around myself and watch the rain course down the hillside in a hundred brown rivulets. "I get it," I say. "And I don't think you're savages. If you knew some of the things they taught me at the Academy . . . Trust me, us pikas are much worse than your people."

Will leans against the rock wall. His voice is weary. "One of the kids got real sick with an infection. No matter what I tried, I couldn't help her. We needed medicine. So we took a chance. We just wanted the drugs. We didn't know about the trenches. Then it all got out of control."

I think about the contractors, the whole setup. If Will's people had appeared in daylight, unarmed, what would we have done? Would we have helped? Or would we have shot them on sight?

"At first, I thought you were toads," I say. "I didn't know what else it could be."

Will doesn't move, but something in his posture stiffens. "Up North we called them draugr. My grandmother used to scare us with tales of how they'd catch children who lied or stole or didn't mind their elders. I never saw one up close until I was ten." He pauses. "They didn't look like she said. No green skin or sharp teeth. They were worse. Because they looked like us. Except they moved funny. Very fast, and jerky." He shudders almost imperceptibly. "You were brave enough to tell me your story," he says with a twisted smile. "Now I'll tell you mine, if you'd like."

"OK," I say, laying a hand on his arm. The temperature has plummeted so far up the mountain, but his skin is hot, almost feverish.

Will watches the rain for a minute. His eyes take on a dreamy, unfocused quality. "My father was in the bow, untangling a fishing line with my sister Greta. It was a calm day for a change. Perfectly cloudless. I had a cat, a gift from another family. He was orange and had seven toes on one paw and eight on the other." He rubs his forehead, arm muscles taut with tension. "It's not as weird as it sounds. The extra toes were tiny. You could only see them if you squeezed his paw a little and made them stick out."

"What was his name?" I ask. I've always liked cats.

"You know, I don't think I'd named him yet. He was so new."

The rain hisses around us and I feel a knot of dread tighten in the pit of my stomach.

Alone . . . drifting for weeks . . .

"So I'm playing with the cat," Will continues, unconsciously switching to present tense, "and after a while I realize I can't hear my father and sister talking anymore. I stand up and walk to the bow. The line they're working on is there, so I figured they went below. I start toward the forward hatch, and that's when I see the blood. Just a few drops, but it stops me cold. I wonder if my sister cut herself and my father took her to bandage the wound. But then I think, I know Greta, she would have yelled her head off. Why didn't I hear anything?

"I start feeling a little scared, but it's the kind of scared where you let yourself imagine that something terrible has happened because you know in your heart that it hasn't really, it's just a game, just your mind playing tricks. Then I hear a scream from the open hatch, and I know right away it's my mother. I freeze, literally freeze. I could not move a muscle. And then I see a shadow on the other side of the sail. I knew it wasn't my father or Greta from the way it stood, so perfectly still.

"I still don't remember moving, but I must have, because the next thing I'm hiding under a rolled-up sail. There was a gap. I saw my mother one last time before they took her over the side. And she saw me. *Don't move*, she whispered. I didn't. I let them go." He says this in a dead voice that matches his eyes.

"You couldn't have done anything," I say gently. "You were just a child."

"I know," he says. "It doesn't really matter."

I touch his braid, damp from the rain, and have a sudden urge to see what his hair would look like unbound, hanging down his back. I think about the gentleness underneath his guarded exterior, and his intelligence, and how he makes me feel when I'm with him.

Like I'm a human being instead of a carefully crafted weapon to be used as others see fit.

"I want to see your hair," I say.

He doesn't answer, but his breath quickens a little as I remove the scrap of string and slowly work out his braid. I use my fingers to unravel it until it hangs down his back in a shining wave. It smells like rain.

He finally turns toward me. "Listen, Jansin," he says, but that's all he has time for because I lean forward on my tiptoes and very softly press my forehead to his mouth. Will's hands cup my face, his fingers tracing my cheeks and jaw. His hair is even longer than I expected, nearly to his hips. I press my palm flat against it, feel the curve of his spine, the lean muscles of his back. His heart beats hard against my throat. I close my eyes and start lifting my lips to meet his when the wail of a siren slices through the storm. It reaches a crescendo, fades, then begins howling again. Will's hands tighten on my shoulders.

"What is it," I whisper, searching his widening eyes.

"Evac," he says, taking a deep, shaky breath. "Time to run."

CHAPTER TWELVE

*Despite, or perhaps because of, the near total trans-
formation of society's physical environment, culture
adhered closely to the old ways in dress, language and
style. Idiomatic expressions like "hungry as a horse"
persisted for decades after the last horse had perished.*

My heart hammers against my ribs as we pound down the
mountain path. It's as if all the pressures that have been building inside since I was taken—my dread of the hypercanes, my
growing feelings for Will, the endless waiting for rescue, for *something to happen*—have all exploded with the storm now raging over
our heads. The warning siren is quiet now but I can still hear it in
my head, urging me on.

*Get away. As far and as fast as you can. Before the monster shows
its face.*

The rain has churned the ground into a muddy river. We slip
and slide as much as run and it's a wonder neither of us break our
necks. When we finally emerge from the jungle, half the tents are
gone. Everyone's moving purposefully, breaking down what's left of
the camp. Will snags the arm of a little black-haired girl whose half-
naked body is streaked with dirt.

"Where's the captain?" he snaps.

"Dunno, try the beach!" she pipes, yanking free.

"Damn," Will mutters. "I hope we get more than a forty-eight hour lead this time."

"What do I do again?" I ask a little breathlessly.

Charlie explained the procedure to me about a million times but of course my mind's gone blank.

"Get your stuff. Use the backpack. I'll meet you at the boats," he says, and then he's dashing off to the infirmary, where Lisa's piling up plastic containers full of supplies.

A steady wind is just starting to rise. It flutters the leaves of the trees, and I try not to imagine what they will look like in a day's time.

"Hurry!" Charlie calls to me from across the clearing. His face is white and pinched. If Charlie's scared, that's a pretty bad sign. "This one's moving in real quick. I mean, quicker than I've ever seen."

"Kelaeno," I say without thinking.

"What?"

And then I realize the name means nothing to him. Kelaeno is the fastest and most destructive of the five storms, although that's a bit like saying a hydrogen bomb is more destructive than an atom bomb. "Never mind. Will we make it?"

"If you get moving right now," he yells, turning away to carry disassembled pieces of the LIDAR down to the waiting ships.

I stuff my few belongings into the pack. The blue dress I wore to the bonfire. One olive drab poncho. An ancient T-shirt Rupert gave me that says, in block letters barely legible anymore, *I Flunked Anger Management.* Four of Will's books. Then I fold up the tarp tent and place it on top of the cot. It's whisked away by two guys I know from class a minute later.

I take the path to the beach, and follow the high tide line towards the cove. The surface of the ocean is speckled with white-caps and the sky is ominous, dark and low. Still, to an untrained eye, it looks like a regular thunderstorm. It's hard to believe there's a hypercane two thousand miles wide bearing down on us.

I time the interval between waves, counting slowly in my head. Six seconds.

That's when I notice the first starfish. I've read about them but never seen one before. The five gracefully curving arms are white in the middle, with orange and pink spots running along the edges. A few yards later, there's another, and then several more. I slow, letting the surf wash over my toes. Suddenly, the shore is full of them as far as I can see, thousands upon thousands stranded on the gravel and sand.

I've heard that big storms can do this, and the terrible waste of life saddens me.

At first, I think they're all dead. But then I see one move. Just a tiny bit. I stare at it, transfixed. It moves again, and so do the ones around it. Which are so definitively dead they're starting to shrivel like dried fruit.

I feel a faint vibration under my feet.

Oh shit.

Oh shit.

I turn and start sprinting flat out as the first mole erupts in an explosion of dirt and gravel behind me.

The whirling drill on its nose makes a high-pitched shriek as the machine emerges fully and slams down, caterpillar tracks gripping the wet ground like it was asphalt. Seconds later, three more spew out of the waves, each a precise distance from the next.

I kick off the flip-flops in midstride and veer for the jungle, head down, blood pounding in my ears, as soldiers in full combat armor pour out of the open hatches. I hear the jagged bursts of machine guns, but don't look back. The tree line is close, maybe a hundred yards. I can run that in ten seconds. But sometimes ten seconds is a long time.

A bullet grazes my arm, searing pain followed by numbness. That usually means nerve damage. I keep running.

All I can think is Will, I have to get to Will.

There's shouting and screaming all up and down the shore now, punctuated by gunfire and the deep rumbling of the moles. I keep expecting another bullet to rip my head off, but then I'm in the trees, leaping over fallen logs and trying not to hit any sharp rocks with my bare feet. At some point I stop and rip a strip of cloth from my shirt for a tourniquet so I don't bleed to death before I find him.

The sounds of fighting fade as I go deeper and turn parallel to the shore until I find the path. I slow to a jog. I'm so afraid of what I'll find.

At the last turn before the clearing, the one where I waved to Will just a few minutes ago, I drop down and start crawling. My left arm is useless, and it takes me forever to reach the perimeter. I don't see any soldiers, and I don't see any moles. I don't see anyone at all. They must have focused on the shore. They might not even know about this camp. Yet.

But it's only a matter of time.

I decide to hell with subtlety and stand up. "Will!"

There's no answer, and his tent is empty.

I hear the faint thrum of laser weapons being discharged not too far away. My left side is soaked with blood, and I can't feel much below the shoulder. I know the whole island will be crawling with soldiers in less than an hour.

We'll head for the hills. Maybe there're deeper caves up there, someplace to hide. No one knows the island better than he does.

I start down the path into the woods, the one we always take in the mornings. I listen hard for any sounds out of the ordinary, and it suddenly occurs to me that I haven't heard a bird sing for days. They knew what was coming.

I'm about ten yards in when I hear a soft rustling in the under-growth, almost masked by the dripping rain. It's too low to be human. An animal, then? But I've never seen an animal here. Not even once.

"Will?" I call softly.

Silence. It has a primordial look, this place, with heavy moss-covered vines draping the tangles of downed trees and a layer of thin mist swirling around my feet. I hear the sound again, off to the left. It has a *slithering* quality that lifts the hair on the backs of my arms.

I start to run then, and something erupts out of the dead leaves. It's shiny, about three feet long, and it moves like a snake. I stumble and it hits my leg, coiling five or six times around my ankle. There's a metallic click as the thing's head locks to its tail. A mobot. Autono-mous kinematic machines with variable morphology. Which means they can reassemble themselves into any shape they want to. Like a manacle.

I feel a pinch as it draws blood. There's a whirring sound.

"Jan!" It's Will. He's running down the path, his pack bouncing on his back.

A light on the mobot clicks from red to green. It's confirmed my DNA. Time slows to a crawl.

"No!" I scream. "Go back! Run!"

But he keeps coming, as the mobot lets out a piercing wail that seems to go on and on and on.

Will lands next to me on his knees and starts yanking at the thing, but it's useless. There's no catch, no lever. My foot would have to come off to get free of it.

"Stop it," I yell, pushing at him. I think I'm crying, but the only thing in my mind is the panic and the knowledge that I've brought this down on him. "Get away from me. Run, dammit!"

"No," he says, and I love and hate him both in that moment.

He pulls me to my feet and then someone shouts, "Over here!"

A dozen soldiers in jungle camo and balaclavas materialize on all sides, gun sights trained at our heads.

"Back away from her!" one of them barks at Will.

He raises his hands and takes two steps to the side.

"Don't you touch him!" I scream. "He saved my life!"

"Kick the pack away!" the soldier orders. "Now get on the ground."

Will complies, and then three of them rush over. One plants a boot squarely on his back.

"Shut that damn thing off," someone says.

One of the soldiers peels back her balaclava. It's a young woman with rosy cheeks and tough brown eyes. She kneels by my leg. I think about kicking her in the face and taking her gun, but I know they'd just end up killing both of us. She does something to the mobot and the shrieking siren quiets.

"I want him on the mole with me," I say.

They ignore me. The woman gets on her radio mic. "Target acquired," she says. "We're bringing her in. Got another one too. A hostile." She cocks her head, listening. "Roger that."

"Hey!" I say. "Did you hear me? He saved my life. And you can't leave him here, there's a cane coming."

"Whatever," she says. She nods at the two soldiers behind me. "Sedate her."

They grab my arms and I feel the sting of a needle in my thigh.

"Will," I croak, but I can't move, can't do a thing.

"We need a stretcher!" she calls.

They slide a spinal board underneath me and then I'm being lifted up into the air, raindrops falling into my open eyes and mouth. "It's OK, Nordqvist, we got you," she says.

As they carry me off, I catch a last glimpse of Will, still on the ground, a soldier standing over him with his weapon pointed down. I hear it fire, and this time I manage to scream.

CHAPTER THIRTEEN

Deprived of the cosmos, our gaze turned inward.
How much deeper could we go?

The drugs I'm on keep the full weight of my depression at bay for a while. But it's always there, lurking in the dark like a chained-up dog. I'm terrified of what will happen when I finally look it in the eye. So I stay medicated.

I don't remember the trip back. The first coherent images are of my mother's hands, stroking my forehead. Her quiet sobbing when I first opened my eyes in the hospital. They treated me for six broken ribs and a shattered humerus, the upper bone in my arm. Plus too many minor lacerations to count.

Will's death replays over and over in my mind. Awake and sleeping both. I'm starting to see details that I'm not even sure are real. His head turning toward me at the last second. His lips moving as if he was trying to tell me something. It always ends with that terrible sound, like a door slamming shut.

I keep thinking there had to be something I could have done differently. But I don't know what. In my heart, I know they would have found me no matter how far we ran.

My parents believe I'm traumatized and that's why I'm not talking and barely eating. I guess I am, but not for the reasons they think.

Since I've been able to get out of bed, my routine is to have black coffee for breakfast and then go walking in the gardens. My father took a week off when I first came home, but now he's back to his usual workload so I don't have to see him much. It's been easy to blame him for everything, even though he did it out of love. Easier than blaming myself, though there's plenty of guilt to go around. I still haven't forgiven him. I might never. But I get it. I would kill in a heartbeat if I thought I could bring Will and the others back. I genuinely wish they had just left me on that atoll. One life against dozens.

My mom's back at work part-time too, so I'm usually alone during the day, which is fine by me. Wandering in her extensive gardens, breathing the humid, richly scented air, lets me pretend I'm not thousands of feet underground. In my imagination, Will walks next to me, pointing out the different plants and flowers. We relive old conversations and I tell him things I've never told anyone, like how I desperately wanted to be a test pilot after reading about crazy Chuck Yeager, the first human being to break the sound barrier. I just couldn't accept that the era of flight was over.

Sometimes Will laughs, and sometimes he lectures, and sometimes he just listens.

Sometimes we finish that kiss.

Those times are the worst. I go back to bed and stay there until they make it night again.

I can't stop noticing all the miraculous little things I used to take for granted. Such as hot and cold running water. A refrigerator packed with food that I can take whenever I feel hungry. Soft sheets. A closet full of dresses and an entire drawer devoted only to underwear. Painkillers. Electric lights. Tampax. The list is endless.

The quantity of *stuff* we have down here boggles the mind, if you actually think about it. Yet none of it manages to fill the swelling void right in my center, like a balloon on the verge of popping. Everything—our house, our neighborhood, the immaculate faux-lawns and sleek cars—has a veneer of falsity, like I'm living on a giant movie set. Life has become a simulacrum of itself. We're all just going through the motions, pretending everything's fine when it's about as far from fine as you can get.

The only thing that seems real and honest and true is my mother, but I can't talk to her about any of this. I'm not sure why. But my mind just freezes up at the very thought. Fortunately, she's one of those rare people who knows how to be with someone and not talk incessantly the entire time. She'll come to my room and read a scientific journal or invite me to help chop vegetables for dinner. We can share a smile or communicate in a hundred other ways without breaking the silence, and it's not heavy or oppressive. Just peaceful.

The first time I saw my reflection in a mirror, I thought it was someone else. Because that skinny girl with the long, sun-bleached hair and crazy bloodshot eyes could not be me.

Could it?

It's lunchtime, not that I pay attention to such things, and my mother comes into my bedroom with a sandwich. It must be a weekend since she's home. I don't bother keeping track of the days. She's obviously worried about me. She says it's been two months. I nod like I am aware of this. But it could have been two weeks or two years, neither would surprise me. Time loses all meaning when you decide to stop living in the present. I do know I've lost a lot of weight, and I didn't have much extra to begin with.

"Hey, honey." She sits on the edge of my bed. I notice that her hair is almost completely grey now. She's still beautiful, with her dark, inquisitive eyes and high cheekbones. "Listen, I've been talking with your father. We think you might be ready to go back to school. See your friends."

She doesn't say, see Jake, but I know she's thinking it. He's come to the house a half dozen times but I won't let him in. I just can't look at his face right now. He was there. I know because my father told me. Described his heroics in great detail. How he distinguished himself in the bloodbath on the island. What a bright, shiny future Jake has before him. When I said there's guilt to go around, Jake is definitely included in that equation.

An army shrink showed up once too, about six weeks ago. I threw a bowl of tomato soup at her head. She didn't come back.

"It's doing you no good lying around here all day. The commandant says you can still graduate if you pass your final."

She pushes the sandwich toward me. I push it back.

"That's two and a half weeks away. Just think about it, OK? I'll support whatever you decide, Jansin. You can always wait until next term. But it might be a good thing to start living again."

"OK, Mom."

She pauses. "We haven't really talked about it, and I understand if you don't want to, but . . . did anything happen to you? While you were with those people?"

She means, was I raped? "No, nothing like that. They were very good to me, actually."

"You sure?"

"Yeah, I'm sure."

"I love you." She kisses my cheek and goes, leaving the door cracked. I get up and close it.

It's fake drizzling outside, but of course there's no breeze to rustle the curtains. They're light pink, like my comforter and wall-to-wall carpet. The posters on the wall are of movie characters and sports heroes I worshipped nearly a decade ago. It's the room of a stranger, or a friend I haven't seen in years. Maybe she's right. Maybe I need to get out of here.

When the doctor comes, he tells me my druggie days are over. No more prescriptions. That's fine, because I've stashed a bunch of pills away. Just in case.

I spend the afternoon thinking about the dead. Not only Will, although it's him my thoughts obsessively turn to, like picking at a half-healed scab. But the others too. Charlie. Nileen. Bob. Banerjee. Lisa and Fatima. The dirty girl with black hair.

My father told me there were no survivors. I didn't expect there would be.

I think about how the clan's ancestors escaped the end of the world against all the odds, *escaped the bloody hypercanes*, only to be gunned down by the very people who abandoned them decades before. Of course, they attacked us first. That's what my father would say. Tit for tat. It just goes on and on. I'm so weary of death. And my father still wants me on that Greenbrier team. He hasn't said it outright, but he's dropped hints.

Tit for tat. Us and them.

There's always a *them*. And if there isn't, we'll find one.

Charlie. Nileen. Bob and Banerjee.

She was a good leader, the captain. I could have followed her without question. Even when she wanted to throw me overboard, she was only doing what she thought was right for the group. Ruthless, yes. Cruel, no. There's a world of difference between the two. People listened to her out of respect, not fear. You can't be soft and make it up there. Not if you're responsible for a bunch of people, including kids.

I bury my face in my hands.

Including kids.

Ironically, they found us because of the clear weather I was so happy about. An orbiting satellite two hundred miles up photographed the activity on the beach at 0900:47 local time and passed the images to Central Prefecture Command, where an analyst who had been assigned to my case full time determined that the new data warranted deployment of military force.

In her report, which I asked for a copy of and read about two dozen times, she estimated there was an eighteen percent chance this was the group that had me, assuming I was still alive. She probably had strong personal doubts that such was the case but was too diplomatic to express them in writing. Apparently, several previous operations had ended with a lot of dead bodies but no Jansin Nordqvist.

Moles were scrambled, hostage extraction teams mobilized, weapons locked and loaded.

Ubi maior, minor cessat.

I wonder what they did with Will's books. If they burned them, or stole them, or just left them for Kelaeno.

Is it possible to have a midlife crisis at the age of sixteen? If so, I'm deep into one right now. If I let my parents send me back to school, if I graduate, there's no questioning orders or choosing missions. You do what they tell you to do, period. And once you're in, there's no quitting, no retiring. You know too much about them for that.

Here's the question that has been plaguing me: What happens if they send me on a hostage extraction mission like the one that killed everyone I knew? It might not even be a real extraction, it might be a wipe-the-slate-clean mission with extraction as a pretext. Because now that they know for sure there are people up there, *insurgents* up there, to use the proper euphemism, do I really think they're going to sit back and let them exist?

Or let's say for the sake of argument that never happens. I'll still be doing some pretty bad things; it's a given in this line of work. I didn't used to think of them as bad things, I thought of them as unpleasant but necessary things. Necessary to protect my prefecture and way of life, et cetera. I'd only be doing my duty, and I happen to be very good at it.

The big problem is that I'm spectacularly unsuited to do anything else. I have no science training outside areas like explosives and chemical weapons, and worse, no aptitude for it. Plus you have to start on that track from a really young age. By the time you're sixteen like me, your career choice has been set in stone for years. The only alternative is a factory job, but I've heard horror stories about the conditions.

Some people go into business on their own, call themselves independent contractors, like the guys who were hired to guard the camp. What they really are is mercenaries, and most of the missions are as bad or worse than what the military does. In fact, the military calls those guys for stuff that's so beyond the pale they want deniability if it comes out. Cushy gigs like the vacation camp are few and far between.

There's something else too. Now that I've been to the surface, *lived* on the surface, the thought of staying down here forever is almost unbearable. Even with the superstorms. Maybe I could pull a Banerjee and go AWOL. She did it, so I know it's possible. I just have to graduate and worm my way into a surface assignment. I might not survive, but at least I'd be free.

All these thoughts are still churning around in my head two days later, when my father drives me to the train station. I'm wearing my uniform to travel, per regulations, but it hangs loose on me now. I had to belt the pants so they don't fall down around my ankles. My shoulder-length hair is pulled back into a severe bun. I plan to fight them if they try to make me cut it again.

"Be safe," he says, giving me a long hug on the platform. "I'm proud of you, baby."

"I will. C'mon, Dad, it's gonna leave without me."

He finally lets go and hands me my bag as I climb aboard. The train is long and sleek, with a sharply streamlined profile to minimize air resistance. It looks like a huge silver crocodile.

"Say hi to Jake!"

I turn away and pretend not to hear him.

It's a mid-morning train, only half full. We ease out of the station and start accelerating. It's a maglev, short for magnetic levitation, which means it hovers just above the tracks, so the ride is perfectly smooth. I find my compartment, drop my bag on the bed, and go buy a cup of coffee. In less than seven hours, I'll be disembarking in Cheyenne, and an hour or so after that, I'll be back at the Academy. If I make it through the final, which is notoriously grueling, I'll be permitted one week of home leave, then given my first assignment. I've been anticipating this moment since I was old enough to understand what had been chosen for me. The problem is I don't want it anymore.

I crave a distraction, anything, so I walk down to the media car. The few people there are all deep into the HYPERCANE NETWORK! ("The Most Trusted Name in Superstorm Coverage!"). I find a corner booth, maybe even the same one I sat in with Jake a million years ago, and flip through the channels until I find a news broadcast.

It seems that our water dispute with Greenbrier has escalated to the point that envoys from both prefectures have been recalled home. Nu London and Sino-Russia just joined Raven Rock in imposing a trade embargo, but Aegyptus and the Pan-Africans are remaining neutral.

The secretary-general of the Union of Prefectures and Associated Subterranean City-States deplores the build-up of troops on both sides and urges a swift diplomatic resolution to the crisis.

When the heavily made-up blonde anchor pulls out an anima-tronic monkey that pees and tells me it's the hottest new toy on the market I switch the TV off. Back in the compartment, I change into a T-shirt and stretch out on the bed. Eat the chocolate on the pillow. Five hours left. I don't think I can handle the rain-swept valley right now, it's too close to what I lost, so I choose a vista of snowcapped mountain peaks with the rising sun in the background.

What would Will think of all this? He'd probably say it's impres-sive and ridiculous at the same time. Ridiculously impressive. Or impressively ridiculous. I wish he were with me so badly. I already know what he thought about the Academy. *Sounds vaguely fascist.* And he was right. Do I want to be one of them?

No. I don't. But I'm going back anyway. So I'm not sure what that makes me.

Four hours and seventeen minutes to go.

A jeep is waiting outside the station, which is bare bones, noth-ing like the glittery bustle of Raven Rock. They don't need to send someone inside since there's only one exit.

"Cadet Nordqvist?" the driver asks as I toss my bag in the back.

"Yessir."

He grins, showing even white teeth. "You don't need to 'sir' me, I'm just a sergeant."

The driver has the usual high-and-tight haircut, with an open, friendly face. Latin stock, I guess, from his flat cheekbones and brown skin. He watches me in the rearview as we pull away from the station.

"How was the trip?"

"Good coffee."

Unlike the urban centers, we don't have manufactured weather out here; it's too expensive, for one thing, and there's just not enough people to bother. The car enters the long tunnel that leads to the Academy. I've driven it so many times, I know every twist and turn.

I can see he's dying to ask and just working up the courage. It takes him about two minutes.

"So what are they like? The savages?"

"Not much different from you and me, Sergeant," I answer.

"I heard they go naked and worship the moon and shit."

"Well, they do, but it's not so bad once you get used to it. Kind of liberating, actually."

He squints at me like he can't tell if I'm joking or not. I try to keep a straight face.

We emerge from the tunnel into a wide open space. A minute later, we reach the first checkpoint. A large red and black sign warns vehicles that they are approaching a restricted area and all visitors will be subject to search. Another, slightly more ominous, adds that the area is patrolled by working military dogs. Everything is enclosed in a fifteen-foot-high barbed wire fence.

The guard in the booth waves us through and we drive for another five minutes. The first buildings of the Academy come into view.

It was built fast and cheap based on the cylindrical Quonset hut design popular in the 1940s, which turned out to translate well underground, especially if you're in a hurry. Each galvanized steel structure can be packed into a dozen crates and erected in a single day by ten men. No special skills are needed to assemble them.

The result isn't very aesthetic—they resemble old airplane hangars—but it's functional, which is always the military's top priority.

I just want to go to my dorm and fall into bed, but the driver bypasses the sleeping dorms and heads for one of the Academy's few concrete buildings. The commandant's office.

"She wanted to welcome you personally," he says, pulling up in front of the entrance. "Good luck, cadet."

I thank him and go inside. The room I'm standing in bears no relation whatsoever to the drab grey exterior. Deep pile carpeting, polished antique furniture, soft lighting. And this is just her secretary's office.

"Nordqvist!" he says, looking up from his laptop. "It's been terribly dull around here without you." He looks me up and down, takes in the long hair. "They won't let you keep that, you know."

Harold Chu has been the commandant's aide since before I was born. He's a small, neat man with an ageless face and acute political instincts, making him the ideal gatekeeper. They say all gossip on the base begins and ends at Chu's immaculate Queen Anne desk. His husband is the Academy quartermaster, so between the two of them, they wield an inordinate amount of power.

"I'll tell her you're here," he says with a wink.

Usually, the commandant likes to keep her supplicants waiting at least half an hour, if not longer. A gentle reminder that she is a very important person and you, sadly, are not. But it's late, so I'm led to the inner sanctum right away.

She's standing by one of the floor-to-ceiling bookshelves leafing through a leather-bound book. The commandant is a collector, and the contents of this room are probably worth more than my parents' house. All publishing is digital now, but many of us still cling to the old ways, and the preservation of pre-Transition printed books is one of those things that certain people find unbearably romantic.

Not that I would call the commandant a romantic.

She looks up as I enter and stand at attention by the door. Like Chu, her eyes linger on my bun.

"You look like hell, Nordqvist," she says without preamble.

"Thank you, ma'am."

She puts the book back on the shelf and removes her granny glasses. "At ease, cadet."

I relax slightly and clasp my hands loosely behind my back.

Commandant Beata Kozlowski looks like a supermodel, which leads most people to drastically underestimate her cunning and ruthlessness. It's not a mistake anyone makes twice. She's about six feet tall, with spiky white-blonde hair, perfect bone structure and spectacular breasts.

Her pale blue eyes, however, inform you that she will not hesitate to have you killed if the mood strikes her.

"Glad to have you back. I understand it's been a tough few months. You may not be aware of it, but there was a strong difference of opinion among the faculty regarding whether you should be permitted to take your final exams. They covered quite a lot of territory in the last term. Territory that you, Nordqvist, missed."

She says this in a faintly accusatory tone, as though I had been cutting class.

"However, you may be gratified to know that I was one of those who recommended that we waive the credit requirements and give you an opportunity to demonstrate the skills that have kept you consistently at or near the top of your class. As a result, I feel personally invested in your success and expect to see you shine. The alternative would be most regrettable. Do I make myself clear?"

"Yes ma'am."

"Good, moving on then. I detect certain alterations to your appearance since last we met."

Here it comes.

"The scrawniness is understandable. We'll bulk you up again in no time. But Section Five, subparagraph (c) of the Training Manual on uniform grooming practices states that the hair of a female cadet shall be neat and conservative. You stick out like a sore thumb, Nordqvist, and I don't like sore thumbs. In fact, I've been known to chop them off."

"Yes, ma'am. But, if I may speak . . . ?"

She nods brusquely.

"It doesn't actually specify a particular length. It just says 'the hair shall not present a ragged, unkempt, or eccentric appearance' and that 'headgear must fit snugly and comfortably'." I studied the manual on the train. "If I keep it pulled back, I believe I still conform to regulations."

"Are you making an issue of this, Nordqvist? Think hard before you answer."

"Yes, ma'am."

She gives me a weary look. "Sometimes you remind me of myself at your age. All balls, no brains. OK, so be it. You're leaving us in two weeks anyway, at which time you can adopt a beehive for all I care. Dismissed."

I give her a smart salute, but she's already turned back to her books.

"How'd it go?" Chu says softly as I pass his desk.

"I get to keep my hair."

He claps his hands in glee.

"As long as I ace my tests. Otherwise, I think I'll end up in a shallow grave somewhere." I'm only half-joking.

"She always did like you, Nordqvist."

"Maybe just a public flogging, then."

He hands me a dossier with my schedule and bed assignment, and offers to call for a car, but I tell him I don't mind walking. It's only about a quarter mile to the dormitories. They've dimmed the lights to simulate night, although it never gets fully dark at the Academy because of the security perimeter. I wonder what it looks like six thousand feet up. It could be raining, or sunny. There could be a full moon. For all I know, one of the hypercanes could be on top of our heads right now. But down here, it's still and quiet.

I cross the hard-packed dirt of the sparring yard, the low walls of Obstacle Course B off to my left. The air at the Academy has a distinctive smell, a combination of sweat, blood, gun oil and army food. It always triggers strong emotions in me when I come back from being on leave; simultaneous feelings of anxiety and belonging, if you can imagine that. I've spent more of my life here than anyplace else.

My bed is in the last dormitory, the one reserved for seniors. In our final year, we're allowed folding partitions that create some semblance of privacy, at least compared to the open dorms of the younger cadets. I sign in with the matron, who gives no sign that I haven't done the same thing every night for the last four months, and follow the numbers on the floor until I find thirty-two. Faint snores drift through the room, and the shifting creaks of a hundred bodies on a hundred metal cots.

My cubicle is about ten square feet. The furnishings are army basic: cot, small dresser, metal chair and desk with a laptop and com pad pre-loaded with the material we'll be covering in class. On top of the pad is a plastic wristband. I've worn one for most of my life. It measures heart rate, blood pressure, body temp and a bunch of other things, and sends the data back to a central computer where it becomes part of our permanent record. There's no doubt in my mind it also has a tracking chip, though they'd never admit it. I strap it on.

The first thing on my schedule the next day is PT—physical training. This consists of calisthenics followed by a half marathon. Before breakfast. It suddenly dawns on me just how soft I've gotten. I haven't even run a mile in months. I hiked with Will, but it's not the same. Not even remotely.

After PT is firing range, obstacle course, lunch, advanced hand-to-hand, and finally some classroom time on unconventional warfare, which is the true purpose of the Academy.

Two weeks to graduation. I feel hopelessly ill-prepared. But I'd better pull it off. Or Kozlowski will eat my liver for brunch, and give the rest to her dogs.

CHAPTER FOURTEEN

The Moho, or Mohorovičić Discontinuity, is the point at which Earth's crust meets the mantle. Seismic measurements indicate a rapid acceleration of waves passing through this zone.

When we turn out in the yard just before dawn, I realize that I'm something of a minor celebrity. I'd been naively hoping to slink unnoticed into the crowd. But that's not how it works around here. Especially not when the tension and fear and cutthroat competition surrounding the final is already thickening the air like a poisonous fog. The eyes of every cadet follow me as I take my place in line. I don't see Jake because I keep my head down, but I know he's there somewhere.

They set the ambient air temperature colder at the Academy, more like fifty-five, to keep us alert. All I know is that I'm not used to it and my arms are pimpled with gooseflesh under the grey T-shirt and shorts we have to wear for PT.

Our instructor is Sergeant Hassan, who I remember from a sabotage course in junior year. He's not a martinet, like some of them, and only barks when it's required. We do push-ups and sit-ups, an ungodly number of squats, and more crunches than the human body was built to endure.

That's the warm-up.

I'm already in pain when the run begins, not a good sign, and struggle along as cadet after cadet passes me. They're not even breathing hard. One boy slows enough to spit at my feet, then scampers off with the rest of the antelopes. I have to walk the last two miles, and come in with one of the worst times ever recorded in the history of the Academy.

I expect to see you shine, Nordqvist. The thought evokes a dismal laugh.

At breakfast, I wolf down a double-helping of everything, then promptly throw it up in the latrines.

"You don't look so good," remarks a cadet named Libby, one of the few who's ever treated me like a human being, as we walk to the firing range.

"I'm fine," I say, rearranging my face into what I hope is a confident smile. "Just a little out of shape."

"I'm serious. Don't kill yourself." She lowers her voice. "We all know what happened. You got nothing to prove to these people."

Oh, but I do.

Once we get to the range and settle in, I start to feel better. I've always been good with weapons of all varieties, and I've trained on them for so many years the skills are like second nature. Plus it only involves moving my arms and hands.

Obstacle course completely destroys me, as I expected it would, but this time my double-helping of food stays put. A small victory, but one I cling to when I'm beat down like a six year-old in the pairs fighting.

I used to dislike classroom time. My grades were good because I liked to read, but the lectures bored me. I wanted to be out in the yards, *doing* something. Today, I couldn't be more thrilled to sit motionless in my seat while the instructor drones on about subversion and propaganda, eroding enemy morale, and food blockades to promote economic hardship. It's pure heaven.

On my way out of the last class of the day, I feel a hand on my arm. A large hand. The fingernails have been chewed to the quick.

He's gaunter than I remember, with lines in his face that weren't there before. The wound must have been a bad one.

"Go away, Jake," I say, shaking him off.

We have one hour of downtime before dinner, which is followed by a mandatory two-hour study session. I just want to get this over with as quickly as possible.

"Why won't you talk to me?" he asks, appearing genuinely confused.

Other cadets push past us, and I feel them watching. Not much goes on here that everyone doesn't know about.

"Nothing to say." I walk away, heart pounding in my chest. I wonder how many he killed that day. I wonder if he was in the woods, hiding behind a black balaclava.

The mess hall is in Building C, which is about halfway between the commandant's office and the dormitories. I join the stream of cadets emerging from other lecture rooms. The light is starting to dim in a simulacrum of dusk. They do it very cleverly, just like day and night, and rain and snow, if we had those things here at the Academy. It's that way in the cities too. You can't really tell where it's coming from except above somewhere, and you can't see the ceiling. Just a smooth indefinite glow. Apparently, even after all this time, people don't like being reminded that they're so deep underground. They find it disturbing.

No one speaks to me at dinner. I clean my plate—synth meatloaf, mashed potatoes, buttered rolls, peas and carrots—and wander over to the rec complex. It has hologames and ultra ping-pong and armchairs for reading, but the main attraction is a giant four-D screen against one wall. About a dozen cadets are slouched on sofas or the floor watching the HYPERCANE NETWORK! ("Nature's Wrath, in Your Face").

Fortunately, none of the worst ones are here tonight. I hit the simulator for a while, selecting a flight path across the Andes. I know there's no snow left anymore but I order the computer to paint the mountains in thick white drifts, circa the early twenty-first century. It's beautiful and perfectly quiet except for intermittent bursts of radio chatter from the tower at El Alto. Flying always helps my mind let go of whatever bone it's been gnawing on—in this case the encounter with Jake and all the attendant memories it dredged up—and I exit the cockpit feeling calmer than I have since I arrived.

The hour is still early. Going back to stare at the walls of my cubicle is a depressing prospect so I find an empty armchair and sit down by the TV. A couple of the cadets glance over, then return to the action. They're watching Kelaeno, named after the Greek storm goddess. Some are placing bets about where she'll hit in two, three or four weeks. At this moment, she's moving through the North Pacific Quadrant, with a sustained wind speed of six hundred and sixty miles per hour.

I don't mention that I've stood on a beach and watched her approach in real life.

"Twenty says she'll turn and take a bite out of the Sino-Russians," says a sky-scraping blonde named Murdoch. "They're due for a good scouring. Can't dodge the beast forever."

The odds master is a skinny, whip-smart kid named Perez. He records all the wagers on his com pad, collects the dues and pays out the winners. I've known Perez since he was eight and he's always had his hand in a variety of black market enterprises. In a place as nailed-down as the Academy, being a fixer is a lucrative sideline.

"Forty-five says she gets passed by Alecto," someone calls out, to a round of hoots and jeers. "Wild Child's pouring on the steam. Laugh now, cherries, you'll be cryin' Friday when I take your money."

Seen from orbit, the cane is a majestic thing, soft and white like a mound of whipped cream. The swirly pattern and hole at the center make me think of water circling the drain of a bathtub. If the tub was a few thousand miles wide.

The view from ground level is different. And with the latest generation four-D screen, you feel as if you're in the middle of it. The sea is whipped into a raging froth, and waterspouts twist and sway like cobras on the horizon. The storm makes a noise that is indescribable. Put it this way: If pure chaos had a sound, what I am hearing would be it. And I have to admit, it's hypnotic.

Nothing we know how to build could survive a direct hit from a monster like that. Nothing. It's like a giant broom, sweeping clean everything in its path. But Will had faith. That there's someplace safe up there.

We were lying on the shore, watching the stars come out.

I wanted to believe it, but there was a ring of truth. The details were so vivid . . .

I wish I had asked him more about the details. Now I'll never know what they were. It was a nice story though.

I half-listen to the other cadets bicker and boast about hot tips on the hypercanes, which they refer to by their nicknames: Alecto, the youngest, is Wild Child. Megaera, the first to appear, is Mother Dearest, or simply Mother. Kelaeno is Roadrunner, and Aeolus is Lucky Day, as in it's your lucky day if you can manage to predict where she'll go next. The four of them roam their respective territories like unleashed hellhounds, and there's not a square mile they haven't chewed up at some point in the last fifty years.

Only Tisiphone has no nickname. She doesn't need one, since no one bets on her. What would be the point? She's an enigma, visible only on LIDAR, and therefore boring to all except a handful of meteorologists.

My mother used to tell me stories when I was little . . . About an island that's hundreds of miles across and sheltered from the storms somehow . . .

In Greek mythology, Tisiphone was one of the Erinyes, a sister of Alecto and Megaera. The ancient Romans knew them as the three Furies. Born from drops of blood in a story too gross to relate here, they specialized in vengeance. This is a concept I can relate to.

The thing is, Jansin, I've heard the same story from other people we trade with . . .

Tisiphone. Locked in place by opposing jet streams.

Locked in place.

A crazy idea starts forming in my mind. It makes my heart beat hard against my ribs. I wander across the room to one of the quiet reading nooks and sit down, but I feel restless and bounce right back up again. There's only a few people left in the rec room now, the diehards for whom every new piece of data on the crawl means money won or lost. Mostly lost, if their faces are any indication.

I pace over to the billiards table and start pushing the balls around, knocking one against the other. It's a game of pure physics. Cause and effect.

Tisiphone is the smallest cane, but her eye would still be several hundred miles across. All the government scientists say she's over water, open ocean, but they're military. And the military likes to keep secrets.

If there is some kind of land mass out there, if the rumors are true, there's only one place on Earth it could be. Only one place that's protected from the other storms.

What if there's something in the eye?

I wish Will was here. I need his actuarial brain to help me untangle the truth. There's not a shred of evidence to support my theory, but if there's anything to it, someone has to know. There has to be a record somewhere. It's too big of a secret to bury completely.

I get back to the dorms five minutes before curfew. I lie on my bunk for a while but I'm way too keyed up to sleep, so I wander over to my computer. The main menu shimmers in the air before me for a full five minutes before I start typing. Then I start searching for every scrap of data I can find on Tisiphone.

I start with the public record: storm tracker sites, scientific journals. I learn that her sustained winds are a mere three hundred mph, although at the eyewall, they reach four hundred mph and beyond. There used to be an observation platform fifty miles from the outermost ring of thunderstorms, but it was shut down during a round of budget cuts a few years ago. Apparently, the bureaucrats felt we had discovered all there was to discover about the hypercane. And the installation was especially costly to maintain because it's in the northwestern hemisphere, which has one other notable feature besides Tisiphone.

It's where the toads live.

That meant the scientists had to be guarded by a rotating detachment of several dozen soldiers at all times. So they finally pulled the plug.

I wonder about the toads. How they changed so *fast*. In just a couple of generations. It doesn't make sense. I wonder why the army hasn't rooted them out of their islands and eradicated them. Or ever even captured one alive. I wonder whether the people at the station were really studying Tisiphone.

When I exhaust the usual channels, I decide to go deeper. It's risky on an Academy computer traceable to me, but I'm reasonably proficient at covering my tracks. I hack into the main prefectural records department and make a list of the divisions likely to finance projects related to the toads or Tisiphone or both. Biosciences and meteorology top the list. I also tag the Novarctic Research

Commission, the Genetically Modified Agriculture Research Service, and a few with cryptic names I've never heard of before, like the Bureau for Adaptation, Innovation and Resettlement.

By the time I finish, it's past midnight. My eyes are burning and my back aches, and I'm still not entirely sure why I'm doing this. It's probably a wild goose chase. But I think I'll keep going until I know one way or another. It's the last thing I can do for Will.

When I sleep, I dream that we're in a tiny boat, drifting on the ocean. The seas are calm and we're lying on the bottom, looking up at the wide blue sky. I feel so peaceful, like I could stay this way forever.

"See, I told you there aren't any storms," he says, stroking my hair like he did that day at the waterfall. His eyes are serious and beautiful. "They made it all up."

He sits up and trails his fingers in the water. I want to tell him not to, that he's made a terrible mistake, but I can't speak or move. And then a scaly hand reaches out of the sea and drags him over the edge.

I wake with a scream trapped in my throat like a knife in a clenched fist.

CHAPTER FIFTEEN

The first expedition to the Moho failed to return, as did the second and third. A decision was made to seek out the other colonies.

The next five days are so bad I can't summon the energy to anything more than faceplant onto my cot at lights-out. But muscle memory is an amazing thing. It took months to get out of shape, and by day six I'm already bouncing back into fighting form. Of course, it helps that I'm eating like a bulimic without the purges, and punishing myself in the gym every chance I get.

By the weekend, I'm near the head of the pack for our morning run. It starts in the exercise yard, winds through a dirt path on the Academy grounds, and then enters a warren of tunnels that used to be part of a mining operation. The ceilings are low and craggy, and I can see my breath pluming in the cold air. We follow glowlights embedded in the ground at ten-yard intervals. The route is crossed by dozens of smaller, pitch-black passages.

Once, a couple of years ago, they sent a bunch of us into the deepest parts where the mines connect to a labyrinth of caves. We spent two days in there, squeezing through cracks and rappelling into lightless pits. The chimneys were the worst, tight vertical passages you ascend without ropes just by bracing your feet and hands. Jake got stuck in one, and I crawled back down and pried him out. He asked me out the next day. I still find it hard to believe people used to do that for fun.

I finish the route in 1:09, and Libby slaps my butt.

"Nice going, Cadet Nordqvist. Glad to see you're out of the geriatric ward."

"Thanks, Cadet O'Conor. Your faith in me is truly heartwarming. Now give me that water bottle before I puke on your boots."

The next week represents the culmination of nearly a decade of training. They're very secretive about the final exam. All I know is that it goes down in a structure known as the Dome, which is in a restricted area of the academy grounds. I've never even seen it. None of us has. As you might imagine, the Dome enjoys near-mythical status among the student body.

Those who fail are permitted one more year of training, and one more chance to take the test. After that you're out. So things have been getting weird: sudden shrieks of too-loud laughter; more fistfights over nothing; the stifled sobs of nightmares in the darkened dorms.

Either way, I'll be out of here in a matter of days. The thought scares me. Not because of the final. I'm OK with it. Whatever happens, happens. I'm much more worried about what will come after. I've decided that my plan is to get to the surface one way or another and then run. I have to make time to keep studying Tisiphone. If there's a safe place up there, I need to find it.

Our instructor in Unconventional Warfare is a lieutenant colonel named Sherwood. Officers have looser rules governing their appearance than us lowly cadets, and Sherwood has long black hair that she keeps in a fancy knot at the back of her neck. She also has a clique of seniors who do her bidding, and if you surmised that they were among the most sociopathic and vicious at the Academy, you would be correct.

On the first day of class, she looked me up and down and shook her head sadly, as if to say standards were really starting to slip if they let in individuals like me. I knew at that point there was no hope of getting on her good side, so we settled into a simmering animosity that flared to life on the rare occasions I raise my hand.

Sample exchange:

"Yes, Cadet Nordqvist?"

"I'm a little confused. If the goal is to force the enemy to their knees through sabotage, assassination, and other clandestine operations, would you say that any target is fair game?"

"Targets are fluid according to the situation and immediate goal, yes."

"Including civilians? And civilian infrastructure?"

"There are aspects of asymmetric or fourth-generation warfare that address undermining the morale of civilian populations through economic and political hardship, and curtailment of civil liberties to induce war-weariness. It's all part and parcel of destabilizing the enemy to the point of capitulation, even if they have the capacity to continue fighting. That is the essence of the strategy."

"But when the other side does it, don't we call that terrorism?"

After a while, she just stopped calling on me. She knows her pets can retaliate once the bell rings.

Today, however, I'm in a dark mood and itching for a fight. I decide to make a pest of myself until Sherwood is forced to acknowledge my existence.

There's about thirty of us in the classroom. It's just a few minutes before the end of class, and most have mentally checked out. There's no written test. Everything is incorporated into the final. If you haven't learned what you need to learn by now, it's too late anyway.

Sherwood's at the big screen reviewing strategies for the recruitment of indigenous subversive forces. I raise my hand and keep it up there. She ignores me for as long as possible, then sighs wearily and nods.

"Cadet Nordqvist?"

"So the enemy of our enemy is our friend?"

"That's right."

"What if they recruit children? Or practice torture? In the unrest of 2057–"

Sherwood cuts me off. "You know where to go, cadet."

On my way to the commandant's office, I think about the day Will asked me what my tattoo meant. *The weak capitulate before the strong.* I used to believe it. That's just the way of things. When the world flooded, we were the chosen few who kept civilization going. The best minds humanity had to offer built huge bunkers and hydro-farms that slowly expanded into the cities we live in now. Half a century later, we take it all for granted, but it was a staggering achievement if you think about it.

Things were supposed to be better. Starting from scratch. An opportunity to build societies that were more altruistic, not constantly at war with each other. And look what we did with it.

Will was a healer. What would he think of us? Of me? And what I could become, but haven't yet.

Harold Chu arches an eyebrow at me when I walk through the door. Somehow, he makes his drab grey uniform look like haute couture.

"To what do we owe this unexpected pleasure, cadet? Or should I say, to whom?"

"Lieutenant Colonel Sherwood sent me, sir."

"Back-talking again, are you? I've heard you two have very lively Socratic dialogues."

"That's one way to put it, sir."

"Well, the commandant is in a meeting. You'll have to wait."

I take a seat on one of those antique sofas that feel like they're made of concrete draped in a thin layer of embossed silk. The room is silent except for the ticking of a grandfather clock in the corner. My left butt cheek has gone completely numb by the time the study door opens.

"Come," Kozlowski barks through the open door.

The top button of her black and gold uniform jacket is undone and her granny glasses are pushed back on her forehead. But her pale blue eyes are about three degrees chillier than a frozen lake when she looks at me.

"I thought we had an agreement, Nordqvist. I overlook certain unorthodox aspects of your presence at this Academy, and you keep your head down and *do your duty*." The words crack like a whip. "Instead, I'm told you are openly questioning the basic doctrine this institution was founded to serve. I have to say, Nordqvist, this does not bode well for your future. Or that of your family."

She looks out the window. It's getting dark, and I can hear the faint shouts of a touch football game in one of the nearby playing fields.

"Are you aware that your father is in line for a promotion? His immediate superior, General Gul, is retiring. Some members of the Council feel he has been less than forceful in his handling of the Greenbrier crisis. At the moment, they view your father in a favorable light to take the situation in hand. But that could change. Very easily."

"Permission to speak, ma'am?"

"Oh yes, please. I'd like to hear it."

Kozlowski has my number, and she knows it. Instead of threatening me personally, which might or might not have any effect, she's threatening my parents. Find your adversary's weak point and squeeze. That's the essence of what they teach us. For Kozlowski, it comes as naturally as breathing.

So I do the only thing I can at the moment: retreat.

"I just thought it might dispel any lingering doubts among the other cadets about our mission to raise these issues. I expect that our forces aren't the only ones employing subversive propaganda to undermine enemy morale. The clearer we are about the righteousness of our cause, the less susceptible we'll be to lies spread by the other side."

Kozlowski seems genuinely amused. "I see. And are you convinced of the righteousness of our cause, cadet?"

"Yes, ma'am," I lie.

"Well, that's very reassuring. If nothing else, you seem to appreciate which way the wind is blowing, and to bend accordingly. With the right friends, you could go far in this prefecture, Nordqvist. Or you could crash and burn." She smiles coldly, and the implication is clear. I wouldn't go up in flames alone.

"Since it's end of term, your behavior in the classroom is a moot point anyway. And you have several points in your favor. I hear you've been working very hard these last two weeks, and your performance now exceeds expectations. This is an admirable achievement in such a short period of time, especially considering your less than stellar debut."

She eyes my uniform, which no longer sags in all the wrong places, and in fact has become a bit tight in the shoulders and thighs.

"You've displayed discipline and determination, qualities that I hold in high regard, and should be commended for it."

"Thank you, ma'am."

"In fact, I've decided to honor you with a special medal for valor under duress. You survived your abduction by the savages and returned in time to graduate despite physical and emotional hardships. Christ knows, we could use some good publicity around here. The Academy benefits, and you start your career on an upward trajectory. Win-win, wouldn't you say?"

What can I do but nod?

"Chu is preparing a press release." One last hard look. "The ceremony will be held Tuesday morning, prior to finals. Don't disappoint me, Nordqvist."

She moves to her bookshelves and selects a slim volume. "*The Book of Five Rings*. There are less than a dozen bound copies left in the world that I'm aware of. A classic treatise on military strategy dating back to 1645. Penned by the samurai warrior Miyamoto Musashi. You should read it."

I have, several times, but I don't bother telling her that. I just want to get out of here.

She leafs through it for a minute, then looks over as if she's surprised I'm still around. "Dismissed, cadet."

Chu glances up at me as I pass his desk on the way out. "That bad?" he says. "I told you, she's always hardest on the ones she likes."

It's a nice thought. But I don't think like or dislike is much of a factor for the commandant; she operates on the level of pure cause and effect, like a game of billiards. She's the cue stick and I'm the ball. Strike me at precisely the right angle, and I'll roll the way she wants. No other outcome is possible.

The yards outside are dark and mostly deserted. No study period tonight. A group of younger cadets passes me, chattering excitedly. Even if you're not in line to graduate, finals are always a momentous occasion at the Academy.

I stop and lean against a wall. One of the fringe benefits of pushing my body so hard is that it keeps my brain from thinking about my time on the surface. But I'm alone for the first time all day and now, for a minute, I let myself open the door. Just a crack.

We didn't have much in the way of possessions, and we were always hungry, and we had to worry about running from the canes, but it was more real. I felt like I knew who I was for the first time in my life. I once told Will that I'm a killer. It's still true. The Academy has shaped me in a million deep and nameless ways, and I'll never eradicate that. Nor do I necessarily want to. But Will showed me that that's not *all* I am. There's room to be other things too.

I miss that feeling of freedom. Of *possibility*.

I miss Charlie's yarns about the storms when we sat around the evening fire. I miss Nileen and her razor-sharp tongue. I miss Banerjee's quiet authority and Fatima's innate decency.

Most of all, I miss Will.

I want him back. I want to know what we could have had but never will, and the pain of that nearly takes my breath away.

Right now I just want to go to my room. But then a figure emerges from the narrow gap between two buildings and blocks my way.

"Jan?"

I stop. "What are you doing here?"

"I've been waiting for you. We need to talk."

Jake is wearing rumpled grey sweats and looks like he hasn't slept in a week.

"No, we don't," I say.

"Five minutes."

I can see he's not going to let it go. Once Jake gets something in his head, he's relentless. One of the reasons he'll make a good agent someday.

"Five minutes," I say wearily.

He rubs a hand through his short-cropped hair and sighs. "For starters, what happened to you? I feel like they took my girlfriend and gave me back a stranger."

I can't help but notice his emphasis on "me" and "my". This isn't about what was done to me, Jansin, it's about what was done to him, Jake. The primary filter through which he views the world.

"We were over before any of it."

"I risked my life for you, and it means nothing. You're a cold one, Jansin."

I feel an overwhelming urge to slap him across the face, hard. All the rage I've bottled up for weeks comes pouring out. "Risked your life? You were wearing body armor and sniping people in the back as they ran away. I know what happened. It was a massacre."

"Some of them had guns . . . Whose side are you on anyway?"

"And what about the kids? Did they have guns?"

There's an evangelical light in Jake's eyes that makes me queasy. "We did what we had to do. Those creatures were vermin. They needed to be exterminated."

Rule one in propaganda is to dehumanize the enemy. Makes it much easier to commit atrocities. I realize then that he has no moral quandary about what went down, none whatsoever.

"Like I said before, you're a dog, Jake, ready to attack for a pat on the head. I'm sure you'll do very well for yourself."

"You've lost your mind," he says calmly.

"Where were you?" I ask.

He doesn't reply.

"During the operation. Where were you?"

"Goodbye, Jansin." Jake starts walking away. But there was something in his eyes . . . Maybe I am going crazy.

"Where were you?" I scream at his back.

Jake turns around and looks at me for a moment. Then he smiles, and I hate him more than I've ever hated another human being. He won't answer me. I watch until he disappears around the corner of the boys' dorms.

CHAPTER SIXTEEN

*The advent of the maglev rail system allowed trade
to flourish and injected new life into a society on the
verge of atrophy. It also brought war.*

We've been given the weekend to do anything we want—train, review military strategy, meditate, throw up, whatever—so after a breakfast of synth eggs that taste like scrambled slugs I switch on my computer and start going over the list I made last night.

Nothing very interesting pops up until I hack into the budget for the Novarctic Research Commission and notice an allocation for Substation 99. There's no indication of precisely where it's located, somewhere in the far north, but I remember seeing the name before. I go back, checking every record. Twenty minutes later, I find it. A reference to a report filed to the Bureau for Adaptation, Innovation and Resettlement. Under something called Project Nix.

I try to locate the report and soon realize that the level of classification is not only beyond my skills to unravel, it's completely firewalled from a lowly cadet computer. After two more hours, I concede defeat. Then I search dozens of databases for any reference to Project Nix, and come up empty. But I keep wondering if Substation 99 is also the Tisiphone observation platform.

And if it's supposed to be closed, then who's filing reports?

There's one person at the Academy who would definitely have access to such a report, and that's Harold Chu. Sweat breaks out on my palms at the very thought of trying to break into his computer. If I were caught, the consequences would be severe to say the least. I'd have to be insane. Totally insane. I sit and stare into space for God knows how long until I realize my foot is tapping compulsively against the leg of my chair and force myself to stop. I hate to admit it, but Jake and I are alike this way. Once we start something, once we gain an inch, we hate to quit. It's a matter of pride. And I'm onto something. I can feel it.

I don't have the skills to hack into Chu's computer. But I know someone who might.

The next day, I corner Perez during our run. The caverns are the only place we're not watched on camera, so they're a notorious makeout spot. Libby gives me an amused look as I break away and drag Perez by the arm into one of the side tunnels.

"I need a favor," I say breathlessly, feeling reckless and stupid and excited all at the same time.

"Sure thing." Perez studies me. He's handsome in an almost feminine way, with green eyes and high, delicate cheekbones. Lucky for him, the high-and-tight haircut and faint acne scars save him from being too pretty. "Whatcha need? Paxilin? Dexies? They're killer to help you focus for the final. I'm waiting on a delivery so the price is a little steep right now."

"Not drugs. Something more complicated."

A spark of interest flares in his eyes. More complicated means more money. Perez always did enjoy a challenge. "Like what?"

"Like Chu's passcode."

Ever the jaded businessman, Perez doesn't react immediately. He mulls it over for a minute.

"You can't get in there remotely," he says finally. "You'd have to physically sit at his desk."

"I know."

"That desperate to hack the final?" he says with a half smile.

"You have no idea," I say. If he thinks my motives are related to the test, I'm not about to correct him. It's the perfect cover, actually.

"OK, listen. Even I can't get you the code itself. I'm not a freaking mind-reader. But I can probably get you a program that would crack it in sixty seconds or less. We'll go the brute force route. And I don't want the regular payment. You have to share the wealth. I want the same info you're getting. Don't worry, I'll keep it tight. Deal?" He looks antsy to go. I am too. If we come in way behind the pack, Sergeant Hassan might get suspicious.

"Deal," I say. "There's just one more thing."

I tell him what I need and he nods impatiently. Easy as pie.

We catch up with the last stragglers out of the caverns. Neither of us speaks or even looks at each other for the rest of the day, but when I return to my dorm that night, I find a small package on my cot. I don't unwrap it, just hold it on my lap, for a long time. Now that I've made my decision, I'm unsure again. I'm scared of getting caught, but I'm more scared of what I'll find in Chu's computer—nothing. That I'm wrong. That Project Nix is just some routine data-gathering operation. I realize I've wanted Will's story to be true so much that I've started believing it. It's a way of keeping him alive. And if it turns out to be a pipe dream, I've lost the last little piece of him that belonged to me.

Would Raven Rock really hide the existence of an entire land-mass?

I don't know.

I turn the package over and over in my hands. Finally, I open it. Inside is a small glass vial filled with a viscous liquid that glows blue when I hold it up to the light. Perez says the hack program's swimming around in there. Nanomites that will march their way into Chu's computer like an army of ants.

I could flush it down the toilet and just forget the whole the thing.

Except that I wouldn't. I'd spend the rest of my life wondering.

I toss the vial into the air, catch it. Slip it into my pocket.

Project Nix. Whatever the hell it is, maybe it's been a secret for long enough.

I've been to the commandant's office so many times at this point that I figure once more can hardly make a difference. As it turns out, I don't even have to try hard to get in trouble. A cadet named Childress is happy to help.

Breakfast in the mess hall. It's too early and too cold and everyone's bleary-eyed from tossing and turning over the final. On the way to my table, I accidentally-on-purpose bump one of Sherwood's pets, a senior with wide blue eyes and a serious Queen Bee complex.

"Sorry," I mutter.

She looks up at me like I have some dread disease and it's catching. "Check it out," she tells her friends. "It's the Speck. You think you're so fucking special, don't you? Guess your daddy forced them to let you come back." She smiles. "Official odds are four-to-one you don't even make it through the first round of finals."

I try to think of a cutting response and come up empty. She's probably right. "Whatever."

"Poor little Nordqvist." Childress raises her voice, and the cadets at nearby tables look over with grins of anticipation. "I think she's scared. I think," Childress says thoughtfully, "I think she knows she's out of her depth. And Daddy can't save her Speck ass this time."

"Bugger off," I say, narrowing my eyes.

"They should have left you with those filthy renegades." She eyes me with disdain. "You look like one of them. You don't belong here, Nordqvist, and everyone knows it. Why don't you just go home?"

My inner ten year-old snarls, "Why don't you make me?"

Childress starts to push her seat back and I sneak my foot around the bottom leg, tipping it to the floor. I jump on top of her and we're rolling around under the table to the tune of a hundred chairs scraping against metal as everyone in the mess hall gets to their feet for a better look. This lasts about twenty seconds before the sentinels arrive and pry us apart. Long enough that Perez had to have noticed what was going on.

The clock is running now.

"She fucking started it! Sir," Childress protests as they haul her off to the dorms, where she'll probably be confined to quarters for a day or two.

As I'd hoped, they have something else in store for me.

Harold Chu gives me a pitying look when I walk in the door of the commandant's office. "Have a seat," he says, humming a funereal march as I cross the carpet.

I take my usual spot on the granite sofa and glance nervously at my wristband. It's 08.03. I can feel the vial Perez gave me in my sweatshirt pocket. Chu ignores me as he methodically goes through the morning's correspondence. I'm amazed he can't hear the rapid thumping in my chest from across the room. I excuse myself to go the bathroom, where I splash cold water on my face. Then back to the couch to stare at the door to Kozlowski's lair, willing it stay closed until Perez plays his part. But as the minutes crawl by, I start to worry. What if he chickened out, or got sidetracked?

Then it will all be over. The term is about to end. I won't get another crack at this, and whatever secrets Project Nix holds will stay buried.

I sit on my hands to keep them from shaking.

Voices from Kozlowski's office, getting louder. The door opens. The Academy guidance counselor comes out, a horse-faced guy named Dr Waring. Kozlowski spots me. Her eyes narrow.

"You," she says, and it sounds like a curse.

I'm opening my mouth to beg forgiveness when the fire alarm goes off. Now Kozlowski does curse, richly and with feeling.

"Go wait with the cadets from Building E," she orders. "I expect you to report back here the moment this drill is over."

"Yes ma'am." I jump to my feet.

"Chu, do we really have to take part in this? I'm in the middle of reviewing the final candidates for fall semester."

Chu purses his lips. I hold my breath.

"Well, it does set a poor example for the staff to ignore the fire drills. We both know the Cheyenne authorities take disaster preparedness very seriously."

Kozlowski scowls. "Fine. I suppose I could stretch my legs anyway." She glares at me. "Why are you still here? Move!"

I scurry out the door, but instead of turning right toward Building E, I turn left and move around the corner of the commandant's office until I'm out of sight. I crouch down behind a recycling bin. After a minute, I hear the door open and Chu and Kozlowski's voices talking quietly about some staff meeting they have planned for the afternoon. They stand there until I start to worry again, thinking they intend to spend the whole drill right outside the door, but then I hear their voices recede toward the playing fields.

The drill lasts precisely fifteen minutes. I check my wristband. Five have already elapsed.

The building blocks me from being seen by anyone on the main part of the campus. I circle around to the far side, where I'd unlatched the bathroom window. Thirty seconds later I'm sitting at Chu's desk.

It's obviously much more than a piece of furniture to him. The wood has been polished to a warm glow and the surface is not marred by even a single speck of dust. I feel a little bad as I open the vial Perez gave me and pour the contents out into a blue puddle. Chu's computer is on, but in hibernation mode. Lights pulse slowly on the main power unit but the home screen projection is inactive.

For a moment, the liquid just sits there in a pool. Then individual globules start to roll away like beads of mercury. The globules break into smaller droplets, controlled by the nanomites inside. I watch in fascination as the program attacks his computer, squeezing inside each tiny nook and crevice until the whole pool has vanished and his desk looks exactly as it did when I sat down.

Suddenly, the root menu appears. It flashes with long strings of number and letter combinations that change every thousandth of a second. The sight makes me instantly dizzy and I take a moment to creep to the windows and make sure they didn't decide to come back early.

The yard is empty.

I wipe the sweat off my palms and return to Chu's desk. It's only been a couple of minutes but I feel like I've been here for hours already.

"Come on, hurry up," I mutter, and suddenly the screen goes black. "What the . . . No. Don't do this to me," I plead. If Chu comes back and finds his computer broken it's only a matter of time until they trace it back to me. "Perez, you piece of . . ." I trail off as the main menu appears. It flickers once, then steadies.

I'm in.

"Perez, you genius," I whisper, fingers flying over the keyboard. I go straight to the intranet of the Bureau of Adaptation, Innovation and Resettlement. With no security firewalls in my path, I quickly locate the report and send a copy to an anonymous email drop I created last night. Then I go hunting for records from when

Substation 99 was ostensibly studying Tisiphone, which is what I'm really interested in. There's enough relevant data to prove that someone did conduct research on the storm at one point, but nothing conclusive about any land mass. I get so caught up in the search that I stay too long.

Voices. At the door.

My heart freezes, then starts beating again triple-time. I hit the power-down icon and drop to the carpet.

". . . making a big mistake," Kozlowski is saying. "She strikes me as unstable."

I scuttle along the floor like a crab until I reach the bathroom door. I push it open just as the main door swings wide.

"Nordqvist has been through a lot," Chu says. "I still think she'll make a fine agent."

I peek through the crack in the door and my eyes bug as I see the blue liquid oozing out of his computer in a long, metallic strand. It crosses the desk and starts slithering down the ornately-carved leg.

"I suppose so. Where the hell is she?" Kozlowski glances at the clock. "Just send her straight in when she gets here."

"Of course." Chu sits down and surveys his desk just as the last of it slides across his wingtips and under the edge of the rug.

I whisper a prayer of thanks as I clamber out the window. Twenty seconds later I'm back through the front door, trying to look suitably chastened. I just hope that stuff doesn't stick around.

Chu flaps his hand at the inner sanctum. "Don't tarry," he warns. "She's already behind schedule today."

Kozlowski is typing on a tablet when I enter. She doesn't look up for a full minute. When she does, her eyes are flat.

"I anticipated behavioral problems from you, Nordqvist, due to the unusual circumstances surrounding your leave of absence.

Contrary to popular belief, I am not entirely lacking in human empathy. I expected there would be a certain degree of residual trauma."

"Yes ma'am."

"Brawling like a wild animal in the mess hall is not within the scope of that indulgence."

"No ma'am."

"Let's start from the premise that as of this moment, you will cease to be a disciplinary problem for me. I like that premise, Nordqvist. I like it very much. Especially since you're about to star in a special awards ceremony, which is a first for this Academy. Are we clear?"

"Yes ma'am."

Chu says something to me as I leave but I barely hear it, my nerves are jangling so badly.

I'd scanned the report so fast, under such intense stress, that its meaning is just now sinking in.

Project Nix is real. It's just not what I imagined.

It's something much worse.

CHAPTER SEVENTEEN

If one were forced to choose the single most effective propaganda tool of the last twenty years, it would be the Hypercane Network. Dazzling entertainment with the clearest of messages: This is what we saved you from. This is where you could still end up.

The document is less than a page long. I lie on my cot and study it yet again.

SITE WSS99
Project Nix, Phase Four
Study Period: Approximately six months
Study Population: Sixteen adults, nine juveniles
Study Design: Double-blind, parallel group, placebo-controlled
Primary Study Objective: Measure behavioral changes over time with varied dosage of AVZ, QPT
Primary Outcome: Two months in, aggressive/violent impulses appear heightened with present course of treatment. Future dosage adjustments could ameliorate or exacerbate this trend. Outcome pending. Cohort trials conducted at the Helix are also inconclusive. Actively seeking new subjects due to rapid attrition of the latter study population, although this depends on amendment of bioethical legal code and/or additional recruitment from the surface. Vigorously pursuing both options.

The report is unsigned. It's dated two weeks ago. The code at the beginning must be Weather Substation 99. I think I have a pretty good idea what the first "study population" consists of: toads. Probably as a new bio-weapon to use against Greenbrier. The reference to a "cohort study" is even more disturbing. It sounds like human trials.

I figure Project Nix started out as someone's pet experiment, or it was always the real purpose of the station, and studying Tisiphone was just a convenient cover. Either way, it obviously hasn't been shut down. But whatever they're doing, it doesn't confirm or contradict my theory that there's something in the eye of the storm. Will's Promised Land.

What started as a game, as a crazy hypothesis to distract myself, has turned into something more serious. I can't sit on this information, even if it's not what I was looking for. They're hurting people, probably castoffs from Chalktown that no one cares about: the drunks and users and other disposable human beings they can disappear without any formal complaints being filed. And they're trying to get more from the surface, to replace the ones they've lost to "attrition".

I have to tell someone, and my mom is the obvious choice. She's popular and respected and has plenty of government connections through her job. In fact, she happens to work at the Helix. It's the main hub for government-funded research, and its circular corridors house hundreds of laboratories and administrative offices. The place is massive so it's hardly even a coincidence that her lab is there. But it means she has access.

Plus, I've always been able to talk to her about what's bothering me. She has the mind of a scientist—logical, dispassionate, always curious—and she's a good listener. She has a way of breaking down problems, piece by piece, that leaves you wondering why you couldn't come up with the obvious solution yourself.

My father though . . . I love him, but I don't think he'd react well to what I've been up to, even if the ends justify the means. He's a true believer, is Anker Nordqvist. I come from a long line of high-profile military officers, back through my great-grandfather, which is why my dad's family got a spot underground. On my mom's side, it was first-rate scientific credentials. They met way back in grade school when they were still struggling to cope with the Transition.

At least my generation never knew anything else. We were born into the prefectures. But our parents were just little kids when they saw the world go to hell. Next thing they know, they're being whisked away to live deep underground, with empty spaces where certain relatives and friends used to be that no one wants to talk about. It's like the generations after the World Wars must have felt: deeply traumatized. Neither of them talked about it much when I was growing up, but I can see it in my father's unswerving loyalty to Raven Rock. The conviction that he lost everything once and won't let it happen again. That this is all we have left, and we'll fight for it to the end, do whatever has to be done to hold onto it.

I can't blame him. But I don't believe that anymore. There's something better out there. And I'll keep looking until I find it.

That night when I dream, I dream of Will, but it's not the bad dream, it's different, for the first time. We're holding hands, and it's the valley and the sheep and the sun pouring through a gap in the clouds, and when I wake up my heart breaks anew in a million sharp pieces.

I lie in bed, staring into the darkness for what seems like hours, waiting for them to turn on the dawn. Why did I come back here? What was I expecting? I'm not the person I used to be, and never will be again.

They don't own me anymore. I think it's time I let them know that.

The medal ceremony commences at exactly 0900 on the parade grounds. Friends and family are not invited to attend; this is strictly a military affair. However, in a break from tradition, Kozlowski has invited the news media to attend. They're in a roped-off area next to the stage, ready to broadcast live once it starts.

I'm the main attraction, or rather, the special commendation she's giving me is. It's an irresistible story, especially since I refused all interview requests after they brought me back.

We're all wearing our dress uniforms, which are pearl grey with a high embroidered collar and a double row of silver buttons running up the right side. They've turned the daylight up extra bright, giving the shadows knife-sharp edges. The band plays our national anthem as we stand at attention. Then Kozlowski takes the stage.

"You, the twenty-second class of this Academy, stand at a seminal moment in this prefecture's history. Our peace and security are threatened by old enemies and new, but we shall not falter. The principles upon which this society is founded—freedom, strength and prosperity for each man, woman and child—are too precious to entrust to the whims of bureaucrats."

She's sending a message, and I suddenly understand that my medal is just a pretext to call out the media.

Kozlowski goes on for a while about honor, values and the need to defend our way of life by any means. She recalls the sacrifices of our forebears, and implies that we, the remnant of a remnant, were anointed by some kind of divine force to carry the torch of civilization. Will once said the Academy sounded vaguely fascist. I'm starting to think he could have dropped the modifier.

Then she glances over at me, eyes sharp and bright the way the gulls get when they spot a shoal of fish, and I know my moment is coming. Last night, I lay awake for a long time thinking about the ceremony. What it means. I don't really care what they do to me anymore, but I don't want my parents to get hurt either.

". . . been exemplary. Cadet Nordqvist embodies the resilient spirit of our founders, who triumphed over adversity through sheer grit and superior intellect."

Kozlowski beckons and I salute, then cross the grounds and ascend the stage to stand next to her.

"For these reasons, the faculty has decided to present Cadet Nordqvist with a medal for meritorious service to her prefecture." The audience applauds as an aide hands Kozlowski a velvet box, from which she removes a silver pin in the shape of two crossed swords. Flashbulbs pop as she attaches it to my lapel.

I look out at the crowd. Six rows of folding chairs have been set up in front of the stage for faculty and visiting bigwigs. Kozlowski is front and center, beaming at me. I smile back, although my chest is suddenly swelling with hate so intense it makes my throat clench like a fist. I want to hit their smug, pink faces, hurt them the way they've hurt so many others. Put *them* in the windowless room with dogs barking outside the door, chains in the ceiling and stains on the concrete floor. That's what defiance buys you in our exalted society. I come close to chickening out then, but I think of Will, of how he risked everything to help me for no reason at all besides the fact that he was a decent human being, and it puts a little strength back in my knees. *I owe him this*, I think.

The crowd is starting to get fidgety, so I clear my throat and start to speak.

"Thank you, Commandant, for those kind words," I say, the microphones carrying my voice across the yard. To my relief, I sound strong and confident, not at all as shaky as I feel inside. "Being a part of this institution has opened my eyes to reality in so many ways. I see now that old orders must give way to new."

Kozlowski nods approvingly and returns to her seat.

"During my time on the surface, I met someone who embodied the values of this new order. Generosity, compassion, hope. Unfortunately, he can't be with us today."

Sherwood looks a little confused, but Kozlowski already suspects things are going off the rails. She whispers something to an aide and he speaks softly into his com link.

"He can't be here because he was shot in cold blood by commandos, who also gunned down every single person on the island where I was being held. Children included."

I see sentinels moving up the aisles. Just a few seconds left.

"Who were they? I'll tell you. Descendants of the ones we abandoned to die up there." I look straight into the cameras. "They hate us, and why shouldn't they? They're not the savages. We are."

As they swarm the stage, I rip the medal off and hurl it at Kozlowski. It hits her square in the chest and falls to her feet. From the look she's giving me, I assume I've made an enemy for life. Well, she can get in line.

The other cadets stare at me in shocked silence as the sentinels escort me down the steps. Then the media section erupts, reporters hollering out questions and poking me with microphones as I'm hauled past. I blow them a kiss.

The disciplinary hearing is mercifully brief. Most of it is taken up by Sherwood, and her testimony is not flattering. She doesn't outright call me a crypto-terrorist, but reports in a voice thick with regret that my mindset in the classroom can only be described as seditious, disloyal and deeply alienated.

The board's verdict is unanimous: expulsion, effective immediately. The only reason I'm not being punished further is because of who my father is. Although considering how badly I've damaged him, that protection will be short-lived.

Two sentinels escort me from my cubicle through the dormitory to a waiting vehicle. As I'm about to get in, a long black car pulls up. Kozlowski. She barely spoke at the hearing, opting to simply stare at me with icy disdain.

"Stand down," she tells the sentinels. "I'd like a few words in private with Nordqvist."

Not cadet anymore, I notice. Just Nordqvist.

They move back a ways and stand with hands loosely clasped, eyes staring into the middle distance, like automatons that have been switched to hibernation mode.

"Our little rebel," she says softly. "You have no idea who you're dealing with, do you? Not a clue." Kozlowski laughs with genuine mirth. "Didn't you learn a single goddamn thing all the years you spent here? If you think you're out of my reach now, that you can go back to being some kind of *civilian*, you're even dumber than I thought. You and your family are completely expendable, and no one's going to care when we pull your lives apart piece by bloody piece."

"Or?" I say mildly. I figure she wouldn't bother to come all the way out here just to berate me. Kozlowski's rants always have an ulterior motive.

"Or you tape a statement saying you were on heavy medication at the graduation ceremony and apologizing for your delusional ravings. Waring will back it up. Then you go on indefinite sick leave until this nightmare blows over."

"And then?"

"Then we'll see."

I know they'll never trust me again. It's just a delayed sentence. And I wouldn't take back what I said if she threatened to shoot me on the spot.

"Tell me something, Commandant. Do you really believe all the things you said in that speech?"

The question catches her off guard and she frowns. "What does it matter?"

"It doesn't." I get in and slam the car door. The driver waits for her nod, then pulls away. I watch Kozlowski in the rearview, staring after us, until we pass through the gatehouse and turn onto the road to the station. It's strange knowing I'll never be back here again. Everything I've taken for granted my whole life has been swept away, but nothing has taken its place yet, and I just feel empty.

I catch a late train back to Raven Rock. Halfway there my hands start to shake uncontrollably and I guess I have my first panic attack. I think about swallowing the stash of pills I saved up. But then I picture Kozlowski's smug grin and decide I can't give her the satisfaction. When we're an hour away, I finally work up the nerve to call my house from the courtesy phone in my compartment. There's no answer, and I hang up without leaving a message.

I know my parents were watching the ceremony live, and they certainly got a personal call from Kozlowski after the hearing. I'm still not sure what I'm going to tell them.

It comes as a huge relief when I step onto the platform at dawn and see my mother. Alone. She starts crying and we hug hard for a long minute without speaking.

"Where's Dad?" I mumble into her shoulder. I'm crying a little too.

"Council meeting," she says. "He'll be home tomorrow." She cups her hands around my face and inspects me. Smiles crookedly. "See, I told you going back to school would do you good."

We look at each other and then we both crack up, the half-hysterical laughter of the doomed.

God, I love my mother.

As we walk to the car, I decide to tell her everything, starting at the beginning. For the first time, I talk about Will and how his passionate study of botany reminded me so much of her. I tell her about the others, especially Charlie and Nileen who I always felt closest to, and how I decided I wanted to stay on the surface, even if it meant never seeing my family again. And then I tell her about Nix. About the report and the human trials and my stubborn belief that there's something in Tisiphone's impenetrable heart.

As I talk, I compulsively check the traffic display to see if we're being followed, even though I know that no halfway competent agents would let themselves be seen. Besides which, they already know where we're going.

My mom listens without interrupting, though she looks over when I mention Nix.

"This was recent?" she says. "Are you sure?"

"Dated a couple weeks ago. Have you heard the name before?"

Maybe it's my imagination, but she seems to pause for a fraction of a second.

"No, of course not. Human trials you say? That's illegal. Experimentation without informed consent has been banned for two decades."

"I'm just telling you what I saw."

"I believe you, honey, it's just . . . This is a lot to take in. I'm still trying to wrap my brain around the fact that you've been expelled from the Academy, probably derailed your dad's career, and have no future." She touches my hand as we pull into the driveway and smiles to take the sting out of her words, but they still cut. "Come on, let's go inside. I've always thought conversations like this go so much better over some Earl Grey."

Two minutes later we're sitting at the kitchen table, drinking tea with lemon, when the phone rings. My mother answers it in the study. I hear her talking in low, urgent tones. When she comes out, her face is grim.

"That was our attorney, Abel Ayela. He says agents will be coming to the house to question you tomorrow. They tore your school computer apart, Jan, and they found something. They know, or suspect, what you've been digging into."

My mother looks ashen. I've never seen her like this, not even the time I fell off a roof during a training exercise and the doctors thought I might not walk again.

"Do you realize what this means? For all of us? It's not just our jobs on the line here anymore. It's our lives, Jansin. You of all people should understand the direction this prefecture has been going in. Mercy is not their strong suit."

"I wiped the hard drive," I say lamely.

"Not well enough." My mother shakes her head. Closes her eyes. "We never should have sent you there. It was your father's idea. He thought it would settle you down, teach you some discipline. The great Nordqvist tradition." She laughs hollowly. "I knew you'd be a thorn in someone's side. I just didn't think it would be the commandant herself." She takes my hand, squeezes it. "Listen, there's someone else I need to call. About this whole Nix thing. Just sit tight and I'll be right back."

"OK, Mom."

I play with the handle of my mug, twisting it around and around. My stomach churns.

Agents. Coming tomorrow. I wonder if my dad will get here before them. I wonder if it makes any difference at this point.

My mother's right. I've made a royal mess of things. And this time it's not just me who's suffering the consequences, it's all of us.

I hear her whispering through the study door and wonder why she's whispering since I'm the only one here. Who exactly did she call? Not my dad. She would have said so. Not our lawyer. She just got off the phone with him. Someone I don't know or she would have said their name, as in, I'm going to call Dick or Harry or whoever. But she didn't say their name. And it's not like her to be so secretive. Her parents are dead. She has no brothers or sisters. Maybe I'm just feeling paranoid, but something seems *off.*

"Who was that?" I ask when she returns to the kitchen.

"An old friend," she says. "He used to be deputy director of biosciences at the Helix. He lives in Nu London now. He's retired but he still has contacts here."

"Well?" I lean forward in my chair. "What did he say? Has he heard of Nix?"

She hesitates. "He said we should check out the biosciences division."

"What's in there?"

"He didn't say, not exactly."

"But what?"

"Jan, we have much bigger problems right now. And I don't want to get your hopes up."

Get my hopes up? I have no idea what she's talking about. "Too late, Mom. Please tell me what he said. Please."

My mother sighs. "He implied that you were correct in your belief that there are human experiments going on. He also suspects that some of the subjects . . . well, that some of the subjects were taken captive on the surface. In the same operation that brought you back to us."

I can't speak. Is it possible?

Even if it's true, they don't have Will. Because he wasn't taken captive. He was killed. Right in front of me. But my pulse starts racing nonetheless.

"Do you have access to the whole building?"

"Well, no. The Helix is enormous. I work in Agrosciences. Different division completely."

"So could you find out if something like that was going on?"

"Jan, this is crazy." She looks at the clock. "And I have to get to the lab in less than an hour."

"Listen to me, Mom. I need you to follow up. Somehow, find a way. Don't get in trouble, but just poke around a little. There have to be records somewhere. And about Will. He's dark blonde, five-ten, a year older than me. Blue-grey eyes."

She hesitates. I can see this whole thing scares her. She's not stupid.

"Look, if there's something going on, something they want kept secret, maybe we can use it as leverage. We'll have something to offer if they want to make a deal tomorrow."

My mother considers this, then nods reluctantly. "OK, I'll see what I can do. Get some rest. There's quiche in the fridge, you just have to warm it up. I'll call Abel when I get to work. See if he's heard anything more. He'll be here at 9 sharp tomorrow morning. We'll wait it out together. Put on a united front."

I hug her and promise to eat something and then lie down in my room, but all I do when I get there is pace like a caged animal. I can't decide which is worse, that Will's really dead, or that he's alive and having unspeakable things done to him. Not to mention the others.

It's been nearly three months.

Fear and rage and despair mingle together until I feel like I'm losing my mind. I replay his death again and again, looking for something I missed. Some loophole. I picture the soldier standing over him, weapon pointed down. What kind of weapon? Black and bulky. A laser weapon. Could it have been set for a non-lethal outcome?

The evac team carried me away before I saw the body. I just assumed.

I wander over to the window and sure enough, there's a car parked at the end of the drive. Two dark silhouettes inside. They're not bothering to be subtle anymore.

Seeing them out there calms me down for some reason. It's like getting an actual glimpse of the monster in the closet. Knowing it's real and not just a figment of your imagination. I spend an hour fantasizing about creeping on my belly up to the car with a garrote in one hand and a Bowie knife in the other. When that gets old, I take a shower and dress in jeans and a dark sweater, leaving my hair down for the first time in weeks. Then I go to my father's gun cabinet. It's locked, but I've known where he hides the key since I was nine. Right toe of a pair of dusty dress shoes on the top shelf of the closet.

My father loves antique weapons, claims they're more reliable than the high-tech laser stuff. I'm sure Quinn would agree. I choose a Smith & Wesson revolver, which holds less ammo but won't jam like the automatics.

Twilight comes, and the car leaves, is replaced by another of identical make and model.

I'm sitting on my bed with the gun in the back of my pants, chewing on my fingernails for some nutrition, when the door opens and my mom looks in.

My heart literally stops beating for a second.

Then she nods. "I think they have him," she says.

I can see that my mother is deeply shaken. She rarely drinks, but now she's nursing a double shot of bourbon on the rocks. The living room is dark, so I go around turning on all the lamps and closing the shutters.

"Tell me," I say, putting the gun on a side table and curling up next to her on the couch. She glances at it and raises an eyebrow, but doesn't comment.

"I couldn't get in there, they've restricted my access." She smiles grimly. "All the data from the entire Helix is backed up automatically on the central server though. It took some digging, but I managed to open a few files. They've been mapping his genome, him and about twenty others. I think they're looking for mutations that would help humans adapt better to life on the surface. I can't imagine they'll find anything in a single generation, it's far too quick for any substantial genetic changes."

"What does that entail? Mapping someone's genome?"

"Mostly a lot of blood work. DNA swabs."

I'm flooded with relief so intense it makes me feel sick. "That's all?"

She doesn't answer right away, and the fear comes rushing back. "No, that's not all," she says finally.

"What then?"

"They've begun testing a variety of drugs and hot agents."

"What do you mean, hot agents?"

"Infectious pathogens."

I try to keep my voice calm. "Is Will one of the subjects?"

"Honey, I'm not even a hundred percent sure it's him. The physical description fits. There's no names, just numbers. Most are adults. There's two teens. The intake forms are dated the same day you came home."

"OK. So what exactly are they testing on him? Or infecting him with?"

"I think he's in Group B. Number eleven. Let's see. They're getting . . ." She opens a file on her work tablet.

"Is it a drug called AVZ, or QPT?"

"QPT," she says, looking up in surprise. "How did you know?"

"They're also testing it on toads. It was in the report I accessed. I think it's some kind of antipsychotic. Or maybe it causes psychosis. Whatever, it made them even more violent."

"Project Nix."

"Yes."

My mother puts her bourbon on the table. "I'm making some calls. This needs to be shut down immediately."

She starts to get up and I put my hand on her arm. "Just think about it for a minute, OK? Someone's protecting this project,

185

someone important. Military or military connected, if they're getting subjects from the surface. There's an entire clandestine sub-station devoted to it. You're not going to shut them down with a phone call. What you are going to do is put them on high alert."

And then I'll never get him out, I think, although I don't say it, not yet.

"Well, I can't sit here and do nothing. It's beyond unethical." She looks angry, which I take as a good sign.

"I don't plan on doing nothing. But we have to consider all the angles first. I think you need to get back on the phone with your friend and find out what else he knows. Maybe he can help." I flick the blades of a porcelain windmill with one finger and watch them spin, a blue and white blur. "We don't have a lot of options here, Mom."

"I know. I just . . ." She trails off.

"What's his name?

"Rafiq. Rafiq Al-Fulan."

"How come you never mentioned him before?"

She takes a mouthful of bourbon and tilts her head back on the couch. "I guess you could say we had a bit of a falling out. This was a year or so before you were born. Allegations surfaced that he mismanaged some key projects. Not from me, but I was aware of the problem. The brass forced him into early retirement and he opted to leave Raven Rock and return to Nu London. His wife had . . . passed away. I guess he saw no reason to remain here."

"So how does he know what's happening?"

"Like I said, Rafiq is still well-connected, on both sides of Novatlantis. A few years ago he got back in touch with me. Said he'd recently recovered from a long illness and was reaching out to people in his past that he cared about, before it was too late. We hadn't spoken in ages, but it was good to hear his voice. He was one of my mentors." She swirls the amber liquid pensively. "Since then we've spoken once or twice a year. Rafiq has his flaws, God knows, but he's a loyal friend. And utterly discreet. He'd never share information if I asked him not to, and he has no fondness for Raven Rock nor the Council."

Something doesn't quite fit, and it bothers me. I don't like ciphers. I'm the type that needs to know why. If I were on a jury, I couldn't convict someone without a plausible motive, even though it's not a legal requirement.

"So how come if he knows about the human trials, he hasn't blown the whistle on them? You'd think it's the perfect revenge for someone with an axe to grind," I say.

My mother gives me a flat stare. "I don't know. How come you're asking me all these questions? I feel like I'm being interrogated. Let's not forget that *you're* the one who–" She cuts off abruptly and takes a deep breath. "Look, I don't want to fight about it. What Rafiq said doesn't matter anyway, we're being sidetracked. They're coming tomorrow, Jan, to the house, for God's sake, do you understand what that means? If they want to arrest you, I can't stop them." The alcohol must be kicking in because my mom's peppy optimism about a "united front" is crumbling in the face of reality, and she's not bothering to hide it anymore. "It doesn't matter if we have ten lawyers. You're a threat to public security and that means you have no rights anymore." She raises a hand to her forehead. It's trembling.

"If Dad was here . . ." I say.

"He couldn't stop them either."

I want to go to her, put my arms around her, but my body feels frozen, like I'm at the bottom of a crevasse with tons of rock and ice pressing down on me. All our years apart have taken a toll. We've been pretending that nothing's changed between us, but of course it has. Or maybe I'm the one who changed.

"How clean is the phone?" I say.

A general's wife, my mother doesn't have to ask what I mean. All our communications operate on TTE, through-the-earth technology. It was developed in the late twentieth century to talk with trapped miners. Low-frequency radio waves relayed by a network of transceivers. The Information Affairs Board keeps tabs on all transmissions, from texts and intranet posts to face-time chats.

"Very clean. Rafiq is obsessive about encryption. We have a system worked out."

"I need to talk to him, Mom. I need to hear his voice."

"Jansin, we need to call the authorities."

"They are the authorities," I shout, and immediately feel bad when she flinches. "Look, how long have they been pumping this drug into Will?"

"A week now," she answers quietly.

"And what do you think they'll do when he's not useful anymore? When he goes insane, or has a heart attack, or even doesn't react at all? Or maybe they'll just move on and inject him with a killer virus." I sit down at the other end of the couch and hug an embroidered pillow that says *Jingle all the way*. "Please, just let me talk to Rafiq."

She sighs. "You're such a stubborn one. I know, you think you can get in there somehow. Fine, he'll tell you it's impossible. Maybe you'll believe him, if you don't believe me."

She dials a long string of numbers and hands me the phone. It rings so long I'm about to hang up when a cultured, upper-crusty voice comes on the line.

"Hello?"

"Dr Al-Fulan?"

"You're not Tamiko." He sounds wary.

"This is her daughter. Jansin Nordqvist. Can we go to video?"

"I'd rather not."

"OK. Can you hold on a sec?"

I smile sweetly at my mother and take the phone through the sliding glass doors that open onto the gardens. She frowns but lets me go.

"Are you there?" I whisper, moving away from the house. It's twilight and the air is perfumed with the spicy scent of hibiscus.

"What can I do for you, Jansin?"

I take a deep breath. Just say it. "I need to get into the Helix. And I think you're the only person who can help me do that."

There's a long pause.

"I watched you on TV," he says. "That was admirable. And very foolish. Which describes you best, I wonder?"

"Mostly the second part," I say. My mother is watching me through the picture window, her face unreadable.

Rafiq chuckles, but there's sadness in it. "I've made foolish choices too. Out of love. And I'd make them again. Can you honestly say the same? I won't get involved unless I know you're fully committed. The consequences are too costly. For both of us."

"I'm fully committed," I say without hesitation. "What they're doing is wrong, sir. I know it seems crazy that I think I can stop it. But you have to trust me. If I can just get inside . . . I think I can do some damage."

"I'm familiar with your history," he says. "You'll have to get yourself in. That's the easy part. I can help you with the hard part."

"Getting out?" I guess.

"Exactly." He sounds pleased, like I'm proving to be an especially bright student.

"So you think it's possible?"

"Anything is possible, with the right information."

"I don't want to involve my mom," I say. "She has no idea what I'm planning."

Now Rafiq does laugh. "I wouldn't underestimate Tamiko. She's not a fool. But don't worry. I would never endanger your mother. She—and you, by extension—are like family to me. So I wouldn't propose anything as crude as you borrowing her identification badge, if that's what you're thinking. It wouldn't work anyway. I have something else in mind."

"Good," I say. "Thank you so much, sir."

"I'm going to tell you some things now. What you do with them is entirely your business. However, you can consider this a favor I may ask you to repay someday. Now, do you need to write down what I say? I won't be repeating it."

"I can remember."

"That would be better. And please, call me Rafiq."

We speak for another ten minutes or so. I hope Rafiq is solid. Otherwise Will and I are as good as dead.

"Where will you go after?" he asks.

"I have no idea." And I don't. I've only been thinking hours into the future, not days.

"Oh dear. In that case, I can only say that the weather in Nu London is lovely this time of year. You might want to look me up sometime."

"Doesn't it rain nonstop?" I ask, but the line has already gone dead.

CHAPTER EIGHTEEN

A child born into the lower classes has three choices: the fields, the factories, or the mines. Her wealthier— and more fortunate—peers have but two: join the military, or train in the sciences.

The building known as the Helix sits on the outskirts of the city, at the far edge of Raven Rock's Industrial quad. White and windowless, it houses four research divisions: Geophysics, Climatology, Agrosciences and Biosciences. It is the premier scientific hub of our prefecture, and much of what goes on there is classified.

As the name implies, it's shaped like a spiral, with the main entrance admitting employees and visitors into a lobby with immediate access to the geophysics labs. Moving walkways continue on to the weather labs where they crunch data on the storms, followed by agrosciences and finally, nestled in the very center, biosciences. The reasoning is that if something nasty gets loose, it should be kept as far from the outer perimeter as possible.

Officially, biosciences focuses on genetics and animal breeding, namely why most domestic livestock seems unable to reproduce in an underground environment. But it's common knowledge within the Helix that other, military-funded research goes on as well. According to the latest rumors, they've begun weaponizing a hemorrhagic swine flu virus. Purely for defensive purposes, of course. In case the other side gets the same idea.

Rafiq told me some of this. Some I knew already. What I didn't know was how tight the security arrangements are. In that regard, he was very enlightening. Long story short, if you're not cleared, you're not getting in. Not without a minimum five-person team and weeks of advance planning.

Fortunately, thanks to him, I know someone who works there.

"Dinner!" my mom calls from the kitchen.

We only eat in the solarium on special occasions, or when we have company. It's pretty there, with all the flowers, but I like the kitchen better anyway. I sit down at the table and start eating my soup, trying to memorize every detail of this room. Of my mother's face. Because after tonight, I may not see either of them again.

We eat in silence for a while—not good silence but brittle silence—until the dismal clinking of spoons and hushed slurping gets to her.

"Look, honey, I can only imagine what you're going through. But I've made up my mind. I'm calling my boss. And a friend at the Network. Once the media gets wind of what's happening, they'll have to pull the plug."

I swallow and bite the inside of my lip to keep from screaming. "They'll pull the plug all right. By making the subjects disappear as if they never existed. Please, Mom. I just need to think a little. There's got to be a better way. Back channels, to let them know it's leaked. Something. Just promise you won't do anything until morning."

She hesitates.

"And I'll promise not to do anything stupid."

Her eyes search mine, then she nods reluctantly. Gets up to serve the noodles. I feel a little bad lying to her, but strictly speaking, what I have planned isn't stupid. Just insane.

After we clean up, she retreats to her study for another conference call with our attorney. I slip upstairs and break into my father's gun stash again. The revolver won't cut it. I need something special. A very rare, very illegal weapon that's one of his most prized possessions. It's heavier than I expected, but also smaller, which is good. After a long search, I finally find the ammo; it's unlabeled and hidden behind a stack of other boxes. These include a collection of antique gold coins, which could come in handy to pay for things off the grid.

I carefully lock up after myself, return the key to the shoe, and go to my room. Turn off the lamp and peek through the curtains. The car's still there, interior dome light illuminating two figures. They must be pretty bored by now. Surveillance is tedious work. It's almost impossible to maintain a heightened sense of alertness for hours on end. The middle of the shift is the worst. Your butt goes numb and the caffeine rush is a distant memory. I figure these guys are about four hours in now. Perfect.

I sit by the window, watching the car and thinking, as the nearest houses go dark one by one. Getting him out is just half of it. Getting away, getting out of Raven Rock, will be even harder. I have no idea what kind of shape he's in. Physically or mentally. Not very good, I expect.

My mind is blank. I can't get around the travel problem. We all carry Pii cards, short for Prefectural Identification Interface. They have a photo and a microchip that links to everything—bank accounts, medical records, school and employment. Criminal history. The first thing that happens if you're wanted by the authorities is they flag your Pii.

They can't be hacked, not by me at any rate, and you can't do anything without one. Such as get on a bullet train, which is the only route in or out of the prefecture. And they'll be looking for us, looking hard. If only I had more time . . . The clock chimes 9 and my mom opens the door, light spilling in from the hallway. She goes to turn on the lamp.

"Don't," I say.

She perches next to me, light as a bird. Her hand moves to touch mine, pulls back at the last second. It occurs to me that I must look a little unhinged sitting here in the dark.

"The lawyers are coming at 8am. We'll be ready for them. No one's taking you anywhere, Jan." She says this so fiercely it breaks my heart a little.

"No, they won't," I say.

That much is true.

"I love you." She rests her forehead against my ear for a moment. She smells faintly of soap and strongly of herself. I lean into her. I hope she can forgive me. I hope they don't make her pay for my actions.

"Me too."

She smiles. I can tell she's scared witless and trying not show it. So am I.

When the door closes, I sit still for a moment, running through everything again in my head. I should be tired, I've barely slept in a couple of days now, but instead I feel razor sharp and humming with potential energy. Ready to hurt someone.

I look out at the car again, and the urge to creep over there and indulge in some retribution is so strong I almost succumb. But I know they'll be checking in regularly by radio. If they go quiet, more will come. A lot more.

So I go to my closet and rummage around for the most conservative outfit I can find. Navy knee-length skirt, grey turtleneck, short navy pea coat. Sensible shoes. Hair in a tight bun. No makeup. The coat has a large inside pocket. I load the weapon, slip it in. Check myself in the mirror. Not bad. No obvious bulge. If they try to pat me down, it'll get ugly, but I hope it doesn't come that.

Last thing: my magic rocks. They look like dark grey pebbles. I used to have a couple dozen, but I lost most of them one by one. They were a present from my dad. When I was little, their powers never failed to blow my mind. Then I figured out how they worked and lost interest. I have five left, in a little felt bag. It goes in my left-hand pocket, along with the coins.

I pass my mother's bedroom door on the way downstairs. The light's on and I hear the low murmur of the TV. It's past 10. I really need to get moving. I'll be making a stop before the Helix, and I'm not even sure where it is.

The computer in her study is hibernating. I wake it up, and go to the staff directory. Whisper the name Rafiq gave me. Luckily, the address isn't all that far. I log out and check the city bus routes, find one that stops within walking distance. Lakeshore District, very affluent. I guess selling your soul to the military brings in a nice paycheck.

I go into the living room and scan the small backyard through the patio doors. My mother keeps a vegetable garden, with special lights to make the plants grow. They're off now, but I can see well enough. It's never completely dark underground. Whoever's in charge of these things just hits a dimmer switch. Everything is quiet. They don't expect me to run. I'm not even supposed to know they're coming for me in the morning.

I silently thank Rafiq. I'm not sure why he's helping us, if it's loyalty to my mother or retribution against his former employer or what. I'm still not at all happy about that. Unknowns have a way of coming back to bite you in the ass, this I learned at the Academy. But I have no choice. The only thing that matters at this point is whether he told me the truth. And I'll find that out soon enough.

I slip through the doors and climb the low stone wall at the back of the yard. Now I'm on our neighbor's property, an old lady who rescues animals that the genetics labs have no use for. Mostly weird-looking cats, which thrive underground for reasons no one can adequately explain. Her house is dark, and I make it to the street beyond without any witnesses other than a pair of luminous green eyes glowing in a ground floor window. There's a bus stop four blocks away. I walk quickly, but not too quickly, head down. Traffic is light at this hour. Moving away from the watchers, I feel as though a tether has snapped, my last connection with the life I've known for sixteen years. It's scary and exhilarating at the same time, like the moment you push off the lip of a cavern wall and hang there for a split second, suspended in air, and suddenly the ground is rushing upwards and rope is slithering in a hiss through the mechanical descender. And then: a light touch, and the free fall is arrested. Controlled descent. That's the goal.

But this is not a controlled descent, I think.

In the space of forty-eight hours, I've managed to completely derail the future that everyone, including myself, had taken as a given. I know I should be more concerned, but all I can think about is Will and the heart-stopping possibility that he's not dead.

I've always had a purpose even if it was just to serve as someone else's weapon. He's my purpose now. And I'm my own weapon.

I see the lights of an oncoming bus and jog the last block. The doors swish open and I look the driver in the eye, smile, swipe my Pii through the console. Right now, I'm still just a wayward cadet, an irritant to be disposed of, but no major threat. If I was, they would have been watching the back of the house too. So my name won't be red-flagged as a fugitive for a few hours yet. At which point, my Pii will become useless anyway and it really doesn't matter what tracks I leave.

The bus is about half full, mainly workers coming off the factory shifts. I find an empty seat and watch the city roll by. The middle-class neighborhood gives way to cheap cinderblock housing, followed by the massive hydroponic farms where nearly everything is automated. By the time we get to Lakeshore, I'm the last passenger. There's no lake, of course, but it sounds good. I figure the only reason they even have a stop out here is for the gardeners and maids who work in the mansions.

I walk a few blocks, turn right, walk two more, start checking the numbers. The one I want is smaller than its neighbors but still impressive. Ultra-modern, with no right angles and walls of computer-controlled windows that look opaque from the outside but let in plenty of light. I know she's unmarried, no kids. I'm not so sure about lovers, which could present a problem. But Rafiq described her as a workaholic, so I'm betting she'll be alone.

There's no point in stealth; I'm sure she's got a state-of-the-art alarm system. So I walk up to the front door and press the intercom. A long minute passes. Lights come on upstairs, then downstairs. The intercom crackles to life.

"Who is it?" Wary, but also curious.

"Jansin Nordqvist." I hold my breath and lean in toward the viewscreen. If she knows, or even suspects, it's over. "My mom sent me," I say into the silence. "I'm sorry to bother you so late, but she said you could help. It's a bit of an emergency."

An eternity passes, although it's probably only a few seconds. Then there's an almost inaudible click. The door swings open.

She's wearing a black silk robe and her eyes are puffy with sleep. If she'd been alert and thinking straight, she might not have let me in. That would have been the wiser choice.

"Hey, Rebekah," I say, leveling my gun at her forehead and kicking the door shut behind me. "How's work these days?"

She doesn't flinch or try to run. Just looks at me with a stony expression. Nothing like the bubbly scientist I dined with under the stars a few months ago.

"Aren't you supposed to be back at school?" she says.

"I guess you don't watch the news. They kicked me out. Are you alone?"

She doesn't answer. Her ash blonde hair is neat, and her patrician face bears no trace of makeup. I listen to the house, listen for any sound that's out of place. It's perfectly quiet. Empty feeling.

"Get dressed. Whatever you usually wear to the lab. Today is bring your favorite grad student to work day."

"It's 11 o'clock at night."

"So what? I doubt your hours are very regular. Not in your line of research."

She looks away and I know I'm right. "Move," I say, extending my arm until the gun barrel is inches from her left eye. "Touch nothing, and don't try to voice-activate anything either, or I'll shoot you." She moves.

"Don't you want to know what I want?" I ask as we climb the stairs.

She sighs. "What do you want?"

"Guess."

"I really have no idea."

"None at all? Think hard."

She stops but doesn't turn around. Her shoulders are hunched, and I notice pale lilac highlights in her bobbed hair. Her feet are bare. "Kidnapping a government scientist is a Class A felony. It doesn't matter that you're under eighteen. I'm talking a thirty-year sentence, hard labor in the mines. Minimum."

"Only if I get caught."

We reach her bedroom door and she looks over her shoulder. Smiles coldly. "You'll get caught."

She's probably right. But something in her tone, the smug confidence, unleashes a sudden fury in me. This is the woman who has been conducting unspeakable experiments on fellow human beings. On Will.

"Let me explain something, Rebekah. I have nothing to lose at this point. Nothing. If I wanted to kill you right now with my bare hands, I could do it in a dozen different ways. Some fast, some slow. Some real slow. So if you attempt anything stupid when we go through lobby security, it will be the last thing you do. I might even let you live. Without a face."

She stares at me, eyes a little wider now, then walks to the closet and pulls out some clothes. She's somewhere in her mid-forties, but her body is still strong and fit. She turns her back on me to change once she realizes I'm not about to look away, not for a second.

"Why did they really close Substation 99?" I ask her.

She pauses for a moment, then zips up her slacks. Doesn't answer. I remember her on the beach that night, regaling us with stories about her work on hypercanes. Toad research seems a radical departure. But what if she was doing both? And then they found something, something they didn't want getting out, so they pretended to shut it down.

"There's a land mass in the eye, isn't there?" I say.

Rebekah studies me. "Why would you think that?"

"Just tell me."

"OK. The answer is no. I spent years gathering data on Tisiphone. I had the same hope once. But we confirmed that she's sitting over ocean, nothing more."

Rebekah says this with perfect sincerity, but something in her body language, in the way she looks away almost immediately, tells me she's lying,

"How did you confirm that? I thought the satellites were blind."

"They are. So we built an experimental plane that can fly through the eyewall."

Maybe the rumors around the Academy were true. "I want to see the data," I say.

She smirks. "Fine. It's about six thousand feet straight up and forty-five hundred miles northeast. In the substation computer banks."

"How convenient," I say, as she finishes dressing. I want to keep pushing her, but time is short. "Where's your car?"

The kitchen opens straight into a garage that holds two vehicles, a green government-issue clunker and a fancy silver sports car. Rebekah starts walking toward the sports car but I shake my head.

"No deviations from the routine."

She shrugs and swipes her Pii through a reader set into the driver's side door of the clunker. "Good evening, Dr Carlsson," a women's voice purrs as we get in. I take the back seat.

"Work," she barks and the electric motor hums to life.

Once we're moving, I place the gun on the floor between my feet and take out the magic rocks. Then I balance my Pii on one leg and dump out the contents of the bag on top. The rocks immediately glom together with a soft click. I just hope they're strong enough.

"What are you doing?" Rebekah asks, glancing over her shoulder.

"Demagnetizing my Pii. Bye-bye data. The guard won't like it, but you're going to talk us through. You're a colonel, aren't you? Pull rank."

"That's against protocol," she says inanely.

"So is testing dangerous drugs on people. Speaking of which, I need to know everything about QPT, what it does, how long it lasts. Side effects. Everything."

"What makes you think I know about . . . What did you call it?"

"QPT," I repeat with exaggerated slowness. "You're also testing it on toads. But it makes them worse, doesn't it? I already read the latest report so don't bother lying."

She frowns at this. Not because I know. Because her experiment is a failure.

And as much as I've been dreading the answer, I have to find out. "So what does it do to humans?"

"That depends," she says, gazing out the window. We're passing the university, a complex of drab metal buildings that reminds me of the Academy, except without the barbed wire and electrified fencing.

"On what?"

"On how much is administered."

"OK. How much are you giving to number eleven? Group B."

"Did you say number eleven?"

"Yes." I realize my hands are clenched into fists, fingernails almost breaking the skin, and make them relax a little.

"I assume you have a . . . personal interest?"

There's something in her voice I don't like. She's stalling.

"You could say that. He's coming with me when I go."

Rebekah stiffens. The moment stretches out, and I have an awful feeling I will remember it as the threshold of *before* and *after*. I don't want to step across, but there's no stopping now. It's as though the world has ruptured and jagged little fissures are running out in all directions. Just hairline cracks to start, but soon they'll widen into chasms big enough to swallow me whole. Bile rises in my throat and I choke it down. Wait.

"That's impossible," she says finally.

"Tell me why not. Tell me, goddammit."

"Because he's infected now."

Infected.

"With what?" I whisper.

"We decided this morning to stop the QPT. Yes, it has side effects—elevated heart rate, muscle spasms, homicidal ideation, seizures. To list a few. We were hoping Group B could be used as a control, but it's pointless. We're too different from the toads. At least the human subjects didn't try to tear each other limb from limb . . ."

She's babbling now, and I can see she is genuinely frightened for the first time since she opened the door and I put a gun to her head. Which scares me to death.

"Anyway, number eleven was in line to be moved to Group C today." She pauses. "What's left of it."

"What's Group C?" I grab her shoulder. "Infected with *what*?"

The car pulls into a vast, mostly empty parking lot and the engine shuts off.

She locks eyes with me in the rearview and says, "Something that can never, ever leave the Helix."

The lobby guard looks up as we push through the double glass doors. On the way there, I reminded Rebekah that I will gladly kill anyone who gets in my way, starting with her. The gun is in my coat pocket, where I can reach it in a heartbeat.

I refuse to believe what she told me, that I'm too late. But her words keep echoing in my head. *Weaponized hot agent . . . no treatment, no cure . . . ninety-five percent fatality rate . . . explosive chain of lethal transmission . . .*

I don't care. I have to see him. And I'm not leaving him here, whatever the cost.

My heart is pounding hard as we approach the guard, but I keep my face composed. He's in his fifties, with thinning grey hair cropped short and round, watery eyes. The lobby is smaller than I expected, and furnished with institutional indifference, not a place designed for lingering. Everything is bright white, inside and out.

Rebekah presents her Pii and the guard swipes it through a console on his desk.

"Thank you, Dr Carlsson." He looks at me questioningly.

"This is my student, Jansin Nordqvist. She'll be assisting me tonight."

I nod and hand over my card. Just beyond the guard's station is a metal detector, and then more glass doors that lead to a moving walkway. I can see a line of doors on the right before the corridor curves out of sight.

He swipes it, frowns. Swipes it again. Examines the black magstrip.

"Is something wrong?" I let a hint of my anxiety leak through, but not too much.

"Let's try once more." He runs it through, shakes his head. "Card malfunction."

"Huh." I stare at Rebekah, willing her to say something.

"All visitors have to be entered into the system." The guard doesn't look happy.

He's carrying at least one visible weapon, a laser gun in a holster, and probably others. I know we're on camera right now. Every inch of the Helix has video coverage, except for the innermost sanctum of Biosciences. So I keep my posture relaxed, unthreatening. A little bewildered.

"What should we do, Dr Carlsson?" I turn to her, put a hand on my hip, right over the pocket with the gun.

She stares at me for a moment, expression unreadable. It's cold in here, but I can feel sweat forming on my palms. Then she looks away, smiles.

"I'm sure we can find a solution. You can still log her name manually, verify her photo. I'll vouch for her. I'm afraid I really can't do without Ms Nordqvist."

He clears his throat apologetically. "I don't think . . ."

"That's an order," Rebekah snaps. "I'll assume full responsibility."

The guard hesitates. He doesn't want to get in trouble, but she's one of the most senior scientists at the Helix. And it's common knowledge that she's in tight with the top military brass. I can see he wants to cave, but needs a way to salvage his pride.

"How about you hold onto the card and I'll pick it up on the way out?" I chirp. "Wouldn't get far without my Pii."

He pretends to consider it. "That'll work. Don't forget now."

He hands me a visitor's badge, which I clip to my lapel. Rebekah passes through the metal detector and walks to the second set of glass doors. I take a deep breath and step into the plastic rectangle. I left the magnets and gold hidden under the back seat of Rebekah's car. I'm not wearing any jewelry. All I have is the gun. And it's a ceramic composite, with 20-millimeter caseless cartridges. Like I said, very illegal.

I step out the other side. The metal detector stays quiet.

Rebekah has her Pii poised over the proximity reader when the guard calls my name. I stop. Slowly turn around.

He's half risen from his chair, brow furrowed. "Sorry, miss, but your name is so familiar. I know I've heard it somewhere."

"Oh yeah?"

I widen my stance a little and get ready for all hell to break loose. I lied when I said I'd shoot Rebekah first. That would be the guard. Rebekah I need, for a while at least. She knows the access codes. I wonder how far we'll get before the Helix goes into full lockdown mode.

Not very far, I'd guess.

Then he smiles. "Any relation to Dr Nordqvist? Agrosciences?"

I make myself smile back. "That's my mother."

The guard beams. "I can see the resemblance now. Such a kind woman. My wife has a bit of a green thumb. Dr Nordqvist gave me some tomato cuttings . . . or, ah, grafts, I think she called it. Anyhow, the wife's been raving about 'em. Make for a mean marinara sauce."

"Sounds like Mom."

He waves as I back through the door. I'm really glad I didn't have to shoot him.

The walkway is weight-activated and starts moving as soon as we step on. Most of the offices and labs are dark, but there are a few hard-working souls still at it.

"Tell me something, Rebekah," I say as we drift through the Geophysics division, where they study things like plate tectonics, heat flow, and how to keep the planet's internal structure from grinding us all into dust. "Because I'm having a hard time getting my brain around it. Why in the world would you deliberately infect someone with a virus that can't be treated, can't be vaccinated against? Just because you can? Why not put a bullet in his head. It's a lot cleaner."

She glances at me, and behind the mask of indifference, I see boundless contempt. She knows her value, knows I won't harm her, *can't* harm her, and feels free to say what she pleases.

"First of all, those people barely qualify as human. I've seen Toads with more intelligence. They're the dregs of the species, and if I can put them to a higher use, I have absolutely no moral qualms about it. For God's sake, you were there, Nordqvist. You saw what they did to the camp." She pulls her hair aside and displays a pink scar that loops up under her chin and around one ear. "I nearly lost my head getting to the mole, so I'm afraid I'm a little short on mercy."

Rebekah lets her hair fall. "Second, how do you think vaccines are developed? In the old days, they used primates. We don't have that luxury. You're a smart girl, Nordqvist. So you tell me something. What do you think will happen if one of the other prefectures unleashes an epidemic on us? How long will it take before every man, woman and child is dead or dying?"

"That would depend on what it is," I say, choosing to ignore the first part.

"Right. Let's say, for the sake of argument, it's a hemorrhagic virus capable of airborne transmission. That means coughing, sneezing, touching. *Breathing.* I happen to know that Greenbrier is working on just such a virus."

We reach the boundary with Climatology and the walkway stops. Rebekah flashes her card in front of the reader, punches in a six-digit number, and the doors swish open. The curvature of the walls is getting gradually more pronounced, and I can't escape the feeling that we're headed into a labyrinth. And that what's waiting at the center is worse than any Minotaur.

"I doubt you've ever seen the effects of a hemorrhagic virus on the human body," she says as we step onto the next walkway. "Unless you were wearing a Level Four space suit, you wouldn't be here right now. Suffice to say, it's spectacular. Like a bomb going off in your internal organs. And every corpse contains billions of virus particles."

The wall to our right is floor-to-ceiling glass, and I glimpse banks of computers humming away in the dimness, busy analyzing oceans of raw data from the storms raging thousands of feet above our heads. They keep sensible hours here, and the place is deserted.

"We've run the epidemiology models. Assuming the most conservative scenario, the answer is seventeen, Nordqvist. Seventeen days for the virus to burn through the population like wildfire. Worst-case? Nine days."

Now we're at Agrosciences. Another six-digit number, and we enter a realm of complicated-looking equipment with little flashing lights and big price-tags. I imagine my mother at work here, white-coated and peering through a microscope at the latest genetically modified carrot. Rafiq told me they conduct some of the livestock research here, but the animals themselves are housed in Biosciences.

"Germ warfare is banned by the Treaty of Nu London," I say.

Rebekah gives me a withering look. "Don't be naive."

We fall silent as a guard passes in the other direction, checking locks on the empty labs.

"So what, you went to the surface to catch some experimental *primates*?" I ask when he's passed us, trying to not think about the symptoms she described, the almost unimaginable suffering. Because if I do, I'm afraid I'll shoot her on the spot.

"No, like I told you, I was there to study the storms and any emerging life forms. Actually, it's thanks to you we had an opportunity to recruit subjects for a small-scale vaccine trial. And of course to monitor the course of the infection. Until I intervened, they were going to shoot everyone." Rebekah shakes her head. "What a waste."

"How did the trials turn out?" I ask, pathetically eager to grasp at any shred of hope she can offer.

We come to a stop. The door in front of us is different than the others, heavy steel with no window. It bears the universal biohazard sign, spiky circles set in a bright yellow triangle. When the door opens, I feel air rushing in; the whole division is under negative pressure so if something leaks, it won't be pulled into the ventilation system outside.

"Not well," Rebekah says, as we step through.

CHAPTER NINETEEN

*The hole we dug for ourselves was so deep as to be
barren of all life beyond what we brought with us.
The long-term evolutionary implications of this are,
of course, unknown.*

I'm standing in a small room. Light blue surgical scrubs hang from
hooks under a sign reading: "Caution: Ultraviolet Light. Wear
eye protection." Two showerheads protrude from the far wall next
to a bank of lockers with stenciled names, and the place has an acrid
chemical odor.

"Not well? What does that mean?"

"It means they were a disaster. Put these on."

Rebekah hands me a pair of plastic booties that fit over my shoes.

"Beyond that door is Biosafety Level Two. Please don't touch
anything. We don't have to worry about decon right now, that's for
people coming out." She looks at me long and hard. "I hope you
were listening when I told you what this thing does. How fast it
spreads. I'm sorry about your friend, but if you try to bring him out
of here, you'll be murdering tens of thousands of people. Yourself
included."

"Growing a conscience, Rebekah?" With the cameras gone, I
remove my jacket, take out the gun. "Tell me who else is in there."

"This late? Just the subjects."

She keys in a code and the second door unlocks. A light on the side turns from red to green. My stomach tightens as we walk through, from fear but also the stench. I've never been close to so many live animals before.

Hundreds of cages line the walls, three high. The chickens and pigs get excited when they see us, clucking and grunting, but the cows just stare. They all look healthy, as far as I can tell.

"We were curious to see if it could jump species," Rebekah says. "The answer, unfortunately, is yes."

"What about the toads? What's your grand plan for them? Some kind of mutant army?"

"That's classified." She's more confident now, on her home turf. This is a woman who's used to being in charge. I'll have to disabuse her of that notion, but not just yet.

We pass the final row of cages. Just beyond is a computer work station and a rack of deep freezers, each bearing a biohazard symbol.

"What's in there?" I ask.

"Virus and tissue samples. Vaccines one through fourteen." She glances at me. "A new one we haven't tried yet."

"Open it."

"What if I refuse?"

I point the gun at her. "Don't be naive."

"You can't help him," she says, swiping her Pii through a reader on the side of the freezer. It opens with a rush of cold mist. She reaches in, pulls out a plastic vial. "Lucky number fifteen."

I put out my hand to take it and she suddenly pivots, slamming into my gun arm. I saw her start to twist and braced myself but the plastic booties have no traction and my leg slips, sending us both tumbling to the linoleum floor. She's fast and strong and desperate, but I'm all those things too, plus a couple decades younger. She gets one hand on the gun barrel, and then I elbow her in the side of the head, right in the temple. I prefer elbows since they hurt a lot less than punching someone with your fist. Her eyes instantly roll up and her body goes limp.

It takes me about four seconds to realize what a bad mistake I've made.

Because there's still another door to get through. And I have no idea what the access code is.

I lie there cursing for a minute, then crawl around until I find the vial, which had rolled into a corner. I check Rebekah's pulse; she's alive but unconscious, and might stay that way for hours.

Why the hell did I hit her so hard?

I laugh, but it sounds more like a sob. I'm so close. So close.

I walk to the steel door to Level Three and rest my forehead against it. Will is on the other side, and he's probably dying right now. I don't know if I can do anything about it, but I have to see him, one last time. To say I'm sorry. I'm sorry I didn't come sooner.

And then I hear a toilet flush. On the other side of a narrow door next to the freezers. It's a faint but unmistakable sound.

It occurs to me that Rebekah lied when she said there was no one else working here tonight.

I silently ease open the door. Creep inside.

To my right is an immaculate sink, equipped with anti-micro-bial soap dispenser. To my left is a urinal, and one closed stall. I bend down. See two bootied feet.

When the stall door swings open, I'm ready, leaning against the mirror with my gun leveled at his belt buckle. This frightens men far more than aiming at the head.

"Howdy, Miles," I say. "You have no idea how happy I am to see you."

He gapes at me, long eyelashes fluttering in amazement.

"Jansin?"

"Just move your ass. I'm in a hurry here."

"What did you do to Dr Carlsson?" he asks in a choked voice as we exit the bathroom.

"Nothing she didn't richly deserve. Don't worry, she's coming too." I grab one of Rebekah's ankles and drag her to the door. Lift the titanium chain holding her Pii and hang it around my own neck. Slip the vial into a pocket. "After you."

"But what are you *doing* here?" he whines, typing in the code. I watch closely and memorize it, as I've memorized all of them up to this point. "You're not supposed to be in here."

The door swings open and we enter the staging area for Level Three. Yellow signs inform me that this is a Restricted Area, and only Authorized Personnel will be admitted. More decon showers, similar to the ones before Level Two. The main difference is a row of positive pressure space suits hanging from one wall. They're made out of blue rubber and come with a self-contained air supply.

"We have to wear those," Miles says.

"No, we don't," I answer.

"But . . . this is Level Three." He seems scandalized.

"I've never trained in one, and they're way too bulky."

He looks at me like I'm insane, then starts getting undressed.

"Miles?"

He glances up.

"If I'm not wearing one, you're not wearing one."

Now he just looks horrified.

"Open the door," I say.

"Oh boy, you're gonna be in trouble," he mutters. "This is *so* messed up."

He has a good eighty pounds and at least ten inches on me but it doesn't seem to occur to him to resist. I think he's the type that just does what he's told and doesn't think very hard about it. A lot like Jake.

"Grab her under the arms," I say, pointing to Rebekah. "And take me to number eleven."

Miles mumbles something that sounds like a prayer, punches in the code, and awkwardly hauls his boss's dead weight backwards through the door.

The room beyond looks like a typical research laboratory. It's long and rectangular and filled with more freezers, as well as incubators, centrifuges, and a row of biosafety cabinets that resemble small ovens. Everything is white and sterile. He leads me to the end, Rebekah in tow, and we pass through another door, this one unlocked.

The dark heart of the labyrinth.

Miles drops Rebekah, and her head lolls to the side, revealing pink scar tissue. He's breathing hard.

The space is empty. Except for five boxes, each about ten feet high and twelve feet wide. They have shatterproof glass windows with built-in work surfaces and holes with heavy rubber gloves attached, so a person standing outside can put their hands in the gloves and do things inside the box without actually coming in skin contact with what's inside.

"Level Four quarantine," Miles says. "I've never been in here without a suit." He sounds like he's about to cry.

They're built so there's no line of sight between one box and the next, ensuring that the inhabitants would experience total isolation. I approach the first box, heart pounding so bad I can feel it in my temples, a dull throbbing pressure. My hand closes tight around the vial in my pocket. I can hear the soft whirring of the filtration system, which scrubs even the tiniest microparticles from the air before it's discharged outside.

The box is empty and so is the one after that.

The third box is occupied.

I peer inside. There's a cot and a steel toilet in one corner. Some kind of slot in the back where I guess they push food and water through. An old guy is lying on the cot, curled into a fetal position. His back is to the window, and all I can see is matted tufts of white hair.

The next box is empty.

I look back at Miles. He's as far from the boxes as he can get, standing by the door, watching.

I reach the last one.

There's two people inside. What looks like a girl, although she's so misshapen and puffy it's hard to tell. She's holding a boy in her arms, his head resting on her shoulder. He's blonde.

I press my gun hand against the glass, tap gently. She turns, looks at me with reddened eyes. Confusion flashes across her face. Her nose is crusted with dark blood.

"Jansin?" she mouths silently.

I can't hear her, but I recognize my name. And then I realize it's Nileen.

I press both hands to the glass, pound on it.

"Miles! Get your ass over here. Is there an intercom?"

He nods.

"Turn it on!"

Miles hesitates, but when he registers the murderous expression on my face, he comes running. Flips a switch under the work surface.

"Oh, God, Nileen. Oh God. I didn't know . . . How's Will?"

She stares at me. Strokes the boy's neck. Shakes her head.

"It's OK, I have a new vaccine." I hold up the vial. "Maybe this one will work. This one will definitely work."

Nileen shakes her head again. Struggles to find words. There's something wrong with her skin. It appears *loose*. Like it's starting to slip down her skull.

"Get me a hypo, Miles. Now, do it!" I yell, as he scurries off. "I'll get one for you too, Nileen, don't worry. There's more in the freezer."

"Jansin," she whispers, and a thin line of darkness trickles from her ear. She's bleeding out right in front of me. I look around the quarantine cell and really see it for the first time. It's a mess. A scene out of a nightmare.

"You don't understand," Nileen says, and even under the gore and bloating, there's a hint of the pretty dark-eyed teenager she used to be. "It ain't Will."

She turns a little and I see the boy's face for the first time. He's thin, with wide-spaced brown eyes and a pug nose. No more than thirteen. He's looks vacant, like he has no idea where he is any more. Like he's already checked out.

I realize I know him. Of course I do. He's Ezzie's little brother.

Miles runs up with the hypo and I grab him by the throat and press the gun against his forehead.

"Where's number eleven?"

Miles's eyes widen in terror. "That's number eleven!" He points to the boy. "That's number eleven. Please God, Jansin, don't shoot me!"

My temples explode and water fills my eyes in a rush as I shove Miles away and steady myself against the glass.

Honey, I'm not even a hundred percent sure it's him . . . no names, just numbers . . .

That's what my mother told me. But I didn't want to listen.

I saw him die. But I didn't want to believe.

In light of what's been happening in here, maybe it's better. I'm not sure I could handle seeing Will with what Nileen's got. I definitely can't handle seeing Nileen this way. A hatred fills me that's so intense, it's all I can do not to kill Miles on the spot.

At least I can still try to help her. And the kid.

"What's his name again?" I ask, scrubbing a hand across my eyes. "I forgot."

"Petyr," Nileen says.

"OK."

I pick up the hypo where Miles dropped it and jab it into the vial.

"What are you doing?" he asks cautiously.

"I'm giving them the new vaccine."

Miles frowns. "There is no new vaccine."

"Then what the hell is this?" I show him the vial.

He examines it. "QPT. See, it says so right there on the label." He points to tiny print I hadn't bothered to read.

"Oh shit. Shit!" I hurl it across the lab. "Where the hell is everybody? You must have started with a couple dozen, at least, to have enough for trials. Where are they now?"

Miles cringes. "Well, a lot of them died. A few were transferred to another secure facility."

"Where?"

"I don't know. Honestly! I don't know!"

I feel sick. The whole thing was pointless. I can't take Nileen, I can't take Petyr. They're almost gone anyway. And pretty soon I'll be wanted by the entire prefectural police force. Not to mention the special ops people. There has to be *something* I can do.

"What about that guy?" I point to the first cell. "Is he infected too?"

"Not exactly."

"Elaborate."

"He's the last QPT subject. I doubled the dosage this morning to see what would happen."

I stare at him until he looks away. "You're a monster, Miles. I hope you know that. So you're telling me he's just drugged up, but no virus?"

"Essentially."

I stride over to the box, look inside. The old man hasn't moved. "Open the door."

Miles quavers a little. "That's really not a good idea. He can be . . . unpredictable."

"Just open it!"

"OK, OK." Miles walks around the corner of the box to a small door, inserts his Pii. There's a series of heavy clicks as the locks disengage. He immediately backs up and returns to Rebekah's side.

I push the door open. The old guy still hasn't moved, and I wonder for a moment if he's dead. It doesn't smell good in the box, a combination of stale sweat and vomit, although the surfaces look clean. I stick the gun in my waistband so my hands are free. I don't want to shoot him if he freaks out; he probably hasn't seen another human outside a space suit in months.

"Excuse me," I say.

Nothing.

He's wearing a thin hospital gown, and I see bruises running up and down his wrinkled arms, most of them greenish yellow, not recent. They're clustered along his inner elbows, so I guess they were drawing blood samples from him, but stopped for some reason. Or started taking it from somewhere else.

I walk to the cot and place a hand on one shoulder to shake it, and suddenly my wrist is seized in a viselike grip. I pry his fingers back and he lets out a howl of rage. He's much stronger than I expected. Incredibly strong, for such an old man. I don't remember ever seeing anyone so old in Banerjee's group. Charlie was in his seventies, but this guy must be at least a decade older.

"Stop it, I'm here to help you," I say, not loud, but he's clearly traumatized and has no reason to believe me, so he just fights even harder. His eyes are wild, I can see the whites showing all around.

His eyes.

Two different colors. Hardly noticeable, unless you really look. The left slightly bluer than the right, which is more of a slate grey.

I stare at him, my grip slackening, and he stares back at me. I sense an emptiness there that scares me more than all the rest of it.

"It's me, Will," I whisper.

I touch his cheek, touch the deep creases and sagging jowls. Seeing his eyes in that face is deeply jarring. But I know him. Without question. I'd like to think that I would even if his eyes matched perfectly.

"Come on, it's me," I say again, and he brings his fist up and tries to punch me but I deflect the blow. "You can't win, I'm stronger. Just listen! I'm taking you out of here."

He blinks, and I can see the effort it takes for him to process this information. "Out?" he croaks.

My heart splinters, then hardens as I think of what I'm going to do to the people who did this. Not today. But someday. Someday soon.

"Yes, out. Can you walk?"

I help Will stand and lead him out of the box. The burst of energy he displayed when I touched him seems to have used him up, and now he does move like an old man. Miles watches me warily as I approach.

"Is your curiosity satisfied, Miles? About what happens when you double the dosage?" I say. Even in his weakened state, Will looks ready to kill someone. And I'm not very inclined to stop him.

"A completely unforeseen side effect," he stammers. "It doesn't seem to alter the muscles or internal organs, just the collagen levels of the outer epidermis, creating an appearance of extreme old age. Rather like Werner's syndrome, although much more accelerated. That's why I stayed so late tonight. To monitor the progress . . ." He trails off as I raise the gun.

"Does it wear off?"

"I don't know."

I shut my eyes. The throbbing has eased up a little, but I feel so tired. I realize I don't care if he's old forever. Or crazy. He's still my Will. And that's when I get the glimmerings of an idea about how we're going to escape, not just from the Helix, but the prefecture.

"Give me your Pii, Miles."

"Are you going to shoot me?"

"Not if you're a good boy and do what I tell you. Now give me the card and put Rebekah in there." I point at the empty quarantine cell.

Will is limping along the row, looking inside each in turn. When he finds Nileen, he lets out a sound no human being should make. He thrusts one hand inside a rubber glove and Nileen takes it in her own. I hear them whispering to each other.

Miles just stands there. "Or maybe you'd prefer to share a cell with them," I say, glancing at Nileen and Petyr, and that gets him moving.

"Sit down and face the wall," I tell him once he has Rebekah stretched out on the cot. Miles complies, nose wrinkling in distaste at the smell.

"This isn't the end, Miles. You should know that. It's just the beginning." He's starting to turn when I kick him in the side of the head, not as hard as I want to but hard enough. He keels over, and I stretch him out next to Rebekah. I slam the door behind me and make sure the locks are engaged.

I can't have Miles conscious and talking when the guards show up. He knows what Will looks like now. Maybe I should have just shot them both; probably I should have. God knows I want to. That's what they taught me to do at the Academy. That would have been the recommended course of action. But it's not my style, and never will be.

Now comes the hard part.

I find the hypo where I'd thrown it across the room, fill it with QPT, replace the plastic tip. I should have asked Miles what "double the dosage" meant precisely, but it's too late now. I put the needle in my pocket and go to Will.

"We have to leave," I say, hating the callousness of the words but knowing they're true, that there's nothing we can do to help Nileen anymore. Nothing. And the longer we stay, the more certain it is we'll be caught.

He rounds on me, eyes blazing, and I take a step back. Then he slams a hand against the glass. Slams it again. He doesn't seem to feel anything, and I start to worry.

"Will!" Nileen yells through the intercom, and he stops hitting the glass, although one eyelid is spasming badly.

"Go," she orders.

He shakes his head, mutely gestures at the door to the cell.

"I wouldn't even if you opened it," she says. "This thing is catching. And unlike them, I ain't a mass murderer." She turns to me. "Jansin, they took Fatima. Had to shoot Bob about a dozen times to get to her, but he weren't no match for the soldiers in the end. They got the captain too, and others. Took 'em away. But they ain't sick like us." She blinks. "Or weren't when they left anyway. Promise me you'll help them."

The odds that we'll even get out of the Helix alive are slim, let alone find some secret military installation and break anyone out. That I've made it this far is mostly dumb luck. But there's only one possible response in such a situation. "I promise, Nileen."

She nods. "Will, you go along with Jansin now. We'll be OK."

"Does it hurt?" he whispers.

"A little, but not too much," she says, and I know she's lying. "Goodbye, Will."

He sobs. She was a good friend to both of us. I wish I could burn this place to the ground.

Nileen turns her back on us, and I take Will's arm and steer him towards the door. He moves like a sleepwalker, turning and going forward when prompted but without any will of his own. I hope he comes back soon, because I need him if we're going to have any chance, any chance at all.

We pass through the laboratory and I swipe Rebekah's Pii, enter the code to the staging area. One of the lockers says *M. Pemberton* on the side. Miles and Will are roughly the same size, and inside I find a pair of slacks and a shirt that look like they'll fit. Will stands perfectly still as I lift off the hospital gown. I have to put each arm and leg into the clothing, like dressing a child.

The animals keep quiet as we walk past their cages; the chickens and cows are sleeping, but some of the pigs are awake. They watch us with intelligent eyes, and I feel bad for leaving them there, really bad. Terrible, in fact. The strength of the emotion catches me by surprise, and all the horrors I've just seen hit me like a tank and I start shaking.

I stop walking and lay my head on Will's chest and cry, telling myself I need to get it out now so I can think straight but really unable to control it. He just stands there, arms hanging by his sides. He smells bad, but I don't care, I've missed him so much, and that makes me cry harder.

"Jansin," he says after a minute.

"What?" I mumble into the damp stain on his shirt.

"That's your name."

I look up at him and his eyes are still shell-shocked but there's a spark of self-awareness that wasn't there before.

"What is this place? Where are we?"

"It's called the Helix. It's an experimental research facility."

"Underground?"

"Yes."

Shadows move across his face. I can see him straining to remember, to comprehend, and failing. I look away before he sees the pity in mine.

"Listen, Will, I'm getting you out of here. Nobody's going to hurt you anymore, I swear it."

I wipe my nose and smile reassuringly. That's when the first alarm goes off.

CHAPTER TWENTY

Finlay's Paradox can be summed up thusly: while engineered genetic mutation is a prerequisite for survival underground, should it go awry, there is no refuge from the consequences.

It's a distant wail, still faint, but the hair on my arms stiffens and I grab Will and start running as fast as I can. Maybe the guards changed and the new one didn't like my scam with the Pii, or even checked my name and realized who I was. The *why* doesn't matter. In seven minutes, the entire Helix will be locked down and then it's just a matter of time until they hunt us into a corner.

We're through the next two doors in thirty seconds, and now we're on camera again. But I have no intention of exiting the way I came in. Thanks to Rafiq, we're leaving by the back door.

I pull the gun out as we pound down the walkway, looking up just in time to see two guards come flying around the curve ahead. The first skids to a stop and raises his weapon but I already have him in my sights.

"Get down!" I scream at Will, firing four times in rapid succession. The recoil of the ceramic gun is tremendous and the last three rounds go wild, but the first hits its mark and the guard spins into the wall and collapses.

Then the walkway behind me explodes. I fly into the air, landing on one shoulder about five yards away, at the feet of the second
guard. Before he can move, I sweep my leg in a low arc, trapping
him in a scissor lock as he falls. The guard thrashes and beats at my
legs, but I've got my thighs around his throat and don't stop squeezing until his body goes limp.

I kick him away and crawl back down the corridor to Will. He's
lying on his side, eyes closed and blood coming out of his nose. He's
so frail, just a bag of bones. I shake him and he coughs. I pray nothing is broken, though I'll carry him if I have to.

Yellow lights are flashing at intervals along the wall and the
alarms are so loud now I can feel them pulsing in my bones. The
main security hub is buried below the research level, but it won't
take long for the rest of the cavalry to arrive.

I drag Will to his feet. He stays there, barely, so I haul him
stumbling around the next curve. Right before the barrier dividing
Agrosciences and Climatology I find what I'm looking for. A white
door, marked Maintenance. I swipe Rebekah's Pii, praying hard that
it works. She must have full access, because the door clicks open,
revealing a wide service corridor that runs parallel to the one we're
standing in. All the Helix's supplies come through here after being
offloaded from trucks.

I half-carry him down what seems like miles of endless, twisting corridors. Will's skin is bone-white and I'm scared he's going
to collapse. How much time has passed? Too much. But the curves
are getting gradually broader, and I know we're close to the outside
now.

Then I see a sign for Bays 4-6. Another door, green this time,
followed by a short hallway. It opens into a cavernous space, with
a series of platforms and hydraulic lifts to transfer crates and heavy
equipment. Three tall steel-reinforced doors give access to the parking lot. I register that one of them is ajar when an arm locks around

my throat, lifting me off my feet. The muzzle of a gun presses against my right temple.

"Drop your weapon," the guard hisses.

I drop it, and he kicks it away.

"Face down, on the ground," he orders Will.

Will raises his arms over his head.

"On the ground!" the guard barks.

Will blinks, and I wonder if he can hear OK, or if the explosion did something to his eardrums.

"Lie down," I whisper with exaggerated enunciation.

"Shut up!" The arm tightens around my throat until I gag.

He's wearing body armor, I can feel it against my back, but only from the waist up. Without moving my arm, I twist my wrist around and slip it into my coat pocket. Extend my fingers as far as they'll go. Where is it?

The guard's radio crackles and I know that in about five seconds he's going to shove me away and order me face down next to Will. He'll call for backup, and it's game over. Then my fingers close around the hypo. I ease it out, flick the plastic off. His arm is just starting to relax when I press the tip against his thigh, not enough to break the skin, but enough for him to feel it.

"Level Four," I whisper. "That's where we just came from. Know what they got in there?" I can't see his face, but his body has gone perfectly still. "Some seriously unfriendly shit, that's what. Which is now a heartbeat away from entering your bloodstream."

"You're lying," he says, but I can hear the doubt.

"This particular strain has been weaponized, which means it'll melt your insides about a hundred times faster than usual. No treatment, no cure." I glance down at Will. "He's only seventeen, you know. What I have in my hand makes what they did to him look like a spa treatment."

The guard curses softly.

224

"First you'll vomit blood," I say, struggling to remember what Rebekah said and make it sound even worse, if that's possible. "The symptoms go downhill from there. It ends with multiple organ dysfunction syndrome. In plain English, your body liquefies and you drown in your own tissue. That includes skin. It's not very pretty. They'll have to torch what's left since your corpse is essentially a virus bomb."

I take a deep breath, as best I can with my windpipe pressed against his forearm. "So what do you say, huh? Can you please get your damn gun away from me? Slowly now."

A few seconds go by. I figure he's calculating whether a head shot would put me down so instantly that I'd drop the hypo before I can poke him with it. In the end, he doesn't like the odds. I wouldn't either. Human skin is less than a tenth of an inch thick. One muscle spasm would do it. He sighs and eases the gun away from my temple. When the muzzle is pointed up, I grab his arm in a hammerlock and twist, forcing him to his knees.

"Grab my gun," I tell Will.

He nods and crawls over to where I threw it. From the awkward way he picks it up, I get the feeling he's never had any firearms training. I should have taught him some basics when we had the chance, but I always thought we had plenty of time. The guard's weapon has fallen next to my left foot; it's small and sleek, one of the newer models. I lean down to grab it, causing my weight to shift ever so slightly to the left, which is a dumb mistake. Because this guy is no rent-a-cop; he's had training.

His free arm whips out and cracks me across the jaw so hard that everything goes black for a second. My ears buzz and suddenly I'm on my back, a crushing weight on my chest. When my vision clears, I see the guard above, pretty brown eyes in a hard face, he's got his gun back and it's pointing straight at me. Then a bullet rips through his throat and he falls to the side, gurgling.

Will glances at the body, then looks away. The hand holding the gun is steady.

I've never killed anyone, he told me once. *And I hope I never have to.*

But that Will is not this Will.

"Are you OK?" he asks.

I nod and make myself get up. The guard's blood is all over me, a sickening wet warmth. I think a couple of ribs cracked. But we have about one minute, probably less, to get out of here. The steel door is starting to slide down as we sprint across the loading bay. I throw myself into the gap and pull Will through the other side moments before it crashes shut. Twenty seconds later we're at Rebekah's car. I use her Pii to open it.

"Good evening, Dr Carlsson," the computer says cheerfully.

"Switch to manual," I say, taking the steering wheel. It's a crappy government car, but I plan to push it to the limit. The whole Helix is lit up, and I hear sirens in the night. Not just from the building, but coming towards us.

"Sit back," I say, placing a hand on Will's chest as our seat belts snake out and click into place. "Let's get out of here."

I screech out of the parking spot, accelerating as we approach the booth. A guy comes running out but I blow past him and skid through a wide turn into the adjoining street. Right, then left, then right again. Nothing behind us, not yet. We merge into the traffic flow, which is surprisingly heavy for this time of night. Some kind of sporting event, since everyone is honking and pedestrians in blue and gold are clogging the streets.

I can't believe we made it out of the Helix. In my heart, I didn't believe it was possible. But we did, and now reality is setting in. The way I see it, there's only one place to run to.

"Will, listen to me now. We're in Raven Rock, my home prefecture. I wasn't too popular to begin with, and now we're both on the most-wanted lists of every police and security agency here and abroad. We could hide for a while, maybe even a few months if we're very lucky, but in the end they'll find us. And we'll disappear. Down into one of the black holes they reserve for detainees that are off the books. Do you understand what I'm saying?"

Will nods. He's calm, but there's still a kind of madness dancing around the edges of his eyes that makes me uneasy. "Yeah, I understand."

"You're probably gonna say we should go back to the surface. Take our chances with the canes. The problem is they found us there too, didn't they? So I'm proposing a third way. It's risky, it might be the worst idea I ever had, but I don't see any choice."

I know they've thrown up a cordon, at least a couple of miles square. Every cop in town has a picture of my face by now. So I need to make this fast.

"I have reason to believe there's a land mass in the eye of Tisiphone. That's where I think we should go. Your safe place, Will. I think I've found it."

He turns to me slowly. "In the eye?"

"In the eye."

His expression doesn't change, but I see a fragment of the old Will, a little of the light and heat. "You're crazier than I am. And how do we get through the eyewall?"

"We fly."

Will shakes his head. Makes a noise that's some kind of cross between a laugh and a sob.

The traffic suddenly slows, which means only one thing. Roadblock.

Time's up.

"Switch to autodrive," I say, "Raven Rock Terminal."

When the computer engages, I take out the hypo, jab it into my thigh, and depress the plunger all the way down. I dimly hear Will yelling something, but the liquid agony coursing through me scours my brain clean of all extraneous thought. I close my eyes and watch colors explode into fragments, reform, explode again.

It's a good thing I'm belted in, because I think I'm going into convulsions. A wave of intense heat rolls through me, followed immediately by wracking chills. I've never felt so sick, not even close. My skin is crawling like I'm covered in bugs.

". . . out of your mind?" Will yells.

His voice is going in and out, like a distant radio station. "First time . . . worst . . . pass but not . . ."

I lean back against the headrest and let the drug wash over me. For all I know, I could have taken double the dosage, or triple, or quadruple. It's not calibrated to my body weight either, which is relatively light. After a little while, I don't know how long, the tremors in my limbs start ebbing, but now my scalp burns as though my hair is on fire. I touch it, and the hair feels weird, fine and brittle.

All my life, I've been strong. Mentally and physically. It horrifies me to think what I've just done. What I've changed into. Maybe forever.

Then bright lights hit the windshield. We're coming up on the roadblock.

Are they looking for this particular car? I try to focus, but the thoughts are all jumbled up, like puzzle pieces that don't quite match. One step at a time. If Rebekah and Miles are still unconscious, no one knows how I got there. We went past the gate guard too fast for him to get a plate number. Probably. If we turn, it'll look suspicious and we'll just hit another roadblock sooner or later. The hunt will only intensify as time passes, and we need to get near the terminal before we ditch Rebekah's car.

If, if, if.

I make myself sit up. The world is too bright, almost cartoonish.

Will cups my face and turns me toward him. He looks furious. "Why?" he whispers.

I glance down at my hand and don't recognize it for a second. "How do I look?"

Will just shakes his head. So I tilt the rear mirror until I get a full view of my face.

"Wow," I say.

As old as Will appears, I could be his mother. Maybe his grandmother.

"They want Jansin Nordqvist." I touch the maze of overlapping wrinkles. Even my eyelashes are white.

"You could have died. Some have."

"Well, I didn't."

"We don't know if this is reversible."

He's right, and the thought suffocates me, so I don't say anything.

The traffic slows to a crawl as we approach the roadblock. It's another stroke of luck that there's so many cars, too many for them to bother checking individual Piis. Instead, they're just scanning the occupants and waving them through. I wonder how much longer our luck will hold.

"Put the gun under the seat," I tell Will.

We're one car away now. There's three cops on each side, with four riot wagons parked at a slant on the edge of the road. He looks down at the forgotten weapon in his hand. Stows it away.

We pass the public bath complex, and I can faintly smell the sulfur from the hot springs.

"I'm not going back," he says in a monotone.

He means he would rather die.

"I know," I say, laying my witch's hand on top of his.

Then we're at the roadblock. I tell the computer to lower the window. The nearest officer leans down, silhouetted against the floodlights, and I wonder if we'd have any chance of running it if necessary, admit the answer is no. No chance. But I wouldn't mind killing her anyway. I feel strange.

There are still flares of color in the corners of my eyes. The sudden urge to reach out and tear at her flesh is strong, but I get control and summon up what I hope is the expression of a befuddled old woman with a healthy fear of the law.

"What's happening, ma'am?"

She looks at me, but her face is already a mask of barely concealed indifference. She looks at me, but she doesn't *see* me. I'm old and therefore worthless. Invisible. She has no clue how close she is to dying at that moment.

And then she waves us through without another glance. The computer steers us back into the traffic flow. I feel as though there's a rabid animal inside me, clawing to get out. Will knows. He can tell.

"It comes and goes," he says in a monotone. "You have to fight it."

I think of the place where I chained the black dog after they brought me back and try to box it in there, but it's not easy. I tell myself there was no other way. It's the truth. I just hope I don't do something bad.

Half a mile from the terminal, I switch to manual steering and guide us north, then west, around the back side of the warren of train tunnels. I park in an alley and kill the engine.

"Be right back," I say.

He frowns. "Where are you going?"

"Chalktown. We need IDs, Will."

"What's Chalktown?"

"Tent camp. Users, people with no family. The underbelly of our illustrious society."

I unbuckle my seatbelt and pain lances through my ribcage.

"Sounds dangerous."

"Only for whoever messes with me," I say, although I'm not sure I could best a reasonably fit ten year-old right now.

The box of gold coins must have slid deep under the back seat when we accelerated through the guard booth at the Helix, but after a minute of groping, my fingers touch metal.

"If you're not back in fifteen minutes, I'm coming after," Will says. I notice the gun is back in his lap.

"Give me twenty."

"Don't be late."

I nod, tuck the box under my arm, and totter across the street on unsteady legs. The way to Chalktown isn't far and it's not hidden, almost the opposite. I've never been there before, but everyone knows about it. Once a year or so, the prefectural authorities send a goon squad to sweep it out, but the residents invariably trickle back within a few months. I think they're allowed to because it's just easier to keep the dregs in one place, and there's nowhere else to put them anyway.

The entrance is grand, in a decaying, haunted house kind of way. Two tall brass doors, one of them slightly ajar, with the words ALL RAINS in tarnished lettering above. I guess the T fell off sometime in the last ten years, when this place was abandoned in favor of the new station, with its high-speed maglev tracks.

I slip inside and the heat hits me like a furnace. No climate control in here anymore. No perfect seventy-three degrees. More like a hundred and three. It's dark, and smoky from the small fires scattered across the main arrivals hall. They give off the only light, except for one TV that someone has jacked electricity for. It's tuned to the HYPERCANE NETWORK!, and about a dozen people sit facing it, slack-jawed and corpse-like. Chalkheads. Not a drug you can take and still blend into society. It turns you pale as a slug no matter what color you started out as.

There's no weather to worry about in here, but some of the residents have erected plastic tents, for privacy, I guess. I hear a few snores and the far-off crying of an infant, but the main sound is the eerie howl of the storm playing on TV. I ignore the chalkheads; they would have sold their Piis long ago, and they're too young anyway. One of them glances at me as I pass, empty doll eyes in a gaunt white face, then returns to the screen.

I scan sleeping faces on the ground, but they're all in their twenties and thirties. Life expectancy can't be very long here. Then I notice a little girl. She's clutching a ragged dog toy, and her eyes are open. I crouch down next to her nest of blankets.

"Hi," I whisper.

She studies me for a minute. "Hi," she whispers back.

"I'm looking for my sister and brother," I say. "They're old, like me. Do you know anyone like that?"

"What's their names?"

"It doesn't matter."

"Are you a cop?"

"No." I open the box, take out a coin. "This is for you if you can show me the oldest people you know here."

She takes the coin, examines it, slips it into a pocket. "OK."

"Take it to a collector, if you can. You'll get ten times what they pay on the street."

I know I'll never find two people who look *exactly* right, but I don't think I need to. We're old and therefore off the radar. If the photos are reasonably close, we might just slip through. If we can move fast enough.

She leads me across the arrivals hall to a side tunnel with Track 44 carved in the stone archway. The platform is cluttered with rusting carts and tools and heaps of garbage. Large cockroaches skitter beneath the rubble. I take quick, shallow breaths, not just because of the smell but the pain in my ribs.

Roaches are one of those species we didn't have to bring on purpose. They hitched a ride.

"How much further?" I ask, acutely aware that our chances of boarding a train without detection are dwindling by the minute. As soon as Miles starts talking, the description will change and the noose will tighten around our necks. That could be happening right now. Why didn't I just kill him?

The girl turns around and her blue eyes flicker for just an instant over my right shoulder. I start to spin but it's too late. Something crashes into the back of my skull, driving me to my knees. The colors still floating at the corners of my eyes erupt into a glowing white starburst. Hands yank the metal box away. I grope blindly, feel a calf, grab the ankle and twist. There's a soft thud as a body hits the ground next to me. I start pummeling it and the guy cries out for his friends, but they're already gone, feet slapping on the stone of the platform.

The guy lands a blow to my cracked ribs and it hurts bad, really bad. He's a scrawny thing, all nose and elbows, with skin just a shade too pale. A first-stage user, then. I kick him in the face and savor the look of astonishment just before his head snaps back. I guess they thought an old lady would be easy prey.

I'm thinking about breaking his neck, one quick twist to the side, when there's the soft crunch of shoes on broken glass in the darkness. The friends are back, one of them at least. I roll away and try to stand, but my brain feels like it's sliding around in my skull. I look for a weapon, anything, and spot a rusty length of rebar a few feet away. Too far. But I start crawling towards it anyway.

The footsteps come faster. I glance behind me and find myself looking into a pair of mismatched eyes.

"I told you to stay in the car," I say as my fingers close around the rebar.

"Well, I followed," Will says, looking from me to the chalkhead sprawled motionless on the platform. "I didn't want to lose you again."

He sounds whiny. Weak. The thing in me stirs, lifts its head.

"Are you OK?" he asks.

I run a hand through my hair and it comes away bright with blood. I stare at it, fascinated. It's warm and sticky. It feels good on my skin.

"Jan?"

"What?"

"You don't look OK."

His voice buzzes like a wasp. I can hear his heart beating, a rapid thump that scrapes my nerves raw. The rebar is heavy in my right hand.

"Go away, Will," I whisper.

He holds my eyes. "No."

The thing shifts, stretches. I feel my pupils dilate. Every speck of dust on the platform snaps into focus.

"Run," I say, and it sounds like someone else talking. "I'm not safe."

"You have to fight it," he says.

I can smell the fear on him, a sour adrenaline stench, and it makes my hackles rise. I'm dimly aware that something is terribly wrong, but the thing is awake now. Hungry. He sees me coming and finally understands, turns to run, and I'm on him, teeth bared, using the rebar to drive him to his knees.

I'm raising it over my head and he's screaming my name, over and over, when the red mist lifts a little and it suddenly dawns on me that I'm about to murder the person I just risked everything for. My stomach clenches hard, and I turn away and vomit onto the tracks until I'm empty. Will holds my hair as the madness ebbs out of me.

"Will it come back?" I ask, when I feel able to speak again.

"It might. We have to be ready. Now you know."

Yes, now I know. But I'm not sure how much good it will do us.

The guy I kicked is starting to twitch a little when my palms, which I'm leaning on, begin to tingle. Faint vibrations ripple through the stone platform and I half expect a mole to burst out of the ground in front of me. Then I feel a breath of wind and remember that this used to be a train station. I'd always assumed they walled it off, but maybe they didn't. Maybe the tunnels still connect to the main terminal.

Which means there's a back way in.

CHAPTER TWENTY-ONE

If a civilization is measured by its cultural appetites, what does it mean that in the year 2065, Raven Rock's number-two rated television show, exceeded in popularity only by the HYPERCANE NETWORK!, was season four reruns of Celebrity Wife Swap?

The chalkhead's name is Luka. He's not happy about being our tour guide, but he doesn't want to get shot either so he leads us through the tunnels with minimal fuss. It's about half a mile to the new terminal. Luka walks in front. He has the only flashlight, and it barely illumines the path in front of us. I keep scanning the shadows, thinking he'll lead us back to his friends, but he must realize we have nothing left to steal. Every few minutes, the wind and vibrations pick up, then fade away.

"Are you sure these tunnels aren't active?" I say. We're walking single-file in the center of the tracks.

"Not for years," Luka says. "One time a guy wandered off to pee and got hisself squished, but he didn't know his way like I do. Was high too."

"Where are the trains to Cheyenne?"

"South side. I'll show you."

In the next hour, or maybe sooner, they'll find the car. When they find the car, they'll have a pretty good idea of where we went. Twenty minutes after that, Luka and his friends and every other pathetic soul who lives here will be sweating it out in interrogation cells. So I have no intention of telling him where we're really going.

The tunnel we're in joins another tunnel. Luka leads us to a small platform and an emergency door that opens onto a flight of stairs.

"Take it to the top," he says. "Can I go now?"

I nod and he disappears into the darkness without another word. We climb the stairs and I press my ear against the door. It's quiet. I turn to Will.

"In junior year, I learned the basics of maglev trains in a sabotage course. Some of the cars have a trap door that opens onto the tracks for maintenance. I intend to find one."

"Where are we going?"

"Nu London. There's a man there, a family friend. He offered to help us. I think."

"So you trust this guy?"

"Not entirely," I say. "But there's no one else."

Will looks at me long and hard. Dried blood streaks his face. It's obvious that something inside him is very close to snapping. Not the drug, just his own emotions. "I'm not staying down here. It's like being buried alive."

I think about the tons of rock over our heads and try to imagine what it's like for him. How much he must hate it. How much he must hate *us*.

"We're not. We're going to a surface substation next to Tisiphone. Then we steal a plane and fly through the cane."

"What about Fatima and the others?"

"We'll find a way to help them. But we have to get out of Raven Rock. Immediately."

Will seems to accept the truth of this because he nods once and eases the door open. We're in a tunnel about thirty feet from a brightly-lit platform. There's a few well-dressed people hugging and saying their goodbyes, and porters pushing luggage carts. Also soldiers. Lots of soldiers. Their gear is black and shiny; the segmented body armor makes them look vaguely insectile.

I realize how naive I was to think we could have boarded a train, even with perfect fake Piis. They clearly expect us to run, to panic and do something stupid. Which almost happened. I whisper a silent thanks to Luka and his drug addict friends for beating and robbing me.

Most of the soldiers are looking back at the platform and the rest are blinded by the lights, so no one notices Will and me sneak across the tunnel to the far side. The tracks in the new terminal run parallel to each other, with yellow-edged platforms in between. We creep across the tunnels, passing through rectangular doorways where train crews can hole up when the tracks are in use.

Then I hear an announcement for Nu London. It sounds like the 12:13. I have no idea what time it is now, but the train is there, its long, aerodynamic snout jutting into the tunnel mouth.

"This is it," I say. "We have to crawl."

Will looks doubtful, but he drops to his knees and follows me. The train is hovering a few inches above the tracks, but the clearance is still minimal. We wiggle on our bellies, which kills my ribs. I try to remember the diagrams we studied in class. Suddenly there's a deep humming over our heads.

"What's that?" he hisses.

"Power," I say, and try to crawl faster.

There's supposed to be a panel under the luggage car, which is either the second or third after the engineer's car. Thank God I don't have any metal on my body, because I'm right in the middle of two gigantic magnets. We clear the first coupling and the humming ramps up a notch. Someone yells on the platform, and though I can't hear the words, I have a bad feeling it was one of the conductors doing a final call.

Then I spot a square on the underbelly of the train. The seams are barely visible in the dim light down here, and I don't see any kind of mechanism to open it. That's probably on the other side. I push against it with my palm. Nothing. There's an ominous series of clicks as the brakes disengage.

Heart hammering, I squeeze my knees up until the soles of my shoes are flat against the bottom of the panel. Then I kick as hard as I can, exerting every ounce of force I can muster. It's not easy, because the tight space won't let me get much momentum behind it. I empty all the air out of my stomach and kick harder. The panel bends, gives an inch, then snaps back into place.

It's not steel, thank God, something more lightweight and pliable. I kick again, grunting with the effort, and this time it pops open. I shove it to the side and pull myself through the hole just as the train starts its slow glide into the tunnel. Fortunately, it's moving *toward* Will, so I'm able to grab his arms and hoist his torso through as it passes over him.

I'm just replacing the panel when we hear voices. Coming closer. Will grabs my arm and drags me behind a stack of steamer trunks.

". . . delayed by three minutes thanks to the extra security protocols. Control says we'll have to make it up during the run."

"Not a problem. We could make up twenty."

"You got the programming codes?"

"Yeah . . . Here, hold my coffee for a sec . . ."

The door to the engineer's car opens and closes.

"How long to Nu London?" Will whispers.

"About six hours."

"We need a better spot, then."

The baggage car is packed with boxes, cases and trunks according to an efficient system that leaves very little extra space. We finally manage to create a small niche in one corner and cram ourselves in. The floor is speckled white and blue and grey, and the compartment smells of pleather and boiled cabbage. I rest my head on Will's shoulder. The ride is so smooth it's like we're not even moving. Still, the nausea I felt on the platform is back, or maybe it never went away. I feel terrible.

"I need a little nap," I say. "Can you keep watch?"

Will murmurs something inaudible. I feel his breath, warm on my cheek, and then I'm sliding down into nothingness.

Someone shakes my arm and for a second I think I'm with Jake on that trip back from the Academy a million years ago when he woke me just before Raven Rock. My head aches, pretty much everything hurts, actually, but I'm still happy when I realize it's Will. More than happy.

I've never needed anyone before, not since I was a little kid. It's an alien concept. Yes, the Academy trains us to be self-sufficient, not to trust anyone but them. There's no place for emotion in the cold calculus of survival. But the truth is I've always been like that anyway. It's why I was drawn to them, why I was so good at it. But Will has changed me. Cracked me open. And I won't let them separate us again, not so long as I'm still breathing and able to fight.

It's ridiculous, but I feel safe with him, like nothing can ever harm us. I know it's not true, that we're very far from being safe, but I am more at peace than I've been in a long time. Raven Rock is behind us, and we're both alive, by some kind of miracle.

Now we just have to find the access point to Substation 99. Which is still about fifteen hundred miles north.

"I think we're stopped," Will says.

He doesn't look as old as he did before. Late fifties rather than seventies. The QPT is wearing off, thank God. When I tell Will, he looks at me closely but says he doesn't see any difference. Probably because my dose was more recent. The alternative—that I'm stuck like this—is not something I will allow myself to consider right now.

We talk it over and decide the best option is to slip into one of the passenger cars and blend with the crowd leaving the train. A few people look at us oddly when we emerge from the baggage compartment, but everyone's tired and impatient to get off and most don't pay us any mind.

A big clock on the platform says it's 10.22am Nu London time. I don't see any soldiers, but that doesn't mean there aren't plain-clothes agents waiting. I scan the people around us. Nothing out of the ordinary.

Except for one guy. He's in his thirties, with a neatly trimmed black beard and heavy shoulders, like a boxer. He doesn't look at us, but I can see he's watching out of the corner of his eye. He's carrying an attaché case and walking purposefully toward the end of the platform, but keeping pace with us just ahead and to the left.

I take Will's hand and signal to him to drop back a little. Now the guy is well ahead of us, but I keep my eyes fixed on him until he disappears around a corner. Just past a sign with an arrow and one word: CUSTOMS.

I stop cold. Of course we have to go through customs to exit the terminal. It's an inter-prefecture train. And that's where they'll be waiting for us. Not legally or officially, since Raven Rock has no jurisdiction here, but they'll be there. At a minimum, we'd be detained as undocumented migrants by the local authorities. I should have thought of this hours ago. It's a glaring oversight. I'm just so tired.

"What's wrong?" Will looks at me questioningly.

"Hold on, I need to think."

The last of the other passengers drift past us, and we're alone on the platform. I go through the various scenarios in my head. It doesn't take long. We could run into the tunnels. Or we could try to find another way out. That's about it. The tunnels don't appeal to me at all, so I start walking again, toward the end of the platform. Behind us, the hum of the train's power supply cuts off and perfect silence descends.

We reach the customs sign and I peek around the corner. It's deserted. White walls, grey carpet, fluorescent lighting. Another arrow at the far end pointing right. And then I spot what I'm looking for. A door about halfway down, unmarked, with a keypad. Probably for the train crew. I'm sure it's alarmed, and I have no idea how to open it, but I'll just blow the lock off if I have to.

"We're going through that door," I tell Will. "We're going to have to run, and we might have to shoot some people if they try to stop us. Can you handle that?" A wave of dizziness washes over me and I put a hand against the wall to steady myself.

Will gives me a worried look. "I can handle that. The question is whether you can."

"I'm fine," I say, taking a deep breath.

But I'm not fine. My skull suddenly feels two sizes too small. I start walking down the corridor, eyes focused on the door. If we can just get through that door, we'll be OK.

It swings open when we're about six feet away and the burly guy from the platform steps out. He's armed and doesn't look surprised to see us. I reach for the gun in my waistband but it's too late, his is already pointed at my forehead.

"Jansin Nordqvist," he says in a thick, almost guttural Nu London accent.

Not a question.

I raise my hands without responding. Next to me, Will does the same.

"Are you aware that diplomatic relations were formally severed between Nu London and Raven Rock at 0930 this morning?" The ghost of a smile plays around his lips. "In fact, our ambassador is being recalled at this very moment. They accused him of being an appeaser because he doesn't support military action against Greenbrier. He's due to arrive on the next train, in about four hours or so."

I wonder why he's not shooting us, or ordering us down to the ground. Maybe he's waiting for backup. But that doesn't make sense, because he was clearly expecting us. Something is off.

"Who are you?" I ask. My arms feel like lead weights and I don't think I can hold them up much longer, but I don't want him to shoot me either.

"Please," Will says. "Can't you see she's sick?"

The guy smiles, but it doesn't reach his dark eyes, not entirely. "I'd like you to surrender your firearm, Ms Nordqvist. Two fingers only, please."

The barrel of his gun has not wavered a fraction of an inch during this exchange, so I do it, nice and slow.

"Kick it over," he says, then glances at Will. "You too."

That bit of business completed, the guy seems to relax a little.

"I'm with the Met," he says. "An hour ago, I would have been obligated to take you into custody for immediate extradition to Raven Rock pursuant to an inter-prefectural arrest warrant issued last night. As it stands, I am no longer required to do so."

"What then?" Will says hopefully. "You're letting us go?"

"Not exactly." He keys the door open and motions for us to step through. My knees choose that moment to buckle and I find myself staring up at the ceiling. The strip of fluorescent lights doubles, then triples. "I'm taking you to my uncle, Rafiq. Unless you'd prefer to go with your friends at Customs." He laughs evilly. "You can't miss them. They're holding up a little sign that says *Nordqvist*."

The next minutes are foggy and endless, but with Will's help, I manage to stagger out. Our escort must be high up in the Metropolitan Police because he knows the code for every secure door in the bowels of Nu London station and gets us through without incident. As expected, it's raining, a steady drizzle. He hustles us into a blueblack Rolls, flips on the wipers, and we're off. Through my blurred vision, Nu London looks a lot like Raven Rock. Grey and crowded. I guess there's only so much urban planners can do underground.

The main difference is that the city is multi-level instead of being spread out. It's like a three-dimensional maze and I quickly lose any sense of whether we're above or below where we started.

"How did Rafiq know to send you?" I ask as we turn left into a long, downward-sloping tunnel lit only by the car's powerful high beams.

"We weren't sure, but he felt there was a decent chance you'd run here. The choices are rather limited." He glances in the rearview. "They amended your description early this morning. How'd you do that anyway? It's quite realistic."

I shut my eyes and rest my head on Will's shoulder. I think I have a fever, a high one. I really hope I didn't pick up something nasty in Rebekah's lab.

"That's because it is real," I say.

He looks like he doesn't believe me, but refrains from commenting.

Will is almost back to normal. I'm not, not at all. I can tell from looking at my hands. Something is wrong. Cold fear grips me and I shake it off. "What are they saying about us? What are we wanted for exactly?" I ask, as if it matters.

"Let's see. You kidnapped a military scientist and broke into the Helix to steal proprietary vaccine research, presumably to sell to the highest bidder, the implication being Greenbrier. Two guards are dead, a third critically injured."

So nothing about Will, or human subjects. Of course. They would have mopped up Level Four in a hurry.

"Do you believe any of that?" I ask.

"I trust my uncle. He wouldn't help you without good reason."

"Who's he talking about?" Will says in a low voice.

"Old friend of my mother's. He helped me get you out."

"Then I like him already," Will says.

I take his hand in mine. Even after all he's been through, what they did to him, what they did to Nileen, he still trusts in human decency. It's his nature, although he doesn't realize it and would probably deny it. I'm different. And right now, it's a good thing. Because as grateful as I am not to be dead or hooded and cuffed on a train back to Raven Rock, I still don't know why Rafiq is doing this, where he's sourcing his information, what he's getting out of it. In my experience, most people are motivated by self-interest.

"Since we're buddies now, can I have my gun back?" I ask in a sweet old lady voice.

He keeps his eyes on the road. "No."

That's the last conversation until he steers the Rolls up a long driveway and parks beneath the carport of a decaying stone heap. It must have been a pretty impressive mansion once, but now a patina of black slime coats the facade and the formal gardens are withered and brown. I figure we're at least twenty miles outside the city; it's very quiet, except for the soft patter of the rain.

"Come, Uncle's waiting," our escort says.

I'm not thrilled about walking in there unarmed. Under different circumstances, I'd jump him and take his weapon, but he doesn't strike me as particularly soft. Plus I feel awful. He seems to guess what I'm thinking because that tiny smile softens his expression for a moment.

"It's not a trap," he says. "And if it were, there's not much you could do about it."

I can't argue with his logic so we follow him inside, down a long, gloomy hallway. The décor is Victorian revivalist, lots of dark velvet and faux wood paneling with oil paintings of pre-Transition English country life. They can't be originals, but must have been commissioned specially. This is a man who yearns for the past.

We enter a large study, with a holofire dancing in the grate and bookshelves covering two walls. Unlike Kozlowski's pristine collection, these are mostly in poor shape, their bindings loose or missing completely, the pages yellow and brittle with age. The third wall is oddly blank, unadorned by even a single picture or photograph.

The fourth is dominated by two tall stained glass windows depicting the Furies tormenting a naked and hunted-looking Orestes, who has just killed his own mother in revenge for *her* murder of his father. The work is beautifully executed, although I have to wonder about a person who enjoys that kind of reminder of our collective sins.

He's sitting in an armchair before the fire, feet stretched out on a hassock toward the imaginary warmth. He's enormous, what they used to call a bear of a man. Let's say Bob's size, maybe bigger.

He looks up at us as we cross the threadbare carpet and I see that any resemblance to Bob ends there. Rafiq's eyes are black, with a fierce intelligence behind them, and the lines on his face are deep and melancholy. He has unruly grey hair and a big knobby nose that looks like it would be right at home hovering over a glass of good red wine.

He's a lot older than my mom, closer to Charlie's age, although the two couldn't be more different physically. Rafiq is twice his weight at least, and much less leathery.

He takes in my appearance, and gestures to a loveseat near the fire.

"I'm very glad you're both here. Now, Jansin, how long ago did you take the drug?" he asks mildly.

"I don't know," I say. "Twelve hours maybe."

"How much?"

"I don't know."

I'm having a hard time focusing on his questions. Everything suddenly seems so unreal.

"From the look of things, you exceeded the safe threshold. That's five milligrams per kilo of body weight. Although in my personal opinion, there is no safe threshold for QPT."

"What does that mean?" Will says, helping me to the couch. "What's wrong with her?"

"Drug reactions vary according to the individual. Age, weight, genetic factors all play a role. You see what it did to her on the outside. It's what's happening on the inside that concerns me." He looks over at his nephew. "Samer, call Aviva, tell her to come right away. Tell her we need a detox."

I lie there, shivering, while Will strokes my hair.

"She's burning up," he says fiercely. "We have to get the fever down. Do you have any yarrow or willow bark?" I feel him shift against me. "No, I guess you wouldn't. Just plain aspirin then?"

Rafiq rises and comes back a few minutes later with a damp cloth, which he lays across my forehead. "She needs more than that," he says. "My friend is a doctor. She can help, and she knows how to be discreet. The new drugs are quite miraculous. It's fortunate we found her within twenty-four hours. After that, treatment options diminish considerably."

I must drift off for a while. When I come back, there's a woman in the room, young and wearing street clothes. She's pretty, with short dark hair and a quietly efficient manner. She checks my vitals and runs some blood tests.

"Her BUN levels are elevated, and creatinine is off the charts," she says, scanning some numbers on a portable lab device. "We're looking at acute renal failure."

I feel Will's arms tighten around me. Where he comes from, bad kidneys are probably fatal. They would be here too, if I didn't get immediate medical treatment.

"Don't worry," she says, swabbing my arm. "I'm going to juice you up."

"How does it work?" Will asks, as she injects me with something.

"The serum delivers custom-designed molecules at the nano scale. That's about a hundred thousand times smaller than the width of a human hair. They identify and lock onto foreign particles in the bloodstream, and purge them through the urine. The applications are almost limitless, but the one I just gave her targets the QPT class of drugs. That's ostensibly an anti-depressant, by the way, but it's so unstable Nu London banned it a decade ago."

"Incredible," Will says. "I mean, that's really incredible."

"It's revolutionizing medicine," Aviva replies. "Imagine being able to precisely excise a tumor while leaving the healthy cells intact, without surgery or radiation. Or being able to knit torn flesh together at the cellular level, without stitches."

Will asks something else, and I fall asleep again to the two of them quietly talking. I must sleep straight through to the next afternoon, because when I wake the house is quiet and dim light is coming through the stained glass windows. I'm on the couch, under a blue blanket, and Will is lying on the rug in front of the fireplace.

I stretch and my back cracks in about fifteen places, but I feel better than I have for days. Weeks, actually. I suddenly have to pee, so I head down the hall and start opening doors. The third is a half bathroom, just a toilet, where I eliminate about a gallon of nuclear yellow urine. It doesn't hurt though, so I guess the shot did its work.

I curl up facing Will and wait for him to wake up. His blonde hair is army short now, but it suits him. I could just watch him forever, but then his eyes open.

"You're back," he says.

"I feel better."

"No. I mean, you're *back*."

I look at my hand and notice that it's not a crone's claw anymore. The skin is smooth.

It's like being told you have a terminal illness and then finding out it was all a mistake. I'll never forget how the cop at the roadblock looked at me. As if I was nothing.

"That's how they looked at us in the lab," Will says, and I realized I must have spoken my thoughts aloud. "Like we weren't even human." He's quiet for a minute. "A few times I just wished I were dead. Many times, I did. They were careful though. After a couple of us found ways . . . Then they watched us all the time. Made us sick, one by one, while they recorded the symptoms. Asking the same questions, over and over. I think they were physics, like me. Why, Jansin? Why would they do that to us?"

I just shake my head. It's not a question I can answer. I could give him the official story, that it was necessary for the greater good. But that's not what he means.

His arms are still green with bruises at the injection sites. I think of how close he came to being infected like Nileen.

"It's all my fault," I whisper.

Will's face hardens. "None of this is your fault. You didn't ask to be taken by the clan any more than I asked to be taken by the soldiers." Will rolls onto his back and stares at the ceiling. "I used to dream of you, Jansin. Awake and asleep both. When they would come for me. You're what I held onto. To keep myself sane."

I don't know what to say. I wish we were alone somewhere, really alone, not on the floor of a strange house with legions of scarily competent people looking for us. I'm not even sure exactly what we are to each other anymore. Friends? Something more? I know what we could have been, but that was another lifetime.

What's been done to Will, what he's witnessed . . . that would drive a weaker person insane. He's not crazy, but he's not the same, that's for sure. I doubt he ever will be. He was already wounded when I met him. I'm just not sure what kind of scars I'm dealing with now.

"I thought you were dead," I say. "I thought you were all dead. That's what they told me."

"Well, they're liars."

"Yes," I say.

We watch the rain wash in sheets down the windows.

"How do they do that?" Will asks after a while. "Make it rain?"

"The people who built the prefectures diverted underground rivers to feed the sewage and drinking water system. They also created a sprinkler network. Fire is one of our biggest worries down here. But it turns out people like having weather. They need it. It breaks the tedium. They can make it snow too."

"I've never seen snow," Will says. "I don't think it exists anymore. Not for real."

"Do you remember how the woods used to smell after a heavy rain?" He nods. "That's one of the things I miss the most. The air. It was always different."

"I miss the boats," he says. "Being out on the water. The world just seemed so endless. I was born on a sailboat and I've probably spent more than half my life out at sea. I'd give anything just to see it one more time."

There's a polite cough at the door and Rafiq comes in with a tray of soup and bread and tea. My stomach leaps at the smell. It's hollow enough to park a tank in there.

"Shower's upstairs, second door on the left," he says. "I've left towels and clean clothes Samer bought this morning."

We thank him and devour the food, then go clean up. When I look in the bathroom mirror, I see that I'm not back to normal, not entirely. My hair is streaked with white, not salt and pepper, but thick swathes from root to tip. I know I should be grateful I'm not dead, or old forever, but it still looks strange, disfiguring, like a half-healed scar.

The clothes fit well, a black long-sleeved sweater and pants similar to agent gear. Sturdy combat boots. My old outfit, which used to be one of my nicest, is so stained with blood and filth I don't even want to touch it with my newly clean hands. It goes straight into the trash.

We regroup in the study about an hour later. Will is dressed the same as me, except he got a black T-shirt. With his cropped hair and pale skin, he looks like a different person from the boy I met less than a year ago. He looks older. Harder.

Like yesterday, Will and I take the loveseat, and Rafiq settles into his armchair. Samer sits by the window, eyes watchful and alert.

The light outside has dimmed. It's raining again.

"I need to know about Substation 99," I say.

Rafiq nods and activates the holofire. It looks perfectly real, down to the glowing coals underneath, although I'm not sure why he needs the andirons and poker. For effect, I suppose.

"Then you're in the right place," he says.

CHAPTER TWENTY-TWO

Did God do it on purpose? Were we being tested? Punished? Or was it all simply proof that there is no God?

Before we start," Rafiq says, "you need to understand what things were like in the early days of the prefectures. My wife, Beth, was stationed at Fort Detrick, so we ended up at Raven Rock. At first, we counted ourselves lucky to be there. Very lucky. What was happening on the surface was . . . Well, some of it defied imagination. Hordes of emaciated refugees. Plague. Wildfires, and then floods that swallowed the ashes of entire cities.

"We had enough food for half a year. After that, the hydroponic farms would be in full production, and we'd grow what we needed. But it didn't work out that way. As often happens, a series of small mistakes cascaded into full-blown crisis. For one thing, there were more of us than we'd planned for, a lot more. Last-minute shuttles kept arriving, relatives of high-ranking officials, others who knew how to arrange a well-placed bribe. A stop was put to it eventually, but it was too late. Everything was already massively behind schedule. The stores that were supposed to keep us alive for six months lasted two."

Rafiq pauses and sips a mug of steaming tea. "We were put on strict rationing, barely eight hundred calories a day, and there were some who began to believe that we'd made a terrible mistake. My wife was among them. She thought we were all going to die down here. Then, on our hundredth day underground, a storm on the surface knocked out one of the ventilation tubes in Sector G."

He looks at me and my insides turn to ice. I never knew about this. I never even knew there *was* a Sector G. The histories make it sound like everything was perfectly planned and executed, down to the last detail.

"Now we understand how to make them cane-proof. But back then, it seems the engineers had miscalculated."

"What happened?" Will asks.

"Why, it flooded, of course. The sea came pouring down and submerged the entire sector and part of those adjacent before it was sealed off. Twenty-five thousand people drowned." He rubs his forehead wearily. "If we were frightened before, afterwards . . . I can't describe the terror, the claustrophobia. Ironically, it was probably the reason the rest of us survived until the first harvest. A tenth fewer mouths to feed."

"That's a horrible story," I say. The image of bloated corpses drifting in the darkness pops into my head and I push it away. "Why are you telling us this?"

"Because you need to know the context in which Beth and I started Project Nix."

"Wait a second. *You?*"

"Well, it was Beth's brainchild. She was a geneticist, a brilliant one. She started to wonder if there wasn't a way we could adapt to the harsh new surface conditions. If, for example, people were given specialized amphibian genes, among others. She and eight others volunteered themselves as experimental subjects. It sounds mad to say it now, but you have to understand the pressure we were under."

Will has gone rigid next to me. I take his hand, but I don't think he even notices.

"You know how it turned out," Rafiq says, his cultured voice relating these horrors so casually I want to reach across the carpet and shake him. "They *changed*. In one sense, it was more successful than we dared to hope. But the changes went beyond the merely physical. Something was missing, something that makes us human. Mercy, perhaps. Empathy for others. And they looked . . . wrong. A recommendation was made that the project be terminated. Clean slate." He holds his giant hands out to us in mute appeal. "I couldn't let that happen. I couldn't let them murder my wife."

"So you set them loose," Will says in a monotone.

"I commandeered a mole and took them to the surface. Six had survived the process. Your mother helped me, Jansin, and I will forever be in Tamiko's debt for it. She was very young then but such a promising student. She worshipped Beth. Me, they punished with early retirement. They knew I'd never publically discuss it. We managed to conceal your mother's involvement. It would have destroyed her career."

Your mother helped me.

I remember the look on her face when she asked what I knew about Nix. The slight hesitation before she denied any knowledge. She must have assumed at first that I'd somehow discovered the original project, her role in it. Then she realized her mistake. *We had a falling out,* she said. Like it was some disagreement over how to split the check at an expensive restaurant. Not that Rafiq's wife turned herself into some kind of monster and then they both unleashed her and five more like her on the surface. I don't think Mom knew about Rebekah, her outrage was genuine, but I do wonder what other secrets she's kept from me.

It sickens me that we *made* the toads, but it has the ring of truth. Nothing natural could evolve that quickly.

"Why take the others?" I ask. "Why not just your wife? Wouldn't that have been easier?"

Rafiq stares into the holofire. "I didn't want her to be lonely. I didn't want her to be the only one of her species."

"Did you know they could breed?" Will demands. He's breathing hard now. "Did you know that?"

"We thought they were sterile."

"Well, they're not," Will spits out. "There's more of them now. And they hunt us for sport. Maybe even food. But I guess you didn't have to worry about that, since you just dumped them and ran back to your hole in the ground."

"I'm sorry. So sorry. If you know what it is to love someone . . ."

"I loved my mother. My father, and my sister." He stares at Rafiq, and his hatred is so raw it's like electricity crackling in the air. "But I'm sure they'd understand, if they were still alive."

Heavy silence descends over the room.

The situation is spinning out of control, and I can't let that happen. I ache for Will's loss, but it's not the toads I care about. It's Tisiphone. And what I hope is inside her.

"What you did is beyond stupid," I say to Rafiq. "But it was a long time ago, and your motives weren't evil, just selfish. Not like what they're doing now."

Rafiq gets the hint. "I found out a year ago that Rebekah Carlsson had restarted Nix, her own incarnation of it," he says quickly. "She was assigned as a senior scientist to 99 when there was a toad attack. Unlike the other times, they managed to capture some alive. I think her grant was about to be cut off, they were getting ready to close the station, and she saw an opportunity to make a name for herself. She had a subspecialty in biosciences. If the toads could be controlled somehow . . .

"Of course, her goals for Nix were nowhere near as complex as what Beth accomplished. Carlsson focused on behavioral modification, primarily through pharmaceuticals. It's all she was qualified for."

There's a whiff of academic snobbery in his tone, which I ignore.

"Now they've promoted her to managing the flu project, even though she has little expertise in bioweapons and Nix failed to deliver concrete results. Typical military. If you know how to kiss the right arses and tart up your data a bit, you're golden." He pauses for breath. "Well, that doesn't matter. I just want to put an end to it. I have no idea if my wife is still alive. If she's one of the *subjects*. But I can't allow her work to be turned into such an abomination."

Will is staring at the wall, and I can sense fury rolling off him in waves, but he hasn't walked out, which shows impressive self-control as far as I'm concerned.

"How do you know all this?" I ask.

"I trade in secrets now. It's the only thing I'm fit for, I suppose. My network of informants is extensive, including one at the station."

Things start to click into place. His story about owing my mother a debt was nice, but he wants something more.

"What are you offering?" I ask.

"There's data in the hard drives. Unhackable remotely, but someone inside could get to it with the right passcodes. You promise to send it back, I give you the precise coordinates and everything you want to know about Tisiphone."

"Why can't your informant do it?"

"Too risky. The price is exorbitant, and most of my savings was exhausted discovering what I've just told you."

I think of the shabby state of his house, the gaping holes in the shelves, like missing teeth, where he must have sold off his most valuable books, one by one.

"There's a classified report in the archives–" I begin, but Rafiq interrupts, voice tinged with impatience.

"Not enough. I need it all. Irrefutable documentation. A single report is too easily dismissed. Or deleted."

I consider the offer and see no harm in it. In fact, it serves our purposes as well.

"What would you do with this information?" I ask.

"Given to the right people in Raven Rock, it would shut Nix down. There's factions within factions over there. Many are dissatisfied with the current state of affairs. The prefecture is rotting from the inside out. They've known it for years, and the draconian handling of the Greenbrier situation is bringing matters to a head. I know the right people. But there's nothing they can do without proof."

"You'll go down, too," I say. "There's no way around it."

"I know," he says quietly. "It doesn't matter anymore."

I turn to Will. "This might be the only way to help Fatima and the others," I say.

He hates to do anything Rafiq wants, I can see that, but after a moment he nods.

"They're holding human subjects at a military facility. You have to make sure they're found, released," I tell Rafiq. "And not just released. Returned to the surface, if that's what they want."

"You have my word," he says.

"OK then. Let's talk about Tisiphone. First, is it true that there's a plane capable of penetrating the eyewall?"

"Yes. It's a holdover from the days when 99 was a real weather station. It's still there, but I don't know much more than that. Any data it may have gathered is under lock and key."

I take a deep breath. Sharing my half-baked theory is harder than I expected. What if I'm wrong? What if Rafiq laughs, and explains why it's impossible? Where will we go then?

"I'll show you," Rafiq says. He touches a hidden button on his armrest. "Queue maps, sixty-four degrees north, sixteen degrees west."

The blank wall comes to life in a richly detailed 3D rendering of Tisiphone, slowly rotating counter-clockwise. There's a glowing red dot off her lower right quadrant.

"That's 99," Rafiq says. "About fifty miles from the edge of the storm."

"Do you have any old maps? Say, from a hundred years ago?"

He looks at me curiously. "Sure. Image same coordinates circa 1990," he says.

The storm dissolves. I see a large land mass to the northwest, with thick glacier cover.

"Greenland before the icecap melted," Rafiq says.

Where Tisiphone sits today, there's nothing but open ocean.

It can't be right. It can't be.

"What's the source of that image?" I ask.

"Official Geophysics archive."

"Could they have altered it?"

"Of course. It's digital."

Geography classes at the Academy focused on the prefectures, the new world. We rarely discussed the surface, especially how it used to look. The past was dead and buried and best left that way.

"Wait," Rafiq says. "I may have a book . . ." He wanders over to a far bookshelf, runs his fingers across the spines. "A rare edition of one of Jules Verne's classics. I couldn't bear to part with it. Aha!"

He pulls a large volume from the shelf. "There's a lovely color plate at the back. Yes, here it is."

He hands me the book. I can't help but smile a little. *Journey to the Center of the Earth*.

Rafiq's eyes twinkle. "You're a clever girl, Jansin," he says.

Because right there is a map, a map of nearly the exact same coordinates as Tisiphone. Except it doesn't show ocean. It shows an island.

A place called Iceland.

I'm tingling all over as I ask, "Can we figure out the elevation?" If it was anywhere near sea level, it would be submerged now.

"As I recall from Verne's quite precise descriptions, Iceland was a mountainous country, with active volcanoes. I suppose you intend to go there?" He says this as carelessly as if he was asking about a trip to the market.

I glance at Will. "*We're* going there. Come see." I hold out the book. "Volcanic is good news. It means they can't send in moles. Too unstable."

"It's not moles I'm worried about," he says in a tight voice. "That's toad territory, Jansin. When you said you'd found a safe place, I didn't realize you meant so far north. You've never been there, but I have. And I swore I never would again. It could be infested."

I hadn't thought of that.

"Or there could be people," I say optimistically. "Survivors."

"Most known toad activity is centered in the Faroe Islands," Rafiq adds. "That's to the southeast. There's no evidence they can swim through seven hundred miles of superstorm. In fact, it's highly unlikely."

"You also thought they were sterile," Will retorts. "In fact, you know little or nothing about what they're capable of." He paces over, looks at the map. "This is in the eye?"

"It looks that way," I say.

"And your government is concealing this because . . . ?"

"Because it might change everything. It might make people think they had a choice. It might make them question. And they won't tolerate that. Especially not with war on the horizon. From the bureaucratic perspective, the truth about Tisiphone is more trouble than it's worth. That's why they shut down 99. That's why they run the HYPERCANE NETWORK! twenty-four hours a day. To keep us afraid."

Will surprises me by turning to Samer, who's sat in silence at his post by the window for the last half hour, listening but not taking part.

"Do you think she's right?" Will asks.

Samer's lips quirk. "I'm a cop. Nothing surprises me anymore," he says.

I decide to plow ahead before Will has a chance to raise any more objections.

"How do we get there?" I ask Rafiq.

"Queue maglev system, north quadrant," he says.

A network of color-coded lines appears.

"Zoom right, up six degrees, zoom. Stop. The rectangle in the center is Nu London station." Rafiq walks over to the image and points to an inverted yellow L. "The tunnel's not under the territorial sovereignty of Nu London anymore. We ceded it by treaty to Raven Rock a decade ago in exchange for trade concessions. But a supply train services the station once a week. It ends at a surface vent tube that leads to 99."

I stare at the tangle of lines until I'm sure I have it memorized. The distance from here to there must be at least eight hundred miles.

"The tube will have defenses. They all do. Can you reach your source and get some specifics? I'd rather not go in blind."

"I can try, yes. We need to get you on that train."

"Give me a name."

Rafiq isn't used to sharing more than he deems absolutely necessary, but I let the silence hang until he caves in. "It's Goodlove."

"Jansin, we haven't agreed on anything yet," Will objects. "We need to talk. In private."

I'm opening my mouth to argue when the phone rings.

Rafiq answers, listens for a moment, and his face goes a little grey. He holds it out. "For you," he says.

My heart is pounding as I put the receiver to my ear. "Hello?"

"Jansin."

It's my father.

"Dad," I say.

He exhales heavily. "I've been worried crazy about you. Are you alright?"

"I'm fine."

"Your mother . . . They took your mother away, Jan." His voice cracks a little. "They've been interrogating her."

I feel sick. They're not only questioning her, they've broken her, or my father wouldn't be calling this number. I don't know what it would take to get my mother to give up Rafiq. To give up her own daughter. I'm afraid to imagine. "Can't you stop them? She had nothing to do with it."

"It's bigger than that now. The Council cut me out. They said I lack *objectivity*. But I still have friends. One was decent enough to fill me in. They know where you are, and they're coming for you," his voice is starting to rise.

"You have to help Mom," I whisper.

"No, *you* have to help Mom." He assumes the commanding, no-dissent-tolerated tone I've heard a million times. But underneath it is something I have never associated with my father before: bone-deep fear. "You're going to go outside and turn yourself in. If you do that, no one will harm you, or her. I've been given assurances." He pauses. "Jake is with them. A strategic decision. You know him, trust him. Don't make this hard, Jan."

I think how little *he* knows me anymore if he thinks I trust Jake, of all people.

"Dad, I can't. I just can't. Do you know they're doing at the Helix? Do you have any idea?" Nileen's face, a mask of blood so dark it looks black, flashes before my eyes.

"I'm not sure what Rafiq has been telling you, but he's mentally unstable," my father continues, more calmly. He's comfortable with this part of the story. They've obviously drilled it into him. He doesn't know, I think. And then: thank God. He's not part of Nix. "The man is a diagnosed paranoid delusional. You need to stop this nonsense and get home, we'll sort things out. The Academy doctor says you're suffering from post-traumatic stress. We can mount an insanity defense."

"You're the one who's crazy if you think I'm going out there," I say. I've never defied my father like this and there's silence on the other end as he tries to fathom this abrupt left turn in our relationship.

"You're being incredibly selfish," he says. "I know what happened topside was a terrible thing, but you need to get past that now. Your family needs you. Your *mother* needs you. Exactly what are you trying to prove that's more important than that? You can't beat them, honey."

The sincerity in his voice makes me waver. Maybe he's right. Maybe there's no other way. They have *my mother*.

Except.

"And if I go outside, turn myself in. What happens to Will?" I say.

There's a brief pause. And that's all the answer I need.

"Goodbye, Dad," I say, and part of my heart shrivels and dies at that moment.

He's shouting into the receiver as I end the call.

"They're here," I say.

Because I know when my dad said "coming", he meant the agents were already outside. Maybe even inside. They were probably listening to the entire conversation. Waiting for the outcome.

There's a moment of silence. Samer walks to the center of the room, his firearm out and pointed toward the ceiling.

"I'm calling for backup," he says angrily. "They're out of their jurisdiction. Nu London will detain the whole lot as enemy spies."

"Your people won't get here in time."
We look at each other.
"Now can I have my gun back?" I ask.
He pulls a piece out of his jacket, tosses it over.
That's when the windows explode.

CHAPTER TWENTY-THREE

*The first plasma charge was detonated on May 6, 2042.
Eight years later, the total mass of subterranean rock
displaced equaled sixteen Manhattan islands.*

If they hadn't been trying to take me alive, we wouldn't have stood a chance. They could have just torched the place with a shoulder-fired missile. That's what I would have done, if I were them.

The gun is arcing toward me when I hear a very distinctive sound—fast rope unfurling through the pulley of a rappelling harness. Once you hear that sound, the window of opportunity to react is one, maybe two seconds. So I snatch it out of the air and bring the muzzle down toward the window on my side of the room just as a pair of boots comes crashing through.

Samer sees me aim, grasps the situation, and brings his own gun up at the other window. We fire almost simultaneously. There's a second guy right behind the first and I shoot him too, then run to the shattered window and look outside. It's dark and rainy. Rope dangles down from the roof but there's no one else on the way.

All this happens in about the time it takes to sneeze.

Samer's lead entry is down, but his partner gets off a shot as he comes through and Samer is hit in the chest. I see Rafiq rush toward him out of the corner of my eye, but there's no time, the agent is inside now, laser weapon up and pointed at Will.

"Get down!" he screams.

I was against the window wall when his feet hit the rug and his Kevlar helmet keeps me just outside his peripheral vision as I slip up next to him, put my gun to his jaw, and fire.

It clicks down on an empty chamber.

Damn.

I should have thought about how many bullets I used at the Helix, but I didn't get around to that. The guy hears the click and starts to turn, and I bring the gun up with both hands and smash the butt down on his head. He falls to his knees, momentarily stunned, and that's when Jake comes through.

Two on one side, three on the other. They do it that way sometimes.

I wonder how many more are outside.

We stare at each other for a split second. Then we both move, but as always, I'm a little faster. I step forward and twist his gun hand down and around until it's hyperextended to the side. With my left I grab his throat in an eagle claw. I have to reach up to do it since he's so much taller, but that doesn't really matter. Once my thumb curls behind his windpipe, his air supply is virtually cut off. Special ops likes it because the victim can't make a sound, other than a thin kind of wheezing.

For a moment I flash back to the last time I saw him. The smile on his face when I asked him where he was during the operation.

I squeeze a little tighter.

Then I see movement a couple feet away. The second agent through, the one I clocked, is getting up. He's reaching for his backup weapon, which is usually a regular handgun in case an EMP has been deployed. He gains his feet and flicks off the safety.

Suddenly there's a yell, and I hear feet crunching on broken glass behind me. It's Will, and God love him, he's got the poker. He sweeps it down and up, and even though the agent has body armor, it's a brutal blow. His knee buckles and Will keeps hitting him, slashing diagonal motions that make contact in all the right places. Will's growling like an animal, but he's not panicking. I'm not either, though it's a close thing. I just killed two agents, people I might even know. I tell myself I had to, and that's true, but it's also true that I feel sick. They were just following orders. It's one thing to cavalierly call yourself a killer. Another entirely to be one. To shoot another human being. If there was any line left, I just crossed it, permanently and irrevocably.

But I can't look back, not now. We have to get away from here. *We have to.*

My whole body is slick with sweat. Jake needs to black out. The last two days have taken a toll, and I don't have much stamina for this kind of thing. Just a few more seconds. The brain can't function long without oxygen. It's a simple and undeniable fact. Some chokeholds actually put people down in two seconds. *Two seconds.* It sounds impossible, and I wouldn't believe it if I hadn't seen it done.

But Jake is well-rested and well-fed and a lot stronger to begin with. He hasn't suffered recent kidney failure, or been blown halfway down a corridor and then brained by chalkheads. And he has really long arms.

The left one grabs me under the rump and just flips me over his shoulder, straight out the broken window.

I land flat on my back in the weeds. The air in my lungs departs with a *whoosh*. I open my mouth and it fills with rain, not the clean rain of the surface but the stale, chemically treated stuff they use down here.

I close my eyes and when I open them, I see Jake leap like a cat over the windowsill. He drops on top of me, pinning my arms with his knees. Inside, Will screams in pain and something smashes to the floor.

"I'm bringing you in, Jansin," Jake rasps. He pulls out a set of cuffs, slaps one side onto my left wrist. "You're lucky I'm here. The others might just kill you at this point." He glances behind the house.

I go limp. Let him think I've given up.

"Where are you taking me?" I whisper.

He snaps the cuffs onto my right wrist.

"Disneyland," Jake says.

He doesn't say it in a gloating way. The opposite, in fact. Like he's a little sorry about it.

I've only heard of the place from rumors around the Academy. Officially, it doesn't exist. It's where the military conducts psy-ops research. Rewires people's brains. Turns your reality into one bad Technicolor acid trip. Hence the name.

"That sucks, Jake," I say.

He shrugs. Yeah, it sucks. But it's the way things are. Orders are orders.

I know better than to appeal for mercy. It won't be forthcoming.

He's shifting his weight to yank me to my feet when a gun goes off inside the study. A single shot, followed by silence.

My heart stops. I struggle to get a glimpse through the window but Jake's armored bulk is in the way. He puts a knee on the center of the cuffs, pinning my hands to the ground, and gets his gun up. I hear a scraping sound. Jake's eyes narrow, and his mouth sets in a grim line. He has a look on his face that can only be interpreted as sizing up the competition.

I know then that he's seeing Will, and he's about to shoot him. So I do the only thing I can. I bite his thigh.

It's an interesting thing about biting. With not much effort, the human jaw can exert pressure of up to fifteen tons per square inch. I read that once. But there's also something uniquely disturbing about being bitten by another person. It elicits a kind of primal horror. Especially when it's near the groin.

Jake is no exception. He howls as I sink my teeth into him, and it buys Will the time he needs to jump from the sill and wallop Jake with a two-handed overhead blow that dents his helmet and knocks him senseless. I scramble over to Jake's weapon and pick it up. The cuffs can be dealt with later. At least they're in front, so I can shoot.

Which I should do to Jake, but can't. Not in cold blood.

"What happened in there?" I ask as we press our backs against the wall of the house, where the shadows are deepest.

"Samer's bleeding bad, he may be dead, I don't know. He's not moving. Rafiq took a gun from one of the ones you shot and got the guy I was fighting. He sprayed me with this stuff that burns your skin." Will shows me his arm. There's an angry red weal running from wrist to elbow. It's already rising in a blister. "Then Rafiq took off, and I saw you outside."

"OK, we're getting out of here. Let's try the back," I say, figuring that the direction Jake looked in is where some of the extraction team is waiting. Hopefully with transportation.

If they did it by the book, there's no more than eight, and four are dead or unconscious. I don't see any of the others, but I know they're out here somewhere.

I get low and peek around the corner of the house. Three stories high, it occupies a large cavern, with about two acres of open space that ends at rock walls on all sides but the driveway. The perfect mousetrap.

I put a finger to my lips and we crouch there for a minute, listening to the soft hiss of rain pattering on stone. Time passes, and the urge to run is almost overwhelming. But that's what they expect us to do. There's not a chance that long driveway is unwatched. Will is stock-still next to me, gripping the poker, eyes scanning the grounds. He's scared but holding it together, and I think that he would've made a decent agent if he was a little more cold-hearted. Also, I'm glad he's not.

Then a radio crackles. It's coming from inside a tall artificial hedge about ten yards to the left. I know it's artificial because it's the only thing that's green, and they take forever to grow in real life. There's a broken stone fountain between us and the hedge, and we use it for cover, creeping across the dim yard on our bellies until we leave the lights from the windows behind. Shadows move on the second and third floors. I hope one of them is Rafiq, that he's still alive.

The hedge is unbroken on this side, and we have to crawl for a way before we find a gap. It leads to a narrow path with blind corners at either end. The path twists and turns like a maze, and I'm afraid if we don't find whoever has that radio soon, they'll find us. And there won't be anywhere to run.

Finally we hit a gap that opens onto a larger square. In the middle are three motorcycles, the very, very fast ones with huge tires and a zero gravity windscreen that are illegal to own unless you're police or military. There's also an agent, but sadly for him or her, they're looking in the other direction. I aim Jake's gun at the vulnerable spot just below the Kevlar helmet, begin to squeeze the trigger. That's when the lights go out.

The blackness is instantaneous and total. Above, on the surface, there's always the tiniest bit of light, even on moonless, overcast nights. But six thousand feet down, it's like the bottom of the sea, or the depths of space. They must have finished searching the house and cut the power.

I can hear Will breathing beside me, and shouts from the yard, near the fountain. They're moving closer. If I shoot and miss, I'll give away our position. And I can't be sure the agent hasn't moved.

So I open my eyes wide and wait for something, anything, to tell me where they are. Ten or twenty seconds go by, and I'm dying to blink but I don't, like the insane staring contests you get into when you're a kid. Then a tiny green light winks into existence, only for a millisecond, but I know what it is: the power indicator on a set of infrared goggles. I fire into the darkness and there's a scream. Boots pound toward us through the hedge maze, about two rows away.

I fire again, and in the white laser flash I see the agent, motionless on the ground. We stumble forward, bumping into the bikes, and I find Will's fingers, give him the gun.

"Shoot the cuffs off," I say. "You have to hit the double hinge in the middle."

"Shit," he mutters. He's thinking he can't see a thing and he might just as easily shoot my hands off.

Together we get the gun positioned so it seems right. He fires. The heat singes the hair on my arms but the cuffs snap in half, leaving the carbon steel bracelets dangling from my wrists. A perfect shot.

I grab the dead agent and drag him or her, I don't know which and don't care, to the nearest bike. Press the still-warm thumb against a reader next to the controls. The dash hums to life, washing the clearing in a green glow.

We jump on the bike and gun it just as an agent bursts through the gap. I run them down, skid around a tight corner and blow straight through the hedge as two others come at us from either side. Their laser fire ignites the hedge, which is made out of something plastic that appears to be extremely flammable. I hope they roast in there.

We hug the side of the fountain and I get the headlight on. Jake is gone. And someone's running at us from the side of the house. Will raises the gun to shoot, but I grab his arm. It's Rafiq.

He's covered in blood.

"Get on!" I yell, braking hard.

Two sets of lights pierce the darkness behind us. I'd hoped the other bikes were burning by now, but no such luck. Why the hell didn't I just fry them with the laser gun? Another stupid mistake.

"It won't take three, you know that," Rafiq gasps. "Forget about me, just go." He thrusts something at Will, as the other bikes roar out of the hedge.

I curse and accelerate down the driveway. When I glance in the rearview, I see one of the agents shoot Rafiq in passing as casually as you'd shoot a rabid dog. He topples over and lies there, still.

Hatred boils inside me, and I swear to myself that I'll get them somehow, someday. For Nileen and Petyr and Fatima and Banerjee and all the rest. For my mother, and what they're doing to her right now. They're going to regret making me what I am. I think they already are.

We enter the long upward-sloping tunnel and I start to wonder why the agents behind us aren't shooting. These bikes are equipped with a virtual armory of lethal accessories. It doesn't take long to find out. Two sets of headlights appear ahead of us. Oncoming, and closing the distance very fast. I guess they don't want to hit the last team by accident, the ones who were covering the exit.

"Hold on tight," I yell at Will, unnecessarily, as he's got me around the waist in a death grip.

I aim for the gap between the lights, knowing it's too narrow. At the last second, I swerve to the left, directly in front of the lead rider, and hit the throttle. The bike screams and climbs up the rock wall of the tunnel in a forty-five degree arc, then thumps down on the big tires. We fishtail badly for a moment, but the bike recovers and we shoot out of the tunnel into a wider, two-lane roadway.

God bless GPS, as I have no idea where the station is.

Tires screech behind us as the agents who were following nearly collide with the ones we just passed. I get the map up on the dash and activate the onboard computer, request directions to Nu London station.

"Proceed straight on King's Road for six point eight miles," a deep male voice instructs. "Then south on the M4 to Interchange Seven."

We lean forward and I open the throttle as far as I can without losing it on the turns.

"Jansin," Will breathes in my ear. "That was . . ."

Four headlights appear in the rearview, maybe half a mile behind.

"Once we're at the station, we can lose them in the tunnels," I call over the thrum of the engine, but Will's already turned away to aim the laser weapon at our pursuers. He's smart enough to shoot at the ceiling instead of trying to hit the bikes, and the blast rains dust and rubble down on their heads. I just hope the whole tunnel doesn't collapse.

"Bear right in point two miles," the GPS advises, and I yank the bike nearly horizontal as we hit a fork in the road. At the rate we're going, point two miles means *right now*.

We scrape through a tight curve and when it ends, there's only three sets of lights behind us. But it's a long straightaway ahead. Bad for us. Because it's the perfect stretch for them to deploy the heavy artillery.

I jerk the bike to the fluorescent center line as a storm of bullets rips through the space we were just occupying. But now I'm in the lane of oncoming traffic, which is picking up as we get closer to the city center. I almost forgot they drive on the opposite side here, and nearly collide head-on with a bus.

Will is cursing fluently behind me, and my legs shake so hard I have to squeeze my knees around the saddle to keep from falling off. Please God, don't let us die here. Not like this. Not after everything we've been through. Not when we're so close to finding out the truth. Maybe even close to being free of them forever.

The tunnel widens, becomes four lanes across. A few seconds later, it opens out in every direction and we're speeding through a commercial shopping district. The streets are clogged with black umbrellas and slow-moving cars. I'm forced to brake and weave through it, and the agents behind us close the gap until they're less than fifty yards back.

A beam sears past the windscreen and hits a garbage truck parked on the side of the street. Flaming trash scatters across three lanes of traffic, setting off a chain reaction of skidding, crunching metal and general mayhem.

"Multiple vehicle accident ahead," the stern male voice warns. "Would you like to retract the wheels? It is the recommended–"

Retract the wheels?

Let's see. Under the circumstances, it seems the prudent course of action.

"Hell yes!" I say.

There's a thunking whirr under the engine as some secondary propulsion system kicks into gear, and suddenly we're airborne, sailing over a sea of astonished, terrified faces.

It's a convertible hoverbike.

Ah.

I've heard of them but never driven one. They're way too expensive for raw recruits to play with.

We clear the pileup and I glance at the map. Nu London station is less than a mile away. Will has gone very quiet behind me.

"You OK?" I call.

"Mmm-hmm," he responds faintly.

I know he's still weak from what was done to him at the Helix. Just because he doesn't look old anymore doesn't mean he's healthy. The arms wrapped around me are thinner than they used to be, and I can feel tremors running through the muscles. *Please God, don't let us die here* changes to: *Please God, don't let Will fall off.*

More beams scorch a row of storefronts as the agents follow suit. Panicked pedestrians run for cover, and I hear the wail of sirens, faster and higher than the ones at home. The locals are about to get involved. It complicates things for us, but also for our pursuers. They're not supposed to be here. Samer said we don't even have diplomatic relations with Nu London anymore.

I lean forward and open the throttle, bringing the bike down to just a few feet above the ground. We tear into a labyrinth of cobblestoned side streets lined with two-story townhouses, the GPS calling out directions so fast that even the computerized voice starts to sound a little frazzled.

"Arriving at destination," it says, as a huge stone structure looms into view.

This is not the time for subtlety, so I go straight through the main entrance. We duck low as the bike smashes through a set of double-doors. The noise is tremendous, but the big windscreen protects us from the rain of glass shards. I swerve to avoid a suitcase-lugging family of four just ahead and barrel toward the information booth at the center of the main terminal. It's capped with a four-sided holoclock that reads 17.57 NLMT.

The perfectly synchronized dance of several hundred people rushing in all directions without bumping into each other screeches to a halt, as if someone just yanked the needle across an old phonograph record.

For a second, I let myself hope the agents have turned back. It depends on what their orders are, and whether Raven Rock wants us badly enough to risk a major international incident.

Then three more hoverbikes roar inside, and total chaos erupts.

There's my answer.

We need to get out of here, get into the tunnels. But which ones? If I get it wrong, we could end up running straight back to Raven Rock. I stop the bike.

"What are you doing?" Will hisses in my ear.

It's the tail end of the commuter rush hour. Nu London's metro underground system also comes through this station, and the terminal is packed. People are pushing and shoving and running in all directions, and the panicked crowds are slowing down the bikes but they're still getting closer by the second.

"I need to think," I say.

"Well, do it fast."

I close my eyes and picture the maglev system map Rafiq showed us. We have to find that L junction. But it won't be advertised, since it's closed to the public. I wish I'd had more time to talk with him.

I wish he was still alive.

"Hourly shuttle to Prussian Alliance departing in five minutes, Track Four," a recorded female voice echoes above the din.

I can't focus. Everything is happening too fast. Colored lines blur and tangle in my mind. We're never going to make it. I have no idea how the map relates to the track numbers in the station. They'll just chase us around in circles until they have us cornered. Or the locals will get us first. Which is definitely the better option.

"We have to move, Jan!"

No diplomatic relations means no extradition. Maybe if we just turn ourselves in . . .

Suddenly, it hits me and I feel like an idiot for not realizing it before.

"The GPS!" I yell.

We just have to get into a tunnel. *Any* tunnel.

I look around. A holo-display is flashing over Track Four. That'll do. Especially since the terminal police have snapped out of their stupor and are now swarming at us from all sides.

"What?" Will sounds exhausted, like he's at the end of his tether.

"Just hold on!"

I weave through the stampeding crowds to the platform entrance. The police are now firing on our pursuers. One of the bikes takes a direct hit and flips end over end into a cappuccino stand. The rider skids feet-first into a table of teenagers. Pastries take flight. I yank the steering hard to the left to miss an elderly couple who are standing in our path, their mouths frozen into Os of surprise. A moment later we're through the archway of Track Four. The platform is deserted, its passengers wisely choosing to locate the nearest exit and run like hell. I accelerate to the far end, where there's a small gap between the train and the tunnel.

"Two still behind!" Will yells.

The Metropolitan police force needs to hit the range more, I think sourly, and then we're flying through the gap and I can finally let the engine open up all the way.

"Seal it," I tell the computer.

A plastic g-force bubble deploys and we go from fifty to two-fifty in about twenty seconds, which does interesting things to the stomach. The good news is that these tunnels were built for things that move much, much faster. They're designed for high speed.

The bad news is that those things are sharing the same space.

"GPS, pull up maglev tracking, real-time," I say. "Locate relative position, please."

The screen comes alive with flashing dots.

"They're coming up on us, Jan," Will says. "I can see the headlights."

He leans over my shoulder and studies the readout.

"Those are trains?"

"Yes. I think we need to get over here." I point to the left, where a tunnel snakes northwest. Now that I'm seeing it, Rafiq's map is starting to make sense. "There's a Y junction coming up. See, it crosses another track, and then runs straight north. It's the only one that goes that way. The tunnel to 99. We'll drive it."

"OK, but . . . it looks like this train is going to get there first."

He points to a dot running parallel and a little behind us.

"No, I think we can make it."

Will's face is hidden, but I easily picture the look I'm getting right now.

I touch the dot and a bunch of data pops up. It's a Trans-Global Shipping freight train, six hundred and twenty cars. Slower than the passenger models. Only 311 miles per hour.

"If we can pass in front, we'll lose them. This honey goes on and on," I say.

Three bursts of laser fire light up the darkness, and that seems to decide him.

"OK, do it," Will says.

I push the bike as hard as I can, until the speedometer reads 287 and the computer informs me that the engines will overheat in two minutes. We only need one and a half.

Trans-Global Shipping is still behind us, but gaining steadily.

"Uh, Jansin?" Will says, as I bring us through a long curve. "What's that?"

I glance down. There's a new dot. On our track.

"Where the hell did that come from?"

We're approaching the Y junction. I see a glow ahead. Filling the tunnel.

"Collision imminent," the computer announces, gratuitously.

The bubble we're in cuts off all outside noise, but I fancy I can hear the roar of ten thousand tons of metal hurtling towards us at speeds that don't bear thinking about. According to the readout, Trans-Global Shipping is almost even.

Too late, I think. Too late to back out. Oh my God, too late, too late . . .

"Now!" I scream, and we fly into the junction.

The whole thing probably takes two seconds, but it feels much longer. Like being a gnat caught between two giant clapping hands. Lights blind us from all sides and it's all I can do to keep the bike upright. The shockwave of the passing trains sends us scraping against the wall of the third tunnel. Sparks trail off into the darkness for a good half mile before we steady out. I ease up on the throttle with hands that barely function and let us roll to a stop.

The engine light is flashing but coolant systems have already kicked in.

Will clings to my back. We're both shaking like epileptics.

"Five minutes for self-service," the computer says.

He takes a shuddering breath. "You are a complete maniac, do you know that?"

"Yes."

"OK. I just wanted to make sure."

I peel my sweater away from my stomach and flap it in a futile attempt to get some air. "Oh my God, I am soaked with sweat," I say. Then: "I mean, I sure hope that's all it is."

Will starts to laugh, and then we both dissolve into the kind of hysterics that leave you sick and aching all over. When we finally get control of ourselves, Will looks at me and whispers, "I think I just peed a little." Which naturally gets us going again. It's the gasping, helpless laughter of two people who really have no right at all to be alive, but somehow are.

They came for us and we beat them. Now there's only one way out. And it's at the end of this tunnel.

CHAPTER TWENTY-FOUR

The geothermal heat that powered the prefectures was also a liability, with ambient temperatures running from 390 degrees Fahrenheit in the Upper Crust to 750 at the Moho.

We shut off the GPS, set the bike on cruise control, and ride north for about three hours. It's boiling hot in the tunnel without full climate control. No lights appear behind us, although we both know they'll come eventually. Once they realize we're not dead, the first team will simply be replaced by another. And I'm not cocky enough to believe we'll get lucky again.

Finally, the tunnel ends at a platform about forty feet long. There are no signs, just a rusty metal door with a keypad. And we don't have the code.

"Hold on," Will says.

He reaches into his pocket. I'd almost forgotten that Rafiq gave him something right before he was shot. I wipe the sweat from my eyes and examine it in the headlight beam. It's a phone. There's no stored contacts, so I press redial and hear a faint ringing. I know in my heart that he's dead, but I can't help hoping that I'll hear his voice on the other end of the line, telling us what to do next. Telling me that he's OK, that he wasn't murdered in front of my eyes. After two minutes, I hang up.

"No answer."

"I'll get the gun," Will says. "We'll shoot the lock off."

"Actually, there may be something better."

We hop back on the bike and retreat a short distance down the tunnel.

"Computer, run a weapons inventory, please."

A brief debate ensues. I'm in favor of something called MAHEM, a Magneto Hydrodynamic Explosive Munition that drives molten metal penetrators into a target and sounds utterly demented. Will convinces me that we'd probably blow ourselves to bits along with the door. Eventually, we reach consensus on a good old-fashioned grenade launcher.

"Fire in the hole," I yell.

We rush through the door with dust still raining down, and stop short. There's only one guard inside, and he's already dead. Will kneels next to the body. No visible wounds, but the guy's lips are blue and his eyelashes are coated with frost. In fact, the entire room is freezing cold. Lights along the walls flash yellow but there's no alarm sound, which makes it eerier.

I shiver as hot air from the tunnel pours into the room.

"There's something in his hand." Will cracks open the guard's fist and holds up a small electronic key.

The poor guy was watching some horror movie with insectile aliens and it's still playing on a 3D console near the desk. Guard duty for 99 must be a boring shift. Most of the time.

The room is otherwise bare, with a bank of three high-speed elevators along the far wall.

"It looks like something already triggered the tube's defenses," I say. "They're all different. Gas, fire, seawater. This one is pretty clever. Deep freezing the room wouldn't damage the tube's infrastructure, and it would preserve the scene perfectly for when backup arrives. They'd want to know exactly who was knocking on their door." I look at the corpse and feel a stab of pity. This kid is chubby and no older than his late teens. Not an agent. Just a low-wager. "I guess he was trying to deactivate it but didn't get there in time."

"What do you think happened?"

I shake my head. "No idea. But we need to keep moving. I guess we'll find out in a minute."

"But why is the body still here?" Will says. "Why haven't they shut down the . . . freezy-thing or whatever it is? Why haven't they replaced the guard?"

He's right. "I don't know."

"Those go to the top?" Will says, pointing to the elevator bank.

"Yep."

He shuts his eyes for a moment. "I thought I'd never see the surface again," he says. "I don't know how you did it. Lived down here."

"I don't either. And I'm never coming back," I say. "Let's go."

"Wait." He puts a hand on my arm. "They're experimenting on toads up there?"

"Yes."

"With the same drug they gave to me and the others?"

"Yes."

"What did it do? To the toads, I mean."

I can't lie to him. "It made them more violent."

"So the plan is to go up there, somehow slip past the super-toads and the guards and whoever else, and steal a plane that we then fly straight into a hypercane?"

"Yes."

"Do you even know how to fly it?"

"I told you, I trained for years on a simulator."

Will gives me a flat stare. "A simulator."

281

"It was very realistic."

"You know this is insane?"

"I'm aware of that, yes. But nobody does crazy better than us."

He looks at me, shakes his head.

"We could leave now," I say, even though it kills me. "Take our chances in the tunnels. Try to get to a different prefecture."

Will is quiet for a long time and I can tell there's a fierce internal struggle going on. Considering what happened to his family, I can't blame him. If I knew there were toads someplace, I'd be running in the opposite direction.

"No," he says finally. "We go up. I just wanted to know what's there."

I nod. "Shoot anyone or anything that moves. They're not going to know what hit them."

Will runs over and hits the call buttons on all three elevators. All three are at the surface. A digital display panel shows the center one start to move, slowly at first, then gaining speed.

We watch the elevator descend until it's a few seconds away. Then we get up and flank the door on either side, weapons ready. I'm shaking so hard from the cold that the barrel is jumping all over the place. Surface security must have watched everything go down on camera. They'll be expecting us.

The light over the doors flashes and they swish open. It's empty.

"Another trap?" Will says.

"Maybe. But there's no other way to the top."

Tinny music is playing, an ancient pop song I've heard before but can't place.

We step inside and I lean against the wall while Will hits a button that says L1. My stomach lurches as we rocket upward. I slide down to the floor and try not to throw up.

"Raindrops keep falling on my head," I say after a while.

"What?"

"Never mind."

"Are you gonna be OK, Jansin?"

"Yeah."

Defying expectations, the elevator does not stop midway or explode or fall. Four minutes later, we reach the surface. The doors open. We step outside.

Cool wind whips through my hair and my lungs fill with salt air. We're standing on a platform in the middle of the ocean. Huge swells lash the steel legs anchoring the structure to the seabed. Squat, windowless buildings occupy most of the space. The rest is devoted to three wind turbines, which must power the station, and an array of meteorological sensors. There's no one in sight.

We follow a catwalk around the perimeter until we come to a door. It's slightly ajar. I push the door all the way open with my boot, both hands on the grip of the guard's pistol. It leads to a hallway that ends in what must be the common room, where the researchers spend their down time. The furniture is worn but comfortable-looking: couch, two armchairs, a pool table, the real kind, with green felt and colored balls. A chalkboard on the wall lists the player rankings: Lewis, Jiles, Garza, Hamilton, Goodlove.

The place is deserted. It's chilly too, like no one's bothered to turn the heat on in days.

Neither of us speaks as we move through a doorway into the medlab, but I know Will feels it too. The *wrongness*. The people here could have been pulled out for a hundred different reasons: contagious illness, bad weather, even unexpected budget cuts. But I keep thinking of that door being ajar. Not the way you leave a multi-million-dollar installation when the evac is orderly.

I share a look with Will and know he's thinking the same thing.

Where are the toads?

"Over here," he hisses, pointing to a rectangular Plexiglas window at the far side of the lab.

A large biosafety cabinet blocks my view. When I clear it, every nerve in my body ramps up a notch. Because on the other side is a row of cages. And all the doors are wide open.

"Oh shit," Will says with feeling.

Oh shit is right.

I think back to the report I found on Nix. It said the study population consisted of sixteen adults and nine juveniles. Twenty-five altogether.

"We need to find that plane," I whisper. "And wherever they keep the weapons."

It would be nice to have something better than a pistol.

"They're loose." Will is standing stock still. He's barely even breathing. "Oh my God, they're loose."

My skin crawls as I look at that row of empty cages. I've never seen a toad. Which makes it worse. Because it gives my imagination free rein to conjure up some pretty awful things.

We just stand there, listening for a minute. It's deathly quiet.

"OK," I whisper, eyes whipping from the doorway ahead of us to the ones on either side. "If you were a toad and you escaped somehow, you wouldn't stick around, right? You'd get the hell out of here as fast as you could."

Will doesn't answer. He's just staring at the cages like a mouse looking into the eyes of a cobra.

"I'm a crack shot," I say. "I placed third in the marksmanship competition at my school two years in a row. And I swear to God, if any of those things are still here, I will fill them with lead. You have my promise, OK?"

He nods, without taking his eyes off the cages.

"Good. But like I said, there aren't any here because they jumped back into the ocean. And they did us a big favor and took out the guards before they left. So really, we should be thanking them. Now let's do what we came to do so we can get the hell out of here too."

I tug his hand and he drags his eyes to mine. They have some of that blankness he had at the Helix, like he's not entirely sure who I am, and it scares me.

"It's over, Will. Whatever happened is over. So here's the plan. We secure this place first, see if anyone's left, then we get to the plane. Can you manage that?"

"Yeah," he mutters.

We go back into the common room, locking doors behind us as we go. Now that he's moving, Will seems to snap out of it a little. He's paying attention, at least, and helping me check any possible hiding places. Now I'm noticing blood spatter, not a lot but enough. Something bad went down here. That must have been what triggered the tube's defenses. I'd assumed it was an attack from below. Maybe even an accident. But the crisis was *up here*. I wonder why they didn't summon help, and get my answer when we reach the com center. All the equipment is smashed to bits. It was a deliberate act, and more worrisome than anything else. It means they're smart.

We clear the cafeteria and start on the individual sleeping quarters. Will instinctively understands how to operate as a two-person team, covering me as I enter the rooms one by one and communicating mostly in hand gestures. I'd said that whatever happened was over, and we don't find anything to contradict that, but neither of us is eager to make a lot of noise either. Just in case.

We don't find any weapons, but we don't find bodies either, and I have to wonder where they are. Would the toads have taken them? I know nothing about how their minds work, what drives them, so all my training on enemy psychology is worthless. There were guards here too, for a resident staff of twelve. Where the hell is everyone?

We're in the sixth room when I notice a white lab coat hanging from a hook with the name Goodlove sewn on a tag at the collar. Rafiq's mole.

"Hurry up," Will mouths as I cross the room to the dresser and open the top drawer. I don't know what I expect to find, maybe some magical microchip with all the data from Nix, but I have to look. What I get is undies, the no-nonsense granny kind that come up to your bellybutton. I'm turning to leave when something under the bed brushes my foot.

I leap back and start squeezing the trigger when I realize that it's a human hand.

The bed's a lightweight army cot, so rather than get down on the floor I just lift the whole thing up. There's a middle-aged guy underneath in a T-shirt and drawstring pajama pants. He's balding, with brown skin and a close-shaved beard. The shirt is badly charred across the chest indicating that he took a hit from laser fire. There was no blood trail because the burns cauterized.

I meet Will's eyes and we switch places without speaking. I have some rudimentary training in field medicine, but this is his area of expertise. He finds a pulse, careful not to touch the burns, and nods. Still alive. We quickly check the remaining quarters, which are all empty, and then put the guy on a blanket and drag him back to the medlab.

"The wounds are scabbing over, so they're more than a day old, probably two," Will says as he breaks the lock on a drug cabinet and scans the contents. Now that he has someone to doctor, his confidence is returning. No more blankness. Just his efficient physic face. "Whatever happened wasn't recent."

"Can you get him talking?" I ask.

"I'll try. He's in shock."

"Will you be OK here if I clear the rest of the station?"

"Just lock the door behind you," he says, setting Jake's laser weapon next to a sink. "And be careful."

"Always," I say.

The rest consists of a dining hall and galley kitchen, storage areas, and a co-ed bathroom with three shower stalls. The kitchen is well-stocked with food and water, which I intend to take when we get out of here. Who knows what Iceland is like now? I want to imagine that it's lush and green, like the valley that used to mesmerize me on the train, but it could be barren. We need to be prepared for anything.

I'm in the bathroom, about to kick open the last opaque shower door, when my butt starts vibrating and I nearly jump out of my skin. It's the phone Rafiq gave to Will.

"Jansin?" a woman's voice says. The connection isn't great—understandably, since it's being relayed six thousand feet down and eight hundred miles south—but I can hear her.

"Who is this?"

"Dr Aviva Sorin. I treated you yesterday."

"How do you have this number?"

"Rafiq gave it to me."

"He's dead."

"No, I'm with him now. I came back to check on you and found him outside. There was substantial blood loss, but he's resting comfortably now."

It sounds so like my fantasy that Rafiq made it somehow that I'm instantly suspicious.

"Why should I believe you?"

"You can speak to him yourself. Not too long, please. He's still quite weak."

There's a pause. Then Rafiq comes on the line.

"Are you there?" he asks. His voice is hoarse, but I'd recognize it anywhere.

"I'm here." I smile for the first time in what feels like weeks. "And so are you. I can't believe it."

"I almost wasn't. Aviva is a miracle worker, apparently. Are you topside?"

"Yes, but there's a complication. The toads broke free somehow, probably in the last forty-eight, and everyone's gone. Communications are down."

"Good God. I wondered why I couldn't reach my source." He's quiet for a moment. "The station sends reports on a weekly basis. It's likely no one back in Raven Rock knows yet. And it doesn't change the basic picture. I still need that data."

"We found one survivor. Will's working on him now. But it's not Goodlove, unless Goodlove has exotic taste in undergarments."

"What?"

"It's a man. Just tell me how to send it, and I'll see what I can do."

"Use the phone. It has a 42-qubit memory that could handle a thousand times what they've got." He coughs painfully. "Promise me, Jansin. Don't leave without finding it. If you do, they'll just mop up and start again."

"I know that, and I won't. What about Samer?"

"He's dead."

"I'm so sorry." And I am. He seemed like a decent person. They've murdered a cop, and I hope Nu London brings a world of pain down on them for it. "I have to go now, Rafiq. This place isn't safe. If you don't get a transmission within the hour, something went wrong. Don't forget the others I told you about."

Every instinct is screaming at me to run to that plane and take off before it's too late, but I remember Fatima bringing me the strappy dress and just can't do it. If Rafiq can do something to help them, we have to try. Besides, I have a personal bone to pick with Dr Rebekah Carlsson.

"Take care of yourself," I say.

"You too, Jansin. And you'll be glad to know you're mother's been released. They got what they wanted."

"Thank you for telling me that," I say, and something tight inside me lets go a little bit. We both know that what they wanted was her connection with Rafiq, but there's no bitterness in his voice. He made his choice that night when I called him from our kitchen, and Will would be dead if he had chosen differently. Will would be dead, and Samer would be alive. "Goodbye, Rafiq."

I end the call and go back to the medlab. Will has cut off the guy's shirt and smeared him with antiseptic burn cream. He also put some on his own arm where the agent sprayed him with Chemnite.

"I just talked to Rafiq," I say. "He's alive."

"Seriously?" Will's eyes search mine. "How is that possible?"

"Aviva found him before he bled out. Got him out of there somehow. They killed Samer. I don't know where Rafiq is now, but he says he can still move the data on Nix if we deliver it. He'll nail them to the wall, Will. He's got the connections. But I can't get into the databanks on my own. Can you wake your patient up?"

Will frowns. "He needs rest. These are third-degree burns we're talking about."

I feel a burst of impatience and make myself take a slow breath. He's just doing what he's been trained to do, like I am.

"Will, the toads could come back at any time. Even if they don't, more agents will be here soon. A lot more. We need to know where that plane is, and how to access the Nix data. Otherwise, Fatima and the captain and all the others are as good as dead. And so are we."

Will looks angry, but I don't think it's directed at me. "Fine, I'll hit him with ten milligrams of calpidem." He retrieves a hypo and fills it from one of the bottles in the cabinet. "This won't be pretty."

Will injects the guy in the thigh and steps back. Nothing happens for about five seconds. Then he takes a shuddering gasp and his dark brown eyes fly open. He makes a high keening sound, like an animal caught in a trap, and tries to sit up. We grab his shoulders and push him down but he's slippery with burn cream and his skin is literally black underneath and I'm terrified it will just come off in my hands.

Will starts talking in a quiet voice and after a couple minutes, the guy begins to calm down. He's *seeing* us, at least, instead of whatever bad trip was going on in his head.

"You're safe now," Will lies. "I'm a doctor. I'm here to help you. What's your name?"

"We should have burned the bodies," the guy says.

"What?"

"We should have burned them post-autopsy, like the others. But we threw them over the side."

"You mean the other scientists?"

"No, jerkoff, the *toads*." He laughs mirthlessly. "It obviously pissed the rest of them off."

"What's your name?" Will asks again.

"Garza." He winces in pain. "Who the hell are you people? Why am I still here?"

Will and I look at each other.

"Advance team," I say. "We were on assignment in Nu London when the call came in. The rest are coming on a shuttle to lock it down at 0300."

"Jesus Christ." His eyes widen. "You mean we're alone here? What about the rest of the crew?"

"They're gone," Will says. "Who shot you?"

He sags back on the gurney. "One of the guards. It was an accident. Afterwards, he dragged me into Goodlove's room and pushed me under the bed. It was pandemonium. They came in the middle of the night . . . Is that door locked?"

"Yes," I say.

"They figured out how to open the electromag cages. I swear to God, if I'd known how intelligent and vicious those things are, I'd never have taken this assignment. I'm a *biologist*, for Christ's sake. I'm supposed to work with animals. The toads may not be human, but they're definitely not *animals*." His voice is starting to rise. "And now they send two kids to secure the station? What if they come back? There were dozens!"

"Take it easy, sir," I say.

"Don't tell me to take it easy! Jesus Christ!" He stares at us. "You have no idea what you're dealing with. None at all."

"We have to restore communications, immediately," I say. "I need all the computer passcodes. And I need to clear the prototype hangar. They could be hiding in there."

Garza rolls his eyes. "Please. Be my guest." He points at Will. "But you'd better leave this one here or I'll have very unpleasant things to say in my debriefing report."

"As you say. Major, is it?"

"Captain."

"OK, *Captain* Garza. Now where do I find the codes?"

CHAPTER TWENTY-FIVE

In his novella The Time Machine, *the late nine-teenth century science fiction writer H. G. Wells imagined* homo sapiens *evolving into two races: the bestial cave-dwelling Morlocks and the docile, parasitic Eloi. Which will we become, I wonder?*

I don't think it even occurs to Garza that we're not who we say we are. This is not a place you stumble across, and we more or less look the part in our black clothing and steel-toed boots. He's also experienced a traumatic event, although his personality makes it hard to feel sorry for him.

I guess if he questions Will too closely, he'll figure it out. But that doesn't matter anymore because he's already given me every-thing. When I ask about the plane, he admits no one's sure it works. Apparently, the Raptor was delivered to the station just weeks before 99's meteorological research was shut down and they never sent a test pilot. Which doesn't surprise me at all. Someone made a bundle on that plane. Who cares if it's never actually flown?

I leave them together and go the perimeter door we entered through. It's bolted shut from the inside now, just like the other three we found. I check my weapon again, hoping the ritual will slow my racing pulse. The guard down below carried a Browning

HP service pistol as his secondary firearm. It's a single-action semi-automatic, so you have to cock the hammer before firing. It has a full magazine. Thirteen rounds.

Garza didn't know where the weapons cache is and I can't waste more time looking for it. The Browning will have to do.

I put my ear to the door. Unfortunately, there's no way to see what's on the other side. The station is windowless, probably because of its proximity to Tisiphone, and all the external security cameras operated through the com center.

All I hear is howling wind.

I cock the hammer and flick the safety off. Then I ease open the door.

Sheets of rain sweep across the deck of the platform, and I'm glad it's enclosed by a steel railing because the waves have picked up in the last hour. The hangar is located at the rear of the station, about a hundred yards away. Nothing is moving out here, although the visibility is lousy. I'm wearing a waterproof slicker I found hanging from a row of hooks in the common area, but I don't dare put the hood up and lose peripheral vision.

I jog the length of the walkway, keeping an eye not only on what's in front and behind, but above and below. For a split second I think I see something in the foaming water but it's gone too fast to be sure. Then I reach a detached building that's low and wide. I key in the numbers Garza gave me and the door clicks open. It's dark inside, but I can see the outlines of an aircraft in the middle of the room.

It's triangular, with twin turbofan engines jutting upward from the back end and curved tails that make it look like the manta ray I saw at Raven Rock's aquarium when I was a kid. They designed it for VTOL capability: vertical takeoff and landing. Standing next to the plane, I'm confronted with the reality that I'm going to have to actually fly it and feel a little nauseous.

Time to see what we're dealing with.

I open the main cabin door to the flight deck and climb inside. It's a two-seater, with a small cargo hold.

"Activate on-board computer," I say, and the cockpit flickers to life. Besides the usual instruments to measure heading, speed, altitude, vertical speed, and vertical and lateral navigation, it has an array of sensors for gathering data on the hypercane: anemometer, barometer, others I don't recognize. I program a flight plan to Tisiphone's eye and am relieved to find that the controls are intuitive and user-friendly, even simpler than the older model X-50s I flew in the simulator.

I leave the Raptor activated but in hibernation mode, and run back down the walkway to the station, eyes squinted against the driving rain. The elevators are still on the surface, which is a good sign. I briefly consider disabling them but I'm afraid of damaging the vent tube. Rafiq's cautionary tale about Sector G is one you don't forget.

Garza is sleeping when I enter the medlab.

"I've done everything I can," Will says. "He really needs to be in a hospital."

"Don't worry, the cavalry will take care of it," I say. "I found the plane. Once it's loaded with food and water, and I send Rafiq his data, we're good to go."

Will looks at me for a moment. "You really think you can fly it?"

"Yes. I just checked the controls. Everything seems to be working. At this point, it's the only way out of here."

"You're sure they're coming? I don't feel very good leaving this guy behind. If he doesn't get medical treatment, he'll die."

"By now, they know we aren't splattered all over the tunnel. Trust me, they're coming."

"Let's get started then," he says, picking up his gun.

I tell him where the hangar is and leave him in the galley, stacking boxes of supplies. Then I go through the trashed com center to a room on the far side of the station where they keep the servers. It's cooler in here, and I shiver a little as I speak the passcodes and jack the phone into an external port. Rafiq's toy has the latest quantum technology, but the station servers are a lot slower. The minutes tick by and I start feeling more and more anxious. We've been here for more than an hour. Past time to be leaving.

The download finally finishes and transmits. I rip the phone out and run to the galley. It's empty, and there's a pretty big dent in their food stores. I guess Will is waiting at the plane.

I take a moment to lock the medlab so nothing messes with Garza until he's rescued. Then I open the door to the walkway and step outside.

Tisiphone's edge may be fifty miles away, but you wouldn't know it standing here. During the time I was sending the data, the weather has deteriorated further. I lean into the wind and start walking. The whole structure is vibrating under the onslaught. I know the computer will help, but I'm not looking forward to taking off in this crap.

I'm almost past the elevator bank when something registers in my brain and I stop. Turn back. A little green light is on. The car on the left is descending.

Eight and a half minutes down, the same to return. Plenty of time.

But I start running as fast as I can anyway.

I skid around the corner of the station and that's when I see them, against the far railing. Will, with Jake gripping him in a headlock and a gun to his face.

The image doesn't compute. Jake? Here? But then I realize that one of the cars could have made a round trip while I was inside. He must have been a little behind the two agents on our tail. He's the relentless type, so it doesn't surprise me that he wouldn't wait for backup.

"Drop it, Jansin!" Jake yells through the roar of the storm. "Drop it now!"

I stop. Toss my gun on the ground. It skitters across the rain-slick metal and halts midway between us.

"Just let us go," I call. "You can say you never saw me."

He's quiet for long enough that my hopes rise a little. Then his face hardens.

"You know I can't do that. Agents are dead."

"They're experimenting on human beings, Jake. That's not what we signed up for."

Will doesn't seem hurt. He's too smart to struggle, but I can read murder in his eyes.

"You're a traitor. I wish to God it weren't so, that it was anyone else . . ." He trails off and looks genuinely stricken for a moment, but pulls himself together. "I don't want to kill you, either of you. But I will if I have to. Face-down on the ground. Do it!"

I drop to my knees.

"All the way!"

I lie on my stomach and press my cheek against the cold steel. I could have killed him back at Rafiq's house, but I didn't. It's a hard lesson.

I turn my head a little so I can see his boots. And then I see something else, behind him. Climbing over the railing.

It's too far to make out clearly, but I have a pretty good idea what it is.

Jake screams as it hits him, and I'm on my feet running for the gun. I reach it just as two more drop from the roof of the station. They're between me and Will, so I take careful aim and shoot them both between the eyes. They fall without a sound. I stand there for a moment, trying to catch up with what I'm looking at.

Humanoid doesn't really describe it. They *are* human, but they're not at the same time. Webbed hands and feet. Small pink slits under the jaw that must act as gills, allowing them to transition between land and water. Pale skin, with fine blue veins visible beneath the surface. And the eyes . . . knowing, intelligent, but utterly alien.

Will steps over the naked bodies, which are as smooth and hairless as children, and grabs my hand. We start for the hangar but more toads are swarming over the railing and we're forced back down the walkway. Jake's still grappling with the first one as we reach a door. Of course, we locked them all from the inside.

I kick it hard twice before I remember I have a gun.

"Hurry!" Will yells, glancing over his shoulder, and I blow the lock off with two shots. We run inside, slam it and put our backs to the door. A second later something hits it with tremendous force. The door shudders and inches inward.

We're in one of the storage areas. Dusty equipment is stacked up to the ceiling, most dating from the days when Substation 99 was a real weather outpost. A jumble of antennas occupies one corner amid boxes of broken gauges and old computers. It smells strongly of mildew.

The toads hit the door again, and this time the steel dents in half a dozen places. We're nearly thrown off, but we bend our knees and *push*, and it clicks shut again. Will has gone very pale.

"We're not dying here," I say firmly, even though my knees are trembling. "We're not."

He doesn't respond. I think he's gone somewhere else. Maybe a sloop on the Novatlantic seas a decade ago.

"Please don't check out on me," I beg, almost crying now. "I need you."

I touch his face, make him look at me, and he takes a deep breath.

"We are going to get to that plane," I say.

"There's too many of them."

Steel screams as the door inches inward. I wedge the muzzle of the gun through and fire, and there's a wordless shriek on the other side. We shove it closed again.

"That's why we need another way out," I say.

"Hold on." Will starts heaping equipment in front of the door. He grabs anything he can get his hands on—broken furniture, boxes of spare parts, stacks of solar panels.

The elevator has to be on its way up by now. We only have a few minutes left.

The big problem is that there's no other door.

"Jansin!" Will calls.

He's climbed to the top of a pile of crates against the wall. Behind the last one is a narrow heating duct. We didn't see it before because it was covered by junk.

"Come on!" he yells.

Telling me to go first.

"Just get in, I'm right behind you," I say, stepping away from the door. Will pries the cover off and starts crawling as it buckles inward. Metal shrieks as the pile shifts, but the door jams on something and stops about six inches wide. Webbed fingers curl around the edge and test it, then withdraw. I can see that the next hit will smash it wide.

I scramble up the crates and dive into the duct, following Will's boots ahead of me. There's a loud noise, then silence. We crawl as fast as we can, twisting and turning, and I'm breathing so hard I can't tell for sure if there's anything behind. I think I hear soft sounds though, the scraping of fingernails on steel maybe.

I scoot along on my elbows, the pistol a reassuring weight in my right hand. But the duct is too tight to turn around and look. Too tight to turn around and shoot. Now I'm sure I hear something. A wheezing hiss. Like air slowly escaping from a tire. My ankles tingle in anticipation of webbed hands closing around my boots and dragging me backwards into the darkness. I may not be able to turn around, but I still can use the gun on myself. I will, if I have to.

Now that I've seen the toads, I understand why Will froze in front of those cages. He was right to be terrified.

Then daylight fills the duct. We crawl another three yards and Will is tumbling out and hauling me to the catwalk. We've come out next to the elevators. We must have taken a tour through the whole station to end up thirty feet from where we started. The moment my feet hit the ground I turn and fire into the duct. Silence. Was it my imagination?

The walkway between us and the hangar looks clear. I check the elevator. It's halfway to the top, about four minutes away. We run to the door and I key it open, my hands shaking so badly it takes me three tries to get it right.

A thin scream cuts through the wind.

Jake.

I peer through the curtains of rain to the railing where he held Will hostage. Jake is lying on the ground, his right leg bent at an odd angle. Three toads are crouched in a circle around him. He's lost his weapon.

The image takes me back to the beach that night, when the raiders hit us. The people who started out as my enemies and became my friends. If I hadn't gone to help Jake then, I would never have encountered Banerjee, or Bob, who in his inimitable Bob way started the whole thing by grabbing me. I would never have met Will.

I'd be just like Jake now. One of them.

I could lie to myself and believe that I would have woken up on my own, but deep inside, I know better. It's not that I liked the way things were. I just didn't know there was any other way.

Jake and I are on opposite sides now. If we ever see each other again, it will be as bitter enemies. He'll never change, he's not capable of it. But I can't let him die here. Not like this. If I did, I'd be just like them.

"I'll meet you in the cockpit," I tell Will. "One minute."

"Where the hell are you going now?" He looks upset, and has every right to be.

"We trained at the Academy together," I say. "I just want to give him a chance. He won't try to stop us again. Trust me."

Will looks extremely dubious.

"You're joking, right? He tried to shoot me, in case you've forgotten. Twice."

"I haven't forgotten. I just can't . . ." I point at the toads, closing the circle. "I can't let those things have him."

If anyone hates toads more than I do, it's Will. He sighs heavily.

"Do it fast," he says. "I'll cover you."

"I will," I say.

I walk toward Jake and start firing as the first one springs. The bullet rips through its chest, and the others spin around but I drop them with two clean shots to the head. It feels more like killing people than animals and my stomach turns. Jake looks up at me, blue eyes wide. He's soaked to the bone and looks about a decade older than he did a few minutes ago.

"Your guys will be here any second," I say.

We both glance down the adjacent walkway as a group of shadows detaches from the wall and starts moving in our direction.

"There's eight rounds left in this gun. Make them count." I hand him the pistol, butt first, thinking I must be insane. But I know Jake. At least, I used to. He's not evil. Just a good soldier.

Jake takes it. "Why are you doing this?"

I hesitate for a moment. He wouldn't understand, and frankly, I'm not sure I do myself. So I say something that will make sense to him.

"Because we never leave a man behind." I start to walk away. Turn back. "One last thing. Just tell me the truth. Were you there when they took me down? In the woods?"

Jake grimaces, left hand loosely cupping his shattered knee, right hand gripping the gun. He shakes his head and I'm filled with relief.

I consider saying take care or something inane like that, but it seems ridiculous under the circumstances. And there's no time to do anything but run.

I'm halfway back to the hangar when I hear a hammer cock behind me. I stop. Turn around.

Jake is aiming the gun in my direction. Our eyes meet, and he fires.

I dive to the side as something drops from the roof above. It thrashes and lies still. Red blood gushes from the bullet wound in the toad's throat. *Go*, Jake mouths silently.

I sprint flat-out then, tearing into the hangar as more gunfire erupts behind me. The plane is waiting and Will is leaning out the cabin door, beckoning me inside.

"Open bay doors," I tell the computer as we seal the cabin and buckle into our harnesses. "Prepare for takeoff."

Like its Harrier jet ancestors, the Raptor uses a two-way toggle to transition between vertical and forward flight. The computer sets ten degrees of flap and I slowly open the throttle. The plane lifts up and soars out of the hangar. We circle around for a pass and I see jump-suited figures pouring out of the elevator. It looks like they brought some serious artillery. Then we're flying into the storm, steadily gaining altitude until we reach a cruising height of 35,000 feet.

"We'll reach the outer edge of Tisiphone in six minutes," I say.

"So what happens when we hit the eyewall?" Will asks.

"I'm not sure. But that's where the highest wind speeds are. About four hundred miles per hour."

Will's face is composed but his hands are gripping the armrest. "I've spent my whole life running from the storms," he says. "I can't believe I'm about to fly straight into one."

I hesitate. "Listen, about Jake and what happened back there . . ."

"It's OK." He stares straight ahead. "I understand."

"I only wanted to say that next time I'll definitely shoot him."

Will doesn't look over but I think his mouth quirks the tiniest bit.

"We could go anywhere in the world, couldn't we?" he says.

"Pretty much." I glance at him. "Having doubts about Iceland?"

So far, the ride has been very smooth. Beautiful, in fact. We're starting to see the hypercane's outer bands of cumulus and cumulonimbus, capped by thin, wispy cirrus. A break in the clouds reveals roiling seas below, with troughs deep enough to hold the entire substation.

It's hard for me to believe thousands of people used to jet across the planet this way every day without a second thought. So much has been lost to us now.

"No, it's not that," Will says, echoing my thoughts. "I've just never flown before, you know? I never in a million years imagined that I ever would. It's like a dream. Ocean crossings by boat are very dangerous. Not just because of the canes, but there's rogue waves out there hundreds of feet high. I guess it's a weird feeling to think that we could cross Novatlantis in a matter of hours."

"I know," I say, checking our location. "And I think the window of opportunity to change our minds just closed."

We enter the storm. Heavy rain streaks across the windshield and visibility drops to zero, but the radar shows red lines of squalls spiraling toward a darker hole at the center.

I point it out to Will. "Tisiphone's heart," I say, when the plane bounces, hard.

"What was that?" Will asks, gripping the armrest.

"I don't know."

I scan the instruments. Everything looks normal, but I'm not exactly a qualified pilot.

"I think we're here," I say.

A second later, the nose pitches down and we're diving into a churning mass of grey cloud.

"You're sure there's land down there?" Will asks.

I make sure the autopilot is engaged. No way I'm doing this part myself, no matter how many hours I've logged in the simulator. Now we're losing airspeed and the Raptor is falling even faster. The airframe shudders ominously.

"She's built to fly through canes," I mutter. "She'll hold together."

But I'm not so sure.

The gusts at the eyewall buffet us like a leaf in a whirlwind, and I can only imagine the terrible forces being exerted just a few feet away. We sink to 20,000 feet, then 10,000. The plane starts yawing violently from side to side. Our harnesses creak under the strain. I think of the waves down there, like small mountains. The radar puts our position at the verge of Tisiphone's eye, hugging the wall in a northwesterly direction.

"Hold tight," I say. "We're punching through."

We hit a pocket of severe turbulence and I hear the cargo of food and water shifting in the back of the plane. Everything is vibrating, like a giant tuning fork. There's a sharp cracking sound and the cabin door flies open. I turn my head and something strikes me just me above the ear. A burst of white, followed by blackness.

I float in the void for a while, quiet and serene. Then my ears pop painfully and a wall of noise comes rushing back in. The desperate whine of the engines, a cacophony of alarms, Will's voice screaming next to me.

". . . something!"

For several long moments, I am gripped by total confusion. I open my eyes, wait for the blurriness to clear. What I see is not good.

I'm dangling in my harness, nearly face-down. Blood is dripping onto the windshield. The plane is in a nosedive. I have no idea how long I was out, how long we have been plummeting toward the earth.

"Do something!" Will yells again.

Crates fill the tiny flight deck. One of them has shattered the autopilot. At that moment, I know we are going to crash. The whole thing was madness.

"Do what?" I sob. "I can't . . ."

"You can!" Will yells. He swipes at my hand, misses it, tries again and grabs me. Squeezes hard. "You can, Jansin! Try! Fly this plane!"

I squeeze back, stomach floating somewhere north of my ribcage. I can't see a thing through the windshield, just dense clouds. I shove debris out of the way and scan the instruments.

"Terrain. Terrain," the computer barks. "Ground proximity warning."

Just like the simulator, I tell myself. You've nose-dived before. You've pulled out of it.

Violent g-forces batter the plane like a giant fist. I feel like I'm going to black out again, and I know we're dead if that happens. For some reason, at that moment, I think of Fatima. Of how Will saved her life because he simply refused to indulge in fear and self-doubt. He just acted.

I seize the controls and pull back, leaning hard into my harness. They judder in my hand and I'm so scared the airframe will just crack apart like an egg, but then the nose starts creeping up, an inch at a time.

"That's it!" Will screams. "You've got it!"

After endless seconds, the plane stabilizes and I let out a huge breath I didn't even know I was holding, then suck in air like I've just emerged from the depths of the ocean. Will whoops and slaps his thigh. I raise a shaking hand to my head and touch the spot where I was beaned. A little harder and I might never have woken up at all.

"Oh my God," I whisper. "Oh my God, that was close."

We're flying low, one thousand feet, at an airspeed of two hundred fifty knots. Will helps me review the landing checklist and make sure the tricycle landing gear is down and the nose is stabilized at a three-degree glide slope. When we hit three hundred feet I reduce the airspeed to fifty knots, drop the remaining flaps and get ready to engage auto-hover. I figure we're better off coming in too high than too low, since VTOLs have no trouble dumping altitude.

I just wish I knew what we were landing *on*.

"Terrain, terrain, terrain . . ."

We're slammed by one last gust, and then bright sunlight hits the windshield. The plane just clears a rocky peak and drops into a valley with a river twisting through the center. It's treeless but covered in grass that creeps up the black slopes like a bright green carpet. Three waterfalls cascade down to the valley floor.

I choose a level area and bring us down to about a hundred feet, then initiate a stationary hover, hold full throttle and let her settle down to earth. The thrust vectoring nozzles rotate to zero degrees as we touch down and I cut the engines to idle before we go rocketing forward.

We're both banged up from the passage through the wall; I'll have purple bruises across my chest and a lump the size of a shotgun shell over my ear for the next few weeks. But I'm barely feeling them now as we open the cabin door and exit the plane.

It's hard to convey what being inside the eye of a hypercane looks like. We're standing in a coliseum hundreds of miles across, except it's made of fluffy white cloudbanks that soar tens of thousands of feet into the air. The circle of sky above is clear and blue.

Just a few miles away, a maelstrom of rain and winds that shatter the Beaufort scale are raging. But here, it's peaceful. A small herd of what looks like reindeer picks its way down the slope. I take the presence of animals as a good omen. If they can survive here, we can too.

As the adrenalin rush ebbs, my head starts to throb. I lean against the cockpit ladder.

"You're still bleeding," Will comments. He takes me by the arm and leads me to a patch of grass. "Lie down," he orders, donning his physic face.

The grass is soft beneath my head. I watch him walk to the plane. His short blonde hair gleams silkily against his neck and his black T-shirt stretches tight across his shoulders and even though I'm dizzy and half-sick, I want him. God help me, I do.

I stare up at the blue sky. A minute later, his face appears, looking down at me. He kneels in the grass and opens up the first aid kit.

"You probably have a concussion," he says, swabbing my forehead with something that feels cool and tingly at the same time. "Hold still." He leans over me and I can feel the warmth from his skin.

"When you were at the Helix . . . You said you thought about me." Will is winding a bandage around my forehead. He pauses for a split-second, then secures it with a metal clip.

I take a deep breath. "I thought about you too. When they sent me back to the Academy."

His blue-grey eyes meet mine and he doesn't look away. But it's impossible to tell what he's thinking.

"I just . . . I didn't know what else to do with myself. I basically stayed in bed for two months after they brought me back. But nothing was the same. I couldn't do it anymore. I got myself kicked out. Right after I found out about Project Nix. My mom . . ." I swallow.

"My mom helped me. If it weren't for her, you'd still be in that place. And now they're going after my parents." I feel a tear slide out of the corner of my eye and trickle down to my ear.

"I'm so sorry, Jansin," Will says. "I know what it means to lose all the people you care about." His gaze softens as he looks at me. "Almost all of them."

He twines his fingers in mine and electricity sparks between our palms. Will smiles, the warmest, most beautiful smile, like the sun coming out from behind a thunderhead. I realize I haven't seen him smile like that since the Helix. Part of me was scared I never would again.

"The first time I saw you . . . you looked even worse than you do now," he says, and I raise an eyebrow. "And you were still the prettiest girl I'd ever laid eyes on."

I start to say something, I'm not sure what, and then his mouth is on mine, soft at first and then with a fierce hunger he can barely control, and I can't believe I ever compared this boy to an actuary. We stay that way, just breathing into each other, for an endless moment. My lips feel swollen and bruised when he finally slides his mouth off mine. He kisses my chin and moves down the line of my jaw, and I can feel my pulse fluttering wildly against his lips. He's so alive in my arms. So real and solid and undeniably *here*. Our tongues touch and the ground spins away. We cling to each other like drowning people, burying our sorrow and grief in the mingled heat of our embrace. He's careful in the way he touches me, he knows where I hurt, and I can tell he's holding himself back. His breath is ragged as he finally pulls away.

"We have to stop now," Will says. "Or I won't be able to."

"Oh," I say, flushing to the roots of my hair.

Will lies beside me, and I nestle my head on chest. "You have no idea how long I've wanted to do that," he murmurs.

"Mmmmm. Maybe I do."

He sighs. "I've been thinking about something, Jansin. If they built this plane, they can build another."

"Yes, they could," I say. "But they won't."

I tell him that I know how they think, the factors that are calculated into every decision. If we were down below, reachable in the ordinary course of things, they would send more agents. Mostly to make a point: No one hurts them and gets away clean. But we're not worth the political capital it would require to finagle a new budgetary allocation and engineer an incredibly complex aircraft for no other purpose than extracting two dissidents from a place that doesn't officially exist.

They also have bigger fish to fry at the moment. Like Greenbrier.

I look around the valley, somehow both lush and severe at the same time. Like Charlie said, life goes on. It evolves. It pushes back. Maybe the canes were nature's answer to a species that was making the whole planet sick. Or maybe we just brought it on ourselves.

Then Will kisses me again and I forget all about being so serious.

We bask in the sun, with the grass tickling our bare feet, until it begins to sink behind the eyewall. He touches my hand and points to a distant ridge. There's a figure outlined black against the dying light. Human. Or human-like.

The clouds catch fire, their edges shimmering with flames of molten gold, as we arm ourselves and start walking towards it.

ACKNOWLEDGMENTS

Like most, this book went through many incarnations. The earliest readers—my wonderful agent, Jeff Ourvan, and my perceptive and generous cousin Eva Thaddeus—were nice enough to get their hands dirty with the raw clay. Their insights kept the whole thing from derailing.

My mother, who believes she's better than me at solving *New York Times* crossword puzzles but is sadly mistaken, was more than happy (gleeful, one might say) to point out typos, plot holes and logical inconsistencies. We still have the prodigious list in a Word document somewhere. Thanks, Mom.

Simon, my beloved, slogged through the drafts again and again, asking important questions and correcting the typos that even my grammar-Nazi mother overlooked. He also dictated every single fight scene, because he teaches krav maga and knows all kinds of wonderful things about full airway chokes and how to grab someone by their eyeballs and nostrils simultaneously, etc. Thank you, my darling! Although not so much for demonstrating them on me . . .

Thank you, Dad, for reading and believing, and Nika, for inspiring me to create a smart, funny, powerful character. Double air punch!

I also owe a debt of thanks to Dr. Kerry Emanuel at MIT, who graciously answered my questions about how hypercanes form and didn't laugh (or maybe he did, since we communicated by email). He is precisely the kind of scientist we should really be putting in charge of things.

ABOUT THE AUTHOR

Kat Ross was born and raised in New York City and worked several jobs before turning to journalism and creative writing. An avid traveler and adventurer, she now lives with her family—along with a beagle, a ginger cat, and six fish—far enough outside the city that skunks and deer wander through her backyard.